BONE

GEORGE C. CHESBRO

THE MYSTERIOUS PRESS

New York • London • Tokyo

Copyright © 1989 George C. Chesbro
All rights reserved.

The Mysterious Press, 129 West 56th Street, New York, N.Y. 10019

Printed in the United States of America

First Printing: March 1989

10 9 8 7 6 5 4 3 2 1

Library of Congress Cataloging-in-Publication Data

Chesbro, George C.
  Bone / George C. Chesbro.
    p. cm.
  I. TITLE.
PS3553.H359B66   1989
813′.54—dc19
ISBN 0-89296-292-5   88-18868
                                                          CIP

Sleeping with Jesus had always saved her in the past, but on this night the electric voices had penetrated even this sanctuary. Sailing on the raw winds of early April, cloaked in darkness and speaking the lisping spring language of rain, the Speakers—three of them tonight—had found her shortly after midnight. On other occasions when the Speakers had found her here Jesus had persuaded them to go away and leave her in peace, but tonight Ho Chi Minh had been very persistent in defying Jesus and persuading the others to do the same; for almost two hours the Speakers had been cursing, spitting and urinating on her from the writhing bundle of black clouds the stone Savior held above her head in his outstretched arms. The pain caused by the Speakers' voices—shimmering electric shocks that made her muscles twitch, her bones vibrate, her eyes burn and bulge—was growing worse, and she knew she would have to escape from the Speakers or she would die.

Marilyn Monroe had told her so.

But she was so terribly cold. The body heat trapped by the five layers of clothing and plastic garbage bags she wore had leaked away into the night hours before, and the urine that had

1

run down her legs into her socks and ragged shoes was beginning to freeze. She had endured nights much colder than this during winter, she thought as she rested her cheek on the gelid granite that was her bed and shuddered—but on those nights Jesus had been protecting her from the Speakers. The fact that this protection had been stripped away, even as the wind had stripped from her the newspapers she had carried all day to cushion and insulate her head at night, made her feel terribly vulnerable, and even colder.

But she had to move. Marilyn had said so.

Mary Kellogg reached inside her thin coat and pulled out the wads of newspaper she had stuffed there for added warmth, threw them to the hungry wind. She did the same with the newspapers stuffed between her garbage-bag skirt and the baggy, filth-caked wool pants beneath. Thus unencumbered, she reached up with a frail, trembling hand to grip the great iron ring on the massive wooden door behind her. Her bare fingers wrapped around the slippery, cold metal and she managed to haul herself to her feet. This exertion, combined with the cold and the wet and the pain caused by the electric Speakers, left her short of breath; she stood gasping and shuddering, leaning for support against a cold stone foot of Jesus. Joseph Stalin cursed at her, and she finally let go of the carved toes, hobbled stiffly to the wrought-iron handrail that ran down the center of the wide stone steps beneath her bed. Gripping the rail with both hands, pausing twice to rest and slap her hands against her thighs in an effort to restore feeling to her fingers, she finally made it down to the street, where she cringed and furtively looked around her, terrified that she might be noticed and caught again by the savage young gray ones who had hurt her and tried to make her do a horrible and disgusting thing. But there was no sign of the gray ones, nor of anyone else. Only an occasional car, tires whistling on the rain-swept avenue, sped by.

Mary turned left and shuffled toward the end of the block. The Speakers followed, screaming at her from their hiding places behind Doubleday, Garrano, Gucci and Fortunoff, across the wide avenue. She paused at the curb, again gasping for breath, feebly trying to brush back the wispy strands of hair plastered to her face with hands that had lost all feeling.

Still standing at the curb in the rain and wind, the old woman's mind began to drift.

2

There were times, usually bad times like now, when for no apparent reason Mary found herself thinking of her husband; she missed him so badly at these times that the pain in her heart became even worse than the pains caused by the Speakers. She remembered the good times they had shared when he was alive, when she was so many years younger, before the Speakers had visited her with their electric torment, before her children had placed her in a mental hospital.

The first place hadn't been so bad, Mary thought, her mind now far away and oblivious to the taxicab that raced past only inches from her, sending up a wall of dirty water that crested and cascaded over her, drenching her from her chest to her feet. She had been almost happy there. The doctors and nurses had been kind, and pleasant volunteers had often taken her out for walks, or rides, or even an occasional picnic when the weather was warm. Most important, the doctors had given her medicine which made her invisible to the Speakers, who had eventually gone away. She'd even had her own television set.

Then the doctors had told her that the state had changed certain rules, and she was no longer considered sick enough to be hospitalized; she was to be transferred to a much smaller, privately operated facility, and the Speakers would not find her there as long as she continued to take her medication.

But the community house where they had sent her had been very crowded, and the small staff had been overworked, impatient and mean to her. Often, they had forgotten to give her her medication, and had shouted at her when she tried to remind them. Once a staff person had shoved her against a wall, hurting her so badly that she had been unable to get out of bed for three days. Then the Speakers had found her, and she'd had to leave in order to escape from them. The police had found her sleeping in a bus station, and had brought her back to the community house; but it had been easy to sneak past the staff, and she had left again when the Speakers ordered her to. This time no one had found her.

So many years ago.

She had been living on the streets ever since. She had to remain on the streets, for it was only in the open that she could escape for any length of time from the Speakers. She could never seem to make the many social workers and doctors who'd talked to her understand this; fortunately, they had never put her in a place that she hadn't eventually found a way

3

to get out of. And on very cold nights, when she had been found and put in one of the blue vans with the smiling faces and forcibly taken to a shelter, she had been grateful for the warmth and food, and had been able to tolerate the pain from the Speakers' electric voices until morning, when she had been free to leave. She had learned where to go for food and clothing when she couldn't find what she needed in the city's garbage, and on nice days she would sit with her friend on the stone steps under Jesus and listen to Zulu, whose deep, booming voice always scared the Speakers away.

She was grateful to kind social workers like Anne and Barry, who came in their blue van and always gave her a paper bag with a sandwich, cookie and carton of juice inside, and who never got angry when she refused to come with them in their van, or when she threw away the card inside the bag that listed their organization's address and telephone number. Even Dr. Hakim, who sometimes traveled with Anne and Barry in the van and made her come inside when it was very cold, seemed to accept that there was no place he could force her to go which she would not eventually find a way to walk away from. Dr. Hakim did seem to understand about the Speakers, and had said that he could make them go away if she would agree to let him put her in a hospital. But she no longer believed that anyone could make the Speakers go away; even Jesus had failed her this night. The only answer was to stay in the open, so that she could move away when they found her.

Mary wondered if Dr. Hakim and the social workers had been telling the truth when they'd said she was in terrible danger now because there was someone loose in the city who was chopping off the heads of homeless people. It had sounded like a story meant to scare her into coming with them in their blue van, but even Zulu, who knew everything, had warned her about the killer and pleaded with her to go to a city shelter. But Zulu did not understand about the Speakers. She was terrified of the young gray ones, but they only seemed to want to hurt, rape and steal. Aside from the Speakers, who were from another world, she could not understand why anyone would want to kill an old woman who wore plastic garbage bags for skirts and meant no one any harm.

Mary was brought out of her reverie by the sudden and agonizing churning of her bowels. Sometimes, when she absolutely couldn't help herself, she went to the bathroom in her

4

pants; she often wasn't even aware that she was urinating until she felt the not unpleasant warmth of the fluid running down her legs. But defecating was something else, transforming her into a vile-smelling creature she could not stand. Horrified at the thought of soiling herself, knowing that she must allow herself time to pull up three garbage-bag skirts and drop two pairs of pants, Mary desperately looked around her for a hiding place that would afford her a measure of privacy.

In the next block a church facade was undergoing renovations, and a covered, wooden mall extended out over the sidewalk for the length of the building. One of the light bulbs beneath the mall was out, and there was a large area of darkness. Mary disliked the thought of relieving herself on the sidewalk in front of one of her stone Savior's many houses, but she did not see that she had any choice; the alternative was to risk soiling herself, and then suffer the ultimate humiliation of having to go to a shelter to beg for clean clothes and water to wash herself.

Slowed by the wide streams of rushing water in the gutters, Mary shuffled across the street, stepped up on the curb and then went faster when a Speaker screamed at her from somewhere inside Lufthansa. She hurried down the mall to the area of darkness, pulled up her first garbage-bag skirt and desperately struggled with cold, arthritic fingers to undo the safety pin that held up her outer pair of pants. She finally managed to lift the skirts and drop the pants, quickly squatted at the base of the stone steps leading up to the church's recessed main entrance and let herself go, sighing with pleasure and pride that she had been able to exhibit such self-control.

A car came around the near corner and started up the avenue, its lights momentarily blinding Mary. The old woman averted her gaze, looked down between her legs—and was startled to see a copious amount of blood mixing with her urine and watery stool; the blood, feces and urine mixed, pooled in slight cracks and depressions in the concrete, then broke into thin rivulets that flowed out over the sidewalk and into the gutter.

Mary's first thought was that she was dying; she had waited too long to leave Jesus, and the Speakers had managed to penetrate her body and mortally wound her. Blood was pouring from her body along with the waste, and soon she would be dead.

5

But she did not *feel* as if she were dying, and the pain from the electric words had begun to ease as soon as she'd left Jesus and descended the stone steps. She did not feel as if her insides were pouring out; aside from the cold and wet, she felt only pride and pleasure at having managed to relieve herself without soiling her clothes. When she finished and tentatively touched herself between the legs, her fingers came away moist with urine, but no blood. Perhaps the blood was not hers, Mary thought, and she wondered if this might not be another abominable trick of the Speakers to torment her.

"Hello, Mary."

This was a different Speaker, one who was hiding somewhere up in the darkness at the church entrance behind her. His tone was gentler, softer, than any she had heard a Speaker use before, and the voice reminded her of a friend.

So it was a trick.

Embarrassed at having been observed relieving herself, frightened by the fact that a Speaker had found her so soon after she thought she had escaped them, Mary stood up, quickly pulled up her two pairs of pants, secured the safety pins and started to shuffle away.

"Don't go away, Mary," the gentle, soothing voice said. "You know me, so you know there's no reason to be afraid. I can see that you're soaked through to the skin, and you must be freezing. You don't want to catch pneumonia. I can help you. Come back."

Mary stopped walking. Perhaps it really was him, she thought, and not a Speaker after all; this voice had uttered many words, yet she felt no electric pain. She slowly turned, cocked her head to one side and squinted, trying to peer up into the night shrouding the recessed entrance.

"I was planning on coming to see you soon anyway, Mary."

Mary shook her head in confusion. "But you see me all the time."

"I think it's wonderful that you're here with me now, tonight. It's a good time. Come up to me, Mary. See what I have for you."

The old woman shuffled back up the sidewalk into the darkness, felt with her foot until she found the first stone step. "What is it?"

"I know how cold and tired you are, Mary. Wouldn't you like

6

to rest? I mean really rest, and never be cold, hungry or in pain ever again?"

"Oh, yes," Mary said weakly, her voice cracking as a violent shudder, triggered by bone-deep cold, suddenly passed through her body.

"Then come to me."

She did—or tried to. She made it up two steps, then tripped in the darkness and would have fallen if a powerful, sinewy hand sheathed in rubber had not reached down and gripped her arm, holding her steady. A car came around the corner across the way, its headlights briefly, dimly, illuminating part of the recess, and Mary smiled up into the face of the man draped in a bright, crimson-streaked orange slicker buttoned to his neck and wearing a rain hat that was only orange.

"Oh, Lord, I'm so glad it really is—"

She abruptly stopped speaking and gasped when a large truck, which had been following the car, came around the corner and its powerful high beams briefly flashed across the recess. Mary had forgotten all about the blood she had seen on the sidewalk, but now she saw where it had leaked from. Beside the carnage that was the fountainhead was a plastic shopping bag stuffed with still more carnage, topped with blood-matted white hair.

"Oh, dear," Mary said in a small voice. "Oh, dear."

"I'm sorry I didn't get to you sooner, Mary," the man said kindly, once more cloaked in darkness. "There are so many who suffer, as you well know. Please forgive me for keeping you waiting so long in your time of need."

"But I don't want to die," Mary said just before the razor silenced the Speakers forever.

CHAPTER ONE

(i)

His first sensation was of vague discomfort, a damp chilliness which almost immediately exploded into wet cold so fierce and piercing it seemed his heart would freeze and shatter; next he was aware of cold rain beating on his head, melting away his hair and scalp . . .

". . . *me, Bone?*" A woman's voice echoing somewhere in the dark depths of his stirring consciousness, a disembodied human sound balanced on the cusp between sleep and wakefulness, or one dream and another. "*Bone, can you hear me?*"

Then came anxiety, which quickly swelled into fear. Something was terribly wrong, but he did not know what it was. A dream? Whose dream? He could not remember anything. He was missing huge chunks of himself, but he could not recall where he had left, or lost, them. Without the pieces of himself that were inexplicably missing he felt reduced to no more than a pair of eyes trapped inside an alien, out-of-control body squatting in cold mud oozing over the tops of his shoes and soaking through the seat of his pants. He sensed that the body was gripping something in its right hand, but he did not know

8

what it was. Fear became terror and he felt as if he were suffocating, the air being crushed from his lungs.

Who was the stranger squatting in the mud?! Who am I?!

Somewhere off to his right in this freezing, black ocean of rain and mud, a man's voice said, *"Look at the poor son-of-a-bitch; he's shaking like a leaf. I'm going to—"*

"No, Barry!" The woman. Her tone sharp, confident, commanding. *"Don't go near him yet. Just let him be for a few minutes."*

"Anne's right, Barry." Another man's voice. Authoritative tone despite a foreign accent that gave the sound a lilting, almost song-like quality. Off to his left. The two men were flanking the woman, who was closest to him. Very close to him. *"I'd say he's trembling as much from fear as cold, and he might very well be dangerous."*

"Oh, come on, Ali," the woman said. *"I just don't want him to be any more frightened than he already is. He's never given any indication that he's dangerous; quite the opposite."*

"He's never squatted in the rain and mud for two days before, either," the high-pitched, lilting voice of authority said. *"Obviously, something's changed in him, and I don't think it wise to approach him until we can determine just what, and how deep, that change or those changes may be. The bone he carries is a human femur which appears to have ossified; it would make a formidable weapon. You're too close to him, Anne."*

"I'm all right."

"I can handle him," the man on his right with the deeper voice said. *"If you give the word that we can take him in, Ali, I'll get him to the van."*

"No," the woman said firmly. *"If you start grabbing at him, we could lose him again. This is the biggest reaction we've ever seen in him. Whatever's happening inside his head is important, and we don't want to rush things."*

"Agreed," the lilting voice said. *"Anne, come back under the umbrella."*

"I'm all right, Ali."

"How long are we supposed to just stand around here in the rain and wait?"

"If you're cold, Barry, go sit in the van."

He blinked—and suddenly he could see. He was crouched in the middle of a very large field which was bordered by trees. Beyond the trees, shrouded in mist and fog, dozens of tall buildings thrust up into a lead-colored sky. Atop one building was a sign, *Essex House;* it meant nothing to him, except that it told him the stranger could read. The sight of the magnificent stone and glass buildings surrounding the meadow and the trees deeply touched him for reasons he could not understand. He had no idea who, what or where he was, and he could not remember ever seeing the meadow or the trees or the tall buildings beyond, but there was no doubt that they reminded him of something. Perhaps it was all a dream, a nightmare, and he would awaken at any moment and remember who he was.

Peel off!

"Give me a break, partner. It just seems to me that it's not going to do anyone any good for two city workers and a psychiatrist to catch pneumonia waiting around for a man to decide if he wants to come in out of the rain. Bone's been here two days already, and there's no telling how long he intends to stay. If Ali will sign the papers, let's at least get the guy's body inside the van, out of the rain, and worry about his head later. As it is, he must be half dead by now. It's freezing out here."

He judged the man with the deeper voice, the one off to his right who had just spoken, to be in his late twenties or early thirties. Under six feet, heavyset, he wore a bright blue windbreaker with a New York Giants logo over a black, woolen turtleneck sweater, jeans which were stretched tight by heavily muscled thighs and tucked into the tops of laced leather boots with rubber soles. His close-cropped black hair with its widow's peak was matted down over a broad forehead. His nose seemed too small for the rest of his face, which was dominated by a broad chin thrust out as if in defiance of the rain beating down on his uncovered head. The bright green eyes, now focused on him, with the rest of his features and the set of his body, revealed a mix of emotions—curiosity, wonder, caution and perhaps not a little hostility and fear.

The features of the other two people were hidden in the shadows beneath the hoods of bulky, gray rain slickers that came down to their knees. The man off to his left had a slight, even frail, build, and seemed almost lost in his oversize slicker beneath the large black umbrella he held over his head.

The woman, about five feet five or six, was standing directly in front of him, very close, no more than two yards away.

"Anne, don't—!"

But the woman ignored the burly man's warning as she

abruptly stepped forward and crouched down directly in front
of him, less than an arm's length away. The sudden movement
caused her hood to slip off, but she made no move to pull it
back up. Before the rain darkened and matted it down, he saw
thick, shiny, dark brown hair, shoulder-length and prematurely gray around the temples. He judged her to be in her
early thirties, attractive if not beautiful, with an aura of both
toughness and tenderness. She had a full mouth, with an
exaggerated cleft in her upper lip, a thin, aquiline nose, high
cheekbones, fair skin, bright hazel eyes that now glistened with
tears. He saw yearning in the reflective pools of the hazel eyes,
hope and a great deal of anxiety; but he sensed that the anxiety
was not for herself, but for him.

Suddenly the woman reached into the deep pocket of her
slicker, drew out what appeared to be a sandwich wrapped in
waxed paper, held it out to him in a trembling hand. The rain
spattering on the waxed paper sounded like machine-gun fire.

"Please, Bone," the woman said in a quavering voice that
was close to a sob. The tears that had glistened in her eyes now
welled, spilled over her lids and ran down her cheeks to be
washed away by the rain. "At least take the sandwich. You
haven't eaten anything in two days, and you must be starving.
You'll die."

He stared at the waxed-paper package in the woman's
outstretched, trembling hand, watched the fat raindrops splat-
ter and pop on its surface. *Rat-tatta-tatta-rat-tatta.*

Dreaming?

The woman withdrew the sandwich, lowered her head and
breathed a deep sigh. Then, without straightening up, she
twisted around and spoke to the short man standing under the
black umbrella. "You've got to give us the okay to take him in
involuntarily, Ali. It's why we dragged you out here."

"I understand that," the man replied easily in his lilting,
singsong voice. "But on what grounds? Who is he hurting?"

"*Himself*, Ali! Damn it, you know that!"

"It isn't really that cold—certainly nowhere near freezing,
which is the critical temperature. After all, it's springtime."

"Ali, he's been out here *two days*! He's going to catch
pneumonia, if he doesn't have it already!"

"I'll be told that's not sufficient grounds for involuntary
incarceration. Your perception of what's happening here is
relatively unimportant, and *you* know that. The increase in

11

tuberculosis among this population is mushrooming, as you also know; but even the fact that a man or woman is dying of tuberculosis—and infecting countless others—is not, by itself, considered grounds for involuntary incarceration. We'll be asked in all seriousness by some half-assed young lawyer how we could be certain he wasn't just trying to wash himself."

"Now *you* sound like one of those goddamned lawyers!" the woman snapped. Her voice was growing husky, as if she might be sick herself.

"You know which side I'm on, Anne," the man under the umbrella replied evenly. "But I'm the one who has to answer to those lawyers and judges, and it's my time that will be wasted answering questions and filling out forms that could eventually lead to a court order freeing him again, anyway. You talk as if you've never been through this business with me before. What is so special about this man? Without too much difficulty, I believe we could find fifty other homeless people here in the park, out in the rain."

"No, Ali! Not like Bone! Not squatting out in the open, unprotected! And not for two days!" She paused, sighed heavily again, and then resumed speaking in a tone that had become plaintive. "At least we can get him inside for a few hours, Ali; get him dried off and put some food in his belly."

"Maybe, maybe not. He might resist—violently—any attempt to undress him, give him medication or food. It's bad professional practice to make a move we know will probably be blocked, Anne—bad for me, bad for you, and bad for the cause we serve. It's the responsibility of the city and the courts to set the guidelines, which they've done. We may know they're totally unrealistic, but all we can do is advise change and keep working within those guidelines. In this instance, we'll probably be told in no uncertain terms that just because a man doesn't know enough to come in out of the rain is no reason to deprive him of his civil liberties. I'm sorry, Anne. I want to help this man you call Bone as much as you do."

"I doubt that," the heavyset man said tightly. "Anne has a thing for Bone."

The woman shook her head impatiently. "Ali, you're the psychiatrist on call, and HRA needs your written authorization to shelter this man against his will. Give it to us, and I promise I'll deal with the lawyers. I think you're being unreasonable.

Bone looks like he's about to keel over from exhaustion, anyway, so why can't you just sign the goddamned papers?!"

Bone? he thought. This was the name of the stranger whose body he haunted?

"I think it's premature, Anne. He's not physically acting out, overtly endangering himself or others. I'm sorry."

He abruptly stood up.

"Anne, watch out!" the burly man in the blue windbreaker shouted as he started forward, his large hands balled into fists.

The woman twisted back around to look up at him, then quickly straightened up and stepped even closer, as if to shield him from the other man. She stood so close that, even through her heavy parka, he could feel the distinctive softness of large breasts pressing against his left arm. "Wait, Barry! Don't touch him! It's all right! He won't hurt me!"

The man with the bright green eyes and short black hair stopped; but his hands remained clenched into fists, and he was balanced on the balls of his feet, ready to leap forward. The man under the umbrella hadn't appeared to react at all.

"I'm responsible for your safety," the man said in a low, tense voice, impatiently swiping at the water collecting on his broad chin. "It's why they send me out with you."

"I'm safe," she replied, and then slowly turned her head to look into his face. There was no fear in her hazel eyes, he thought; excitement, hope and compassion—but no fear. He was still very conscious of the feel of her breasts against his arm, the confident gentleness of her voice. "We're not going to hurt you, Bone. Please don't try to hurt any of us."

Then she slowly lowered her gaze, to his right. He looked down and was startled to see that he was holding a large bone in his right hand, and that his arm was half raised, as if to strike with the strange object, which, now that he was aware of it, felt as heavy, cold and hard as stone; he could understand the burly man's concern, and was struck anew by the woman's confidence and fearlessness.

He was the one who was afraid.

He lowered his arm—but did not release the bone. He wondered why anyone would carry a bone around with him, yet realized that the stranger whose body he inhabited did— had. Indeed, these people seemed to know the stranger, called him "Bone." *Where* had the stranger carried the bone? *Why?*

He was afraid. And, suddenly, he was ravenously hungry.

13

The woman stepped away and once again, slowly, held out the sandwich to him.

Tat-tatta-rat-tatta.

He transferred the bone to his left armpit—slowly, deliberately, so as to show he was not threatening anybody—and then took the sandwich from the woman's outstretched hand. His own hands shook as he fumbled with the wrapper, and he finally tore it off, dropping the pieces of waxed paper into the mud at his feet. He bit into the sandwich and groaned aloud with satiated need and pleasure at the taste and texture of the bread, ham, cheese, lettuce and mayonnaise. He wolfed down the first sandwich, accepted a second, which the woman, beaming with pleasure, had produced from the deep pockets of her gray parka. When he had finished this he felt better, if a bit dizzy. He licked mayonnaise off his fingers, then glanced up to find that the two men had moved closer, and now stood on either side of the woman. At this distance he could see that the slight man under the umbrella had a dark brown complexion, accented by a thin, very dark moustache that matched the color of his hair, and very large, limpid black eyes that were now staring at him with intense curiosity.

"Who the hell are you?" he asked, looking from one face to another.

The dark eyebrows of the frail-looking man under the umbrella lifted slightly. "I am Dr. Ali Hakim," he said, his lilting voice now carrying more than a trace of amusement as well as surprise. "This is my colleague, Miss Anne Winchell, and her assistant, Mr. Barry Prindle. And who the hell, may we ask, are you?"

He searched his stranger's mind for an answer that wouldn't appear. His fear, which had been forgotten as his terrible hunger had been recognized and partially assuaged, now returned, and was worse. "I . . . don't know," he said hoarsely, looking around him at the mud and wet grass, the trees, sidewalks and lampposts, the tall buildings that rose like a circular mountain range all around them. "Where am I?"

The woman's broad smile vanished as she frowned with concern. "You're in the Sheep Meadow. Don't you remember coming here?"

His stomach muscles tightened as his fear continued to grow in him. Reflexively, he took the bone from under his left arm

14

and gripped it tightly. The heavyset man to his right tensed, and the woman quickly put her hand on his arm.

"Sheep meadow? What sheep meadow? Where?"

Still frowning, the woman exchanged glances with the brown-skinned man under the umbrella, then looked back at him. "The Sheep Meadow in Central Park—New York City. Don't you know who or where you are, Bone? Don't those names mean anything to you?"

Again, he searched the stranger's mind, and again found no answers. He studied the faces of the people standing in front of him—the woman's, anxious and pensive; the burly man's, cautious and suspicious. The expression on the face of the man under the umbrella was impassive, with only the brightness of his limpid, expressive eyes revealing his continued keen curiosity.

"Not at the moment," he replied at last, glancing down at the bizarre object he held in his hand. "You call me 'Bone.' I presume because of this." He paused, looked hard at the woman. "But you also talk as if you know me. Do you?"

"Yes," the woman replied softly, in a strained voice that clearly reflected dismay and disappointment. "At least, I feel as if I do."

"For how long?"

"A little over a year—since Barry and I approached you over on Eighth Avenue."

He swallowed hard, found that his mouth was very dry. He licked rain from his lips, then closed his eyes and probed desperately into the stranger's mind for some feeling, however vague, of recognition or familiarity. There was none, and he opened his eyes. "I've been here a *year*?" he said to the woman as he gestured around him, making no effort to hide his fear. A *year*!

The woman nodded. "It was about a year ago that we first spotted you on the street. You were mute; this is the first time any of us have heard you speak. Since you were always carrying that thing around with you, it just seemed natural to start referring to you as 'Bone.' You can't remember your real name?"

He started to search the stranger's mind again, but gave up quickly; there were no answers there, only fear, bewilderment and frustration. He slowly shook his head.

"Look, Bone—oh, I'm sorry if that bothers you."

15

Despite himself, despite his fear and the surrealistic nightmare he found he had awakened to, he suddenly laughed. "You've got to be kidding me, lady," he said as the laughter quickly died and left a raw feeling, a bitter taste, at the back of his throat. He suddenly felt flushed and very dizzy, and he had to concentrate on remaining steady on his feet. "I don't know who I am, where I am, where I came from or how I got here, and you think I'm going to worry about what you call me?"

That received a faint smile and slight nod from the brown-skinned man under the umbrella. The younger man's expression of caution and concern remained unchanged, while the woman laughed uncertainly.

"Bone," she said, tentatively reaching out and touching his hand, "obviously, we have a lot of things to talk about, but there's no reason for us to stand out here in the rain. Is there? Will you come with us?"

He stepped back, away from the woman's touch and the soul-deep chasm of loneliness the touch had opened in him without warning. "Where?"

"To a place where we can get you dry clothes, proper food and a thorough medical check. Right now you don't look too good, and we don't want you to get sick."

"I don't think I have any money."

Again, tears welled in the woman's hazel eyes. "You don't need any money, Bone."

"You said you first saw me on Eighth Avenue, wherever that is. Where else have you seen me before?"

The woman wiped water off her face, pushed her rain-matted hair away from her eyes, then shrugged and gestured around her. "All over the place, Bone; you liked to walk. But I think you spent most of your time in midtown and lower Manhattan."

"Manhattan?"

"It's where we are now. That name really doesn't mean anything to you?"

"Right now, lady, nothing means anything to me."

"Manhattan is a borough—a part—of New York City. It's really a big island, and I wouldn't be surprised if you've walked over most of it."

"Where have I been staying? Where do I sleep at night?"

"I don't think anybody knows, Bone," the woman replied quietly. "You've been seen at soup kitchens at a number of locations, but you've never signed in to any of our shelters or clinics. Nobody has ever—"

He held up his left hand, and the woman stopped speaking. "I don't know what you're talking about," he said. "I don't know anything about shelters, soup kitchens or clinics. I don't remember anything."

"We've approached you on a number of occasions, Bone," the heavyset young man said as he walked forward and stood next to the woman. The change in his voice and demeanor was striking; the tension and vague hostility reflected in his body language was gone, and his voice had become soft, even gentle. This man was deeply protective of the woman, Bone thought, and perhaps even loved her. For whatever reason, he had apparently decided that this stranger with his bone posed no threat to her. "Like Anne said, you never talked—but you obviously knew how to take care of yourself. You always looked clean when we saw you, and you knew the locations of the soup kitchens, churches and Salvation Army centers where you could get food and clothes. You never bothered anybody, at least not that we know of. Sometimes you'd be carrying things— "

"What things?"

Barry Prindle shrugged his broad shoulders. "Just stuff you'd apparently picked out of trash piles—clothing, old blankets, odds and ends you must have felt you had some use for. The one thing that never changed was that bone in your hand; you always had it with you." He paused, squinted slightly. "You don't remember where you got it?"

"No."

"It doesn't mean anything to you?"

"No. You say I've been out here for two days?"

Anne Winchell nodded. "Somebody called in and told us you were here; it seems you plopped yourself down on this spot the day before yesterday, Thursday, around dawn. You've been squatting here, just staring off into space, until now. This is the fourth time Barry and I have been here."

Dr. Ali Hakim abruptly walked forward, cleared his throat. "This is a very intriguing conversation, lady and gentlemen," he said wryly, "but, considering the rather adverse weather conditions, I suggest we get to the point. Mr. Bone, my colleagues and I work for the city's Human Resources Administration. What we try to do is convince those of the city's homeless who are without any visible resources to accept the city's offer of food, shelter, medical care and employment counseling. However, the fact of the matter is that we can't force anyone to accept our help against that person's will— unless he poses a clear and present danger to himself or others. I'm a psychiatrist, and it's my responsibility to make that kind of determination. At the moment, you obviously don't appear to fall into that category. You have a decision to make."

Anne Winchell suddenly reached out with both hands and clasped Bone's hand, gripping it tightly. It was a gesture that made Barry Prindle stiffen perceptibly. "Bone," she said, "what Dr. Hakim is saying is that you must *choose* to come with us and let us help you. How about it? We've got a van parked not far from here. Wouldn't it be nice to get into some warm, dry clothes, eat some hot food and get some proper sleep?"

Without warning tears sprang to his eyes and rolled down his cheeks, and he had to stifle a sob. This woman's face and voice, her words and the strong yet gentle feel of her hands around his seemed to offer so much at the same time they made him feel even more vulnerable and lost. Lost. He was so cold, tired, hungry. And sick. Now, suddenly, he felt fever heat blazing in his body. His vision was beginning to blur, and he was afraid that his legs would collapse under him. "I want to go home," he whispered, his voice breaking.

"And where might that be, Mr. Bone?" Ali Hakim asked in an even, matter-of-fact tone. "Do you recall?"

Tears continued to spill out of him as he picked at the stranger's mind, found nothing but silence and emptiness. He swallowed hard, shook his head, whispered, "Where will you take me?"

"First, to a hospital," Anne said with a heavy sigh of relief. She squeezed his left hand hard, smiled up into his face. She, too, had begun crying again. "We'll get you fed, washed up and into some dry clothes. Then the doctors will examine you. Who knows? Maybe they'll even be able to figure out why you've lost your memory, and then help you get it back. Okay?"

He nodded.

"Thank you for letting us help you, Bone," Anne said, and suddenly began to sob. "I've been trying for so long . . ."

Barry abruptly took off his windbreaker and started to drape it over Bone's shoulders.

"Don't patronize me!" Bone snapped, pushing the jacket

18

away. "If I've been sitting in the rain for two days, I really can't get much wetter, can I?! Put your damn jacket back on!"

But when his knees began to buckle, he allowed the two men to support him under the arms.

"Proud, even defiant," Ali Hakim said to no one in particular. "Good vocabulary, intelligent. Cognitive processes seemingly intact, for the most part, but apparent total loss of memory. Most interesting."

(ii)

With Anne leading the way, frequently and anxiously glancing back at him, he was half escorted, half carried across the meadow, along a sidewalk, then up a flight of wide stone steps to the sidewalk next to a street filled with slow-moving cars and trucks. He was led to a bright blue van that had a bright yellow and black smiling face painted on its side, next to the city's official seal. Anne, who looked increasingly concerned, slid open the door on the side, and he was helped up and into a seat. Anne sat down beside him and gripped his left hand tightly as the two men got in the front. Barry drove, while Bone—sweating profusely now, and with his vision going in and out of focus—gazed in bewilderment out the window at the throngs of people and vehicles slogging through the rain, the enormous buildings—great stone, steel and glass monoliths built side by side on both sides of the street and extending in all directions as far as he could see. Suddenly, for no reason at all that he could understand, he had the unmistakable sense that this world of stone canyons that were city streets was at once totally alien to the stranger and totally familiar, an impossible paradox that was nonetheless true in the unknown universe of the stranger's heart.

Barry maneuvered the van with confidence and skill through the traffic as Bone, now drenched in sweat, drifted in and out of consciousness. Once, in a moment of consciousness and clear vision, he found himself looking out the window at a magnificent stone church, with an intricately carved facade. There were two sets of stone steps leading to two entrances. The wide steps leading to the main entrance were bisected by a steel guardrail. At the top of the steps, beneath a stone overhang, close to two dozen people, in all manner of dress, were huddled

19

together as they sought protection from the rain. At the front of this group was the bizarre figure of a very tall black man dressed in a brightly colored, flowing robe that billowed in the wind. The man stood very erect, both hands grasping a stout wooden pole of polished wood which he had placed in front of him, and which was almost as long as he was tall.

Again, Bone experienced the effects of the paradoxical emotional laws at work in the universe of the stranger's heart: he was at once native and alien, at home and very far from home.

He dozed, had fever dreams of dark, cold, wet places, graveyards, the rotting smell of dying things and things long dead, drowning in darkness, falling, blood, a forest of bones, flashes of bright orange and red and purple, flickering lights of giant candles . . .

He awoke as the van slowed and made a turn. He glanced out the window and saw a sign that read *Bellevue Hospital Center*. Then the fever in him took complete control and he passed out.

CHAPTER TWO

(i)

He was not aware of time passing, consciousness or unconsciousness, in the usual sense; he felt like a large body of water
controlled by powerful psychic tidal forces that waxed and
waned in totally unpredictable patterns. In passing moments
of dim, blurred consciousness he was vaguely aware of lying in
bed in a small room with pale pink walls and a white plaster
ceiling spiderwebbed with cracks. People—white-coated doctors and nurses, the two men and a woman who had brought
him here—came and went, and were occasionally joined by a
well-dressed, powerfully built black man who would simply
stand by the bed, unmoving, for long periods of time and stare
down at him. He heard snatches of conversation about the
danger of dying from exposure, double pneumonia, serial
killings, murder and horrible mutilation.

Or he imagined he heard these conversations.

Once, he awoke to find himself shivering violently on an
inflatable plastic mattress that seemed to be filled with ice,
simultaneously burning with fever and chilled to the core,
another paradox in the stranger's universe. It reminded him of
how cold he had been when he had "awakened" in the meadow.
And before that . . .

There was nothing before that. Attempts to probe beyond that barrier in his stranger's mind only exhausted him, and he would lapse back into unconsciousness.

And he would dream. His stranger's crippled mind would torment him with flickering, candlelit images of being trapped underground, buried alive, sinking in quicksand, of a great stone chamber where bones protruded from the walls, floor and ceiling like stalagmites and stalactites erupting from hell. Tunnels. Orange streaked with crimson. Purple. And there was something waiting for him in the chamber, stalking him through the tunnels, something unspeakably horrible. He had found the thing's treasure, and he must die for it . . .

He dreamed of falling through space . . .

Peel off!

(ii)

When he awoke it was morning, and he knew his fever had broken. His white cotton hospital gown was wet and clammy with his night sweat, but aside from this discomfort he felt better, if very weak.

He sat up on the edge of the bed, then had to brace himself with both hands as a wave of nausea and dizziness passed through him. The spell passed, and he looked around.

The room was not the one he had been in before. The walls and ceiling of this room were painted a dark brown, and the two windows in the wall, as well as the small one set at eye level in the door, were covered with thick wire mesh. A small television camera was mounted in a corner, near the ceiling, and it was pointed at him. Without knowing how he knew it, he realized he was in the hospital's secure ward.

What had his stranger done to be considered dangerous?

His heart began to beat rapidly, and he closed his eyes and took a series of deep breaths to calm himself. Then, once more, he slowly began to probe the stranger's mind to see what else besides the recognition of a secure ward he might know, or could remember. He remembered Anne Winchell, Barry Prindle and Dr. Hakim bringing him to the hospital after he had awakened in the park. He remembered the first words he had heard there; the clinging, gelid touch of mud in his shoes, and on his seat; the sudden pangs of hunger, and the incredible pleasure eating the two sandwiches had given him. He remembered the frightening thrill he had felt, along with the numbing blow of loneliness, at the touch of Anne Winchell's hand, the feel of her breasts. He remembered everything that had happened—from the time he had awakened. And nothing before that. He did not know what he knew.

He did not even know what he looked like.

The woman with the hazel eyes had told him he'd been wandering the streets of New York City for at least a year. That year was completely lost to him. Where had he come from? What had he done before? How many more years had he lost? How old was this stranger whose body he inhabited?

He stood up, walked to the foot of the bed and picked up the chart that hung from a cord there. He was listed as John Doe. He walked into the small bathroom, bent down over the sink and peered into the small square of polished steel that was anchored to the wall to serve as a mirror. What he saw was the reflection of a man in his early to mid-thirties. His eyes were a deep blue, and there was a thin, jagged scar that bisected his left eyebrow and tracked up his forehead to his hairline. He had a full head of light brown hair—matted and stringy now with dried perspiration—which he remembered as falling around his shoulders when he had been in the park, but which had been cut, and not badly, during the time when he was unconscious. He was fair-skinned, with a smallish nose that looked as if it might have been broken once. Strong chin and mouth. When he examined his teeth, he found them reasonably clean and white, with none missing. All in all, he thought with a thin smile, this stranger wasn't all that bad-looking, and some people might even consider him handsome. He estimated his height at around six feet.

He was turning away from the polished steel when something on the right side of his head, an inch or two above his ear, caught his attention. He put his hand there, pulled back the hair and was surprised to find a depression the size of a half dollar covered with puckered scar tissue.

He stepped back from the sink, untied the laces of his baggy hospital gown and let it drop off his shoulders to the floor. Examining his body, he found that he had a flat, hard belly, heavily muscled legs with thick thighs. After a year living on the streets, he thought, not to mention an unknown length of time in a hospital in a coma, the stranger still looked remarkably fit, if a bit on the thin side in the stomach and around the ribs and gaunt in the face. He even had good teeth and gums, and he wondered how that could be possible. It had to mean that the stranger had well-honed survival skills. He knew how to take care of himself in the most adverse circumstances, and he found that reassuring.

He certainly was in adverse circumstances.

When he looked down at the palms of his hands he was startled to see that they were covered with large calluses—not just on the palms, but from his fingertips to the heels of his hands. They were softer now, surely, than they had been a year before, but large and thick nonetheless. It was, of course, possible that he'd done some kind of very rough work with his hands during the year he'd been on the streets, but he doubted that calluses such as his could build up in only a year; they had come from the time before his year on the streets, from the other—the first—life lost from his memory.

When he turned his hands over and examined the backs, he found the same evidence of incredibly hard use—in this case a network of scars, indentations, gnarled fingers. Two nails on the fingers of his left hand, and three on the fingers of his right, had somehow been torn off, and the tips were overgrown with flesh and scar tissue.

Construction worker? he thought. What kind of work could he have been doing that could possibly cause such kind of damage? And why wouldn't he have worn heavy gloves to protect himself? An accident? No; accidents don't leave calluses. Whatever he had been doing to wreak such damage to these large, obviously powerful hands, he had been doing by choice.

Except for the absence of memory, he thought, the stranger's mind seemed to work fairly well. It allowed him to speak, to read, to think and even—apparently—to reason. There was an emotional toughness to the stranger; he no longer felt the anxiety approaching panic he had experienced in the first moments in the park when he had awakened and found he did not know who or where he was. The situation was presently as bad—or worse, since he *still* could not remember anything before awakening to find himself squatting in the rain and mud in the middle of the Sheep Meadow—but he seemed to be dealing with it. His stranger was apparently cool, level-headed.

He hoped he stayed that way.

24

He felt lonely, but not overwhelmingly so. Was there no one who loved him, who would have reported him missing?

Whatever had happened to cause him to lose all memory of that first life and end up on the city streets, it was nonetheless true that he had apparently been taking care of business, so to speak—meandering around Manhattan, obtaining food and clothing and finding a place to sleep. What had happened to cause the stranger to suddenly stop taking care of business and squat down in a field, in the pouring rain, for two days?

Had he wanted to die?

Why had he been placed in a secure ward? The woman had said he'd never been considered dangerous before, despite the bizarre trophy he'd carried around with him. Why, suddenly, was he considered dangerous now? What had he done?

There was a small shower stall in the bathroom. He washed, dried himself off with a ragged towel hanging on a rack next to the toilet, then put on a clean cotton gown he found in a white metal cabinet on the wall next to the sink. Directly above the cabinet was another television camera, pointing directly at him. He looked up at the camera and patted his stomach; suddenly he was very hungry.

Was he insane?!

Without warning the thought with fangs had leaped out at him from the dark depths of the stranger's mind, attacking, making him short of breath and knotting the muscles in his stomach.

Leave it alone, he thought as he leaned on the sink and took deep breaths to ease his fear. There was no sense in worrying now about what he might find out about himself. His job now was to try as hard as he could to retrieve the mental records of both lives he had lost, regardless of what those records might show.

Even if the monster chasing him through the caves of his dreams turned out to be himself.

He had not been comfortable with the physical appearance of the stranger's body, had been pleased with his thought processes; now he had no choice but to trust the stranger himself.

When he came out of the bathroom he was startled to see the well-dressed black man—the same one whose presence he had been aware of at times during his brief periods of consciousness—leaning against the wall near the foot of the bed;

he had not heard the door open or close, had not heard footsteps.

The man had strong features—high forehead, gray shadows on the sides of his head where he had shaved the hair. Bone judged him to be in his mid-forties. There was a milky spot in his left eye, suspended in the black iris like a thick cobweb. There was no humor in the man's thin smile, but rather mild curiosity and a great deal of suspicion. He wore a well-tailored, three-piece, gray pinstripe suit, pale blue shirt, maroon tie. His black shoes, when he stepped around from behind the bed, were highly polished, and looked expensive. He was, Bone thought, obviously a man who cared about his appearance and was probably more than a little vain. He was a man who was very sure of himself.

"Good morning," the man said simply.

Bone sat down on the edge of the bed, met the man's gaze. "Good morning."

The door to the room opened to the sound of a buzzer, which Bone had not heard when the black man had entered. A young, frowning doctor with a stethoscope draped around his neck hurried in, followed by a husky orderly carrying a tray containing juice, cereal and milk, a carafe of coffee, a covered dish and a small paper cup with two blue pills in it. The orderly set the tray down on an adjustable table next to the bed, then turned and hurried out; the door closed behind him with a loud click—another sound Bone had not heard previously. The black man in the three-piece suit, who obviously knew something about clicks and buzzers, retreated to the wall at the opposite end of the room, where he continued to stare at Bone with the same mixture of curiosity and suspicion.

"I'm Dr. Graham," the young man announced perfunctorily as he stopped in front of Bone, crossed his arms over his chest and gazed down into Bone's face. This man's pale brown eyes also revealed curiosity and suspicion, and perhaps disgust. Bone wondered why. "How are you feeling?"

"I'm not sure," Bone said carefully, watching the other man's face. "I seem to have lost my memory."

"Do you know where you are now?"

"A place called Bellevue Hospital Center, in New York City."

"How do you know that?"

"The people who brought me here told me the name of the

city, and I saw your sign when we drove in. I remember waking up in a field in the rain, but nothing before that."

The man leaning against the wall put a hand over his mouth and coughed lightly. The doctor grunted, then abruptly put the plugs of the stethoscope in his ears and listened to Bone's heart and lungs. After a few moments he straightened up and took the plugs out of his ears.

"You still have some fluid in your lungs," the doctor said curtly, "but the antibiotics we're giving you should clear that up in a day or two."

"You don't seem very interested in my loss of memory."

"I'm an internist, not a psychiatrist or neurologist," the doctor replied in the same abrupt tone. "Amnesia isn't my field. What you describe is interesting, but unfortunately my schedule here doesn't permit me to indulge curiosity."

"What about you?" Bone said to the man standing against the wall. "Are you a psychiatrist?"

The man shook his head—a slow, deliberate motion.

"What's the day and month?" Bone asked the doctor.

"April seventeenth—a Saturday."

"How long have I been here?"

"Seven days. You had a severe case of double pneumonia complicated by other factors associated with exposure. For a time, we thought we were going to lose you." Graham paused, blinked slowly, continued, "You seem to remember the meaning of months and days; obviously, you haven't lost the concepts of time and date."

"Is that unusual?"

The man against the wall coughed again.

"I told you amnesia isn't my field," Graham replied as he cast a quick, annoyed glance at the other man.

"I seem to have a background of general knowledge that wasn't lost," Bone said, looking back and forth between the two men. "I suspect I'm fairly well educated, because that background of general knowledge seems broad; I keep finding out things that I know. But I can't remember specific events in the past, or anything at all about myself."

The doctor ran a hand through his thinning, light brown hair. "I must say, considering the fact that you're just recovering from a serious illness, you look remarkably fit for a man who's been living on the streets. You have no idea of the condition some of the people the street squads—"

"Street squads?"

"That's what we call the mobile squads that work for the HRA—the city's Human Resources Administration. The people they bring us are usually suffering from things like tuberculosis, scabies, frostbite and even an occasional case of plague or cholera. Almost all of them have to be deloused before we put them in a bed. During the winter and early spring, hardly a day goes by that we don't have to amputate some homeless person's fingers or toes because of gangrene caused by frostbite—and it's not unusual for us to be cutting off the digits of somebody we've worked on before. You're a striking exception to the usual kind of homeless person we usually get in here."

"Why does the city allow it?"

"Allow what?"

"People to live on the streets who are dying of tuberculosis and the other things you mentioned. How can they let people freeze in the winter?"

"If you want to discuss social reform, you've got the wrong person. It's not my field."

"That's right, I forgot," Bone said. "You're an internist."

If the young physician detected the sarcasm in Bone's voice, he didn't indicate it. "That's correct."

"Why am I in a secure ward, Doctor?"

The other man's brown eyes searched Bone's face, then looked away. "That's an interesting bit of the 'general knowledge' you mentioned; you not only have the concept of a secure ward, but you know you're in one."

"What have I done?"

"That would be my department," the well-dressed man with the milky eye at the far end of the room said, speaking in a casual tone as he walked to the foot of the bed and rested his forearms on the brass rail there. "Are you finished, Doctor?"

"The pills," Graham said, pointing to the cup on the tray. "They're your antibiotics; take them, please."

Bone put the pills in his mouth, washed them down with orange juice.

"He's all yours, Lieutenant," the doctor continued matter-of-factly as he made a note on Bone's chart, then walked quickly from the room.

"You're a policeman?"

"Detective Lieutenant Perry Lightning, New York Police Department. Why don't you eat your food before it gets cold?"

Bone drank the rest of his juice, then started in on the two eggs and three strips of bacon he found under the metal top of the covered dish. The food was already cold—but it was good, and he wondered if they would bring him more if he asked for it. As he finished the bacon and eggs, sipped coffee, then turned his attention to the cereal and toast, he felt oddly at peace. For better or worse, he thought, he was about to find out something about the stranger; if the stranger was a criminal, well, there was nothing he could do about it. To have a kind of witness, even a hostile one, to the behavior of the stranger in the past that was lost to him was a relief, and strangely reassuring. He thought he would trade almost any bad dream for the nightmare of having no past at all.

"Sometimes, for a man in my position, it helps to have an unusual name," the detective continued in an easy, conversational tone. "It helps people to remember him. What about you? What's your name?"

Bone ate the last slice of toast, then looked up into the other man's face. There was a straight-backed chair in the room, but Lightning gave no indication that he wanted to sit. Instead, he came around to the side of the bed and stood over Bone, very close, and this magnified his strong physical presence. Despite the man's easy tone, there was no doubt in Bone's mind that Detective Lieutenant Perry Lightning meant to be intimidating, and he found that this didn't particularly bother him.

Interesting, he thought; the stranger was not easily intimidated. "I don't know," he replied evenly, pushing the table with the tray away from him and forcing the detective to step back. "I can't remember."

"Well, people have to call you something. You like the name John Doe?"

The man had moved forward again, and was standing so close that his broad chest was only inches from Bone's nose. Bone pushed himself back in the bed, drew his legs up and crossed them Indian-style. "Bone," he said.

"Bone? You call yourself 'Bone'?"

"It's what other people called me during the year or so I spent on the streets—and I think you know that."

"I like to get my information firsthand. Do you remember people calling you that?"

"No; not before I woke up in the park. Do you think I'm putting on some kind of act?"

"Are you?"

"No."

"Is that what you were doing in the park, sleeping?"

Bone leaned his back against the wall and studied the other man's stern features, the hard light in his black eyes only partially eclipsed by the milky spot in the left, the compressed, grim line of his mouth that contrasted so sharply with his casual, almost friendly, tone of voice. "I don't know what I was doing in the park before I became aware of those three people from the HRA standing in front of me. The first thing I remember is hearing the woman's voice, and it sounded far away. It was dark; I couldn't see anything. Then I got my vision back and I could see the three of them. I remember everything that's happened since, except for the time I was unconscious. I use the term 'wake up' because that's what it felt like, and that's how I think of it. Have I committed a crime?"

"Have you?"

"This is going to get us nowhere, Lieutenant. You do think I'm putting on an act, so you're playing games with me. Believe me, I really want to know what it is you suspect I did—or what I did. It would make things easier for me."

"You really think so?"

The tone had changed, and something in the other man's voice and eyes made Bone extremely uncomfortable. "I don't know," he replied softly. "What I'm saying is that I very much want to regain my memory."

"Sometimes the mind plays very strange tricks on people, Bone," Perry Lightning said, his tone once again easy, conversational. "You say you want to remember, but maybe you really don't. Maybe you have the need to block one or two things you don't want to remember, and the only way for you to do it is to block out everything."

"Does that mean you're giving me the benefit of the doubt when I tell you that—for whatever reasons—I can't remember anything that ever happened to me before I came around in the park?"

The policeman took a cigarette from a pack in his suit jacket pocket, placed it between his lips but did not light it. "I'd like to ask you some questions."

"I thought that was what you've been doing."

"What I've been doing is enjoying a casual conversation with

30

you about the state of your physical and mental health, Mr. Bone."

Bone smiled thinly. "Just 'Bone' will do, Lieutenant."

"Before I formally ask you any questions, I have to tell you that anything you say to me could be used against you in a court of law, and I have to ask if you would like a lawyer present while I question you. If you can't afford a lawyer, which clearly seems to be the case, the city will provide you with one free of charge. Do you want me to get you a lawyer, Bone?"

"No, thank you."

"Does what I just said mean anything to you?"

Bone thought about it. "It's the Miranda ruling," he said at last, not knowing where the knowledge had come from.

Perry Lightning's thick eyebrows lifted slightly. "I'm impressed. Has anyone ever said those words to you in the past?"

"I don't remember. I just know what the words mean."

"Let me tell you something, Bone: for a man who supposedly can't remember anything, you seem to remember a whole hell of a lot of things. How do you explain that?"

"I can't," Bone replied evenly, meeting the other man's steady gaze. "I've told you that I seem to have a fairly good background of general knowledge; and certain facts, or knowledge of what things mean, surface from time to time. But I can't remember anything about myself. I'm being straight with you, Lieutenant."

Perry Lightning grunted noncommittally, then stepped back and went around to the foot of the bed. He bent down to the floor, came up holding a large paper bag that had been hidden from Bone's view. Lightning reached into the bag with his left hand, drew out a small tape recorder and microphone. He turned on the recorder, then set the apparatus down on the bed a few inches from Bone's right thigh. He came back around the bed, placed the paper bag close to Bone's feet.

"Bone, have I informed you of your rights under what you yourself informed me is the Miranda ruling?"

Bone sighed. "Yes, you have, Lieutenant."

"And have you waived your right to have an attorney present while I question you?"

"That's correct. Let's get on with it, Lieutenant."

"Let me tell you something, Bone," the police detective said in a low, rumbling voice that now seemed almost tinged with sadness. His eyes, as they stared into Bone's, seemed even brighter. "I've been in the police business a long time, close to twenty years, and I've seen some of the damnedest things; but this business about you supposedly losing all but bits and pieces of your memory has to be the strangest. You can cite the Miranda ruling to me, and yet you say you can't remember even the tiniest detail about yourself."

"That isn't quite accurate, Lieutenant," Bone said evenly. "I told you I don't remember anything about myself prior to a week ago, when I first became aware of events and my surroundings."

Lightning's gaze shifted to the ceiling, as if he were looking for cracks. "I mentioned before how, and why, a man will let his mind play very powerful tricks on him. For example, in the past I've come to know very hardened criminals—murderers, some of them— who, deep down, really wanted to be caught. Maybe they got tired of the hassle of offing people and then worrying about having the police on their trail. Or maybe their consciences began to catch up with them. For whatever the reason, Bone, I've seen many a killer roll over, drop right off and sleep like a baby after he became convinced that we really had the goods on him and he was going to be put away. These men are deeply relieved, Bone. It was peace of mind they were looking for."

"I've been sleeping very well, Lieutenant, thank you."

"You've been very sick."

"I don't feel guilty about anything."

"But then, you're a special case, aren't you?"

"Why don't you just tell me what you're getting at, Lieutenant? What are you accusing me of?"

"Do you still claim not to remember anything before you squatted down in the Sheep Meadow?"

"I don't even remember squatting. I don't know where I came from, or what I was doing there. I only remember waking up. I don't 'claim it,' Lieutenant; it's true."

Lightning removed the unlit cigarette from his mouth, carefully put it back in the pack, then replaced the pack in his suit jacket pocket. He pulled a chair over next to the bed, sat down and casually crossed his legs. Apparently, Bone thought, the other man's attempt to intimidate him with his physical presence was over; yet, rather than feeling relieved, he felt the tension in him increasing. The police detective was a dangerous adversary, certainly in possession of knowledge he had not

32

yet revealed, and the stranger had nothing with which to defend himself but the truth.

"All right," Lightning said easily, "just for the sake of argument, let's say I believe you. Why do you suppose you ended up in that particular place at that particular time?"

"I don't know. It might help me remember if I knew the precise locations where people had seen me in the past, and if these people would tell me what I was doing. Did you ever see me out there on the streets, Lieutenant?"

"I'd like to ask you some specific questions concerning certain crimes—"

"Why won't you answer my question?"

Lightning slowly uncrossed his legs, leaned forward in the chair. "We're here to have you answer my questions, Bone, not the other way around. I was about to say that I want to ask you about certain crimes that have been committed within the confines of New York City." He paused, and without taking his eyes off Bone's face reached with his left hand into the paper bag on the bed near Bone's feet. He drew out an object that was sealed inside a translucent plastic bag that had a large, yellow, numbered tag on it. "Do you recognize the object inside this bag?"

Bone nodded. "It looks like the bone I was carrying—holding—when I woke up in the meadow."

"Where did you get it?"

"I don't know."

"Do you know that it's a human bone?"

"I heard Dr. Hakim mention it. It's a femur—a thighbone."

"Now, why do you suppose you'd have carried a human thighbone around with you for a year?"

"I don't know—and I want to know. Obviously, it meant something to me." He paused, glanced over the detective's shoulder at the closest of the two mesh-covered windows. It was raining outside, and, as if echoing from another world, he could hear the faint sound of wind and rain lashing against the side of the building. He continued quietly, "When I find out where I got the bone, and why I carried it with me everywhere, then maybe I'll have the key to who I am, and what happened to me."

"Did you ever hit anyone with it?"

Bone looked quickly from the window to the other man's

face, which remained impassive. "I don't know, Lieutenant; I hope not."

"Our lab technicians found traces of human blood and hair in the cracks at one end of this little trinket of yours, Bone. It's amazing what those lab boys and girls can do, don't you think? Even after being deluged with rain and sunk in the mud, the traces of blood and hair were still there—and the lab people found them. It looks to me like you used this bone, at least once, to club somebody. Does that bit of information tickle your memory at all?"

Lightning again raised his eyebrows slightly, obviously waiting for a reply. Bone said nothing. Despite his former resolve to give himself the benefit of any doubt, he was becoming increasingly suspicious of the stranger, and was once again feeling split—a pair of eyes haunting someone else's body.

Lightning put the bone back into the bag and drew out a much smaller object, also wrapped in plastic and marked with a yellow tag. "Do you recognize this?" he asked in a soft, flat, neutral tone as he held the object out to Bone.

Bone took the plastic bag, held it up against the bank of fluorescent lights directly over his bed. Inside something metallic gleamed—a small heart-shaped locket, inlaid with mother-of-pearl, on a fragile-looking gold chain. On the back of the locket, just barely legible on the time-worn metal, were the engraved initials *MHK*. He turned the bag around repeatedly in his fingers, staring intently at the inlaid front, the engraved initials on the back, straining to find some link between this object and the stranger's past. There was nothing, and finally he gave it up.

"No," he said quietly, holding the bag with the locket out to the detective.

Perry Lightning ignored the locket, kept staring hard into Bone's face. "Are you sure?" he asked tightly. "That locket doesn't mean anything to you?"

Bone set the bagged locket down next to him on the bed, next to the running tape recorder. "It doesn't mean anything to me, Lieutenant. It might help if you told me why you think it should mean something to me."

"You were wearing it around your neck."

Bone snatched up the locket and chain inside the plastic bag, once again held the bag up to the light. *MHK*. "It's a woman's locket," he said tightly, feeling his heartbeat quicken. "It could belong to a relative. It's old. The initials; maybe my mother . . ."

"It didn't belong to your mother unless she was a bag lady," the other man said in a voice that had again become soft, neutral.

Bone glanced up into the detective's dark eyes, saw the intensity there behind the impassive features, knew the man was gauging his reaction.

"We got lucky with that locket," Perry Lightning continued in the same flat tone as he continued to stare hard at Bone. "An acid bath brought up those initials, and a date which you can only see if you look at it just right, from an angle. There were also traces of hair and body oils that weren't yours. One thing led to another, and we were finally able to match that locket to a crazy but harmless old bag lady by the name of Mary Kellogg. Middle name: Helen. There are lots of records on Mary. Mary heard voices, and it seems those voices made her do a lot of crazy things. Almost thirty years ago her two children and some other relatives decided that she'd be better off in a mental hospital. As a matter of fact, she was; the doctors found a proper balance of medication, and she functioned pretty well, considering the fact that she was a schizophrenic. Then the state started emptying the mental hospitals, and Mary was sent off to a residential treatment facility in Queens. It seems she didn't much like it there, so she split. They brought her back, and she split again. Finally, she just fell through the cracks. Either her kids and relatives didn't care enough to take the trouble to look for her, or she didn't want to be found—a lot of them don't. For the past twenty years or so she's been living on the streets of New York."

Bone swallowed hard, found that his mouth was very dry. He had thought the truth about the stranger could not be worse than the void in his mind, and now he realized that that wasn't necessarily true at all. He thought of a tormented woman growing old on the streets, suffering in the wind and the snow and the sun and the cold and the rain, and his eyes misted with tears. "Maybe my name is Kellogg," he said in a choked voice, clenching the locket in his trembling fist and looking away. "Maybe I'm one of those relatives. The woman could have been my mother—or grandmother. Maybe I did come looking for her, and something happened. Lieutenant, if I could just talk to

35

this woman, there's a possibility—" He stopped speaking when he glanced back, saw Perry Lightning slowly shaking his head.

"Her two children are a lot older than you, Bone. They've been accounted for, and so have their children. And you can't talk to Mary Kellogg. She was murdered nine days ago, sometime between two and four in the morning—the same morning of the same day, incidentally, when you plopped yourself down in the Sheep Meadow. Her body, and that of a homeless old man we still haven't been able to identify, was found on the steps of a Presbyterian church on Fifth Avenue. The church is less than five blocks from Central Park, by the way."

Bone clutched the plastic-wrapped locket even tighter as he watched Perry Lightning once more reach down into the paper bag which for him had become a sack of horrors. The detective slowly drew out four enlarged, glossy, color photographs, slowly and deliberately set them down one by one on the sheet next to Bone's thigh.

"Oh, Jesus Christ," Bone said, his voice a kind of distorted groan as he stared in revulsion and horror at the photographs. He gazed, transfixed, at the pulped and ragged flesh, the pooled and spattered blood, and tried to link the obscenity of what he saw to . . . himself. Tentatively, like a man reaching out to see if a grill is hot, he probed the stranger's mind—but almost immediately withdrew, afraid to sear the tender flesh of the only mind he now possessed. He no longer wished to enter the stranger's mind to any great depth, for he was very much afraid of what he would find there. If this was the work of the stranger . . .

Finally, he managed to tear his gaze away from the photographs. He forced his fist to unclench, and the locket dropped to the sheet, landing on top of one of the photos with a sharp smacking sound. "Did I do that?" he asked in a voice that had suddenly grown very hoarse.

"You tell me, Bone," Lightning replied, his own voice just above a whisper.

Bone could only shake his head.

"Are you saying you didn't do it?"

"Don't . . . know."

"Now, why would anybody want to butcher an old man and an old lady like that?"

Bone brushed away tears with the back of his hand, sighed

deeply. He felt so tired, so *burdened*, that he could hardly keep his eyes open. Then he remembered Lightning's remarks about some criminals wanting nothing more than to be caught and to sleep, and he struggled to keep his eyes open, his mind alert. "It's insane," he said softly. "If I did that . . ."

"Did you?"

"I don't know; I can't remember."

"Come on, Bone. Tell me about it. It's what you really want to do, and that's what all this hunkering down in the mud and amnesia bullshit is all about. What did you do with the heads? You couldn't have carried two bloody heads very far in New York, even in the middle of the night."

Bone's jaws ached. "Lieutenant," he sighed, "I just can't remember. I'm not saying I didn't do it; I'm saying I don't remember doing it. Obviously, I can't explain the locket or why I was wearing it around my neck, because I don't remember anything before waking up in the meadow."

"We know you did it, Bone. You're right when you say that anybody who'd slaughter helpless people, cut off their heads and cart them away is insane. That will be taken into account by the courts. The part of you that's sane—and decent—had to find a way to stop the madman, and you did. But you've only gone part of the way; you exposed yourself to us so that we could lock you up, which is good, but you're going to feel a whole hell of a lot better when you stop playing these other mind games with yourself. You'll remember when you let yourself. So tell me the details, and tell me what you did with those people's heads."

Bone took a deep breath, then looked directly into the other man's eyes. "I told you I can't explain why I was wearing the locket, Lieutenant—but just because I had it doesn't mean that I killed either of those people."

Perry Lightning snorted derisively and made a dismissive gesture with his left hand as he once again leaned back in his chair and crossed his legs. "You started your mud-squatting routine on the same morning those two old people were killed, and only a few blocks from the murder site."

"Even that doesn't—"

"You had traces of blood on your pants and shirt cuffs, Bone. There were two blood types, and neither was yours. The blood on your clothes belonged to the old people slaughtered on those church steps."

These last words, somehow made even more powerful by the casual manner in which they were delivered, had the effect of a series of brutal physical blows that threatened to beat away the last of his resistance to guilt and his tenuous attachments to the stranger. Now he loathed the stranger, feared him. He felt like he was drowning in horror. Now he was ready to make the leap to memory the detective insisted was within his capability; he was willing to remember killing an old woman and an old man and hacking off their heads, was willing to condemn the stranger—and he couldn't. He felt nothing but revulsion at the acts of murder and mutilation, but, try as hard as he could, he could not remember ever doing such things. The close proximity in both time and place between the murders and his squatting in the field, the locket and the blood on his clothes, certainly seemed to indicate that he was guilty, but he could find no evidence of it in his mind. Before awakening in the rain and wind-swept park there was—nothing.

He was not aware of time passing, but when he looked down at the bed he realized that he must have been thinking for some minutes, absorbed in his nightmarish search for the memories that would condemn the stranger; there were more photographs, and they were strewn all around him, turning the sheet into a garish patchwork of color. Of blood. The photographs showed more headless corpses, of all sizes and shapes and races, of both sexes, dressed for the most part in rags.

"These, too?" he asked in a voice he did not—or would not—recognize as his own.

"These, too."

"How many?"

"Don't you know?"

"How many, Lieutenant?"

"Twenty-eight, counting the old man and old woman you killed last week. The first murder and decapitation occurred roughly just around the same time I'm told you showed up on the city streets—which is another factor I think you'll agree smacks of a good deal more than mere coincidence. Also, there haven't been any killings in the past nine days—since you came in from the cold, so to speak. You've been a busy beaver, Bone, since you came from wherever the hell you came from, and I can tell you that you've sold a lot of newspapers and scared the shit out of a few million people. There are lots of different sorts of homeless people on the streets of the cities these days, but your victims were always those who were worst off: hopeless cases who couldn't even begin to help themselves, and whom nobody seemed able to help. For the past ten months—after the first six killings—thousands of our homeless have gone to city shelters, at least at night; people who'd never set foot in a shelter before headed for one when the sun went down. But not your victims. You've been killing the psychotics and the stone-gone alcoholics who couldn't even tell you if the sun was shining, people who were slowly dying out there anyway, but whom nobody could reach. In a very real sense, I think it can be said that what you did were acts of mercy—although I'm not sure your victims would have felt that way. What I'm saying is that even your crimes show that there's a basic decency in you, and it's that basic decency that finally made you stop. It was probably that decency that kept you from being caught—until you wanted to be caught. From what I'm told, nobody ever would have guessed that this clean-cut young man—obviously troubled, or he wouldn't be in that situation, but not harming anyone—walking the streets during the day was killing people at night and cutting off their heads. You want to tell me about it now, Bone? If you start by telling me what you did with the twenty-eight severed heads, it would help. You can understand that the families of these victims, where there are families, would feel a lot better if the heads were given a proper burial along with the rest of the remains. You can start atoning right now for what you've done by telling me what you did with those heads."

"If I did those things, I'm grateful that you've got me locked up where I can't harm anybody else," Bone said in his tortured stranger's voice. "But I still don't remember. It seems I'd have nothing left to lose now by remembering—but I don't. I'm sorry, Lieutenant. I really am."

Perry Lightning pursed his lips and shook his head, then stood up and began collecting the photographs, putting them back into the paper bag along with the locket. Only the tape recorder, which continued to run, remained on the bed.

"I'm sorry too, Bone," the detective said with what sounded like sincere regret in his voice. "We know that you did it—but now I think we also know that you're a very sick man. Maybe the doctors here can help you get well, and then someday, maybe, you'll be free to try to build a new life. But that's going to take a long time. Certainly, I might venture an opinion that you weren't responsible for what you did. But the first step in the healing process is to get all this other shit behind you. The way you do that is to remember, and then to tell the police all you know. You'll feel better when you do that; I want it for you. I was hoping you were ready."

He was lost, Bone thought. There was nothing he could say for himself—the himself that was in his eyes, the himself that could not remember. He was alone.

But . . .

The stranger whose body he inhabited was alone, too. And the stranger had no voice other than his own. Everything he had been saying had been on behalf of *himself*—the eyes, ears, voice and consciousness that were only slightly more than a week old. Who would speak for the stranger?

He sat up straight, pointed to the shopping bag which the detective had picked up and was holding in the crook of his left arm. "The people in those photographs you showed me certainly weren't beaten to death with a bone," he said in a voice that was much stronger than he'd thought it would be. "Twenty-eight heads weren't cut off with a bone."

"A razor, or a large, very sharp knife," Lightning said, cocking his head slightly, as if to view Bone from a different angle. His tone had changed, for the first time betraying an edge of genuine surprise and uncertainty. "I'll be damned; you really don't remember, do you?"

Bone met the other man's steady gaze, sighed. "No. Thank you for believing that, at least."

"Hey, Bone, I don't need to be told that anyone who squats in a field for two days in the cold and rain obviously doesn't have all his marbles. I've got a pretty good bullshit antenna, and that antenna tells me that you may be telling the truth on that point—you can't remember. Now. But you will. It's inevitable. You can't suppress the memories forever, because you really don't want to. You wouldn't have stopped and put yourself in the Sheep Meadow unless you wanted to be found out and stopped for good. You trust me on that; I know what I'm talking about."

"You want me to confess to incidents I can't remember, Lieutenant?"

"No. I want you to start concentrating on one thing at a time.

40

Why don't you begin by trying to remember where your stash is?"

"Stash?"

"Where you keep your personal belongings—odds and ends that you don't feel like carrying around with you. Almost every homeless person has some kind of stash, somewhere, even if it's just in a shopping cart."

"But how do you know that *I* have a stash?"

"Because you were sighted wearing different sets of clothes at different times, and the only thing you always carried with you was that bone. It means you had to be keeping your extra sets of clothing somewhere—maybe near water, since you always seemed to be fairly clean. You'll have slept close to your stash; it could be somewhere in Central Park. That could also be where the twenty-eight missing heads are. When you remember where your stash is, a lot of other things will start coming back to you, if only in bits and pieces. I'll take the bits and pieces. You tell me what you remember, and then we'll get this all cleared up so you can start getting it behind you. There are some pretty good mental hospitals in this state, and you'll find it a hell of a lot more comfortable in one of those than on the streets. The people there will understand."

"Lieutenant, you're patronizing me. Are you guaranteeing me that I'll be sent to a mental hospital if I remember the killings and confess to them?"

The detective reddened slightly, darted a quick glance at the tape recorder on the bed. "No," he said tightly. "I can't guarantee that. But I do have your best interests in mind. I know that deep down you want to get those terrible things off your chest."

Defend the stranger, Bone thought. Speak for him. Give it your best shot. "Your concern is touching, Lieutenant. I'd very much like to talk to anybody—everybody—who's seen me on the streets over the course of the past year."

"No," Lightning replied curtly. "Not yet."

"Why not? What harm could it do? Maybe someone who's seen me knows where my stash is."

The detective shifted the bag to his other arm, turned slightly and gazed out the window. "First let's see what you can remember on your own, Bone. Let's not complicate things with other people's memories or ideas. It won't do any good to have

41

a lot of people putting things into your head before even you know what's there."

"But it's all right for *you* to put things into my head, isn't it, Lieutenant?" Bone said, suddenly feeling an odd sense of exhilaration as he realized that something was bothering the other man. Doubt? "It seems I have a pretty good bullshit antenna of my own, and it's sending me very strong signals right now. You've had a week to check me out, talk with people who knew—or at least had contact with—me during the past year. If any of those people knew where my stash is, you wouldn't be asking me these questions. Well, what harm can there be in letting *me* talk to them? Maybe you're not as certain I'm the killer as you pretend to be. Could you be trying to get me to confess to things even you're not certain I did?"

Perry Lightning, his face flushed and his jaw muscles knotted, abruptly stepped back to the bed, set down the bag and shut off the tape recorder. A film of perspiration glistened on his shaved skull. "Who else could have done it?" he said tersely. "You had traces of blood from both the man and woman on your clothes, and you were wearing the old woman's locket around your neck."

"What about my hands? Did I have blood on my hands?"

"Two days of rain would have washed the blood off your hands."

Bone put a gnarled hand to his forehead, pressed his thumb and forefinger into his temples. The stranger could think, but he had to do the talking, had to defend as best . . . there was something . . . "Fingerprints," he said suddenly, dropping the hand. "You must have fingerprints from the scenes of all the killings. Do any of them match mine?"

Anger and frustration glinted for a moment in the other man's dark eyes, then was gone. "You don't have any fingerprints, Bone," Lightning said in an oddly flat tone of voice. "They've been worn away."

Bone slowly turned his large and powerful but strangely scarred and ruined hands over and examined the tips of the crooked fingers. It was true; they were all hard, thick callus and scar tissue. There were no prints.

Peel off!

There was a scene, a fleeting image of . . . Bone reached for it, and it was gone. It was all right, he thought. It was there; it would come back, but he must be patient and not try to force

42

it. For now, he must defend the stranger against a dangerous opponent who wanted to put him away in a place and situation where he might never be able to find what he had lost.

"What could have caused this?" he asked, thrusting out his hands.

Lightning shrugged. "Beats me."

"What do the doctors say?"

"What do you say? They're your hands."

"Come on, Lieutenant!" Bone snapped, experiencing a rush of anger, a positive sense of outrage, that felt good. "Now that we've dispensed with the bullshit about you being my good old buddy who's just trying to help me clear all these terrible things off my conscience, why don't you at least give *me* a little cooperation?! You want to put me away so you can say you've got all the murders solved? Go for it. But at least be good enough to share some information with me. Who knows? Maybe I'll end up hanging myself with it. Now, what do the doctors say about my hands?"

Lightning's thin smile almost, but not quite, reached his eyes—eyes that reflected a newfound respect. "They say lots of different things could have caused those injuries, including masochistic self-mutilation."

"I don't feel masochistic, and I wouldn't call my hands mutilated. I feel like I have a lot of strength in them."

"Agreed. What I'm saying is that they don't really have the foggiest notion how you managed to do that to yourself. You've got scars in funny places all over your body, but it's only your hands that are really beat up like that."

"You say you found blood from the two people who were killed at the church on my clothes. What about the twenty-six other victims, Lieutenant? Any traces of their blood on my clothes?"

"You could have been wearing other clothes."

"Which means that maybe you can tie me to the scene of the one crime, but not the others. What about the traces of blood and hair you found on the bone?"

It was some time before Perry Lightning answered. "There are only so many blood types, Bone," he said at last. "And the traces they found on the femur were microscopic samples."

"Which means that it's impossible to tell."

"Well, let me tell you about something else the lab people found in the cracks of that femur," Lightning said evenly.

"They found traces of powder which they're almost certain is dried aqueous humor."

"What?"

"You bashed out somebody's eye with that thing, Bone."

For a few moments, Bone was shocked into silence. Then, using this new information as a kind of psychic digging tool, he began to tentatively probe the stranger's mind. Since there was no doubt that the stranger had carried the femur for a year, there seemed no doubt that the stranger had put out somebody's eye with it. He didn't know the circumstances, and he would continue to defend the stranger until it was proven beyond a doubt that he was a crazed mass murderer, but he was not certain that he wanted to remember destroying somebody's eye. And he didn't.

"Have you checked reports of missing persons for the past year?" he said at last.

"For the past two years—from all over the country. That's a lot of time and territory to cover, and not every police department has the complex facilities we do, so we're still working at it. So far we haven't come up with a physical description that matches you."

"I must not be married, or have children." He paused, frowned slightly as a sudden wave of sadness washed over him, leaving behind a sense of loss that had nothing to do with memory. Now he felt pity for the stranger. "I must have lived alone, and had few, if any . . . friends."

"Not necessarily," Lightning said evenly. "You may have told your wife, children or friends that you were going someplace."

"For a *year*? Without *contacting* them?"

Lightning shrugged. "Maybe they think you're dead."

"What about prisons? Mental hospitals?"

Lightning shook his head, then put the tape recorder in the paper bag, which he picked up. Now he seemed distant, thoughtful, as if his mind were now on other things.

"Lieutenant?"

"What is it?"

"Help me."

"That's what I'm trying to do."

"Tell me something about myself."

"I already have."

"But you know more than you're telling me. And you could let me talk to the people you've talked to."

"For now, you just concentrate on what you can remember on your own."

"You've already said that you've given me the benefit of the doubt when I tell you I can't remember. Now give me the benefit of the doubt when I tell you I want to remember—even if it means I'll die, or be locked away in prison or a mental hospital for the rest of my life. If I did the things you believe I did, then, at the very least, I should be put away where I can't harm anyone else. There isn't a whole hell of a lot I can do for myself while you've got me locked up. Give me something that I can work on."

Lieutenant Perry Lightning's response was to turn and head toward the door; he nodded in the direction of the television camera, and the door opened with an accompanying buzzing sound. He started to leave the room, hesitated, then turned back to face Bone. His eyes now seemed strangely hooded, as if he might be trying to hide his true feelings. His voice, when he spoke, was flat.

"Wherever you got that femur you were toting around, it wasn't from one of your victims. People who know about these things tell me it's at least four hundred years old, undoubtedly American Indian. In fact, it's ossified—more stone than bone. I don't know where the hell you would have found something like that, unless you've been camping out in the basement of the Museum of Natural History. You think on that."

CHAPTER THREE

He had not realized how much he'd missed the woman with the hazel eyes and gray-streaked, dark brown hair until now, when he saw Anne Winchell again clearly for the first time since the day when he'd awakened to her voice and touch in the park. Only now, looking at her, did it occur to him that, in large part, he had been operating from strength and confidence she had given him. He remembered well his terror at finding himself cold, lost and alone in a world that was totally alien to him. It had been her voice that had pierced the darkness and lighted his way out of whatever terrible place he had been in; it had been her touch that had reassured him and given him warmth, her willingness to stand close to him that had told him he was not in danger. Anne Winchell and her warmth—as opposed to the suspicion and vague hostility of Barry Prindle, and the detached, almost bemused curiosity of Dr. Hakim— had pulled him from the strange, black sea where he had been drowning. She had demonstrated her faith in the stranger— and Bone now realized the great extent to which that faith had allowed him to believe in the stranger, and to defend him.

Without her, he thought, he would almost surely be dead.

In the rain she had seemed a dream of life, her tear-misted eyes and rain-soaked features a kind of beacon beckoning to him. She had seemed beautiful to him then. She still seemed beautiful, although he knew other men might not agree. Anne wore jeans and sneakers, and a silk blouse of bright blue. Her long brown hair was combed out, and fell softly over her shoulders. She wore little makeup, and large-rimmed glasses with lenses that were slightly tinted. Barry Prindle, his bright green eyes once again clearly reflecting suspicion and caution, walked stiffly behind the woman as they entered the room, and the door clicked shut behind them. Both the man and woman carried packages. Barry reached out for Anne's arm as she started toward Bone, but she shrugged off his grip and approached the bed.

"Hi," she said brightly, putting her package down on the bed and extending her right hand.

"Hi," Bone replied as he pushed himself up in bed, then shook her hand. As in the park, he found the woman's touch warm and reassuring; as in the park, she seemed totally unafraid—although, surely, she knew of Lieutenant Perry Lightning's certainty that he was a mass killer, and was aware of the evidence against him. As in the park, she was giving the stranger even more than the benefit of the doubt; she was saying that she believed in him.

He found he was deeply touched, on the verge of tears, and he wondered how, when, he would find words to tell this woman how her simple trust had strengthened, filled, him.

"How are you feeling?"

"A whole hell of a lot better than I'd be feeling if you people hadn't come along." He paused, looked into the tense features of the broad-shouldered man standing at the foot of the bed. "I want to thank both of you for pulling me in out of the rain. I'd get out of bed to properly greet you both but the police took all my clothes, and this hospital gown leaves me a bit drafty in the rear."

Anne smiled, patted the package she had set down on the bed, then pointed to the one Barry still held in his hands. "Barry and I have brought you something to wear. I think they'll fit—I'm pretty good at guessing sizes."

"The clothes should fit," Barry said drily, relaxing just a bit as he leaned forward and placed his package on the bed. "Anne's been sizing you up for a long time, Bone."

Bone glanced from the man to the woman, saw Anne's face flush with embarrassment, then clench in anger. "I don't understand," he said quietly.

Barry ran a hand back over his close-cropped hair. "Anne has always thought that you're quite a hunk," he said in the same dry tone.

"That's enough, Barry," Anne said in a low, husky voice, without looking at the other man. Her face was still red with embarrassment and anger, and Bone could feel her distancing herself from him. He found himself resenting the effect the man's words had had on her.

"I still don't understand," Bone said.

"My partner's trying to be cute," Anne said, looking up at him with a smile that now seemed forced. "Barry is saying that you've been a kind of special project of mine ever since we first spotted you on the street."

Bone frowned. "Why?"

The woman shrugged, then brushed a wisp of hair back from her eyes. "It's difficult to explain to somebody who doesn't remember anything about what he was doing out there, but there are lots of reasons why people end up homeless—and many different kinds of people out there. But they all share one thing in common: for one reason or another, they've reached the ends of their ropes—economically or emotionally, and usually both. Yet, you didn't seem to fit any pattern at all." She paused, smiled wryly. "That's not to say that there wasn't something obviously wrong with you."

Bone smiled, laughed softly. "No kidding?"

The woman's smile vanished. "You were totally mute. Yet, you never seemed helpless. Again, it's hard to explain, but even when you were obviously just wandering around, you never gave the *impression* that you were just wandering around. You always appeared to be alert. When we'd want to talk to you, to try and convince you that you should let us take you to a shelter, or help you in some other way, you'd always stop and listen—but you always gave the impression that you were doing it out of politeness, so as not to hurt our feelings. You'd take the food we offered you—but, again, you seemed to be doing it out of politeness, because you knew we were just trying to do our job."

"Then why did you keep at it?"

"Because," she said, flashing an angry glance at Barry, "you

48

were so obviously in need of help, even if you didn't realize it. It just seemed to me that you had . . . hidden depths. You were an enigma. And, of course, the bone you carried intrigued us all. I became convinced that if I could *somehow* reach through to you, then you'd 'come back,' as it were, and be able to get on with your life."

Bone smiled thinly. "Well, I guess you were half right."

"Do you . . . remember anything?"

He shook his head. "Not before waking up in the park." He glanced at Barry Prindle, then at Anne. "You know, of course, that the police think I've been killing people."

Prindle remained silent, averting his gaze. Anne said quietly, "What do you think, Bone?"

"I don't know," he replied evenly. "It's very obvious that I'm possibly insane; nobody can say for sure what an insane person will do."

"Well, maybe I know you—at least the 'you' that was on the streets for a year—better than you do. You were always calm, and I don't believe you would have hurt anybody."

"But we don't know for sure—and until we do, I guess I'm just as happy I'm in here. Where did you see me?"

Anne looked at Barry, who simply shrugged his broad shoulders. "Like I told you, we first spotted you on Eighth Avenue, between Thirty-ninth and Fortieth. After that, we'd see you all over midtown and downtown Manhattan."

"Meaning south of Central Park?"

Anne nodded. "That's the area we patrol. But you liked to walk, and I'm sure you probably explored other parts of Manhattan, as well. If you'd like, I'll check with the other teams."

"Thank you. Do you have any idea where I slept? The detective who questioned me is sure I have what he calls a stash somewhere."

"You probably do, but I don't think anybody knows where it is. The teams in the other vans may not have paid much attention to you because, in their opinion, you didn't fit into the category of the kinds of people we're tasked to help."

"I can understand that," Bone said evenly.

"We have upwards of five thousand potential clients just in our sector of Manhattan alone."

"Forty thousand people, Bone, maybe more," Barry said in a low voice. His features had become more relaxed, and for the first time Bone was aware of the passion in the man, a deep caring that had been hidden before by the man's caution and protectiveness toward Anne. Bone could understand the man's attitude; if their positions had been reversed, Bone was sure he would have reacted in the same way—he would certainly not have trusted the wild-eyed stranger with the heavy bone in his hand. He would still not, and he would be anxious every time Anne Winchell approached too closely.

"That's the number of homeless people in New York City?" Bone asked quietly.

Barry nodded. "And the numbers are growing every day. What you might feel is a callous attitude toward you—on my part, at least—isn't anything personal. In this business, your nerves get stretched pretty thin at times."

"Especially if you care," Bone said to the man with the green eyes and sharp widow's peak, "and you obviously do." He paused, smiled wryly. "I can understand why you might be more than a bit reticent toward a man who might be a mass murderer."

Somewhat to Bone's surprise, the heavyset man suddenly grinned, came around to the side of the bed and extended his hand. "Well, they haven't proved you're a mass murderer yet; and until they do, you're still our client. You know I'm going to be keeping my eye on you when you're around Anne, but that's my job. That doesn't mean I don't feel for you. Okay?"

"Okay," Bone replied as he shook Barry's hand. "And thank you. Where's Dr. Hakim? I'd like to thank him, too."

"Ali—Dr. Hakim—is a professor of psychiatry and neurology at NYU Medical Center," Anne said. "That's where he is now. He works for Helping Hand on a volunteer basis; we need a psychiatrist to certify that someone is in imminent danger of hurting himself or others before we can bring that person in for help against his will. I'm certain he'll be around to see you. You intrigue him."

"Why?"

"Because he says your symptoms don't match any syndrome of amnesia he's familiar with—and Ali's an expert."

Bone sighed. "Meaning he doesn't believe me."

"On the contrary," Barry said. "I think he does believe you—although he didn't come right out and say so."

"Ali is a very good man, Bone," Anne said as she reached out and touched his shoulder. "Your 'waking up' in the Sheep

Meadow was just a first step. Although you're technically not his responsibility any longer, I'm sure he'll help you—or find you another doctor almost as good. You'll regain your memory; I'm sure of it."

Perhaps only to find out that he was a mass murderer, Bone thought. A maniac. Those were the memories he would have to live with, of killing people and then cutting off their heads. Frightened by that thought, embarrassed by the woman's touch and the deep feeling of vulnerability it caused in him, he looked away, touched the package by his side. He opened it, found two shirts, khaki slacks, underwear and toilet articles.

"There are shoes in this one," Barry said, handing him the other package. "Now, at least, you'll have something besides that hospital gown to wear."

"Thank you. I'll pay you back."

Barry smiled, shook his head. "It's not our money; it's the city's. We were able to set up an emergency service grant for you, and we drew on that. Depending on circumstances, there may be quite a lot we can do to help you, Bone. We'll have to wait and see what happens."

"Meaning we have to wait to see what the police decide to do with me."

Anne nodded. "You haven't been formally charged yet, Bone."

"Why not? The detective who questioned me seemed absolutely certain that I'm the murderer. He has physical evidence linking me to the murder scene and to one of the victims—Mary Kellogg."

"What evidence?" Anne asked in a small voice, obviously taken by surprise.

Bone swallowed, found that his mouth was dry. He wanted to look away from the woman's hazel eyes, found that he could not. "I was wearing a locket that belonged to her around my neck," he said evenly. "And I had her blood on my cuffs and sleeves."

"Oh," Anne breathed. She did not move back from the bed, but some color drained from her face, and the muscles in her jaw tensed. Shadows moved in her eyes, and suddenly Bone felt terribly alone.

"You didn't know that?"

Anne slowly shook her head. "No," she said in a voice that was just above a whisper.

"You almost sound as if you believe you did it," Barry said in a tone that seemed carefully controlled, flat.

Bone met the other man's gaze. "I'm just telling you what I was told."

"Then Lieutenant Lightning pulled a fast one on us, Bone," Anne said. Her voice was tense, and she sounded slightly out of breath. It meant, Bone thought, that for the first time she was considering the very real possibility that he was, indeed, the killer, and she was not sure how to handle the fear that stirred in her. He understood the feeling very well. "He had someone on the staff here inform him when you woke up, so that he'd be virtually the first person you spoke to. He had no right to come barging in here and asking questions without you having a lawyer present. If we'd known that you were a primary suspect in the killings, we'd have made sure that you had a lawyer. We have a number of good attorneys who work for us *pro bono*."

"He asked me if I wanted a lawyer; I told him no."

"That was a mistake, Bone," Barry said in the same flat tone.

"Why?" He paused, took a deep breath and shifted his gaze to the woman's face. "Anne, I just don't *know* if I did it. I don't remember a damn thing before waking up in the park. If I'm a killer, then I *should* be found out and put away—in prison, a mental hospital, whatever. Until I can be reasonably certain that I may *not* have killed those people, I don't want to be free. The most important thing to me is to remember who I am, and how I ended up on the streets of New York. A lawyer's not going to help me do that."

"You're missing the point, Bone," Barry said, moving closer to Anne. "The cops don't care whether or not you get your memory back; they *do* care about finding somebody they can lock up so they can say they've caught the killer. They've been taking a lot of heat over these murders. As far as they're concerned, the fact that there haven't been any more of the beheading murders since you've been in here is enough reason for them to want to keep you in here."

"I can see their point."

"So can I; so can Anne. But the fact that there haven't been any murders like that for a few days doesn't prove that you're a killer. There have been lapses before, some a lot longer than this, between beheading murders. A lawyer would try to make sure that you're not railroaded for something you may not have done. You want your memory back—and they want somebody they can label a killer. Don't for a moment think that their interests are the same as yours."

"Next time any detective talks to you, we'll make sure you have a lawyer present," Anne said. Her voice was still tense, her tone breathy.

Bone looked away from the two social workers, toward the wall with the mesh-covered windows. "Are you free to answer my questions?"

There was a pause, and Bone sensed that the man and woman were exchanging glances. Barry replied, "We haven't been told not to."

"I know there have been twenty-eight beheading murders," Bone said, struggling to keep his voice even, trying to think of himself as a kind of lawyer for the stranger. He had to find the stranger, find out the truth about him; but he also had to defend him. "Why didn't the police put undercover agents in among the homeless?"

"They did," Barry answered, "and they do. But the numbers of homeless people are just too great for any kind of effective long-range surveillance. Also, the killer is certainly a maniac, but he's no fool; he's always chosen his victims carefully— loners who were caught alone, at night."

"As far as I know, the last two killings are the only ones the police can link me to. Do you know anything about those two old people?"

Anne sobbed as tears formed in her hazel eyes, rolled down her cheeks. "They haven't been able to identify the man, but Mary Kellogg—we certainly knew her. She was a feisty old broad, Bone. We just couldn't keep her anyplace, although God knows that we all— social workers, psychiatrists, city and state officials—tried hard enough."

Anne paused, withdrew a tissue from her pocket. She wiped her eyes, blew her nose, then continued, "Mary suffered from what psychiatrists call undifferentiated schizophrenia. She had a mix of symptoms—hallucinations, obsessions, voices in her head telling her what to do; she had it all. A psychiatric social worker noted on one of her files that she was a great 'breakout artist.' There just wasn't any appropriate facility for Mary that she'd stay in. She was one very sneaky old lady, and the law limits us in how far we can go to keep even someone like Mary locked up against his or her will."

Bone said, "It certainly sounds as if she was a threat to herself."

Anne shrugged. "You'd be surprised how many civil rights lawyers and advocates for the homeless would disagree with you; it gets tricky when you try to deal forcefully with people who've committed no crimes, even when the guidelines are changed—and when the guidelines are changed, as they have been from time to time, then the city doesn't have nearly enough beds to accommodate all the people we bring in. We did manage to get Mary committed a few times—then she was either released too soon in order to make room for somebody who was even sicker, or she wouldn't stay put long enough for the doctors to get her properly stabilized on medication. I know she was terrified of being in closed places. For years she slept on the steps of St. Patrick's Cathedral, but then the Fifth Avenue merchants' association managed to get the police to drive her away—bad for business, they said, and I can't really argue with them. So Mary moved up the street a few blocks, to St. Thomas Episcopal Church. It was only a block or two from there where she was murdered, along with the old man. It was relatively safe for Mary at St. Thomas, more in the open, and I guess we'll never know why she suddenly decided to leave there in the middle of the night."

"What about the other victims? What can you tell me about them?"

Again, the man and woman exchanged glances; Barry pursed his lips, shook his head.

"We don't really know that much about them," Anne answered. "As I said, there are so many . . . without the heads, it's difficult. So few of these people carry any kind of identification. We only know what we read in the newspapers at the time."

"But it's possible that the police could have made positive identification after the initial stories in the newspapers?"

"It's possible. We wouldn't necessarily be informed."

"What's your point, Bone?" Barry asked.

"I was just wondering if there might not be some common link between the victims—aside from the fact that they were homeless." He paused, looking at the dark possibility in his mind, then forced himself to voice it. "We know that I was *somehow* in contact with Mary Kellogg—even if it was only to rob her. I was just considering the possibility that I could somehow be linked to all of the victims. I wonder if any—or all—of them knew me?"

"My God," Anne whispered. "You'd search for that link, even if it condemned you?"

"I want the truth, Anne—even if the truth is that I'm a madman and a murderer."

"I think that makes you a very brave man."

Embarrassed, Bone averted his gaze. He did not see his attitude as reflecting courage at all; he felt more terrified at the possibility that he could be executed, sent to prison or a mental hospital, virtually as a passenger, a prisoner inside the body of the stranger, without ever learning who he was. It was not enough to know what the stranger had done; he had to know *who* the stranger was, and why he had acted as he had. Asking questions was all he could do now for the stranger, and it could not be helped if the answers he received were meaningless. If he could retrace his steps, go back to the places where the stranger had been, perhaps he might remember—but he could not do that while he was locked up in the secure ward of a mental hospital. And so there was nothing else to do but keep asking the questions as they occurred to him, wait, and hope that something would turn up to show that the stranger might be innocent of the terrible crimes he was accused of.

The streets held memories of at least one of the two lives he had lost, but he could not get out on them.

"Bone," Anne continued quietly, "are you all right?"

He nodded. "Yes; I was just thinking." He paused, looked back and forth between the two social workers. "I want to thank you both again for . . . everything."

"You're welcome," Anne said, and smiled warmly. "It's what we're paid to do."

Bone shook his head. "You don't do it for the money; you do it because you care. How did the two of you end up on this 'street squad' of yours?"

Anne brushed a strand of brown hair away from her eyes. "I trained for social work; it's what I took my degree in." She paused, squeezed the arm of the burly man beside her and laughed good-naturedly. "Now, Barry here is a frustrated priest. His bark is really much worse than his bite. Most of the time you've seen him, he's had a frown on his face; but he's really a great big pussycat—and a very good human being. You should see how some of those poor people on the street respond

to him." She paused, winked coquettishly at Bone. "Except for
you, of course; you didn't respond to anyone."

Barry flushed slightly, obviously embarrassed, then grinned;
it made him look younger, almost boyish. "I'm not a 'frustrated
priest,' Anne, and you know it. If I'd wanted to become a priest,
I'd simply have stayed in the seminary."

"But you were studying for the priesthood?" Bone asked the
man.

Barry nodded, lowered his gaze. "I thought I had a calling,"
he said quietly. "For as long as I can remember, I felt God
wanted me to devote my life to helping people who were less
fortunate than I was. Being Roman Catholic, naturally I
interpreted this strong urge to mean that I should become a
priest. But I was wrong. I entered the seminary and studied for
a couple of years, but . . . I just couldn't connect with what
was going on around me. It seemed to me that I was spending
my time there studying to be a kind of administrator, admin-
istering, for the most part, to people who shared my personal
beliefs. I didn't want to be an administrator. I realized then
that God wanted me to play some other role; I didn't know
what it was, but I felt that God would eventually show it to me.
So I left. To tell you the truth, that was a very upsetting time in
my life. I ended up knocking around New York for a while,
taking odd jobs and devoting almost all of my free time to
doing volunteer work for various charitable agencies. But the
fact of the matter was that I was spending so much time doing
volunteer work that I was barely making enough money to
support myself. So I cut back on the volunteer work and landed
myself a job with an outfit called Empire Subway Company
Limited. It was the grace of God that sent me there."

"Why the grace of God?" Bone asked, intrigued. Nothing in
the man's previous behavior or demeanor had indicated the
religious fervor and genuine urge to do good that was in this
man. He wondered what similar surprises he might find as he
probed deeper into the mind of the stranger; even people in
command of their memories were not always what they
seemed. "I'd like to know. What's the Empire Subway Company?"

Barry seemed hesitant, but Anne nodded encouragement.
"Tell him, Barry. You usually love to talk about your work with
Empire Subway."

"Down there," Barry said, pointing to the floor as he obviously warmed to the subject, "is a world you wouldn't believe, Bone. I mean under the streets of Manhattan. The Dutch started digging there, near the tip of the island, in the sixteen hundreds, and we haven't stopped since. There are underground lakes, streams, caves—and these are *natural* formations. For more than three hundred years they've been building aqueducts, subway and train tunnels, laying water and sewer pipes, gas lines and electrical cables. I won't bore you with the details, but now, before anyone can put up a new building or do anything that requires digging, they have to know what they're going to run into down there. All the systems—electric, gas, steam, sewage, high- and low-pressure water mains, the transit subways—are all entwined down there, and they often interlace with very old systems that go back to the time of the first settlers, structures that have never been mapped. Grand Central Terminal, for instance, goes down seven stories below street level, and there are people who think there are older structures or systems beneath it. No one map shows it all, and a lot of the old maps have been lost. For example, we know that the Treasury Department used to use underground pneumatic tubes to deliver financial notes and securities; they didn't *want* a lot of people to know about the system, so only a very few maps were made—and these were lost over the years as the underground system was abandoned. A hundred and fifty years ago, the post office used to deliver mail through their own tunnels—and a lot of those maps were lost. You've got three different water systems which were constructed at different times.

"Anyway, you get the idea. Before anybody—construction company or utility—can poke so much as a shovel into the ground, they have to know what they may be digging into. Empire Subway acts as a consultant that supplies that information. They've been doing it for a long time, and they know more about what's under the city streets than anyone. What they don't know, they find out. Before any new tunnel is built or electrical cable laid, Empire Subway checks out the terrain underground and files a report or map; this information is then shared and used by all the utilities and transit companies to expand and update whatever maps and records they may already have. I worked as a member of a team of 'moles' down there, checking out the situation whenever somebody wanted to build something. There are areas down there where different cables are laid so close together that they look like spaghetti, and workers literally use spoons to dig around them. Anyway, that was my job, and it paid well."

Barry paused, and Bone was startled to see tears suddenly well in the man's green eyes, brim over and roll down his cheeks. He quickly looked away, wiped at his eyes as Anne reached out and touched his arm.

"I found other things down there besides old aqueducts, sewers and tunnels," the social worker continued in a voice that seemed slightly muffled. "People. There are men—and even an occasional woman—living in those tunnels down there, all over the city. They live in perpetual darkness, and God only knows what they eat. Some of them, I think, just go down there to die. They live there with the rats and the spiders and the filth. That's when I finally knew what it was God wanted me to do—work with the homeless. I applied for a job with the Human Resources Administration, and they temporarily waived the college degree required; I'm taking courses now. So, that's how *I* ended up doing this."

Down there is a world you wouldn't believe.

Bone closed his eyes, listening intently as the words echoed in his mind, struggling after them to see where they might lead. Why did the words produce such strong reverberations? Bones; he must have picked up the ossified bone somewhere underground. Maybe. But he had certainly not found it in a subway tunnel or water main.

Dark places.

He opened his eyes. "Do you go underground to try to work with those people?"

Barry shook his head, and when he spoke there were traces of anger and bitterness in his voice. "The city won't allow us to go down there; it's considered dangerous."

"Most of the people down there are really crazy," Anne said. "They're usually all right as long as you leave them alone—but totally unpredictable if you try to approach them. City policy is that we try to reach them if they come up, but we don't go down into the darkness after them. It's a sound policy. There's far more work than we can handle on the streets without going underground to look for more, and at least up here we can see what we're dealing with."

"They won't even let me go down on my own," Barry said tersely. "If I do, and they find out, I get fired. It's not right."

"What would you do if they did permit you to go down there, Barry?" Anne asked in the tone of voice of someone who'd had this conversation before. "Those people aren't going to come up with you, and you know it. All you'd manage to do is get your throat slit."

"At least I could take them food and water."

"Which would remove any motivation they might have for coming up. The administration is right."

"Now you sound like the bureaucrats who favor cutting off these people's welfare benefits if they miss one meeting with a counselor, or leave one official letter unanswered, because this offers them 'incentive.' That's insane, and it's inhumane."

"I'm not in favor of that approach, Barry, and you know it," Anne replied tightly. "You're new at this, and what you have to learn is that you'll help more people, in a more efficient manner, if you let your head rule your heart once in a while. We're professionals, and we're not going to do anybody any good if we start poking around with the underground people and get ourselves mugged, raped, beaten up or even killed. There are skeletons down there too, Barry; I know, because you told me about them."

Barry flushed, and suddenly the veins in his thick neck stood out. "I'm not so sure I want to be so professional that I ignore a whole segment of people who desperately need help." He paused, slowly looked back and forth between the woman and Bone. "Besides," he continued in measured tones, "I don't think you're in any position to lecture me about professionalism, or about helping the greatest number of people with the most efficiency."

Now it was Anne's turn to flush. "You're way out of line, Barry. Now you cool it."

Barry Prindle's bright green eyes glinted with anger. He glared at Anne for a few moments, then abruptly turned and started for the door. There was a buzz and click as the door opened, and Barry walked quickly out. Anne hesitated, then started after him.

"Please don't go," Bone heard himself say. The words surprised him, as did the sudden surge of emotion that had accompanied them.

Anne stopped in the middle of the room, turned back, cocked her head slightly and smiled. She again brushed hair back from her eyes, walked back to the bed, took his right hand in both of hers and squeezed it.

Suddenly Bone was embarrassed—and afraid. Up to the point when he had found himself asking the woman not to go, the stranger had seemed reasonably complete unto himself— anxious, afraid of what the truth about himself might reveal, yes, but not lonely, not needy in an emotional sense. Now he realized that had been an illusion. This woman, with her very special beauty, had a strong grip on his soul, he thought. It had been her voice that had formed the trail of sound he had followed to emerge from oblivion, her persistence and caring that, finally, had probably saved his life.

Why had he apparently wanted to die?

Down there is a world you wouldn't believe.

It was dangerous for him to be vulnerable like this, Bone thought. He could not afford to need—much less risk falling in love with—anybody. He would only stand to lose even more in the end, be crushed even more by the truth about himself. Being too close to this lovely, tough yet gentle woman was extremely dangerous for him—and maybe for her, if he was indeed insane and ultimately unpredictable.

But he did not take his hand away.

"I'm sorry," he mumbled, averting his gaze from the face that was beginning to increasingly occupy his thoughts. "I have no right to keep you here. I know you've got more work than you can handle, and you've already been far more than kind to me. I don't want to keep you."

"It's all right," Anne said, squeezing his hand again. "Barry needs some time to cool off, anyway. You put up a great front, Bone, but inside you must be terribly afraid and lonely. I try to imagine how *I* would feel and react if I were in your place, not able to remember my name or past; I'm sure I'd be curled up in a corner, bawling my eyes out. Or screaming."

It was too close to how he did feel, too close to what he feared he would come to. It was what he feared his affection for this woman might trigger. Not trusting himself to speak, he said nothing.

"Barry can sometimes be just a bit too full of himself," Anne continued. She spoke quickly, as if conscious of Bone's misgivings, and sensitive to the discomfort he felt in the silence. "He's a big boy, to be sure—but in many ways he *is* still a boy. He means well, he's exceptionally good in dealing with our clients, but he can be very immature. Sometimes I think he spent too many years in the seminary, even if he never finished. He has an annoying tendency toward male chauvinism, and the fact that I'm his trainer and supervisor doesn't always sit too well with him. He tends to get upset when he realizes that I don't really need or want him hovering around all the time to protect me."

"He's jealous," Bone said simply. "His interest in you is a lot more than professional."

"Barry can also be very naive. I don't mean to criticize him, but he had no right to talk to either of us the way he did."

Down there is a world you wouldn't believe.

"What he had to say about what's under the ground around here interested me," Bone said carefully.

Anne nodded, shrugged. "I guess it is interesting, at least from a historical point of view. You've got stuff downtown, around Wall and Canal streets and the Bowery, that dates back hundreds of years. Aaron Burr built one of the first waterworks down there underground somewhere, and that waterworks indirectly led to his duel with Alexander Hamilton. Do those names mean anything to you? Do you recall any history?"

Bone shook his head. "I haven't really thought about any history but my own."

"There was even a guy who built a private subway in the late eighteen hundreds. It was closed down and forgotten about. Then, in nineteen twelve, workers were digging the BMT— that's a subway line—and suddenly found themselves in the first subway's waiting room. Surprise, surprise." She paused, shuddered slightly, grimaced. "There's a lot of history down there, but there are also things like rats—probably as many rats underground as there are people in the city. Some of them are mutants, immune to poison, and they can grow to the size of terriers. There's disease, and death." She paused again, laughed nervously. "But then, I'm prejudiced. I'm afraid of the dark, Bone—like a child. Maybe it's because I'm legally blind in my left eye."

"How did that happen?"

"A congenital defect. Anyway, probably because I'm so afraid of losing sight in the other eye, I hate the dark. I sleep with a night-light on, and I never ride the subway for fear that it will break down and I'll have to walk out through one of the tunnels." She paused, released his hand and laughed again as her face grew slightly red. "Good grief, look at the things I'm telling you. My *friends* don't even know why I refuse to use the subways."

"Barry said there are also people down there," Bone said distantly, again tentatively probing the stranger's mind. Dark places; fear of darkness. When he now searched for the stranger's memories, he felt like a man groping around inside a pitch-black room in which there were unseen hazards— madness, mutilation and death.

Anne sighed. "There are an awful lot of homeless people in this city, Bone—and in other cities across the country. It's true that some of them go underground for warmth, for . . . whatever."

"I may have been one of those people, Anne."

The woman frowned."Why do you say that?"

"First, the bone I carried; bones come from under the ground."

"Bones come from graveyards, and nobody's hinted that you rose from the dead."

"But in a way I did, didn't I?" he said very softly.

"That bone is a fossil," Anne said tightly. A tremor had appeared in her voice. "It's a museum piece. A fossilized bone is not, by any means, the strangest thing you'll find in garbage cans or on the streets of this city, believe me. You could have picked it up anywhere. I agree that it must have had some very special meaning for you, but you didn't necessarily find it underground."

"I . . . have dreams."

Anne abruptly sat down beside him on the bed, looked at him intently. "*What* dreams, Bone?"

"Of dark places; wet places."

"Tunnels?" Excitement now vibrated in Anne's voice.

"I'm not sure what you mean by tunnels."

"I'm talking about subway tunnels—concrete, steel rails, lots of noise and echoes. Do you ever dream of anything like that?"

Bone shook his head. "No; this is moist earth—and there are bones all around, under my feet and over my head." He paused, swallowed hard. "Like inside, under, a graveyard."

"Oh, Lord, Bone," Anne said as she once again gripped his hand. "How terrible."

He debated whether or not to tell her about the orange and purple figure, his fear that it was himself, and decided not to.

62

"The dreams tie in with the bone; they mean something. It means that the bone I carried *did* come from somewhere beneath the streets of the city. I'm sure of it."

Anne frowned, absently bit her lower lip. "I just can't connect you with the people who live in those tunnels, Bone. They're virtually all . . . crazy. And if they weren't crazy when they were above ground, living on the streets, then living down there like a rat or mole drove them crazy. They live *worse* than animals down there. God help them, they are animals. You . . . if you could have seen yourself walking the streets, Bone. There was pride in you, life, such a sense of *vitality*. It was what . . . drew me to you. There was such a mystery about you, and I just had to know *who* the hell you were. I know you can't connect with what I'm saying, but you just weren't—aren't—like any of those tunnel people."

"At least not during the day." He paused, took a deep breath, slowly let it out. "You said nobody knows where I went at night."

"I said *I* didn't know."

"There's obviously something very wrong with me, and I have to consider the possibility that I'm insane. I may have been quite different during the day from what I was like at night— *as* different as day and night. Did all of the killings take place at night?"

"I really don't know," Anne replied after a pause. "Even if they did, it's only logical that the killer would operate under cover of darkness. After all, the police were looking very hard for him."

"It's also only logical that the killer knew his victims very well. The killer may have been—may be—a street person himself."

"Why do you say that?"

"The police must have used decoys—lots of them. But the killer was never fooled by them."

"I hadn't thought of that," Anne said softly.

"You can be sure Lieutenant Lightning has." He thought of the orange-draped apparition, felt his throat and stomach muscles tighten. "I think the police should search underground."

"Why, Bone?"

"Lightning said there have been twenty-eight of the beheading murders—but he was talking about corpses that had been

63

found on the *streets*. I'll bet some of those victims still haven't been identified; nobody ever noticed them, or at least paid much attention, until they became murder victims, and then only because their bodies were cluttering up the streets."

"You're saying there could be a lot more corpses under the streets," Anne said tightly.

"Yes."

"Even if you're right, it doesn't mean you left them there."

"No, but I *could* have—and I can't deny that possibility. Maybe when I came up and walked around during the day I was looking so good because I'm crazy as a loon and felt great because I'd killed somebody during the night. I want the police to look around down there, Anne. And I want Lieutenant Lightning to know the idea came from me—if he hasn't thought of it already, which he probably has."

Anne, her face suddenly pale, got off the bed, slowly turned to face him and moved back a step. "Bone, do you . . . are you saying that maybe you *do* remember . . . killing people down there?"

"No, Anne," he said evenly, realizing how much he had frightened her. "I'm just saying it's possible; and the bone and my dreams underline that possibility. If I'm ever going to remember who I am, then I have to have the courage to say what comes into my mind. I'm sorry if I upset you."

"I don't believe you murdered anyone."

"Tell Lightning what I said."

"I'm not going to tell the lieutenant anything, Bone," Anne said curtly. "It sounds to me like you're trying to hang yourself."

"I want the truth about myself, Anne, no matter how ugly that truth may turn out to be. Finding out the truth is the only chance I have to be free—from places like this, and in my own mind. But if I have . . . harmed people, then I don't want to be free to do it again."

"Well, I'm going to insist that you have a lawyer present the next time the police want to talk to you. And a lawyer will tell you to keep your notions about where to look for bodies to yourself. First of all, they don't have the manpower to search the hundreds of miles of subway and train tunnels, sewer and water mains that are beneath the streets of this city. What Lieutenant Lightning will say is that your kind of out-loud

64

thinking is really the plea of a guilty man who wants his guilt proved beyond a doubt."

"Maybe that's true, Anne—even if I'm doing it unconsciously."

Anne's response was to glance at her watch, then head for the door. She knocked twice, and a few moments later the door buzzed and clicked open. When she turned to look back at Bone, there were shadows in her hazel eyes that might have been uncertainty, confusion, perhaps pain. "Tell Dr. Hakim about your dreams and conjectures, Bone," she said quietly. "He'll be in this afternoon, and he's very eager to talk to you."

And then she was gone. Bone wondered if he would ever see her again—and, if he didn't, how long it would take him to recover from the damage he had already done to himself by accepting her warmth, savoring the sound of her voice, thrilling to the touch of her hand. Now, he thought, the stranger would be haunted by another ghost.

CHAPTER FOUR

(i)

She had to face up to the possibility that the strange, ascetic man she was so powerfully attracted to was, in fact, a serial killer, Anne thought as she walked through the lobby of the Bellevue Hospital Center toward the First Avenue exit. And a liar—which was the prevailing opinion among virtually all the professionals involved in the case: police, social workers and medical staff. And if not a liar, then a man who was hopelessly insane, and very, very dangerous. She had broken protocol by staying alone in the room with him, as Barry had broken protocol by leaving without her.

And yet . . .

She simply could not match the figure of the bright-eyed, jaunty man she had seen striding so purposefully through the streets of Manhattan, or sitting on the steps of St. Thomas listening to Zulu, with a murderer who had moved in the night slaughtering helpless men and women and cutting off their heads. And if he was a liar, if the majority of consulting psychiatrists were right about the form of amnesia he was describing being impossible, what was his motivation? Why had he stopped and squatted down in the Sheep Meadow? To die, or be caught, as Lieutenant Lightning claimed?

She did not hear a liar when he spoke, did not see a killer. What she saw, sensed, when she looked into the startlingly blue eyes or held one of the strangely battered yet powerful hands, was a man of integrity and courage. She had no real explanation for the strong attraction she had felt for the brown-haired man from the first time she had seen him. Sexual desire? Certainly. Bone exuded strength, self-confidence and sensuality in his every movement. But there were certainly other men she had been physically attracted to, and they had certainly been more appropriate than a mute, homeless man who walked the streets of New York City carrying a bone like a swagger stick. Was this feeling really a "Messiah Complex," which she had been warned against through so much of her training? Perhaps—but she doubted it. As Barry had pointed out countless times over the course of the past year, Bone had never looked like he needed anyone's help, and there were any number of people in New York City who did things that were far more offensive and self-defeating than walking around with a bone.

Then why the powerful attraction? Why the powerful need to trust and believe in him? She had been in New York too long, seen too much misery brought about by self-delusion and had had too many of her own dreams shattered, to believe in anything as naive as love at first sight.

And yet . . .

She had not been in New York so long that she had given up all hope for love and happiness, all belief in the mystery and magic of the human heart. And that, she knew, was what Bone represented to her—mystery and magic, feeling, hope. And she would trust that feeling, she thought, believe in *herself* and her instincts, until she was proved wrong. She might be a minority of one, with Ali's attitude—as in most things—uncertain, in considering the possibility that not only was Bone telling the truth when he said that he couldn't remember anything, but that he was innocent of the killings; but until such time as the police proved their case against Bone, she was determined to serve as his advocate and see that his rights were protected. That was, after all, her job.

Barry was waiting for her just outside the hospital entrance. He was leaning against the side of the van, which he had left idling in a No Parking zone at the curb, and was idly smoking a cigarette as he stared off into space. The anger that had been in him before seemed spent. Anne playfully slapped him on the rear, then climbed up into the passenger's seat at the front of the van.

Barry threw away his cigarette, came around the van and got in behind the wheel. "What's next on the agenda?" he asked quietly as he put the van into gear, cut in front of a cab and eased into the heavy traffic on First Avenue.

"Let's go check on the schizo in rags who's been hanging out on Sherman Square," Anne replied distantly, still distracted by thoughts of the man locked up in the secure ward of the hospital they were leaving behind. "He accepted a sandwich the day before yesterday. Maybe he's ready to let us take him to a shelter."

Barry grunted, turned the wheel sharply and headed crosstown. "So, what do you think?"

"Huh?"

"What do you think?"

"About what, Barry?"

"About the character we just visited. I'll say this for him: he sure as hell is disarming. I can't believe we were up there casually chatting for a half hour with a mass murderer."

Anne looked at the man beside her, saw now that he was not as subdued as she had first thought. His voice was soft, but his mouth was set in a tense, thin line, and his hands were clenched on the wheel. "You think it's all an act, don't you?"

"I'm not the only one, Anne, and you know it. I agree with the doctors who say he's been watching too many old movies. They all say amnesia doesn't work that way."

"Not all; Ali thinks there's a possibility he's telling the truth."

"Ali's out to lunch half the time. All those shrinks are."

"Then his opinion is just as good as the others', isn't it? And Ali Hakim just happens to be one of the world's foremost neuropsychiatrists. Do you know what that man's time is worth? It probably costs him a thousand dollars every time he comes out with us on a call."

"Ali's got other fish to fry with this Bone."

Anne frowned. "I don't understand what you mean."

Barry was silent for some time. Finally he shrugged, said, "I'm not sure what I mean. It just seems he's a lot more interested in this guy than I've ever seen him before. Ali's not really big on people, you know; he only cares about their brain waves."

"You're wrong about Ali, Barry. And why shouldn't he be interested? What Bone is suffering from falls right into the area of research that Ali is noted for."

"He's not the first amnesiac we've ever picked up."

"The others were alcoholics with Korsakoff's syndrome. Bone's no alcoholic."

"Every other shrink who's watched his tapes and read his record says it's almost certain he's putting on an act."

"If it's an act, it's a pretty good one, isn't it?"

"Is it? All of the shrinks, except for Ali, agree that the odds against being both anterograde and retrograde at the same time are at least a million to one, and that it's virtually impossible that such a person would then continue to track mentally the way your friend Bone does."

"What they mean is that they've never come across a patient like Bone before."

"For a man who supposedly can't remember anything that happened to him before a week ago, he doesn't seem all that distressed to me."

"Oh?" Anne asked coolly. "Just how distressed should he be?"

"More than he is."

"Has it ever occurred to you that he may be a lot more frightened—distressed, as you put it—than he lets on?"

"He's the serial killer the police are looking for, Anne," Barry said firmly. "He's killed twenty-eight people."

"You don't know that."

"He's a killer, and he thinks he's going to get off on an insanity plea."

"Serial killers rarely get off on insanity pleas," Ann replied tightly. "If you haven't learned that already in any of your sociology or criminology courses, you soon will."

"Maybe so, but he doesn't know that, does he? Come on, Anne; he had the old woman's locket around his neck, and her blood on his clothes. What more do you want?"

"The answer to why, if he's the serial killer, he just suddenly stopped one day and squatted down in the rain and mud in Central Park, " Anne said distantly.

"You defend him because you like him," Barry said evenly. "We both know you liked him from the very first time you saw him." He paused and made a harsh, barking sound that might have been an attempt at laughter, but came out ugly. "I've heard about physical attraction, but chasing after a mute, homeless man for a year is ridiculous."

Anne bit off her sharp retort, swallowed her anger and turned to look out the window. There was too much truth in what Barry said for her to defend herself—which she did not want to do in any case. She was troubled by her feelings, and she did not want to exacerbate them any more by getting into a disagreeable, defensive argument with Barry, whose odd, emerging possessiveness was also beginning to increasingly trouble her. She would be silent, Anne thought, and let some time pass. Then, at an appropriate time when she hoped the man sitting next to her would be least offended, she was going to ask to be assigned a different partner or trainee. Bone's awakening had brought out a side to Barry's personality, a jealousy, she hadn't imagined existed, and it made her decidedly uncomfortable.

Barry was heading uptown on Broadway; as always, Anne was struck by how the mall-like traffic islands in the center of the avenue attracted the worst cases of the city's homeless. Sick people, many clad only in rags and carrying all their belongings in shopping bags, slumped on benches on the traffic islands, or occasionally rose to harangue passersby, as did the young man they were now on their way to see. Anne recognized many of the people—the old woman who always sat in the same place, on the island across the street from the apartment which had been her home and from which she had been evicted three years before; alcoholics who had drifted like human flotsam up from the Bowery, where they would eventually drift back; the former advertising executive who'd started drinking heavily after his wife had left him, taking with her their five children, and who had then proceeded to lose his job, his home and his self-respect, and who had ended up . . . where he was, living on a traffic island; the old man who was constantly looking up at the sky and talking, insisting that he was being interviewed on Martian television; the pretty young woman who proudly sat on a blanket by day, politely chatting with pedestrians and graciously accepting the money a few of them gave her, who at sundown moved three blocks to the west and spent most of the night screaming obscenities into the darkness. It was like driving through an open psychiatric ward,

Anne thought, and in the time it would take them to drive to Sherman Square they would pass by perhaps a hundred homeless people, most of them mentally ill. And why were they passing by all these people on their way uptown? Because a young man in desperate need had accepted her offer of a sandwich, Anne thought, and she now dared to hope that he was ready to accept their offer of food, shelter and medical treatment. He was being targeted. She had already approached, on many occasions, most of the people they were passing by, and she would approach them again. But first she would approach the young man on Sherman Square again. You had to target; otherwise, a person would burn out in a day, hurrying from one apparition on a traffic island to another sleeping inside a cardboard box in a doorway . . .

"I'm sorry, Anne," Barry said quietly, after they had driven a few more blocks.

"There's no need to apologize, Barry," Anne replied evenly. "I think we should just drop the subject of Bone, and leave it dropped. He's just a client, like any other. If you don't want to help me service him, that's all right; I'll handle it myself."

"He's more than just a client to you, Anne."

"Barry!"

On one of the malls, a woman—draped from head to toe in black and green plastic garbage bags, wearing torn, filthy bedroom slippers on her feet and a wool cap pulled down around her ears—slowly pirouetted, arms held out and face to the sky, like an aging, unwashed ballerina dancing to an invisible, celestial orchestra only she could hear.

"Anne," Barry said in the same low voice, "I'd like you to have dinner with me tonight. Will you?"

She turned toward the man behind the wheel, forced herself to smile. "Oh, Barry, that's sweet," she said, touching his heavily muscled forearm. "But I never go out with co-workers. It's kind of a private policy with me."

"You won't make an exception for me?"

"No, Barry. I'm sorry."

Two cabs had collided at the intersection of Broadway and Sixty-fifth, causing a massive tie-up. Ignoring the hand signals of a brown-uniformed traffic policeman, Barry yanked the wheel to the left, cutting into an inside lane where traffic seemed to be inching along. "Anne," he said tightly, "I think I'm in love with you. I know I'm in love with you."

"Barry, that's silly," Anne said lightly, trying to find the right tone of voice that would fend off the man without offending him. Most definitely, she thought, it was time for a new partner. "It's a lovely compliment, but—as a friend—let me tell you that I don't think you know what you're talking about. First of all, you're five years younger than I am, and—"

"Hear me out, Anne," Barry interrupted curtly. "Now that I've managed to get some of it out, let me get it all out."

"Barry, I really don't think it's a good idea—"

"I made a mistake in not telling you earlier—right after I started working with you, I knew I was in love with you. It's the first time. You probably think that I'm immature, but I'm not. When I was in the seminary, I remained chaste because that's what I thought God wanted. I didn't even think of women. But when I realized that God had other plans for my life, I opened myself up to love. And I found you. I think of you as a gift from God; I believe we're meant for each other."

"Barry, are you putting me on?"

He flushed. "I love you, Anne."

"Stop this."

"Let me finish. I didn't feel there was any hurry; I believed that everything was going according to God's plan, and that we would just naturally come together when the time was right. I believed that you would realize that I loved you, and that you would come to love me. It was *natural*. Then I saw the way you reacted to Bone, and . . . well, it just hurt me terribly. I saw the look on your face when you looked at him, and, finally, it made me very jealous. Well, it was my own fault for not speaking out sooner, for not announcing my feelings, for not fighting for you. All right, I was naive. But now you know how I feel, and I think if you look into your heart—if you'll let yourself—I believe that you'll find that God means for you to love me."

Again, Anne looked out the window. There was a momentary break in the traffic, and she caught a glimpse of a young Hispanic woman sitting on the sidewalk. The entire left side of the woman's face was covered with a dirty bandage that seemed ready to fall off; in the woman's arms was a small dirty child dressed in ragged clothes, holding a hot dog smeared with ketchup. Propped up next to them was a crudely lettered sign that read: *Please pardon our appearance. Will you help?*

"Anne . . . ?"

Anne cleared her throat, turned to him. "I don't share your feelings, Barry," she said, making no effort to soften the firmness or warm the chill in her voice. The time had come, she thought, to stop being polite. "Nor do I share your theology. I'm sorry this whole thing has come up. Under the circumstances, I think it might be better if we found new partners."

Barry paled. "What are you saying, Anne?"

"Oh, *Jesus*, Barry!" Anne said with frustration. They were standing still, and Anne yanked open the door of the van, stepped out into the street. "Why the *hell* do you have to be so difficult?"

"Anne, where are you going?"

"You go check out that guy in Sherman Square," Anne called over her shoulder as she angled through the stalled cars toward the woman and child on the sidewalk. "I'll take a cab back to the office."

(ii)

His thoughts drifting easily in the semi-trance he entered between performances, oblivious to the crowds of pedestrians that eddied around him at the corner of Fifty-third Street and Fifth Avenue, Zulu stood very erect, his staff held close to his body, staring over the heads of the people. Without looking around, he knew there would be a large number of men and women—hot dogs, kebabs, sausages, falafels and cans of soda in their hands—gathering behind him on the broad steps of St. Thomas Episcopal Church to hear his next story. He was not ready; he had an inexhaustible wealth of stories to tell about the colossal, cruel, fantastic host-creature that was New York City, but the right words and rhythms in which to tell the next one had not come to him yet.

He was thinking, worrying, about the bone-man, who in the past had almost always come to hear his noontime performance.

It had been more than a week since Zulu had seen the blue Human Resources Administration van heading down rain-slick Fifth Avenue, with the social worker he knew as Barry driving, and the worker Anne in the back with the bone-man, who'd looked lost, forlorn and bewildered as he'd stared out the window. Zulu had raised his staff in greeting, but the bone-man

73

had given no sign of recognition. And then the van had been gone. Zulu, who knew that the bone-man was much like himself, had not been able to understand what the other man was doing with the social workers.

And then he had read the newspaper stories the next day.

Zulu usually read at least five newspapers a day, pulling them out of the wire trash basket on the corner as soon as they were thrown away. He normally started the morning with *The Wall Street Journal*, discarded by well-dressed, fast-walking businessmen who had already read it over breakfast, or during their commute by train, subway, bus or taxi. But it had been the *New York Post*, not the *Journal*, which had given Zulu the most graphic description of what had happened to the strange, mute man he had come to think of as a friend.

The papers had said that although formal charges had not been filed, the bone-man was undoubtedly the killer who had been murdering homeless people and chopping off their heads.

He didn't believe it. Zulu was a writer—a sonic creator of short stories, essays and epic poems; he believed he could see into the hearts of men and women, sometimes with no more than a glance into the eyes of a pedestrian, or an exchange of looks with someone who had stopped to hear him, perhaps to drop money into the intricately carved and painted ceremonial wooden bowl at his feet. He had glimpsed petty thieves in three-piece suits, saints in leather and beads, closet alcoholics, embarrassed adulterers on their way to trysts in some mid-town hotel, homosexual priests, rapists, charitable people, writers like himself, insane people ready to explode at any moment. He had told stories about all of them, often feeling the inexorable surge of inspiration and beginning his recitation of the images in his mind even before the subjects had passed out of earshot.

But the person he had told the most stories about was the bone-man, and Zulu had never seen a killer in the bone-man's eyes or his strangely impassive face.

"Mister . . . ? Excuse me, mister?"

The papers said they had found him squatting in the mud in the rain; for two days he had been squatting in the mud, staring off into space.

That was not the bone-man he knew. The bone-man knew how to take care of his own needs as well as any man Zulu had ever known, even including himself.

Zulu didn't believe the bone-man had killed the old woman, Mary, or the old man on the steps of the Presbyterian church up the street. The bone-man was not a murderer, and Zulu didn't care what the "unspecified evidence" was that the police supposedly had. The one thing Zulu knew for certain was that something terrible had happened—

"Sir . . . ?"

—to the bone-man a year ago. Now something even more terrible might have happened to cause the bone-man to squat in the rain for two days. But, whatever had happened, Zulu was convinced the bone-man had not killed crazy old Mary, or anyone else—who had not deserved it.

"Sir, may I speak to you a moment?"

When in a trance, Zulu could normally block out all sounds and movement around him. But today he was distracted by thoughts of the bone-man, and the right words for his stories were not coming to him; consequently, he became aware that someone was persistently trying to get his attention. He looked down from his seven-foot height at the middle-aged, bespectacled woman with gray hair who was standing very close to him, almost touching his staff, craning her neck to look up into his face. There was kindness in the face, Zulu thought, compassion in the gray eyes magnified by her thick eyeglass lenses. And curiosity. Hers was a face being gently eroded by open countryside, displaying none of the sharp, tense lines sometimes etched into even young faces by the city. He had seen the woman before; each day for the last three days, after eleven but before the crush of the noonday crowds, she had come to sit on the steps of St. Thomas and listen to his stories, and she had always dropped at least a dollar into his wooden bowl.

"How can I help you, ma'am?" he asked in his resounding, mellifluous bass.

The woman smiled warmly. "I just want you to know how much I enjoy your stories, sir. They're like poetry, and when you speak it's almost like you're singing. My husband and I are here on vacation—we're from Indiana. This is my first trip to New York, and it's all too much, but I must say that I enjoy listening to you as much as anything else I've seen or heard. I think you're a remarkable man."

"Well, I certainly thank you for saying that, ma'am. I'm glad you enjoy my work."

"Are they true?"

"My stories? Oh, yes, ma'am."

"You tell them so well. Are they things you've memorized?"

"No, ma'am. I tell them as they come to me."

"But you said the stories are true."

"To describe something which has happened is not the same thing as telling a story, ma'am. A good storyteller must use just the right words if he is to accurately re-create the events in the listener's imagination." He was glad he had broken from the trance; the right words for another story were beginning to form in his mind.

"You mean you tell those stories right off the top of your head, here on the spot?"

"On the spot, yes, ma'am; not off the top of my head. The words come from somewhere deeper than that."

"Oh," the woman said quietly, somewhat surprised and obviously disappointed. "I was hoping . . . I very much wanted to buy some of your work."

"My work is not for sale, ma'am; it's given away. If people enjoy what I do, then they are free to give me what they want. You have given me donations, and I appreciate your generosity."

"I was hoping to take a book, or something else of yours, home with me."

"If you remember me, if my stories linger in your mind, then you've taken me home with you."

The woman smiled wistfully. "We don't get many street poets in Indiana."

"In New York you expect to find such people, and so you do; you don't expect to find such people in Indiana, and so they would be easy to miss. Is it possible you weren't listening with the same ears and seeing with the same eyes when you were in Indiana?"

The woman stared up into his face for some time before finally nodding. "Yes. I think you may be right. I'll bear that in mind when I go home. I just wish, sir, that I had something of yours which you could autograph."

"The memory of me and my work is my autograph, ma'am. It would please me if I thought that my autograph would be easy for you to find, and to share with your friends."

"But you haven't published anything, sir?"

"My name is Zulu, ma'am. I publish here; every day."

"May I take your picture, Zulu?"

Zulu blinked slowly, then averted his gaze, hoping to mask his disapproval and disappointment so as not to hurt the gray-haired woman with so much kindness and curiosity in her eyes. He said softly, "If it is a photograph of me that you want, ma'am, go right ahead."

The woman removed a small Kodak Instamatic from her purse, waited for a break in the pedestrian traffic, then backed away to the curb and raised the camera to eye level. Zulu gazed stonily over her head, across the street, and saw the four youths in gray leather jackets, gray denims and black boots coming from the direction of Central Park, moving with the crowds. They abruptly stopped by the entrance to Fortunoff's, then moved back behind the flowing wall of people, disappearing from sight—but not before Zulu had seen the tall albino leader of the Wolfpack nod in his direction. They were in the next block, on Fifty-fourth Street.

The attack would come from his left.

He looked back at the woman, and knew that she had not released the shutter on the camera, which she was now putting back into her purse. She had a puzzled expression on her face as she walked back toward him.

"I don't know why," the woman said distantly, "but I don't think I want to take your picture. It's like it would take something away from that autograph you mentioned."

"You must go now, ma'am," Zulu said in a low voice.

"Oh," the woman said in a small voice that clearly reflected distress. "I hope I haven't offended you."

"No, ma'am."

"I still have an hour before I have to meet John, and I was so hoping to hear another of your stories. Isn't there any—?"

"There's going to be trouble, ma'am. If you stay here, you could be hurt."

The woman looked around her in alarm. "Trouble?"

"Yes, ma'am. Please go now—or at least move up on the church steps with the other people."

The woman blinked. "I'll get the police."

"That won't do any good, ma'am. If you bring the police here, it will only postpone the trouble. Please go. Hurry, now."

The woman, clearly frightened, clutched her purse to her chest. She once more looked around her, then back at Zulu; but Zulu was in another kind of trance now, one which sharpened his senses and heightened his awareness as he waited for what he knew was coming. The woman started to say something to him, then abruptly turned and hurried away, moving with a knot of pedestrians across Fifty-third Street.

The attack came five minutes later. The Wolf—this one a pimply-faced white youth of fourteen or fifteen—came at him on the run from behind a tightly packed knot of pedestrians. To his left, out of the corner of his eye, Zulu caught a flash of gray moving at right angles to the pedestrian traffic. Then the youth cut sharply and came at him at full speed, at the last moment reaching down to grab the money-filled bowl at Zulu's feet.

With what appeared to be a minimum of effort, without even glancing down, Zulu reached across his body with his left hand to grasp his staff in its middle, then used both hands to bring the heavy wooden rod smashing back into the youth's face and chest. The impact of the staff stopped the running youth in his tracks, straightened him up. His hands shot to his nose and mouth, which were gushing blood over his clothes and onto the sidewalk. He uttered a low, mewling cry, spat blood and teeth, then toppled backward. There were startled gasps from the people on the sidewalk and on the church steps behind Zulu. Somebody screamed, but a few seconds later there was a spontaneous burst of applause. More people started to clap as the youth, retching and spitting blood, crawled across the sidewalk, collapsed at the curb and rolled into the gutter.

Suddenly there was the howl and whoop of a police siren close by, and then a squad car came squealing around the corner of Fifty-third Street and braked to a halt at the curb— missing the fallen Wolf's outstretched hand by only two or three inches. The policeman driving the car, a slender man with strands of fiery red hair visible from beneath the edge of his cap, took in the scene at a glance; he casually glanced down at the bloodied youth lying in the gutter before getting out of the car and stepping over the Wolf, spitting as he did so.

"Wolfpack," the policeman said to Zulu in a thick Irish brogue as he perfunctorily jerked his thumb back in the direction of the street. "I'm sorry I didn't run the fucker over. You all right, man?"

"Yes, Jim," Zulu replied evenly. Once again he was standing very erect, his staff planted firmly on the sidewalk in front of him. "Thank you. I believe, though, that the young man in the street has some trouble; he's missing teeth, his nose is definitely broken and his jaw may be as well."

The red-haired policeman grinned wryly. "Shit. Was he trying to rob *you*, Zulu?"

"He gave that indication, Jim," Zulu replied in the same even tone. "He seemed to be reaching down for my bowl as he sprinted along the sidewalk, and I'm afraid he miscalculated and ran right into my staff."

From somewhere in the crowd on the church steps, an angry woman shouted: "That's right, Officer! The kid was trying to rob the man! It was self-defense!"

There was a chorus of assenting, angry shouts which turned to jeers as the youth, still holding both hands to his face, struggled to his feet and staggered across Fifth Avenue against the light, causing a cacophony of blaring horns, screeching brakes and shouted obscenities from drivers.

"You want to press charges, Zulu?" the red-haired policeman asked as he casually watched the gray-jacketed Wolf stumble over the curb on the opposite side of the street. "If you want, I'll go get him."

"Don't bother yourself, Jim. I don't think he'll be back."

"Others will. The Wolfpack gang is getting to be a real pain in the ass. Juvenile Division's been trying to handle the Wolfpack, but I think they've underestimated the problem. When those kids start doing numbers like this in broad daylight, on Fifth Avenue, it's time to kick some ass."

"They've been watching me for a week, and I knew they'd be coming at me sooner or later."

The policeman nodded. "You could be right; maybe they won't come back—at least not for you. They're not used to having their victims fight back." He paused, looked at Zulu. "I was over on Park and this woman came running out into the street and flagged me down. She told me you were in trouble. You don't see that kind of concern for fellow citizens much these days."

Zulu nodded. "She's a lovely lady."

The policeman headed back toward his squad car, called over his shoulder: "Take care, Zulu. And make sure you pay the taxes on the bundle in that pot of yours, or I'll turn you in to the IRS for the reward. The Irish know a silver tongue when they hear it, and you've definitely got one. I'm damn sure you make more money in a year than I do."

"Jim?"

The policeman opened the door to his car, turned back. "What is it, Zulu?"

"I read in the papers that you think the bone-man is the one who's been killing all those people and cutting off their heads."

The other man gave a noncommittal shrug of his shoulders. "It looks that way, Zulu. Homicide says they've got the goods on him."

"He's not the kind of man who would do that, Jim," Zulu said evenly.

"I know he's a friend of yours, Zulu—but you know he's a loony. Have you ever heard him talk?"

"No."

"Well, you tell your stories, and let us take care of the police work. And the next time you swat a member of Lobo's gang with that stick of yours, see if you can't knock his head off. So long."

Zulu watched the patrol car drive off down Fifth Avenue, and within moments a new story began forming in his mind; and this time the words crystallized easily. He struck his staff once on the sidewalk, then, in a booming voice, began to speak of good and evil and the gray marsh between the two where most people live. He began a tale of a great city with thousands of people living on its streets. He spoke of how some men and women, for various reasons, suddenly find themselves with no home, and how they often gather the few smaller valuables they have left—jewelry, family heirlooms, sometimes a map indicating where they have hidden larger valuables—and wear them on their bodies, around the neck or wrist, or carry them in a pocket. Sometimes, Zulu said, even the dirtiest person dressed in the filthiest rags would be wearing a ring, necklace or bracelet of some value, a last memento of another life.

Zulu told of how a particularly vicious, multiracial street gang had discovered that these tiny treasures often could be found on lice-infested bodies, and of how this band of youths had come to specialize in robbing these most helpless of people—often raping and sodomizing them in the process. He described the Wolfpack as a gang which prided itself on its viciousness and what it considered its clever tactics which left them virtually invulnerable to successful prosecution; their victims were usually so helpless, so mentally ill, that they could rarely even remember what happened to them, much less present a coherent report to the police. With so many thousands of potential victims, the Wolfpack always worked quickly, roaming through the night streets, as well as bus and train waiting rooms and the network of tunnels beneath Grand Central Terminal and Penn Station, mugging, robbing, beating and raping, then meeting at dawn at various sites around the city to pool and divide what they had captured during the night.

Laced through Zulu's tale of a great city with merciless beasts of prey and thousands of homeless people living on the sidewalks beside buildings where countless fortunes were made and lost every day was the theme of how this city had a powerful attraction for both the best and worst of people from all over the world, the best and worst of many things; people traveled to see the masterpieces at the Metropolitan Museum of Art on buses, trains and subways stained with the tortured art of the city, graffiti, desperate attempts to forge identity.

The story, a long one, turned out to be one of Zulu's best—and it had fortuitously come to him at the height of the noonday rush. Many people stopped to listen, creating a growing blockade on the sidewalk which in turn caused even more people to stop to see what was happening, and to be caught up in the rhythms of Zulu's words and the near-hypnotic power of his voice. Many of the men and women in business suits or dresses kept glancing at their watches—but they did not move away. Vendors at the corners and down the length of Fifty-third Street ran out of food and soda, and wheeled their carts away; vendors from other sites hurried to take their places. People listened intently to this tale of their city and themselves, occasionally glancing at the others around them, or up and down the stone canyon of Fifth Avenue, perhaps seeing themselves and their environment with new eyes. More than a hundred dollar bills were dropped into Zulu's bowl—and one elderly man climbed to the top of the steps of St. Thomas and began handing out dollar bills to the ragged people sitting in the shadows there, beneath the carved stone statues of Jesus and the saints.

And then the story was finished. It was past one o'clock, and the people began to drift away. Zulu, now standing erect and silent on the sidewalk, waited for the crowd to thin out. He gathered up the money from the bowl and put it into a pocket inside his robe, then went to a vendor and bought hot dogs and soda for the homeless people who remained on the church steps. He had not eaten all day, and as he passed out the food he realized that he was very hungry. He bought two kebabs and a soda for himself, then sat down on the steps near the sidewalk to relax and chat with the people who passed by. He might wait awhile to see if one more story came to him, Zulu thought, and then—as he did on most days—he would spend the rest of the afternoon in the Forty-second Street library, before going home.

He was eating his second kebab and thinking of buying a third when he glanced up and saw Lobo standing on the corner across the street, watching him. Zulu sipped his soda, stared back placidly.

The gray-clad leader of the Wolfpack wore a black patch over the hole where his right eye had been, and even from this distance Zulu could see the pink left eye of the albino gleaming with the kind of unnatural light Zulu had seen in the eyes of so many psychotics, dangerous or not, he passed on the streets. This young man with chalky skin, tightly curled white hair and pink eye was very dangerous, Zulu thought. This boy-man had an aura of savagery about him which was almost palpable, causing pedestrians to make a wide circle around him as they passed. The albino was a little over six feet, Zulu judged; around two hundred pounds, perhaps quicker than he looked; seventeen or eighteen years old. He would carry a variety of weapons, in hidden places.

Zulu unhurriedly finished his kebab as Lobo walked across the street, came up on the sidewalk and stopped a few feet away from where Zulu was sitting on the third step. Zulu wiped his hands and patted his mouth with a napkin, which he put into the paper bag beside him. Then he placed his seven-foot staff across his knees and casually glanced up at the one-eyed albino youth standing in front of him.

"You're pretty good with that stick, nigger," Lobo said quietly, his slight lisp somehow making him seem even more threatening. "You hurt one of my people. When you do that, you hurt me; you make me look bad. I think it's only right that you fork over your money so we can pay his doctor bills. That way, you won't get hurt."

Zulu grunted. "What's the matter, Lobo? The Wolfpack doesn't provide health insurance for its cubs?"

The albino frowned. "How do you know who we are? How do you know my name?"

Zulu studied Lobo, considering the odd question and what it told him about the albino. Finally, he said, "Don't any of you creeps read the papers or watch the news on television? There's a story about the Wolfpack at least once a week."

"I'm too busy to pay attention to the news."

"Too busy doing what? Roughing up and robbing helpless people who can't defend themselves?"

Lobo's reaction was unexpected. Zulu had meant to anger the youth and perhaps provoke an attack with the insult, but the albino with the pale light in his eye merely shook his head. "We're not doing anything to anybody that the fat cats of this city don't do—only they do it worse. Why do you think all those people are homeless, anyway? Somehow, in some way, somebody else ripped them off good. And if they can't take care of themselves, they shouldn't be out on the streets. This is the United States of America, nigger, and you don't have to read newspapers or watch television to know that in this country it's survival of the fittest. Hey, we're doing the people of this city a favor. If those bums want to clutter up the streets, then I say we have a right to take from them. Whatever they have obviously isn't doing them any good, but we can sure as hell use the money. That's called capitalism, nigger, and that's a word I remember real well from school. If those bums get scared off the streets and into shelters, so much the better for everybody else. They shouldn't be out on the streets; it makes the United States look bad in the eyes of the world. The goddamn communists are laughing at us."

"You should be a speechwriter for the Republican Party."

"What?"

"Get out of my face, asshole," Zulu said evenly, without any change of expression.

Now the albino reacted—first with surprise, then with anger that brought blood to his ashen face, making his flesh appear as if it had been badly sunburned. "What did you say, nigger?!"

"I called you an asshole, and I told you to get out of my face. You're ruining your image with me. From everything I've read about you, I thought you were a real mean guy; now it turns out that down deep in your heart you're really a social reformer and zealous patriot, obviously misunderstood by the people you rob and rape. Now you'd better haul ass, sonny, or I'm going to put out the one eye the bone-man left you."

The albino youth's right hand shot to his eye patch as he flushed an even deeper red. "You know about that?!"

"I know about a lot of things, Lobo. That was just a rumor going around on the street, but now I can see that it's true. The bone-man did put out your eye, didn't he?" Zulu paused, slowly smiled. "He smacked it right out of your head. Son-of-a-bitch. You city wolves are sure as hell pretty dumb critters. You should be more careful about who you try to bring down."

"I'll kill him when I find him," Lobo said, his lisping voice seething with hatred. "I'll do more than just kill him; I'll take him apart like a fucking chicken. I'll slice off his nuts and feed them to him before I slash his throat—just like the communists used to do in Vietnam. He's been hiding from me, but I'll find him."

Zulu resisted the impulse to laugh; he wanted to know more about the strange landscape of the albino's mind "You think the bone-man is hiding from you, Lobo?"

"I just got out of the hospital last week, and we've been looking for him all over the city. He's hiding, all right. But I'll find him; and when I do, he's dead meat."

"So you've been looking for him for a week?"

Lobo's eyelid fluttered. "That's what I said, nigger. You know where he is?"

"How would I know where he is?" Zulu replied evenly, glad now that the bone-man was in police custody; if he weren't, he'd undoubtedly be dead. "I guess you'll just have to keep looking for him, won't you?"

"I don't know why the hell I'm wasting my time standing here talking to you, nigger!" the albino snapped. "You're just another homeless bum fouling up the streets. Give me your money!"

Now Zulu laughed loudly. "Why don't you tell me a good story, sonny? If I like it, I'll maybe lay a dollar on you. If you want to try to roll me like you do all those other people, you're welcome to try—anytime. Like I said, I'll put out your other eye for you."

The albino's gaze flicked up over the faces of the other people on the steps, then came back to Zulu. He unbuttoned the front of his gray leather jacket, pulled back the flap to reveal a huge bowie knife in a leather scabbard hanging from his belt.

"I don't know whether you're seeing and hearing me, nigger;

if you're not, you'd better start. We own these streets, and the people like you who live on them. Think of the Wolfpack as your landlord. Now, I can't have you making me look bad by beating on one of my collection agents. Today you're going to give me all your money to pay for my man's medical bills. After that, it's ten dollars a day, which is what we charge all the street performers; you use our streets, you have to pay for the privilege."

Zulu's heartbeat had quickened at the sight of the bowie knife hanging at the youth's side—not out of fear, but at the thought that he might now know who had been killing and beheading the homeless people. He wondered if the albino was stupid enough to allow himself to be goaded into admitting it.

"If I don't give you my money, are you going to cut off my head the way you did to the others?" Zulu asked evenly.

"I may cut off your balls and feed them to you, just like I'm going to do to that crazy bone-man when I catch him."

It was not the response Zulu had hoped for. "Don't try to tell me you're not the one who's been killing those people, sonny. There's plenty of killer in you, and that knife you've got looks like it would do the trick very nicely. What have you been doing with the heads?"

"I haven't got time to stand around here all day bullshitting with you, nigger; you're crazier than I thought. Hand your money over, or I'm going to come up there and cut you."

Zulu's response was lightning-quick. He leaped to his feet and, in a series of fluid, unbroken movements, swung his staff once around his head, then brought it flashing down through the air fully extended—stopping it at precisely the point when its tip was touching the youth's curly white hair.

There were gasps of astonishment from the onlookers on the church steps and the sidewalks; it had all happened so fast that the albino had not had time to react in any way. But now he began to tremble, and sweat broke out on his forehead as his one eye rolled up to look at the hardwood weapon resting on his head; the pink eye gleamed with humiliation, rage and hatred as the albino's gaze traveled down the length of the staff, came to rest on Zulu's face.

"You have no idea of how close you just came to getting one hell of a headache, sonny," Zulu said easily. "I don't much like being threatened, and I suppose I should have bopped you good, but I'm feeling kindly today."

"I'm going to kill you, nigger," Lobo said in a trembling voice.

"Not with your brains running out your ears, sweetheart. I'm beginning to wonder if you've got a brain up there at all, and I'm really tempted to open up your skull to find out."

"There are too many of us, nigger. I'll be back for you, and I won't be alone. You're a marked man; you can't fight all of us."

"Well, you know where to find me—*don't touch that staff!*" Lobo had started to reach up to push away the staff, and now Zulu bore down, making the albino's knees buckle. "Move, and I'll break both your collarbones!"

"We'll . . . get you . . . where you sleep, wherever that . . . is. We'll find you. You're a . . . dead man."

The flashing lights of a police squad car were suddenly visible above the heads of the crowd of gaping pedestrians who had formed a semicircle on the sidewalk around the gray-jacketed youth.

"Hear me good, sonny," Zulu said quickly, in a low voice. "You and the rest of your gang are the ones who are marked. I'm declaring this block a Wolfpack-free zone. If you think you can take me on this corner, be my guest—any day. But I tell you that if I see one punk in a gray jacket around here, I'm going after him. If you think there's safety in numbers, you'd better think again, because then I'll just have more skulls to split open. You spread the word, Lobo; any Wolf who doesn't want his bones broken had better stay out of my sight. I have a strong feeling that the police are going to look the other way if and when I start busting you people up. So now get out of my face, like I told you to."

Zulu withdrew the staff from the youth's head as a patrolman pushed his way through the crowd. Lobo flashed one more hate-filled glance at Zulu, then pushed through the crowd in the opposite direction and disappeared.

"Was that the Wolf king himself?" the patrolman asked, taking off his cap and running a hand through thick, unruly locks of black hair.

"None other, Harry," Zulu replied evenly, glancing around him as the crowd began to disperse.

"I was talking to Jim earlier; you've had a busy day with the Wolfpack."

"I laid a heavy threat on him, Harry. I told him I'd bust up him or any other member of the Wolfpack I see on this block. I meant it. If I see any Wolf around here, I'm going to break bone. I'm telling you up front, Harry, so you can get a jail cell ready for me, if you've a mind."

The policeman tilted his head back and squinted at the pale sun overhead. "I'm sure you impressed him, Zulu," he said with a sigh. "But it's not Lobo or any of the Wolfpack I'm worried about. You humiliated him, and now he's going to be after you. Lobo's psycho. I'm not asking where you crash at night, Zulu, because it's none of my business, but I just hope to hell it's a safe place where Lobo and his gang can't get at you."

"It is."

"Then they'll try to ambush you someplace else. Killing you, or putting you in the hospital for a good long stay, is going to be Lobo's top priority."

"I can take care of myself, Harry, but I thank you for your concern. In any case, I'm not Lobo's top priority."

"I'm telling you you are, Zulu. Nobody's ever stood up to Lobo like that. He's lost face, and that's one thing he won't tolerate."

"He wants the bone-man even more; the bone-man put his eye out. The papers say you have him in custody; he should be warned about Lobo."

The policeman frowned slightly. "You know that guy?"

Zulu's answer was a curt nod.

"Well, the Wolfpack is the least of that loony's problems. The only place that guy with the bone is going is death row, and I don't think Lobo will be inclined to follow him there."

"He should be warned, Harry."

"How the hell do you know that guy put out Lobo's eye? Did he tell you that?"

"No. As far as I know, the bone-man never spoke to anybody."

"Then who told you?"

"An old woman named Mary—one of the people he's supposed to have killed."

CHAPTER FIVE

The dark-skinned Pakistani psychiatrist with the large, soulful eyes and lilting voice listened impassively as Bone told him of his dreams of graves and being buried alive, of a great chamber with bones growing from the walls, floor and ceiling. Bone described the recurring image of a ghostly figure chasing him, a spectre dressed in a shimmering orange cloak that was streaked with blood; he shared his thought that the twenty-eight bodies found so far might be only a fraction of the total, that there might be more in the underground world beneath the city that Anne had told him about—nameless, homeless people whose deaths would go unnoticed.

Finally, Bone shared with Dr. Ali Hakim his abiding fear that his thoughts and dream-images might mean that he was indeed the killer. Through it all, Ali Hakim's expression had not changed; in fact, he did not seem all that interested—and Bone told him so.

The Pakistani psychiatrist sat in a straight-backed chair facing Bone, who sat on the edge of his bed. Ali Hakim closed the small memo pad in which he had occasionally been making notes, closed the cap on his fountain pen and put it in the plastic-shielded pocket of his gray shirt. He leaned back and casually crossed his legs.

"What you say is only logical," Ali said, a slight shrug in his singsong voice. "You dream of bones under the ground, and it is only natural that you connect these images to the possibility that there have been other murders under the streets. You are an intelligent man, and you seem absolutely sincere in your desire to know the truth about yourself, no matter what the cost. Any intelligent person experiencing your dreams would conjecture as you have. But not everyone would have the courage to voice those conjectures. I'm certain the police have already considered the possibility you mentioned—but even if more decapitated corpses are found, it doesn't mean that you committed the murders."

"Thank you, Doctor."

"For what?"

"I'm not sure . . . I guess for giving me the benefit of the doubt. For making me feel better."

The psychiatrist looked genuinely surprised. "Is that what you think I'm trying to do?"

"It's what you've done."

Ali Hakim grunted noncommittally, opened his pad, took out his pen and made a note.

"I see your point," Bone continued wryly. "It's also possible that the dreams and thoughts *do* mean that I'm a murderer."

"You still remember absolutely nothing before waking up and finding us standing in front of you in Central Park?"

Once again, Bone took time to think, to probe, trying to see past the dark curtain that had risen only to the sound of Anne Winchell's voice. "No," he said at last.

"The aftereffects of your physical illness aside, you are in remarkably good physical condition for a man who's lived on the streets for a year. Your medical workup indicates no parasitic infections, no lung problems not associated with your pneumonia, outstanding muscle tone, few cavities in your teeth and no gum disease. Yet your hands and the scars on your body strongly suggest very rugged physical stress, suffered over a long period of time. It's very interesting."

Bone suppressed a bitter laugh. "Aside from the fact that I don't know who I am or where I came from, and aside from the fact that I can't remember a damn thing prior to eight days ago, and aside from the fact that I may have cut off the heads of twenty-eight people, I'm in great shape and doing just fine. Is that what you're saying, Doctor?"

"Yes," Ali replied evenly, with no change of expression. "That is what I'm saying."

"Do you believe me when I tell you I can't remember anything?"

"Why shouldn't I believe you?"

"I got an indication from Anne that a number of psychiatrists had examined my story, and presumably watched a videotape of my conversation with Lieutenant Lightning, and you're a minority of one who thinks I may be telling the truth. Apparently, I don't fit some pattern."

"What would be your motive for lying, Bone?" Ali asked in the same easy tone. "To escape punishment? You certainly haven't managed to do that, have you?"

"To escape responsibility."

"Ah." The psychiatrist made a note on his memo pad, looked up. "A conscious desire to be stopped, yet evade responsibility? But if you planned to do that, it clearly implies a conscious decision to lie about your loss of memory, and it seems to me that you're sufficiently clever to have done a bit of research on the symptomology of various kinds of amnesia so as to make your act more convincing to skeptics."

"That would be the behavior of a sane man, not a lunatic—which I may well be."

Ali made a very slight derisive gesture with his right hand. "Describing someone as insane explains nothing."

"That seems like an odd remark for a psychiatrist to make."

"Only laymen believe that so-called insane people aren't responsible in some way for their behavior. 'Insanity' is a legal term, not a medical one."

"What's happened to me, Doctor?"

"Now, that's a very good question," Ali replied. For the first time, what could have been a note of excitement had crept into his voice.

"You and the other doctors must have some idea."

"As you pointed out, most of the other doctors don't believe that anything 'happened' to you in the sense that you mean."

"But you have some idea."

"Much of it is only speculation."

Bone sighed, fighting back a growing sense of impatience

and frustration. "Well, would you mind sharing your speculation with me?"

"Approximately one year ago, you suffered a grave injury to your head. The most massive trauma occurred on the right side, but there are also indications of trauma suffered on the left—and your symptoms indicate that there was damage to both sides of the brain. There are no signs—or records that anyone can find—of medical attention, and so it seems that you somehow managed to survive without medical treatment; it's most remarkable that you're alive at all, Bone, and so I don't find it unreasonable to speculate that there may be other remarkable aspects to your case.

"It seems incontrovertible, judging from your subsequent behavior, that the blow, or blows, to your head caused global retrograde amnesia, which is the inability to remember events that occurred before the trauma. I believe—and most of the other doctors concur here—that once you had physically recovered from your concussion, you began an entirely new existence on the streets of New York.

"Research indicates that global retrograde amnesia results from damage to what we neurologists call the limbic system, specifically two structures in the brain called the hippocampus and the amygdala. Now, we have no way of knowing what your memory pattern was on the street, since you're unable to tell us. However, since you apparently survived quite easily, it is safe to assume that you were able to form *new* memories, both short and long term, and made use of them in your daily life. That is not inconsistent with retrograde amnesia. Also, clearly, the cause of the retrograde amnesia was—is—organic, as evidenced by the signs of injury to your head."

"Dr. Hakim," Bone said in a flat voice, "could such injuries also have caused me to start decapitating people?"

"Possibly," the psychiatrist replied evenly. "Some serial killers—which is what this murderer is—display organic brain damage; that can be one characteristic of a serial killer."

Bone swallowed, found that his mouth was suddenly very dry. "Do I display any other characteristics of a serial killer?"

"It's too early to tell," Ali replied softly. "Neither of us knows all that much about you yet, do we?"

"What are the other characteristics of serial killers?"

"I'm not sure it would be appropriate for me to discuss that with you, Bone."

Bone nodded. "I understand. Go ahead."

"For approximately a year you managed to survive on the streets, despite the fact that you were suffering global retrograde amnesia. Then, eight days ago, I think we can assume that you suffered another severe trauma. Since there is no evidence of recent physical injury, we may reasonably conclude that this shock was psychological in nature."

"Why did it have to be a shock? Why couldn't I have just 'come around'?"

Ali responded with a slight shrug of his shoulders. "Possible, but unlikely."

"Why? My head injuries had healed."

"But not the damage to your brain," Ali said, his tone flat. "Nerve cells are not capable of repairing themselves."

"Then my brain damage is permanent?"

"Yes."

"Then I may never—?" He stopped speaking when the neuropsychiatrist held up his hand.

"Let's not get ahead of ourselves, Bone," Ali said not unkindly. "Before we concern ourselves with what's *not* going to happen, let's continue to try to draw a picture, however blurred, of what *has* happened to you.

"During the year you spent on the street, you suffered not only global retrograde amnesia, but global aphasia as well— the loss of all forms of communication. Then, suddenly, you awakened. Obviously, you are no longer aphasic; but you still cannot recall anything that happened before the original trauma, and in addition can't recall anything that happened *after* the original trauma—up to the point where you found us with you in the Sheep Meadow. This is called global *anterograde* amnesia. It is the combination of the two kinds of amnesia, along with your spontaneous recovery from aphasia with your intellectual abilities remarkably intact, that my colleagues—and, of course, the police—find extremely difficult to accept."

"But not you?"

"I have neither accepted nor rejected anything; at the moment, I am observing. Perhaps you are the serial killer the police say you are, perhaps not; that question must remain open for now. But since I have difficulty understanding what your motive would be for concocting such a complex and improbable condition as yours, I must lean toward the hypothesis that your syndrome is exactly as you describe it."

Bone suddenly felt slightly dizzy. He let out a long sigh. "Thank you, Doctor."

"Please," Ali said abruptly. "Don't thank me. We are in a rather unusual situation here, and my personal and professional ethics compel me to tell you certain things at the outset. It did not take me long after becoming a psychiatrist to realize that I was only a so-so therapist; now my time with patients is limited to volunteer work of the sort that brought me to you, and counseling HRA employees who may benefit from short-term therapy of one sort or another. What I am very good at is research, and my particular area of expertise happens to be memory function. Do you understand what I'm saying?"

"You're telling me that your mouth waters at the prospect of having me as a research subject."

"Precisely."

"And you're being very candid in telling me that you're more interested in what you can learn from me about memory function than you are in healing me."

"Not *more* interested—but *as* interested. It is essential that you understand this, because I propose that we spend a good deal of time together—as much as the police will allow—testing you and trying out certain techniques I have developed. I want you to understand completely that I have a very personal interest in this."

"Could these techniques help to restore my memory?"

"Perhaps; perhaps not. I cannot guarantee anything. I am saying that your syndrome interests me more than the question of your guilt or innocence."

"Okay," Bone said evenly.

"You can accept these conditions?"

"First of all, Doctor, I think you paint too harsh a picture of yourself. If you cared so much more about research than people, you wouldn't give as much time as you do to helping the homeless and counseling city workers."

"I'm asking if the professional posture I've adopted bothers you."

"No. In fact, I think I like it. I don't need a sympathetic therapist or friend; I need someone to help me get my memory back. You help me search for my memory, and I'll look for friends elsewhere."

Ali, his face impassive, studied Bone for some time with his limpid, dark eyes, then hurriedly made a series of notes in his pad. "The fact of the matter is that we really know precious little about how long- and short-term memories are formed, or how they are maintained," he said evenly as he closed his notebook and set it aside. "It seems indisputable that it is a biological process, one which can be disturbed by drugs or injury, and we can map certain areas of the brain that are identified with that process. But beyond that . . ." He paused and shrugged.

"Beyond that?"

"Beyond that is where you and I will attempt to go. I have mentioned to you the limbic system, and how damage to your amygdala and hippocampus has resulted in your loss of memory. Current mainstream theory in neurology would predict that these memories can never be recovered—but current mainstream theory cannot account for your spontaneous recovery from aphasia, and it would dictate that you should be suffering from a host of related symptoms, such as acalculia, agnosia and a lot of other ailments which I won't bother describing since you don't suffer from them.

"There is a second theory—of which I am considered a primary proponent, by the way—which speculates that there is a supplementary system of memory formation and retention which is outside the limbic system, and which, in evolutionary terms, is very ancient. This system, if it exists, is almost certainly in the striatum—a complex of nerve structures in the forebrain. According to your CAT scans, your forebrain is undamaged.

"In this system, memory formation occurs as a result of stimulus-response, below a conscious level or will to 'learn something.' In this system, learning is noncognitive—based not on knowledge or other memories in the usual sense, but on subconscious connections between a stimulus and a response. In short, the basis of this secondary system is *habit*."

"Doctor, I don't have the slightest idea what you're talking about."

"Your brain knows more than you think it does, Bone, and the key to recapturing your memories may be a kind of reverse stimulation. You must begin paying close attention to the things you find yourself *doing* automatically. For example, pay particular attention to what you find yourself doing with those

94

hands of yours, or what you may *want* to do. Pay close attention to your *emotions*. Emotion is what plants and secures long-term memory in both systems. What are the things you *want*? The things you *don't* want? Whenever you find yourself behaving in some particular way, catch yourself; take note. But these are not things that you *try* to do. At once you must be conscious of what you are doing, while at the same time—as paradoxical as it may seem—being free enough to allow yourself to do these things unconsciously. Since your *body*, controlled by the undamaged parts of your brain, may automatically respond to certain things the same way it has in the past, it is your body that may lead you back to conscious memory of just who you *were* in the past; at least, it will indicate to you the things you did. The *emotion* connected to movement, behavior, sights, sounds, touches, smells, tastes; these are the things to which you must pay close attention. For you, the immediate present may present the key to your past. Now, do you understand?"

Bone looked down at his gnarled hands, then around him at the pale walls, the mesh-covered windows. The stranger's past was not here, he thought; and since he was powerless to leave, he felt smothered by the difficulty of using this room to recapture the past. The stranger's past—a year of it, at least— was outside on the streets, and perhaps under the streets, of this behemoth of a city. But he could not—and perhaps should not—get there, and so he saw no value in brooding over it.

"I think so," he said at last. "Yes."

Ali abruptly leaned forward in his chair, resting his elbows on his knees. "Up to now, you have been trying to remember *anything*, Bone," he said, his voice suddenly taking on a new intensity. "Now let's try something different; let's try to remember *something. One* thing. Can you?"

Bone tried, but the curtain remained intact. "No," he said quietly.

"It is not necessary to *try* so hard, Bone. It is enough simply to try. If there is no response at first, simply let it go. Since waking up in the park, have you experienced anything that reminds you of anything else?"

"I . . . no."

"A smell?"

". . . No."

"A sound?"

". . . No."

"A sight?"

"I'm . . . not sure."

"Explain, please."

"When I woke up and first looked at the buildings ringing the park, I thought they were something else."

"What did you think they were?"

"I don't know. I've thought about it a lot, but it just won't come to me."

"You say you dream of being underground, of being buried alive; you dream of bones, and a strange orange figure."

"Yes."

"Buildings are not under the ground."

"No."

"Underground and graves are low; buildings are high."

Peel off.

Bone felt his breath catch in his throat. Wide-eyed, he stared at Ali as he tried to capture the fleeting image that had just raced through his mind, but it was gone.

"You felt something?" Ali continued.

"Yes."

"What?"

"Fear . . . but also exhilaration; tremendous excitement."

"Are the fear and exhilaration still there?"

"No."

"What do you feel now?"

Bone shrugged. "The obvious."

"Nothing should be obvious to a personality that was born only eight days ago."

"All of the feelings that I can identify are associated, as far as I can tell, with my present situation. Tremendous anxiety—"

"About what?"

"About the possibility that I may have hurt—killed—people; fear that I may never find out who I am, or remember the things I've done; fear that I may never go up again."

"Go up again?"

Bone was silent for a long time. "I don't know what I meant by that, Doctor," he said at last.

"When you said it, was there any emotion that might be identified with a past experience?"

"I don't know."

"What about touch? Since you woke up in the park, have you

touched any object or surface that brought about a sense of familiarity?"

". . . No. But I haven't been thinking about it."

Ali leaned back in his chair and once again crossed his legs. If he was disappointed, he didn't show it. "But now you will think about these things, won't you?"

"Yes."

"But don't press. You must not try to pressure yourself into remembering; you must try to *catch* those feelings when they come into your mind."

"Do you think I can't remember because I don't want to remember?"

"What do you think?"

"I don't know."

"Then I don't know, either."

"If I can remember something—anything—from my life, either before or after the injury to my head, will I remember all of it? Both lives?"

"I don't know."

"You said that my awakening in the park was caused by some kind of psychological shock?"

"That's speculative. But *something* caused you to come around; since there is no evidence of recent physical injury, we must assume that the stimulus was psychological trauma."

"Like . . . killing somebody?"

"Trauma."

"But then, if I'd killed at least twenty-seven people before the last, why would the one killing have had such an effect on me?"

Ali said nothing as he gazed steadily at Bone with limpid, unblinking eyes.

"I feel that I'm a good person, Doctor," Bone continued quietly.

"Really?" Ali replied matter-of-factly. "And why is that?"

Bone poured himself a glass of water from a carafe on a table beside the bed, sipped at it. "You've been asking me how I feel, how I cope."

"I haven't asked you how you cope." Ali paused, cocked his head. "But, under the circumstances and considering the anxiety you tell me you feel, you seem to be coping quite well."

"I . . . I constantly feel like I'm some kind of ghost who's stranded in this body."

"But you're a friendly ghost, as it were."

"Yes. I know it sounds ridiculous."

"No. It does not sound ridiculous."

"I feel like a pair of eyes hanging inside a stranger's body and soul. I have no choice but to be here, and so I feel I have no choice but to defend this stranger as best I can while I search for . . . his . . . identity, and the truth about him."

"A most interesting formulation," Ali said. As before, his tone was matter-of-fact, but his eyes gleamed with interest as he quickly took his memo pad out of his pocket and made a series of notes.

"The stranger's accused of being a mass murderer—"

"A serial murderer. There's a difference, and it might help you to know that as you search for this stranger's identity and formulate his defense."

"Will you tell me the difference?"

"The mass, or multiple, murderer usually kills all his victims in a single outburst of uncontrollable frustration and rage," Ali said as he glanced up from his notebook. "Often, his target may be only *one* person within the group of his victims, but his rage is so great that it spills over into the act of killing anyone else who may be around. This type of killer usually has a paranoid personality, and in that one instant this personality explodes across the threshold of rational thought. The explosion usually occurs after a series of rejections or personal defeats—loss of a job, divorce, that sort of thing."

"And the serial killer?"

Ali studied Bone for some time before speaking, and he answered with a question. "How do you feel sexually, Bone?"

Bone smiled thinly, momentarily disoriented by the sudden, and apparently arbitrary, change of subject. "I don't know what you mean," he said at last.

"Have you felt sexually aroused since awakening and discovering yourself inside the body of this stranger?"

"Are you kidding?"

"No," Ali replied evenly. "I am not kidding. Have you had any wet dreams?"

"No."

"Have you felt sexually aroused at any time?"

Bone remembered the feel of Anne's breasts touching his arm in the park, the thrill he had felt when she had come to visit him. He thought of his loneliness. Finally he said, "Yes."

"Has the object of this arousal been male or female?"

98

"Female."

"And has your sexual fantasy involving this person included an act of violence?"

Bone flushed as he stared into the impassive face of the psychiatrist who, for all the expression in his voice, might have been asking if he would like a glass of water; then he looked up at the television monitor on the wall.

"I'm not the police, Bone," Ali continued in the same even tone. "While it's true that everything we say and do is being recorded, it's also true that nothing you say to me can ever be used in a court of law. The tape of this session will not be made available to the police; if they wish to prove you guilty of the crimes they've accused you of, they must build their own case. We are engaged in a search for answers— for the 'truth about the stranger,' as I believe you put it. I took you, the ghost haunting the stranger, at your word. If you're no longer quite so sure you want that truth at this time, I'll get off the subject."

Bone shook his head. Then, feeling like a man about to plunge into unknown waters that could either burn or freeze him to death, he focused specifically on thoughts of making love to Anne. He fantasized doing as he pleased with her body—and then he tried to imagine how he would feel if he physically hurt her in the process. He experienced a wave of revulsion and remorse. He did not want to hurt Anne—only love her, please her and have her please him. There was no pain in this universe.

"No," he said at last.

"If you will, fantasize about making love to this person."

"I just did."

"Do you believe that you could get an erection just by thinking about her?"

Again, Bone smiled thinly. "I just did."

"And you experienced this erection without fantasizing acts of violence toward her?"

Bone sighed. "Yes, Doctor."

Ali studied him for some time, then made a series of notes. "The serial killer is a much more mysterious character," he said when he had finished writing. "We believe, judging from the latest research, that most serial killers are sexual sadists. A serial killer derives satisfaction from the abuse or mutilation of his victims. As often as not, this kind of individual has never experienced a normal sexual relationship with anyone. Killing, or the thought of killing, is the only stimulus that will provoke sexual arousal—and the arousal is very powerful.

"Unlike the mass murderer, whose profile can be quite clear and predictable, it is very difficult to draw a profile of a serial killer, except for the sexual angle—which is hidden from all observers who are not his victims. Even under the most expert examination, many of these individuals will display no evidence of overt psychopathology. Serial murderers usually evince absolutely no sense of guilt; they do not distinguish between people and objects. When they are not killing, they go about leading their lives, which in some cases can include extraordinary achievement. They are usually extremely clever, and can be most charming."

"Then the fact that I appeared harmless during the day doesn't mean that I wasn't murdering people at night."

"Precisely."

"And my loss of memory?"

"Uncharted territory. For now, I think your construction of a 'you' inside a stranger is healthy, and may prove useful to you. From listening to you and observing you, I would say that you don't display the single strongest characteristic of the serial killer—sexual aberration and hostility toward women."

"Unless I'm lying. You said that serial killers can be very clever."

"Unless you're lying. But I don't believe *you* are. However, the question remains as to whether your stranger was, or is, a serial killer. If he was, it seems he became one as a result of the same blow on the head that caused your initial, retrograde amnesia and disintegrated your personality. Another trauma, I believe, caused you to reintegrate, but with accompanying anterograde amnesia."

"Lieutenant Lightning said . . . Is it possible that I *choose*, in a way, not to remember because what the stranger did during that year is something just too horrible to cope with? Is it possible that, unconsciously, I prefer not remembering living as a man who, in a year, killed and beheaded at least twenty-eight people?"

Ali shrugged. "Who knows? As I said, we are heading into uncharted territory. First, we must see if we can help you to recover your memory; then you may be able to answer your own question."

Bone licked his dry lips, sipped more water. "If the stranger did those things, then he has to be . . . punished."

"'Punishment' is not necessarily what the stranger who did those things might merit."

"Whatever—punishment or treatment; they would be dealing with a person who no longer exists."

Ali raised his eyebrows slightly, once again made a series of notes; he had filled more than half the pad with his large, scrawled handwriting.

"I'm glad I'm maintaining your interest," Bone continued wryly.

Ali looked up. "Does my manner offend you?"

"No. We both have the same interests: to find out the truth about the stranger, and to track his past."

The psychiatrist gave a slight nod of his head that might have indicated approval.

"I have to give him the benefit of the doubt, Doctor," Bone continued.

"But of course."

"The most damning evidence against him is the blood of the man and old woman who were killed last, which they found on the cuffs of his shirt and pants. Then there was the locket around his neck that had belonged to one of the victims, and the fact that he was found in a peculiar trance at a spot only a few blocks away from where the last two murders were committed. Have I left anything out?"

"From what I understand, that seems to just about cover it."

"But the detective never said there was any evidence linking me to the twenty-six other murders. Do you know of any?"

"I told you I'm not the police, Bone."

"All I'm asking is if you know if the police have any evidence linking this stranger of mine to the other beheading murders— or any crime at all."

"No, I don't know. But the police wouldn't necessarily provide me with that kind of information, Bone." Ali paused, and a faint smile tugged at the corners of his mouth. "The police tend to think of psychiatrists as the enemy—until they need one."

"But Lightning would have told *me* if they had other evidence," Bone said distantly, gazing out one of the mesh-covered windows just behind and over the psychiatrist's head. "He went out of his way to lay everything on me about the blood and the locket in an attempt to get me to confess to the murders on the church steps, so it's only logical that he would have told me if the police had evidence linking me to the other murders. Do you agree?"

"I agree that what you say sounds logical," Ali replied evenly. "But the police, like all of us, do not always act logically."

"The stranger could have stolen the locket at some time before the murders—or even have taken it from the old woman's body."

"Or the locket could have been given to you," Ali said in the same neutral tone.

Bone slowly blinked, then looked hard into the other man's face—but he could read nothing there. "Thank you for saying that, Dr. Hakim."

"Don't thank me. It's simply logical that the locket could have been a gift. We do need to consider all the possibilities, don't we?"

Bone nodded. "The stranger was definitely at the site of the last two murders; the blood on his clothes proves that. But it doesn't prove that he *killed* those people. When you cut off somebody's head, blood must spurt all over the place. If the stranger had butchered that man and woman, why wasn't there blood all *over* his clothes?" Bone paused, hoping for a response. When Ali continued to merely stare at him, Bone leaned forward on the edge of the bed. "Tell me, Doctor: why wasn't there blood all over his clothes?"

"I told you I'm not the—"

"Pretend you are the police."

"I'd rather not," Ali replied drily. "You must remember that Lieutenant Lightning thinks you're a liar—as do the vast majority of my colleagues."

"Then pretend you're the police, and break down my lies."

Ali sighed, and for the first time his features displayed a hint of emotion—annoyance. "You were wearing a raincoat or some other kind of garment over your clothes, leaving only your cuffs exposed," he said curtly.

"Then what did I do with the raincoat? It wasn't on me at the park. I had nothing with me but the bone."

"You hid it somewhere, along with the murder weapon, before you went to the park. Perhaps the raincoat and murder weapon are hidden in the same place where you took the victims' heads, which have never been found either."

"Why didn't I leave the locket there too? I might not have realized I had blood on my cuffs, but I certainly would have realized that the locket could condemn me. Why didn't I leave it with the other things?"

"Because you didn't realize that it could be traced. Or you simply forgot about it."

"*Why*, after a year spent busily running around chopping off people's heads, would I suddenly go and squat down in a field in the rain for two days? And don't give me any crap about this being my way of getting the police to stop me; I'd already stopped, and without your intervention I'd have managed to stop myself permanently. So, if I'm the killer and I'm lying about my loss of memory, why would I go and do a crazy thing like that?"

"Precisely because you are crazy," Ali replied drily, his initial annoyance replaced by what might have been a trace of amusement. "Who can explain the things a crazy man does? We policemen can't explain why you did everything you did, but we sure as hell know you killed all those people, and we sure as hell wish you'd stop being a pain in the ass with all this amnesia nonsense and just tell us all about it."

Suddenly Bone felt light-headed and fatigued, yet exhilarated, like a man who has come to the end of a long journey, fearing the worst, and finds himself in a place of wonders he never expected. He took a deep breath, slowly exhaled. "It's not enough," he said, somewhat startled by his own discovery—and not a little afraid. "My God, it's not enough." He paused, gazed hard into the Pakistani psychiatrist's eyes. "It's possible I could get out of here, isn't it?"

"Not if the district attorney and police can help it," Ali replied evenly. "We have a legal practice in this state called preventive detention, and the district attorney is lining up a rather large group of psychiatrists to testify that you shouldn't be set free—even if the circumstantial evidence against you is suspect. On the other hand, Anne is lining up a rather large group of very good lawyers who are associated with the Coalition of the Homeless to argue that you should either be formally charged or let loose. A grand jury isn't likely to indict you on the basis of the present evidence against you—or so I've been told. Psychiatrists often make fools of themselves in court, and so my guess is that you will be freed."

Bone closed his eyes as he felt a new rush of euphoria, laced with fear. "What will you say in court, Doctor? What will be your recommendation?"

"I won't be appearing in court, Bone, because I won't be making a recommendation. I have always maintained that psychiatrists shouldn't try to predict behavior, especially in the courtroom. Fortunately, I don't need the appearance fee."

Bone opened his eyes, found that the other man was smiling faintly. He could think of nothing to say.

"How do you feel about the possibility of being free, Bone?"

"I feel a lot of things, Doctor," Bone replied quietly.

"What's your overriding feeling?"

"Right at this moment? Fear; anxiety."

Ali nodded with approval. "You understand, of course, that the other psychiatrists will recommend against your release because they believe you are lying about your loss of memory. I believe you, but I think we agree on something else; we simply don't know if you—your stranger—did the killings."

"We agree."

Ali wrote something in his memo pad, then tore out the sheet and handed it to Bone. "This is my telephone number, and the address of my office over on Lexington Avenue. I would like to set up regular appointments with you on Sunday mornings, if that will be convenient. I want to spend extensive time with you, and that's the only day I have free."

"You really do think they're going to let me out, don't you?"

"As I said, I would like to meet with you on Sunday mornings at my office, if you are released."

"I'll be there."

"Also, I would like to hear from you immediately, any hour of the day, if you feel the need to talk to me. I emphasize 'any hour,' Bone. You'll rarely be able to get me directly, but as soon as you identify yourself, my answering service will forward the call to me. Call me at once if you begin to feel disoriented in ways other than can be expected. I think you understand what I mean."

"You mean that there's a possibility that my personality could begin to disintegrate again."

"I repeat: we're going into uncharted waters."

"You also mean that if I did kill those people, there's a chance I could start killing again."

"Same reply."

Bone looked away. "You'll hear from me if I begin to feel . . . strange. Or the police will."

Ali rose and walked to the door, which almost immediately buzzed and clicked open. "Anne is spending an enormous amount of time on your case, Bone," he said in a mild tone as he stood in the doorway. "I wouldn't be surprised to find that she's personally attracted to you."

There was a prolonged silence, and Bone sensed that the other man was waiting for a reply. Bone said nothing.

"Anne is a very special lady, Bone," Ali continued at last, and now there was a sharper edge to his voice. "Her toughness and professional competence are evident, yet she is very vulnerable. If she chose to commit to someone, that commitment would be total—and perhaps unwise. I am sharing a personal feeling with you, not a professional opinion."

"I understand."

"Do you understand why?"

"I think so," Bone replied softly.

"If you continue to choose to work with me, we will probably spend a considerable number of Sunday mornings together. The rest of the time you will be free to pursue your memories, the two lost lives of your stranger. You—the eyes I'm looking into—have indicated that you've experienced sexual arousal since awakening, and that it's been within normal parameters. I will not ask you who your fantasy subject was, because for professional purposes it's irrelevant—and because I think I know. But bear in mind that because you, the 'ghost,' has experienced normal sexual arousal doesn't mean that the stranger always did. You awakened in response to an unknown stimulus, and it's not inconceivable that an unknown stimulus could reverse the process."

"And if I was dangerous before, then I could become dangerous again . . . and hurt somebody who was close to me. I'll call, or turn myself in, if I feel that happening. If I'm set free."

"If you have time."

"I'll pay attention."

"Keep a close eye on the stranger, Bone," Ali said, and left the room.

CHAPTER SIX

(i)

Bone stared for some time at the grayish-brown, ossified bone and the locket on the bed, then finally looked over to where Perry Lightning stood leaning against the wall next to the open door of the hospital room. As before, the police detective with the shaved head and milky eye was immaculately dressed, this time in a light brown suit, pale blue shirt and tie, highly polished cordovan shoes. Outside the mesh windows, rain was beating against the glass and brick with a sound like snare drums.

"They're yours," Lightning said in a flat voice, gesturing toward the objects on the bed. "Those represent all your worldly possessions when you were picked up."

"I'm free to go?"

"Yeah. The HRA people are waiting for you outside, in one of their vans."

Bone's hand trembled slightly as he reached out and picked up the locket and chain which had belonged to an old woman he might have beheaded. "The locket should go to the woman's children," he said, and realized he had a lump in his throat.

"They don't deserve it. If you want to mail it to them, be my

106

guest; I'll give you their address. On the other hand, as your lawyer so skillfully argued, it's possible that the old woman gave it to you, the same as it's possible you got that blood on your clothes when you came across the bodies and stooped down to examine them."

Bone studied the other man's face. "Does that mean *you're* willing to consider the possibility that I'm not a thief and murderer?"

"No, man," Perry Lightning said matter-of-factly. "You killed those people, all right."

"Oh," Bone said as he quickly looked away. He was surprised at how the other man's words—the certainty in them— could hurt the stranger. Suddenly he felt very much alone.

"The blood on your clothes, the locket, your proximity to the scene of the last two murders and the fact that we haven't had any more beheading killings in the week and a half we've had you in custody are, in my opinion, ample proof that you're the guy we want. Unfortunately, Detective Perry Lightning's opinion isn't what counts in a courtroom. That Winchell woman has good contacts; she had some normally very high-priced legal talent in that courtroom this morning."

Bone picked up the human femur, slowly turned it over in his hands. It felt very hard, cold—yet somehow familiar. "The stran——I passed a lie detector test, Lieutenant. You know that."

"That doesn't mean jack shit."

"Then why did you ask me to take it?"

"I could tell you stories about serial killers and polygraph tests that would make your hair curl. Polygraphs don't detect lies; they detect *stress*. Serial killers are great liars because they don't feel guilt; and they don't feel anxiety or stress because they don't believe there's any way they'll ever be caught. Serial killers don't have normal emotions."

Bone looked up, meeting the other man's hard, steady gaze. "I feel a lot of things, Lieutenant."

"Now."

Bone frowned slightly, trying and failing to read something in Lightning's face. "What does that mean?"

"You don't even know if you killed those people."

"That's what I've said from the beginning. You didn't believe me."

"Well, *that* I've come to believe, Bone. Hakim says he tends to

107

believe you, and I put a lot of stock in what he says. Hakim is a pretty straight shooter for a shrink; he talks so that you can understand him, and he doesn't try to throw a lot of bullshit at you. The fact that he wouldn't recommend that you be released from custody jacks up his credibility with me. He says that the injury to your head *could* have caused you to lose your memory, and even have caused you to kill people without really being aware of it. Now, maybe, you're back to your old self again; you're different now, and might never kill again. We might never be able to pin those murders on you."

"Which would bother you a lot, wouldn't it, Lieutenant?"

"Yes. There's an accounting to be made."

Bone turned so that he was directly facing the other man. "If I remember that I killed those people, I'll tell you," he said evenly. "I agree that an accounting must be made, and that's not something I could live with."

Lightning did not say anything, but simply continued to study Bone.

"You don't believe me," Bone continued.

"Actually, I think I do," Lightning said quietly.

"I thank you for that."

"But it's not how you think and behave when you're like you are now that we're worried about, is it?"

"No."

"We're going to be keeping a close eye on you, Bone."

"I should hope so."

Perry Lightning abruptly pushed off the wall, walked across the room and stopped very close to Bone, looking hard into his eyes. His manner and the expression on his face seemed almost friendly. "I understand that the HRA people wanted to place you in a residence, a halfway house, in the Bronx, and that you turned them down."

"That's right."

"That was a mistake, Bone."

"I was out there on the streets for a year; but I wasn't in the Bronx, and I wasn't in a halfway house. I have to go *where* I was if I hope to find out *who* I was—and who I am. I had no job, no money and no identity. That's what I have to go back to."

"The HRA will give you some money, but it won't last you long here in Manhattan. And the only place they can put you in Manhattan is in the Men's Shelter down on the Bowery. You're not going to like it much there."

"I doubt that it will make a difference to me one way or another."

"With a proper residence, you'd be entitled to welfare payments. Also, I know the HRA people offered to give you employment counseling so that you might be able to find a job, and you turned them down on that, too. Why won't you let them help you?"

"They are helping me. You have to understand, Lieutenant, that I'm not interested in starting a new life. I already *have* a life—somewhere. I have to find it. I'll need work, but I'll look for it somewhere around the shelter; that's one area I used to wander around."

"I know I'm repeating myself, but you're not going to like it in the shelter. You're not like the men on the Bowery, or in the shelter."

"Obviously; the difference is that they know who they are."

"That's not what I'm talking about, Bone. There are lots of homeless people on the streets of this city, but they're not all there for the same reasons. Believe it or not, some actually *prefer* to live on the streets. But the men down on the Bowery are defeated. They're life's losers—alcoholics, drug addicts, crazies and just generally broken people. Where you're going is just a warehouse for people who are *never* going to make it back into society. You're different because you were never defeated. Christ, I hear what you're saying about the need to recover your memory, but why not at least accept all the help you can get?"

"I appreciate your advice, Lieutenant."

"But you're not going to take it."

"The person who wandered those streets didn't accept the kind of help you're talking about. He's the person I have to find, and in order to do that I have to get as close as I can to the life he was leading."

"If I heard Hakim right, that was a different person. You may never find him. And life on the streets, especially with the people you're going to run into down around the shelter, just might squash you, Bone."

"I guess that's a chance I'll just have to take."

"You can get yourself killed real easy in this city, Bone—especially in the places where you plan to go."

Bone hesitated, then slowly and deliberately hung the old woman's locket around his neck. Then he again picked up the femur and, feeling slightly foolish, put it under his arm. "I'd like to go now, Lieutenant. I have two lives to find."

Lieutenant Perry Lightning's response was to abruptly turn his back and walk quickly from the room.

(ii)

Bone had sensed tension between the two social workers from the moment he had walked out of the Bellevue Hospital Center and stepped into their blue van, which had been parked with the engine running beside the curb just outside the entrance. Anne Winchell's greeting had seemed oddly distant, and Barry Prindle had seemed almost hostile. Clutching his femur, Bone had settled back in the seat in the rear, then gazed out the window, looking for familiar sights or figures, as Barry headed downtown on Second Avenue.

There seemed to be signs of homeless people everywhere— cardboard cartons used for shelter pushed back into doorways, men and women in dirty clothes squatting or sitting in desultory solitude on the sidewalks, some holding signs begging for help.

He saw nothing that looked familiar. This passing landscape had nothing to do with the stranger, he thought; the stranger had not squatted on the sidewalk, nor had he begged for help.

It felt very good, if slightly disorienting, to see Anne. Once again it occurred to him that the attraction he felt toward this woman could be distracting, even damaging, to him. Also, he wondered if the palpable tension he sensed between the man and woman in the front seat had something to do with him.

As if in response to his thoughts, Anne half turned in her seat. She was smiling, but her eyes seemed clouded. "There's no *reason* for you to go to this place, Bone. Believe me, the residence in the Bronx where we want to place you is a hundred times nicer."

"I wasn't in the Bronx; you said I was always sighted in Manhattan."

"The chances are that you were never in the Men's Shelter, either. You have to register to get in there; if you couldn't—or wouldn't—speak, somebody would have assigned you to a social worker. There'd be a record of a mute man staying there, and there isn't."

"At least it's in Manhattan, Anne. I was in this territory."

They passed a one-legged man on crutches leaning against the side of a building, wearing a huge overcoat that was at least three sizes too big for him. The man's mouth was open, as if in a silent scream, and he was violently shaking his head back and forth.

Anne pushed a strand of shiny brown hair back from her hazel eyes, breathed a small sigh of frustration. "Bone, I've talked to a number of doctors. Most of them think that you're faking at least some of your symptoms; you know that."

"I know that."

"But there is one thing that they *do* agree on. They agree that *if* you really can't remember *anything*, it's because of your head injury—and this form of amnesia is incurable; you'll never get those memories back. Even if we could find somebody who'd been around you all during that year, somebody who could tell us what you did, where you went and where you stayed, it *still* wouldn't mean anything to you. The same is true of the memories of the life you lived *before* the injury. Those memories are *gone*, Bone. You have to face that fact, and then let us work with you and help you to build another life. This searching for the past is a waste of time, and a few of the doctors think it might even be dangerous. Going to the Men's Shelter when there's a choice of something better is a big step backward for you. I really wish you'd reconsider."

Bone watched Barry Prindle shake his head slightly, as if in annoyance. The heavyset man's shoulders were hunched forward, the muscles tense, as he drove the van. "Not all of the doctors think that my memories are necessarily lost forever," he said quietly.

"You're talking about Ali and his theories," Anne said with thinly concealed anger. "I love Ali, Bone, and he's given us more of his time and help than we have any right to expect. But I have to tell you that he's a very strange man."

Bone smiled, laughed quietly. "Then he sounds like just what the doctor ordered for me, doesn't he?"

"It's not a joke, Bone."

"I wasn't joking."

"It's your life we're talking about, Bone. Ali is very, very good at what he does, but his primary interest is *research*. I know that he sees in you a way to test some of his theories. His

111

interests aren't necessarily yours, and it seems to me that he's putting his interests above yours. He's using you."

"He told me the same thing from the beginning," Bone replied evenly. "I accepted the situation. I understand that the odds are against me, and I understand that I could be wasting time. But I've lost two lives, and it seems to me that it's worth a bit of my time to search for them."

"Where you're going is the pits, Bone."

"So people keep telling me."

"They had a shooting there last week."

"I understand there are a lot of shootings every day in New York."

"Why don't you let him be, Anne?" Barry said tightly. "If he wants to pass up a chance to get into a residence, so be it. Lord knows there aren't that many residence beds available. Bone's a big boy, and he doesn't need you to mother him."

Anne glanced sharply at the man behind the wheel of the van. "Why don't you mind your own business, Barry?"

"I was just—"

"Why don't you go over the procedures with Bone?" she interrupted coldly. "There are things he should know."

Bone said, "I'm sure I'll find out what the procedures are soon enough."

"They're expecting you," Barry said in a flat voice, turning his head slightly. "The first thing you'll do is sign in. I take it you remember how to write, so you can use the name Bone if you want to. I'll explain things to them."

"I can do my own explaining, Barry," Bone said evenly. "For now, Bone is the only name I have, so I think I'll stick with it."

"Suit yourself. You should be there in time for lunch, since the meals from Creedmoor almost always arrive late."

"What's Creedmoor?"

"A mental hospital. All the meals for the city shelters are prepared there, then trucked around to the centers." He paused, glanced at Anne. "Bone should be thankful he's not going *there*."

Anne flushed angrily. "He's lost his memory, Barry, not his mind."

Which wasn't quite true, Bone thought, and suddenly felt cold. He had lost his mind for a year; and there was the possibility he could lose it again—perhaps forever.

Barry said, "You're in luck, Bone. Up until two months ago

112

they didn't have sleeping quarters in the Manhattan shelters, so you'd have been trucked someplace else every evening. Now they've got beds, but you have to sign up for one early in the day—every day. You'll have preference, since you'll be an official resident, but you still have to sign up; forget, and you'll find somebody else in your bed that night."

"I understand," Bone said drily. "I'll try to cope."

"You have to sign up in the morning, but you won't be allowed into the sleeping quarters until five. During the day, you can do whatever you like."

Anne handed him an envelope over the back of the seat. He opened it, found a hundred dollars in small bills inside.

"That's an emergency grant," Anne said, smiling warmly. "You have to have some money in your pocket."

"That's Anne's own money, Bone," Barry said in the same flat voice. "It's true that you're eligible for an emergency welfare grant, but you'll have to apply for it at the welfare office in the shelter."

Bone started to give the envelope back, but Anne pushed his hand away. "That's walking-around money, Bone. You may need it. Filling out forms and meeting the requirements for getting money from city agencies is no easy task, believe me. You'll pay me back, won't you?"

"Yes," Bone said. He folded the envelope and put it into the back pocket of the pants that were part of the clothing parcel he had been given, then looked away in order to hide the sudden surge of emotion he felt. "I'll pay you back."

"You'll find the Social Services office on the second floor of the shelter. Would you like Barry and me to go with you?"

"No, thank you," he replied quietly, once more gazing out the window at the moving panorama of hope and despair, wealth and poverty. The stranger had apparently not needed the city's shelters, food, clothing or money, he thought. The stranger had been able to take care of himself. "I think I can manage to find it."

Barry said, "If you want to sign up for the shelter's work-employment program, it pays thirteen dollars a week. You'll have to clean up the shelter itself, city parks, subway stations—whatever. Thirteen dollars isn't much, but it'll give you some pocket money. We also have an employment counseling office up there, in case you change your mind and decide you want us to help you find a job."

He had to find two lives. "Thanks for the information, Barry. I appreciate it."

"Bone," Anne said quietly, "there's so much more we can do for you, if only you'd let us."

"For now, Anne, I feel that I have to do it this way. I got along for a year without your help. If I'm ever going to recover my memory of that time, I believe I have to follow the same pattern of living, as closely as possible."

"You mean Ali believes that," Anne said tersely.

Bone did not reply.

"A word of advice, Bone," Barry said, his tone warmer, almost friendly. "In the place where you're going, you're going to stick out like a sore thumb. Some people may mistrust you; the guards at the shelter aren't the most highly educated people you're ever likely to meet, and you never know what the residents are thinking. People are going to wonder just what the hell you're doing there, and paranoia is not an uncommon characteristic of this city."

"Do any of the people there know that the police suspect me of killing all those people?"

Anne answered, "A couple of the people on our staff have been briefed, but the guards and residents won't know unless they read the papers and somehow connect you to the stories. Maybe you should leave that bone somewhere; it will only attract attention to you. Would you like me to keep it for you?"

"No. It means something to me—or it did. I prefer to keep it with me."

Again, Barry turned his head slightly. "You want a few more words of advice?"

"Yes, I would. I'd appreciate anything you have to tell me."

"You're hunting for something you've lost and think you may be able to find; the people you're going to be sharing living quarters with have lost everything, and they have no hope of ever getting it back. For them, all they have left to hang on to are a few scraps of dignity. On the other hand, you have a bunch of poorly trained and poorly paid guards who, if only subconsciously, realize that *they* could end up as residents in the shelter if they lost their jobs. That can make for a touchy situation sometimes. Things like respect and macho are very important to those people."

Anne shook her head slightly. "What are you trying to tell him, Barry?"

Barry looked over at the woman. "I'm talking about his attitude. Bone, you can get into some funny situations in there. You've been offered a bed in a halfway house—something most of those people in there would give just about anything for. But a halfway house wouldn't work for them because they don't have any job or living skills left—if they ever had them. My point is that some people might accuse you of playing games."

"Because I want to recover my memory and find out who I am?"

"Because of the way you're choosing to do it. I'm not saying you're wrong; I'm saying that some people might resent your attitude. Just watch yourself."

"Thanks for the advice, Barry."

"Are you going to be seeing Ali, Bone?" Anne asked quietly.

"Every Sunday morning."

Barry grunted. "Sunday is the only time he has to himself. He's really giving you the royal treatment."

Bone noted the slight trace of resentment in the social worker's voice, wondered what it meant. "I think he wants to spend more time with me than he has available during the week."

Anne said, "Do you know where his office is?"

Bone nodded. "Lexington Avenue. I have the address and his phone number."

"His office is a long way from the shelter."

"I'll find it."

"How will you get there?"

Bone shrugged, smiled at the woman. "I suppose I'll walk. Walking seems to be about the only thing we know for sure I do well."

"There's a bus that'll take you there. And if you don't want to spend money for bus fare, I'll pick you up and drive you."

"It's all right, Anne; I'll manage to get there. Thank you for the offer."

"I'll get you a bus schedule."

"Thank you."

Barry turned on Fourth Street, went around the block, came up Third Street and pulled over to the curb at the small side entrance to a mammoth, grayish-brown stone building. The door was dwarfed by the facade, which was soaring, bare, oppressive. The sidewalks on both sides of the street were crowded with men, blank-faced, sitting on trash cans or slumped against the sides of buildings. Some stood in groups of two or three, talking. A few feet from the entrance, four men stood facing the stone wall, urinating.

"Home, sweet home," Barry said tersely.

Anne reached into her purse, drew out a manila envelope and handed it back to Bone. "I've put some things in here which I think you might find useful. There's an overall map of Manhattan, and more detailed maps of different areas. I've marked the places where Barry and I sighted you during the past year, and I figured you might want to check out those neighborhoods first. The numbers next to the Xs indicate—approximately— the number of times we saw you at that particular spot. There's also a subway schedule; if you can't make sense of it, just ask the people in our office at the shelter—or give me a call. My card is in there, and I've written my home number on the back. If I'm not in my office or at home, leave a message on my machine. If you need anything in an emergency, or you're in trouble, don't hesitate to call me—day or night." She paused, flashed a broad grin. "After all, we did manage to get you out of the rain and the hospital, and we kept you from going to jail. Now we have to keep you going. Don't be afraid to ask for help if you need it. Okay?"

Bone's hand touched Anne's as he took the second envelope from her; he left his hand outstretched, and she did not take hers away. Their eyes met and held, and in that moment he clearly sensed the woman's openness and sincerity, her affection for him, her vulnerability—and his own.

And he remembered what Ali Hakim had said.

He had no right, Bone thought; he could not love until he had found the stranger.

"Thank you," he said, averting his gaze as he took the envelope. "I owe you both"—he paused, looked hard at Anne so that she would know it was really her he was talking to—"more than I can ever repay. Goodbye."

He quickly opened the back door of the van, got out and slammed the door shut. Barry immediately put the van into gear, and as it pulled away Bone could see Anne looking back at him with open affection—and worry.

He held her eyes, answering in the only way he could—in silence—until the van turned right on the Bowery and disappeared from view. He sighed, placed the femur under his right arm, where he hoped it would be as inconspicuous as possible. Then he headed for the door to the converted armory, nodding to a knot of curious-eyed men as he passed through the doorway into a world of strange smells and dank semidarkness.

(iii)

Barry drove three blocks up the Bowery, then abruptly pulled over to the curb behind an appliance truck that was unloading and turned off the engine.

"What are you doing?" Anne asked. "We have a staff meeting in half an hour, and we're probably going to be late as it is."

Barry turned to her. He looked pale, the ashen color of his face accentuated by his dark widow's peak. "I need to talk to you, Anne."

"Won't it wait?"

Barry shook his head almost angrily, and his large hands tightened on the wheel. "I wish you hadn't done that; you shouldn't have given him your home telephone number."

"Why not?"

"The man could be a killer."

"He's not."

"You don't know that; even *Bone* doesn't know whether or not he's a killer."

"I know he's not, even if he doesn't. I don't believe a man's character could change so much just because he lost his memory."

"It was the blow to his head that could have caused the change in character; that's what Ali says."

"Well, Bone can't kill me over the telephone, can he?"

"It was unprofessional of you to do that."

Anne stiffened. "I don't need lectures from you on professionalism, Barry; I've been at this business just a bit longer than you have. Bone is a special case. You have to give him credit for voluntarily going right back into the bowels of this city, because he thinks he has to, even when we offered him an easy way out."

Barry looked away. "You talk like you're in love with him," he said, a strong note of petulance in his voice. "Or at least sexually attracted."

"Oh, come on, Barry. If I were, it wouldn't be any of your business. But I still think you're missing the point. We spend our days, our careers, applying Band-Aids to the gaping wounds of this city, and we both know it doesn't really do too much good in the long term; most of the people we try to reach out to were destroyed long before we ever got to them. But Bone *can* be helped, both short and long term; he already has been. It's true that I now think of him as a friend as much as a client, but I don't understand why that should bother you. You've had a kind of nasty thing about him ever since he came around in the Sheep Meadow. Now, I think we'd better get going, or—"

"Anne," Barry interrupted in a thick voice that was slightly muffled by the window. "I know you've requested that you be assigned a new assistant. I'm asking you . . . please . . . not to do that."

Anne sighed, glanced at her watch; they were going to be very late for the staff meeting. "Barry, I just think it would be best for both of us, kind of a change of pace. You'll learn new things from a different partner, and it will be good for you." She paused, met his gaze, continued in a firm voice, "Besides, you've really been acting kind of weird for the past week or so; frankly, you make me uncomfortable."

"It's because I love you, Anne!" Barry said quickly, his green eyes shining brightly. Beads of perspiration had formed on his forehead, and on his upper lip. "I knew I loved you, but I never realized how much until I . . . saw the way you looked at that man!"

"Barry, I seem to recall having a similar conversation with you once before," Anne said in the same soft but firm voice. "It's why I—"

"I took you for granted, Anne! Now God is threatening to take you away from me unless I make things right!"

Anne slowly blinked, instinctively shied away from the man beside her until her forearm was pressed painfully against the door handle. *"What?!"*

"I know I've been acting badly, Anne, but it's because I'm afraid of losing you!"

"Barry," Anne said in measured tones, enunciating each word clearly. "I was never yours to lose. Do you hear me? I never had any *idea* that you felt this strongly, and if I had—"

"I believe God wants us to be together, Anne! I know it was

118

God's will for me to leave the seminary and work with the homeless, and I believe God meant for us to meet and—"

"I'm going to take a cab, Barry," Anne said as she shoved open the door of the van and quickly stepped out on the sidewalk.

Barry shoved open his door—narrowly avoiding having it torn off by a cab that swerved away at the last moment and continued up the street, its driver shaking his fist. Barry rushed around the van, caught up to Anne on the sidewalk. He started to reach out for her arm, then dropped his hand when she again shied away from him.

"Anne," he murmured, distressed by the shock and alarm he saw in the woman's hazel eyes. "Anne, I'm sorry. That's all I really wanted to say, and . . . I just don't want to lose you as a partner. Please."

"I spend all day talking to people who talk to God, Barry," Anne said coldly as she stepped to the curb and raised her hand to signal for a cab. "I sure as hell don't need another one sitting next to me in the van."

"Please get back in, Anne. I said I was sorry. I'll never mention the subject again."

He waited, but Anne did not reply.

"Anne . . . ?"

"I'll see you at the meeting, Barry. Give yourself a break; buy yourself a cup of coffee and calm down. We'll talk later."

A few moments later a cab pulled up to the curb, and Anne got in. The cab immediately pulled away with a screech of spinning tires, leaving Barry Prindle standing on the sidewalk looking after it with eyes that had misted with tears.

CHAPTER SEVEN

(i)

Inside the massive converted armory that was the New York City Men's Shelter, Bone waited patiently in line in a large, stone vestibule with two dozen or more shuffling, disheveled men. There were three metal detectors set up at the front of the line, near the opposite end of the vestibule, but none of them appeared to be working. Instead, frisk-searches were being conducted by two uniformed, surly-looking HRA security guards who wore gauze masks over their noses and mouths, and rubber gloves. Beyond the metal detectors, at the foot of a stairway leading deeper into the interior of the armory, a bored-looking, middle-aged woman with dyed red hair sat at a desk, taking down the names of the men as they passed through the security check and handing out slips of paper of various colors.

When it was Bone's turn to be searched, he stepped forward and raised his arms over his head as he had seen the others do. The guard on his left, a man with cold, suspicious black eyes showing above his gauze mask, squinted as he looked up at the femur Bone held in his left hand.

"What the hell is that?" Even muffled by the mask, the voice was harsh, rasping.

Bone met the man's hard gaze, shrugged. "It's just something I carry around with me."

"You've got to be kidding me, blue-eyes. You can't bring a weapon in here."

"It's not a weapon."

Without warning, the guard on his right, a young, prematurely balding man who smelled strongly of body odor, reached up and snatched the femur from his hand. "Jesus Christ," he said to his partner in a squeaky, high-pitched voice, "this fucking thing is hard as a rock." He paused, thrust his pinched face close to Bone's. "You could bash somebody's brains out with this thing."

"It's just something I carry around with me," Bone repeated quietly, looking back and forth between the two guards. "I've never . . . I don't use it as a weapon."

"Well, you're sure as hell not bringing it in here," the pinch-faced man with the body odor said.

"Fine," Bone said, lowering his arms and holding out his hand. "Then I won't come in. Give it back to me, please."

The two men exchanged glances, then pulled down their gauze masks and turned their eyes back to Bone.

"Frank didn't say he was taking it away from you, or that you wouldn't get it back," the raspy-voiced guard with the cold black eyes said in what seemed to Bone a guarded tone. He pointed to his left. Bone looked in that direction, and saw beyond the metal detectors a large, glassed-in room; two walls of the room were lined from floor to ceiling with metal storage baskets labeled with strips of paper tape. Inside the room, three more uniformed guards stood next to a huge coffee urn, smoking and talking. "We'll keep it in there for you, and you can have it back when you leave."

"All right," Bone said evenly, and lowered his hand.

"What's your name, blue-eyes?"

"Bone."

"What's your real name?"

"I don't know. Bone is what people call me."

The young bald man named Frank took a step closer to Bone, thrust out his chest. "Hey, you son-of-a-bitch," he said with quiet menace, "are you trying to jerk us around?"

Up close, the smell of the man's body was almost unbearable. Bone resisted the impulse to step back. "No," he said in a flat voice. "You asked me my name, and I told you what I'm called. I don't know my real name." He paused, stared back into the pinch-faced man's light brown eyes, smiled thinly. "If you want to call me by some other name—even son-of-a-bitch, if it makes you happy—be my guest. And if you want me to turn around and walk out of here because you don't like my name, that's all right too. Just give me back my property."

"Now, whoa, hoss— !"

"Just a minute, Frank," the raspy-voiced guard said as he put a hand on the other man's shoulder and pulled him back. "Take it easy."

"Look, Burt," the bald man snapped as his face flushed a deep red, "I'm not about to let some prick come in here off the streets and try to make a fool of me!"

"Shut up, Frank," the other man said evenly, without taking his eyes off Bone's face. "Are you righteous, blue-eyes?"

Bone replied, "I don't know what you mean."

"I'm asking if you're righteous—if you really have any business here."

"I still don't understand what you mean."

"You wouldn't be a reporter, would you? Maybe a spy sent here to check up on us to see if we're doing our jobs right?"

The bald man named Frank glanced sharply at his partner; when he looked back at Bone, his small eyes were clouded with anxiety and open hostility.

"I'm just somebody with no place to stay," Bone said quietly.

The man with the cold eyes shook his head. "You don't exactly look like the kind of guy we usually get down here, blue-eyes."

"I wouldn't know."

"Shut the fuck up!" Frank shouted over Bone's shoulder in response to grumbling among the men behind him. Bone glanced around, saw that the steadily building line now snaked back into the street. "If you don't like waiting around for free food, shelter and clothing, get your filthy asses back out on the fucking streets! I don't want to hear any more fucking belly-aching!"

"You look to me like a man with things on his mind, blue-eyes," the guard named Burt said quietly, his black eyes continuing to search Bone's face. "Men who come in here usually don't have anything on their minds, except what's to eat, which cot they sleep on and where they're going to get their next drink when they walk back out onto the street in the

122

morning. You don't look to me like a man who's been missing too many meals; what you do look like is a snoop of some kind. We've been taking a lot of shit in the newspapers lately about the way we run things down here, and I'd hate to think that you're here to spy on us and make more problems."

"I am exactly what I told you—somebody with no place to stay."

"Look at your clothes; they're brand-new."

"They were given to me by HRA people—the same people who told me I could come here. They said I was expected."

"Not by us, blue-eyes."

"Check upstairs."

"Fuck upstairs. What's in the envelope?"

Bone handed the man the large manila envelope. The guard looked inside, examined the maps, pushed them to one side. "What's with the maps?"

"They're just things I carry around with me. Like the bone."

"What are you, a fucking eccentric?"

Bone choked back laughter. "You could say so."

"What's in the smaller envelope?"

"A hundred dollars."

"Where the hell did you get a hundred dollars?"

"It was given to me. It's all the money I have; these are the only clothes I have."

"Most of the men in here haven't seen a hundred dollars in cash in years; some of them would kill you for this. You want us to keep it for you?"

"No, thank you."

"Empty your pockets."

"I don't have anything in my pockets."

"Frank and I are the naturally curious types; show us."

Bone pulled out the pockets of his pants to show that there was nothing in them.

The cold-eyed man continued, "No identification?"

"No. The bone, my clothes, the maps and the money are the only things I have."

"What the fuck? Were you born yesterday?"

Just about, Bone thought. But he said nothing. Once again the two guards exchanged glances, then Burt handed him back the envelope with the maps and money.

The man with the body odor mumbled, "Well, if you are snooping for some newspaper or the HRA, make sure you

123

report that we're doing our jobs as best we can. You can see that we're searching for weapons, and we won't let you carry that club. Burt and I aren't the ones who let that guy with a gun slip in here."

"I'm neither a reporter nor a spy."

The cold-eyed man shrugged, reached into his shirt pocket and withdrew a slip of blue paper. "Hang on to this," he said, handing the paper to Bone. "We'll sign you in. That piece of paper will get you lunch and a care package."

"Care package?"

"There's a room upstairs, down the hall to your left. Show the guy there this slip of paper and he'll give you some things you may need. Also, the blue slip means you've got a bed reserved for the night; don't lose it, or you'll spend the night on the street."

"Thank you," Bone said as the two guards stepped aside to let him pass.

"Don't forget to report that Burt and I are taking care of business!" the young bald man called after him as he walked past the woman with the red-dyed hair and passed under an arch into the musty interior of the armory.

To his right, men were lining up at the head of a stairwell that appeared to lead to a lower level; Bone caught the smell of fried chicken wafting up the stairwell, and he realized he was hungry. He walked to the end of the wide corridor, stopped at the entrance to a huge hall that was blocked off by a heavy chain secured at both ends by bent, rusted nails. Beyond was the main hall of the armory; an area as large as a football field was filled with row upon row of steel-frame folding cots, each with a pillow, sheet and olive-gray blanket. There was a strong antiseptic smell.

Nothing seemed familiar, and Bone was certain the stranger had never been inside the shelter. But, he thought, that did not mean that others who were here might not have seen the stranger on the streets, or even have known him. Someone in the shelter might be familiar with the stranger's routine, know where he had slept—and kept his stash. He would study the maps Anne had given him, but he knew he must also study, while he was here, the maps of the human faces all around him, hope that he might catch some sign, however faint, of recognition.

(ii)

Lunch consisted of greasy chicken served with two slices of bread, a slice of tomato on a wilted leaf of lettuce, rice, and coffee in a Styrofoam container. The portions of chicken and rice were ample, but the food was bland, and there were no seasonings on the table; Bone noticed that a number of the men carried their own containers of salt and pepper, sugar and even plastic packets of ketchup and mustard which bore the familiar labels of various fast-food chains. Also, there were no napkins, and Bone used a corner of his handkerchief to wipe his hands and mouth after he had finished the chicken. Although his hunger was quickly assuaged, he forced himself to eat everything on his plate; he knew he would need all his energy, and he could not afford to get sick.

When he had finished eating he pushed away his paper plate, then looked around at the faces of the men sitting at the long table with him, seeking to make eye contact, looking for some sign of recognition in other eyes. But most of the men were vacant-eyed, eating like automatons as they stared off into space at some distant vision of their own, perhaps a past—a wife and children, a bed they slept in every night, perhaps a house, even a lawn to mow. Those who were not simply staring avoided eye contact with anyone, and when they found Bone staring at them they would quickly turn away.

Since he'd had his hair cut at the hospital, Bone assumed that he must look different now than he had while he was living on the streets; his clothes were different as, certainly, was his behavior. Even someone who had been close to the stranger might not recognize him now.

But he had time, Bone thought. He had a place to stay, food to eat, clothing and the maps Anne had given him to aid in his search. Most important, he had his freedom. Eventually, he would find a job—but not until after he had devoted sufficient time to going back over all the routes indicated on the maps; as for money, the hundred dollars he now had in his pocket might be more cash than he had had during the entire past year.

After thirty minutes they were cleared out to make room for the next shift of men coming down to eat. Bone went to the second floor of the armory, to the room the guard named Burt had mentioned. A thickset, unshaven man in jeans and a dirty T-shirt sat on a chair in the doorway, reading a comic book. Over the man's shoulder Bone could see piles of used, presumably donated, clothing—slacks, shirts, shoes, racks of gaudy ties. There was also a cardboard box filled with eyeglasses.

"If you're here for a shopping visit, pal, you're two hours too early," the man said without looking up from his comic book.

"Excuse me?"

"No shopping visits until four."

"I don't think I want to go shopping."

"What do you want?"

"The guard downstairs told me to come up here and show you this," Bone said, holding out the blue slip of paper he had been given.

The man looked at the paper, grunted. "Care package," he said as he rose, went back into the room and disappeared behind a rack of worn shoes.

The man in the dirty T-shirt reappeared a few moments later carrying a package wrapped in brown paper, which he handed to Bone. Bone thanked the man, then walked a few yards down the hallway and opened the package. Inside he found underpants and a T-shirt, two pairs of socks, a small tube of Colgate toothpaste, a disposable razor, a bar of soap and a pink plastic comb. Bone rewrapped the articles, put the package under his arm, then followed some men up another flight of stairs. On the next floor, across from the head of the stairs, was a large room; upwards of fifty men sat on rickety folding chairs, heads back as they stared at a game show playing on a small color television set supported by brackets suspended from the ceiling. Bone entered the room, grimaced slightly at the strong smell of unwashed bodies. He walked around the chairs, stood just below and behind the set. He looked into the faces of the men seated before him and felt a pang of sadness.

All of the faces seemed oddly vacant—except for an air of hopelessness, etched in the men's faces as if by some kind of psychic acid. All of the men appeared to be wearing more than one layer of clothing, including jackets and overcoats, despite the fact that the room was quite warm. All were unshaven, with glassy eyes. Many were staring at the television set with their mouths open, revealing black, broken or missing teeth. No one spoke, and only occasionally did anyone move to change position or scratch himself. As he had done in the dining area, Bone stared at the men, seeking to make eye contact. Few seemed to even notice his presence; those who did meet his gaze quickly looked back up at the television set over their heads. No one gave any sign of recognition. After a few minutes Bone felt the sadness and depression weighing on him like a rough, heavy cloak, and he walked from the room.

At the end of the corridor on the third floor was a large recreation hall containing two broken-down pool tables with ripped felt covers, a ping-pong table and a number of card tables, some with chess or checker sets on them. Bone stopped just inside the doorway, studied the faces of the two dozen or so men before him. One man who looked to be in his early or mid-thirties sat alone at a table, idly tapping his foot and staring at the chess piece he rolled in the fingers of his right hand. The man was clean-shaven, and his clothing—baggy khaki slacks that looked at least two sizes too large, worn tennis sneakers and a pale yellow dress shirt buttoned to the neck—looked very worn but clean. Bone walked across the room, stopped in front of the man.

"Mind if I sit here?"

Startled, the man dropped the chess piece he had been holding, quickly looked up. He saw Bone, relaxed somewhat.

"Sorry," Bone continued evenly. "I didn't mean to sneak up on you like that."

"No. It's all right. I was just . . . Sit down." He paused, picked the chess piece up off the floor, set it down on the board between them. "Do you play?"

"I don't think so," Bone said as he sat down at the table across from the man.

The man frowned. "You don't think so?"

Bone studied the squares on the board, the chessmen; he picked up a piece that was shaped like a horse, rolled it in his fingers. "Chess," he said distantly.

"Yeah, chess," the man said in a slightly puzzled tone. "Do you play?"

"No," Bone replied, setting down the piece. "Sorry."

"Nothing to be sorry about," the man said, smiling shyly. "I don't play, either. Are you a supervisor in this place or something?"

Now it was Bone's turn to be puzzled. "No. Why would you think I was a supervisor?"

The man shrugged. "You don't look or act much like the rest of us in here. I figured you might be a supervisor."

"I'm here for the same reason I assume you're here," Bone said evenly. "I have no other place to go."

"I haven't seen you in here before."

"I just got here a couple of hours ago; it's my . . . first time in the shelter. I don't suppose you've seen me anyplace else before? I mean on the streets. Do I look familiar to you?"

The man in the pale yellow shirt slowly shook his head. "No, I've never seen you before."

"My hair would have been much longer."

"No; I'd remember." The man paused, added distantly: "I never had to live on the streets, thank God." He paused again, looked at Bone, frowned slightly. "You don't look like a man who'd be living on the streets, and you don't look like you belong here."

"Neither do you."

The man sighed, shook his head slightly. "Yeah. I guess I'm still trying to figure out just how I did get here, how I let things . . . Would you believe that I used to be in advertising?"

"Why shouldn't I believe you?"

The man reached out to the board, picked up the king and gently set it on its side. "A year and a half ago I got fired. In itself, that wasn't a big deal—it happens all the time in that business. You expect to get fired sooner or later, with account shifts or whatever, and usually you just go out and look for another job. But just about the time I was getting fired, I found out that my wife was having an affair with a guy I thought was a friend of mine. I confronted her, and she told me she wanted a divorce. She asked me to move out of our house, and I did—to a hotel. It's just about impossible to find an affordable apartment in this city, especially in Manhattan, or any apartment inside six months. I had some savings, so I figured I'd be okay for a time, and then I'd start looking for another job after I got over my depression. A week went by, then two . . . and then more. Then a friend of mine hanged himself; he wasn't even thirty yet, and he hanged himself. That really threw me. All of a sudden it was all I could do to get out of bed in the morning. I got sick; made myself sick, I suppose. I just couldn't handle things. And I just couldn't seem to get around to looking for a job. One day the money ran out, and I came back to the hotel to find my room double-locked with all my stuff in it; I owed two months' rent, and I just didn't have it. So I walked out and came here; I couldn't think of a single other thing to do. That was over a year ago. And so, here I am."

"I'm sorry," Bone said quietly.

The man flashed a wry grin. "Yeah, me too. I remember reading about this plane load of Russians who were voluntarily going back to Russia after living here—some of them for years. They said they just couldn't adjust to life here. Me, with my hundred-thousand-dollar-a-year job, I couldn't understand why anyone would voluntarily give up the freedom of this country. Now I think I do. You're free here—but that also means you're free to fail; to be hungry, to be sick, to lose the roof over your head. Oh, hell, they're not going to let you die. But here, when you lose it, you really lose it. And you're given just enough to keep you alive, and in return they take your self-respect. This society doesn't let you die; it just makes you want to. So now I understand why the Russians went back. The United States is a tough, tough place to be in if you slip off your rung on the ladder, or if you never managed to even find the ladder in the first place." He paused, smiled wanly. "Hey, but I really think I'm ready to start putting things together again. I'm feeling better, and maybe tomorrow I'll get out of here and go look for a job; any job. I guess I really didn't like advertising anyway, and I think I'd like to work out-of-doors somewhere. I'll bet I'd make a good gardener, if somebody gave me the chance. The thing about a place like this is that you find out a lot about yourself, whether you want to or not. When you lose everything, and you're down to just yourself, you find out how many wrong ideas you had; you find out who you are at the core, after you've been stripped of all the things you once used to define yourself—your job, especially, but also your car, your clothes, your boat, your television, your stereo. You'd be surprised how many guys like me there are in the city shelters—people like the Russians who, suddenly, just can't cope with all the freedom and choices that are supposedly left to us. But we don't have a Russia to go back to; we're 'free,' whether we like it or not. Sure, you've got drug addicts, alcoholics and crazy people here—but you've also got truck drivers, merchants who lost their businesses after sinking all their savings into them, working people . . . and advertising executives. But I'm going to get back on my feet; you'll see. I just need a little more time to get my thoughts and my act back together again."

"I'm sure you'll be all right," Bone said, smiling and nodding encouragement.

The man grinned, extended his hand. "I'm Dave Berryman."

"Bone," he said, shaking the other man's hand.

"Bone? That's it?"

"That's it."

"What on earth did you do to your hands? They look like they've been all mashed up—more than once." Dave Berryman paused, nodded thoughtfully. "Strong, though."

"I don't know what happened to them," Bone replied evenly as he studied the other man's eager, almost boyish face. "I've lost my memory. I know— because I've been told—that I spent a year living on the streets; but I don't know how I got there, what I did while I was on the streets, or what I did before. I don't know who I am."

"Holy shit," Berryman said with a slight shake of his head. "And I thought I had problems. That's really heavy."

"I've been hoping someone here might recognize me, maybe know something about me that I don't."

"Most people around here are pretty much lost inside themselves and with their own problems," Berryman said quietly. "Like me. I haven't lost my memory, but ask me what I've been doing for the past year and I'd be pretty hard pressed to tell you. That's what severe depression does. The people in here look, but they don't see; they'll look at you when you talk, sometimes, but they don't hear. Like I said, I'm finally beginning to feel better."

"I'm glad," Bone said simply.

"You know the routine around here?"

"I'm learning it."

"Just about everything revolves around mealtimes. Incidentally, they lock the doors at ten, so if you're out you want to be sure you're back before then if you want a bed." Berryman paused, smiled wryly. "When you live here, the two most important things in life are getting fed and having a place to sleep."

"I would think that's true of most people—even if they don't think about it."

"And watch yourself. This place can be dangerous."

"So I've been told."

"It's the reason a lot of people prefer sleeping on the sidewalk to coming here; they've had bad experiences. You've got some real crazy people in here who don't always know what they're doing. And there are weapons. Those metal detectors downstairs haven't worked the whole time I've been here, and the security guards don't always search people the way they should. Give a wide berth to anyone who even looks funny. And try not to let anyone cough in your face; there are men in here with everything from pneumonia to tuberculosis, not to mention AIDS. You look like you can handle yourself pretty well, so I don't think anyone's going to try to rip you off—at least not while you're awake. At night, it's usually a good idea to slip your shoes under the legs of the cot, so they'll be there when you wake up in the morning. Put anything else of value right inside your pillowcase." Berryman paused, shrugged. "It isn't the Waldorf, but it's better than living on the streets."

Bone wondered. "Thanks for the tips, Dave. I appreciate your sharing them with me."

"My pleasure."

Bone sensed a presence behind him. He turned in his chair, found himself looking up into the harsh features and cold black eyes of the guard called Burt. Burt had removed his rubber gloves to reveal thick hands with torn, dirty fingernails. His gauze mask hung around his neck.

"How are you making out in your new quarters, Mr. Bone?" Burt asked in his rasping voice. His lips were pulled back in a sneer.

"I'm doing fine," Bone replied in a flat voice, meeting the guard's hostile stare. "And I want to thank you for giving me the paper that allowed me to get the package of underwear and things."

"Don't thank me, pal. It's the city that's paying for it, the same as it pays to keep all you bums. You still claim you're not a reporter, blue-eyes?"

"I'm not a reporter."

"In that case, you probably feel rich with that hundred bucks in your pocket. Still, money runs out. Have you thought of looking for a job?"

"Yes."

"Well, we've got a little work-employment program here you might be interested in—saves you the trouble of going out and looking for a job, if you know what I mean. It don't pay much—about thirteen bucks a week for ten hours of work—but it means you always get to go down to dinner right at six, with the first shift. You interested?"

Bone caught the slight head movement of the man sitting across from him, the frown of warning. Against this Bone weighed his needs—time, and freedom of movement. He had the hundred dollars, but he preferred to think of this as an emergency reserve to travel on the city's transportation system when he had to, and for unforeseen needs. Ten hours a week was not a lot of time, and the thirteen dollars could help keep him from dipping into his reserve.

"I'm interested," Bone said.

The security guard grinned. "That's a very good attitude, Mr. Bone. You come on with me, and I'll get you started right off."

Bone rose and nodded to Dave Berryman, who still looked concerned. Then he followed Burt out of the room, down two flights of stairs to the first floor, then down a long side corridor to a utility room. He took the mop, bucket and rags the guard handed him, then followed Burt down another stone corridor which ended at a half-open door.

"The head needs cleaning," Burt rasped. "That should keep you busy for a couple of hours. Go to it, Mr. Bone."

Bone stepped through the door into the huge, marble-tiled lavatory and almost retched. Now he understood why the men outside the shelter had been urinating on the wall. The lavatory looked like it had not been cleaned in weeks, and all the urinals and toilets were blocked up. There were puddles of urine and vomit on the floor, smears of feces everywhere. The room was an open sewer.

Sewer!

Bone blinked rapidly, momentarily feeling short of breath and oddly disoriented. These smells, this *sewer*, meant something to the stranger, he thought. But not this place, this room, this sewer. Someplace else.

Underground.

Above ground.

Over and under the ground, filthy smells under, yet something overhead, very high. Over and under . . .

Peel off.

The stranger had been in sewers, Bone thought. But where was the sky in sewers? Why should he think of the two things,

132

blue skies and filthy sewers, at the same time? It made no sense.

Orange, streaked with crimson. Blood. Something buried alive. The orange figure was down there, coming at him. Himself? Purple flashes. Bones, bones, bones . . . underground. The stranger couldn't possibly see the sky from the sewers, or the sewers from the sky, and yet the fetid odor of this room made him think of both.

Who am I?!

"At the rate you're going, blue-eyes, we're both going to die of old age before you get finished. You're not getting paid to just stand there."

Bone turned to find the burly security guard standing very close to him, his gauze mask once again in place over his nose and mouth. For a moment he felt rage at the man with the cold eyes for interrupting his thoughts; he felt he had been close to something, his senses prodding his brain and the ancient, secondary memory system Ali Hakim had told him might exist. It did exist, Bone thought; he had felt its stirrings. But now it was gone. He must be patient; there would be other sights, sounds, smells. Dreams.

"Here, Burt," Bone said, abruptly handing the mop, pail and rags to the startled security guard. "I've decided to make a career change."

"You're a wise guy!" Burt shouted after him as Bone strode quickly out of the lavatory. "You've got a bad attitude, and I'm telling you right now that you're going to be waiting in line one hell of a long time before you go down to dinner tonight! You lazy, fucking bum!"

Sky and ground, Bone thought to himself as he walked away, the security guard's angry words echoing in the long stone corridor.

Climbing. Underground.

CHAPTER EIGHT

(i)

He spent the rest of the afternoon wandering through the recreation rooms of the shelter, then walking the streets ringing it, studying faces, hoping for some sign of recognition. But in the multitude of faces he looked into—old and young, male and female, black, white and Hispanic—he saw only despair, loneliness and defeat. And sometimes he saw nothing at all, a curious and frightening vacancy in the eyes of men and women who slumped in the shadows of doorways, or shuffled along the sidewalks, like zombies. There were dozens of drunks sprawled on the sidewalk, or occasionally vomiting into the gutter. The street called the Bowery seemed to be lined with drunks, and by late afternoon Bone found that he was severely depressed. He fought his sadness by pressing even harder to find someone he recognized, or who recognized him, trying—usually unsuccessfully—to strike up conversations with some of the other men. Most merely eyed him suspiciously, and then asked for money.

The shift of security guards came at five-thirty. Bone, standing in the outer vestibule just behind the metal detectors in order to study the faces of new arrivals coming in for supper, watched as the cold-eyed Burt and malodorous Frank held a whispered conference with three of the replacement guards. Occasionally, one or more of the guards would turn his head and furtively glance at him with open suspicion and hostility. Bone, now virtually certain that he would find nothing of value to him in the shelter, merely stared back.

He did not even bother getting in line to go down to eat until seven, when it appeared that most of the men who would be arriving were already there. Dave Berryman found him, and they waited in line together. Berryman's boyish face was flushed with excitement; he had been out since early afternoon, and although he had not actually spoken with anyone who might hire him, he had dared to take a bus uptown and had walked past the advertising agencies on Madison Avenue, including the one where he had last worked. He had stopped in a bank and converted part of his welfare allowance into rolls of quarters and dimes, and the next day he hoped to work up the courage to actually make some calls and inquire about openings.

Bone gave an occasional polite nod as Berryman talked throughout the meal, but he was only half listening to the other man's excited recitation of his adventures uptown; he continued to search faces, but to no avail. He was already thinking about his next step. He was now thoroughly convinced that the stranger had never been in this place, and it was highly unlikely that any of the members of this particular underclass of the homeless would recognize him. Tomorrow he would begin using the maps Anne had given him; he would walk uptown, begin searching through the streets, soup kitchens and temporary shelters there.

After dinner he resumed walking through the shelter and on the adjacent streets, still searching for someone who might come up to him and say, "Hello, Bone." Nothing. At five minutes to ten he came back inside, just before they locked the doors. Tense, depressed and very disappointed, he suddenly found that he was exhausted. But he found there was something the stranger insisted he do before sleep: wash. He had used the first of his emergency funds to purchase a gallon jug of spring water. He took toothbrush, toothpaste and soap from his package, which he had retrieved from the place where he had hidden it, then brushed his teeth and washed himself as best he could in the corridor just outside the stinking lavatory.

Then he gave the package to one of the guards to put in his wire basket, and went into the vast main hall of the armory. The cots nearest the entrance were already filled with men, most already asleep and snoring. Bone went to the rear of the hall, found an empty cot at the very end of a row and slumped down on it. He was asleep almost immediately.

(ii)

He was awakened in the middle of the night by the hard, persistent, spasmodic coughing of the man on the cot across from him. Bone sat up, looked over at the man and felt a sudden wave of revulsion and fear pass through him. The man was slumped over the edge of his cot, both hands to his mouth as he vainly tried to stifle the coughing. His sheets and the floor beneath his head were speckled with blood. He whooped, coughed again, brought up thick, bloody sputum, which fell to the armory floor.

Tuberculosis.

Bone shuddered, quickly turned away and put a hand to his mouth to keep from retching. His first reaction was fear, for he had been breathing tiny droplets of the man's infected sputum for hours. Then came concern and pity for the man, whom Bone could see was old, and who was coughing away his life alone, helplessly adrift in the middle of a vast city which Bone was certain must have among the best medical facilities in the world. It was not right, Bone thought. The old man should be in a hospital.

He sat up, put his feet on the floor, retrieved his shoes from where he had anchored them under two steel legs of the cot. Then he rose, intending to go to the guards at the front of the armory to report the old man's condition. In the dim light cast by the naked, low-wattage bulbs suspended from the ceiling, Bone peered down the vast length of the armory filled with sleeping men—and stiffened.

At the opposite end of the hall, near the entrance and backlighted by the harsher bulbs in the outside corridors and vestibule, four men stood huddled together, speaking in whispers. One was an on-duty guard, in uniform. There were Burt and Frank, dressed now in civilian clothes. The fourth figure, in a gray leather jacket, jeans and black boots, looked to Bone to be younger than the three guards, perhaps no more than a teenager. He carried an empty paper shopping bag folded under his arm.

As Bone watched, the teenager in the gray leather jacket handed money to each of the three guards, who then stepped back outside into the corridor. The gray-jacketed youth, whom Bone could now see was Hispanic, with long, stringy hair falling down over his shoulders, removed something from his pocket which glinted briefly in the harsh backlighting. Then he began moving up the center aisle.

Bone quickly moved back into the shadows at the rear wall of the armory, beneath a broken exit sign, and watched as the young man paused and stooped down beside the first sleeping man. The youth reached under the man's cot, dragged out what appeared to be a lumpy laundry bag. The youth searched through the laundry bag, removed a few items and put them into his shopping bag.

The second man in the row started as the youth approached, sat up. The youth darted forward, held what Bone could now see was a knife against the man's throat and whispered something in his ear. The man fumbled with the buttons of his heavy flannel shirt, removed something from around his neck and gave it to the young man, who dropped it in the paper bag.

Bone found the fingers of his right hand reflexively clenching and unclenching, and he knew what the stranger wanted—the iron-hard femur, which was locked away in the guards' room. The stranger had, indeed, used the femur as a weapon, Bone thought—perhaps in self-defense against someone like this gray-jacketed youth who might have tried to rob him.

In fact, Bone thought there was something familiar about the youth—although the face meant nothing to him. His clothes?

But he had other things to think about now, and Bone let the thought go. There were, Bone estimated, upwards of a thousand men sleeping in the armory—all relatively helpless, disarmed by Burt and Frank, who would also have taken note of anything of value which the homeless men carried.

Even if the young man with the knife only got a dollar or two from each man, Bone thought, he was going to make quite a haul in the two or three hours it would take him to maraud through the armory.

Unless someone stopped him.

"Wake up," Bone whispered urgently as he knelt down in the aisle between the two men closest to him.

The man on his right, whose breath smelled of cheap whiskey, snorted, then stirred. "What—?"

"Wake up!" Bone repeated, shaking the frail shoulder of the man on his left. "You're going to be robbed."

The man on his right nodded, then rolled over on his side and began to snore loudly. Bone, shaking his head in frustration, moved down the aisle to the next man, shook him. "Wake up, damn it. You're going to be robbed."

This man sat up quickly; he looked around him in alarm, then clutched at something he wore around his neck.

"Wake up as many of the men around you as you can," Bone continued curtly when he saw that this third man was sober and alert. "Tell them they're going to be robbed if they don't get up and stand together."

He straightened up and started down the aisle—then stopped when he saw the gray-jacketed teenager with the stringy hair standing still, glaring at him from perhaps twenty yards away; even in the dim light, Bone could see hatred smoldering in the youth's dark eyes.

The youth slowly raised his hand to show Bone the knife he held—a switchblade, with a notched, six-to-seven-inch blade. He motioned for Bone to back away.

"Wake up, everybody!" Bone shouted, keeping his eyes on the youth. "Wake up! There's a thief in here! Get the guards!"

"You motherfucker!" the boy snarled, his lips pulling back to reveal uneven, discolored teeth. "I'm going to cut you!"

By now a number of men closest to him had begun to stir, and a few had jumped to their feet and were milling about. The steady, low murmur of voices rippled out across the hall. Then the youth, his face flushed and clenched in rage, started toward him, knife extended, pushing people aside and kicking empty cots out of his way. Bone whipped a blanket off the vacated cot to his right, quickly wrapped it around his left forearm and hand, which he held out in front of his chest as a kind of shield as he waited for the knife-wielding youth's attack.

The men around Bone scrambled to get out of the way, knocking over cots and each other as they did so. The youth, his eyes wide and drug-bright, stopped a few feet away from Bone and slowly waved the knife in front of him in a figure-eight motion. Bone, his blanket-wrapped forearm still held out in front of him, turned slightly, flexed his knees.

"Who the fuck do you think you are, motherfucker?" the youth said in a voice thickened by drugs and alcohol. "You must be really crazy."

"Go away," Bone replied evenly, keeping his eyes focused on a spot in the center of the figure-eight pattern formed by the weaving switchblade. "Don't these people have enough misery without you adding to it? Why don't you leave before the cops get here?"

"First I'm going to teach you a lesson you won't—" The youth suddenly stopped speaking as he squinted, leaned forward on the balls of his feet and stared into Bone's face. Then he dropped his hand to his side, took a small step backward. "Holy shit," he continued, more in amazement now than anger. "It's *you*."

Bone felt his stomach muscles tighten and heartbeat quicken, and he almost dropped his guard. "Who?" he breathed, willing himself to keep his gaze focused on the knife in the hand at the youth's side. "What are you talking about? Who am I?"

"*Hooee!*" the youth shouted as he feinted with the knife, grinned, then did a little pirouette. "Is Lobo ever going to be one happy son-of-a-bitch when I bring him your balls."

Then the youth lunged in earnest, feinting toward Bone's right thigh, then slashing up and over the extended arm toward his face. Bone sidestepped the lunge, kicked at the youth's left kneecap, missed. He went back into a slight crouch, turned with the youth, who had now begun to slowly circle him.

Where were the guards? They had to know something was wrong; everyone was up and milling about.

Waiting for him to be killed?

"Who's Lobo?" Bone said to the knife.

The youth, clearly surprised, abruptly stopped circling. "Are you kidding me, man?"

"Who's Lobo? Tell me."

"He's the guy whose eye you put out with that bone you used to carry, motherfucker," the youth said tightly. "And he's been a time hunting you. Well, motherfucker, I've got you, and you're *dead meat!*"

The Wolf lunged like a fencer and kept coming, slashing with the switchblade at Bone's forearm.

Bone spun away from the attack, waving the blanket in the youth's face. Then he abruptly spun counterclockwise, flapping his left arm to unwrap the blanket. When the Wolf turned and came at him again, Bone flung the blanket over his head, then picked up a cot and hurled it at the shrouded figure. The cot crashed into the youth's chest, and he went down. Bone clenched his fists and started forward—then leaped back as the knife blade ripped through the blanket. The Wolf thrashed beneath the blanket, finally managed to free himself. He leaped to his feet, slashing with the knife. Blood flowed down over his left eye from a deep gash on his forehead.

"Who are you?!" Bone snapped, once again turning sideways and flexing his knees slightly as the bleeding, knife-wielding youth glared at him with frustration and hatred. Unwilling to take his eyes off the knife for even a split second, Bone inched backward, groping for a blanket—anything—with which to defend himself. His hand touched nothing but empty air. "Who's Lobo?! Tell me what happened! *Where* did it happen?! Where can I find Lobo?!"

Where were the guards?!

The Wolf went into a crouch, preparing to attack again, then glanced at something behind Bone and abruptly straightened up.

"Hey!" a deep voice boomed from just over Bone's left shoulder. "What the hell's going on here?!"

The youth spun around and began running toward the broken exit sign at the rear of the armory.

"Wait!" Bone shouted, and started after him.

Suddenly someone leaped on his back and put an arm around his neck, carrying him to the hard tile floor. Another man piled on. Bone pulled in his chin to protect his windpipe, managed to get both arms over his head to protect it as fists began to pound at him. Finally the blows stopped. He was grabbed under the arms, roughly pulled to his feet. Each arm was gripped by a uniformed guard, and he found himself facing two other guards. The guard standing to his left, a man with a huge paunch and fiery broken blood vessels in his lumpy nose, was the guard who, with Frank and Burt, had taken money from the gray-jacketed youth. The other three guards, middle-aged men, were pasty-faced and puffy-eyed, as if they had just awakened from deep sleep. All of the men stank of gin.

At the rear of the armory, a heavy steel door banged shut, the sound echoing in the hall like distant thunder before gradually fading away. The youth who knew who he was was gone.

The one person who had recognized him was a criminal, Bone thought, and had wanted to kill him. Someone named Lobo wanted him dead; the stranger had put out Lobo's eye.

"What the hell's going on here?!" the guard with the lumpy nose shouted, spraying Bone with his gin breath. His muddy brown, bloodshot eyes flashed with anger—and perhaps, Bone thought, with fear.

Bone glanced at the guard on his right, who wore a badly fitting toupee. Dandruff speckled the shoulders of the man's blue shirt. He wondered if the guard on his right and the two guards holding him had shared in the bribe given by the youth—and, if so, how much danger he was in. He sensed that he could easily break the grip of the guards holding him, then run from the armory—if he wanted to. But now there were important things here to be discovered; the guard with the lumpy nose and muddy eyes, at least, would know who Lobo was, and might know where he could be found.

"The guy who ran out of here was trying to rob these people," Bone said evenly. "I was just trying to stop him."

"That's what we're here for, pal," the lumpy-nosed guard who had taken the money said. "Why didn't you report it to us? We'd have taken care of it."

"There wasn't time. He attacked me with a knife."

The man holding his right arm snapped, "Nobody gets in here with a knife! Are you saying we let someone in here with a knife?!"

"He's telling the truth," the man on his left arm said quietly. "I saw; the kid did have a knife. He was Wolfpack."

"Bullshit," the other man said tersely. "If it ever got out that a Wolf with a knife managed to sneak in here, we'll all lose our jobs."

"Shut up, both of you!" the guard with the lumpy nose shouted. "We don't have to take the word of some shit-for-brains who'd starve to death if we didn't take care of him. There was nobody with a knife, no Wolf." He paused, fixed his bloodshot eyes on Bone. "It looked to us like you were beating up on that guy, pal."

"No," Bone replied quietly, meeting the other man's gaze. "He had a knife. Ask the other men."

The guard with a toupee and dandruff on his shirt snorted. "Ask these wet-brains? They wouldn't know what they saw."

"He came into the hall about ten minutes ago," Bone said in the same quiet voice as he continued to stare into the muddy eyes of the guard who had taken the money. "Somebody must have let him in."

Suddenly his right arm was twisted painfully behind his back. "Those doors out there are locked tight at ten, pal. Nobody gets in here after that."

"We got the word on you, pal," the guard with the lumpy nose said, once again moving close enough to spray Bone with his breath. "That word is that you're a troublemaker. We don't need troublemakers in here."

The guard on his left arm probably didn't know about, or share in, the bribe, Bone thought. But the guard on his right arm and the one with the dandruff might well be involved. And now, with his right arm twisted up behind his back, it wouldn't be so easy to break free.

Danger.

"I think I'd like to go now," Bone said evenly. He paused, repressed a smile. "I don't much care for my room."

"A wise-ass, to boot," the man holding his right arm said tightly. "Well, we know how to handle wise-asses."

"Did Frank and Burt tell you I was a wise-ass?"

The guard with the lumpy nose flushed. "How the hell do you know their names?"

"I'm learning a lot about this place. Who's Lobo?"

The two men in front exchanged startled glances, and he heard a soft grunt from the man on his right.

Bone continued, "What's the Wolfpack?"

"What the hell are you talking about?!" the lumpy-nosed guard said curtly. Shadows that were fear moved in his muddy eyes, and Bone knew that meant increased danger for him. He sensed that if he remained passive, he could be seriously hurt by three of these four guards. He could not afford to be hurt; he had things to do. He had to find the right pressure to apply— but not too much.

"The kid who attacked me with the knife said he was doing it because somebody named Lobo wanted me dead. I figure if

I can find out who Lobo is, I can go to him and save him the trouble of looking for me."

"Let's take him to the office," the lumpy-nosed guard said in the same curt tone, and turned on his heel.

Bone, both his arms now twisted painfully behind his back, was marched down the length of the armory, then shoved outside, across the vestibule, into the glass-enclosed guards' station. He was roughly shoved against a bank of wire baskets, heard his shirt rip and felt a jagged metal tip scratch his back, drawing blood. The man who had held his left arm quickly hurried back out. The other three guards stood in a semicircle around him, feet slightly apart, the expressions on their faces at once both hostile and anxious. The man who had held his right arm was thinner than the others, and kept nervously licking his chapped lips.

For some reason that he could not fully understand, Bone felt sorry for the three men; he remembered Barry saying how many of the guards were themselves afraid of ending up homeless.

"Now, pal," the lumpy-nosed guard said in a low, menacing tone, "what's your story?"

"I don't have any story. All I want to do is walk out of here. There won't be any trouble."

The thin man with the chapped lips frowned. "Trouble? Why should there be trouble?"

Bone said nothing, but he kept his gaze fixed on the lumpy-nosed guard, who now stepped closer.

"You act like you know something that could get us in trouble, pal. All this talk about Frank and Burt, and some guy named Lobo. You wouldn't be a reporter working on a story, would you?"

"No," Bone replied in a flat voice. "That's Frank and Burt talking again; they're wrong. I'm not a reporter."

"There you go again, dropping names. You know, if you *were* a reporter, I don't think your bosses would like it much if they found out you'd gotten into a fight with one of those poor, homeless men in there—and we had to rough you up in order to stop you. That would be *our* story—and it would be the word of the three of us against yours. Believe me, we'd have no trouble getting a dozen men in there to back up anything we say. Then anything you have to say against us wouldn't carry much weight, would it?"

He was going to be beaten, Bone thought—and all because the murky minds of the three guards standing in front of him could figure no other way to provide a defense against charges of drinking and sleeping on the job, not to mention taking a bribe from a knife-wielding youth who would enter the shelter to rob, and possibly hurt, the very people the guards were supposed to protect.

"I think we should give you a taste of just how hard we work to protect the people in our care," the man in the toupee said, moving forward as the other two guards moved to flank him and grab his arms once again. "And you know what our story will be, so it may be just as well if you kept yours to yourself and count yourself lucky that you got away with only a beating; a man could easily get killed in this part of the city at this time of night."

There was nothing to do but take the beating, Bone thought, and hope that they quit before they did too much damage. If he made a blunt threat to tell what he had witnessed, they might only beat him harder; or, out of panic, they really might kill him and dump his body on some street blocks away. It was useless to try to fight back against the three of them. He braced himself, put his forearms across his face and awaited the first blow.

Suddenly there was a pounding on the glass wall to his right. Bone took his forearms away from his face, glanced in that direction and saw the anxious, angry, boyish face of Dave Berryman on the other side of the glass.

"Let me in!" Berryman shouted, his voice muffled by the thick glass. "Damn you, let me in there!"

The lumpy-nosed guard pointed a thick finger at the ex-advertising executive, then balled his hand into a fist. "You get the fuck out of here!"

Berryman, his face pale, swallowed hard, shook his head defiantly, then resumed his pounding. "Let me in! I have something to tell you! You'd better not hurt that man, because I'm a witness!"

That got the security guards' attention. The men exchanged startled looks, and then the guard in the toupee rushed across the room, yanked open the door and dragged Berryman in by the front of his pale yellow dress shirt, ripping it.

"You little son-of-a-bitch—!"

"*Don't* you talk to me like that!" Dave Berryman snapped,

slapping the guard's hand away from his shirt. The anxiety was gone from his face, and now his dark brown eyes flashed with anger and outrage. He stepped back, straightened himself up to his full height, spoke in clear, measured tones. "You have no right to talk to me like that, sir, and you have no right to treat this man the way you've been treating him. This Men's Shelter is, as I'm sure you're aware, run by the Human Resources Administration of this city to help its citizens, and you are employees of that agency. I have a good mind to file a complaint—and I *will* file a complaint, unless you listen to what I have to say. Have I made myself clear?"

Bone watched, somewhat bemused, as Dave Berryman, his narrow chin thrust forward in pride and defiance, glared at the three speechless guards. On the other side of the glass walls, faces of other men were beginning to appear.

The thin guard with the chapped lips was the first to find his voice. "Just what is it you think you're a witness to, shithead?"

"My name is Berryman; David Berryman. And I *insist* that you treat me with respect!" He paused, glanced at Bone. "Are you all right?"

Bone nodded, smiled. "I'm all right. It looks like you are, too."

"Why the hell shouldn't this man be all right, Berryman?" the guard with the lumpy nose and muddy eyes asked warily. "Are you saying we mistreated this man?"

"I'm saying that I saw what happened in the sleeping hall, and you didn't."

"Yeah? What is it you think you saw?"

"A kid in a gray jacket was attacking this man with a knife. This man was only defending himself—and doing a hell of a job of it, I might add. You came in, and the kid started to run away. This man tried to stop the kid, but then four of you jumped on his back and started punching him. You should be thanking him for doing your jobs, not pushing him around."

The guards exchanged wary glances. The man in the toupee said, "You talk pretty smart for a guy who's been living off the taxpayers for a year."

"*That* kind of talk will get you reported!" Berryman shot back, pointing a trembling finger at the guard. "*I'm* a taxpayer! I paid taxes before, and I'll soon be paying them again! *I've* paid your salary, sir, and you will treat me with respect!" He paused, dropped his hand, continued evenly: "But I didn't come in here to make trouble."

The lumpy-nosed guard said, "Why did you come in here, pal?"

"I came to volunteer information as an eyewitness, because it appears there has been a misunderstanding. You're treating this man as if he'd done something wrong."

"It looked to us like he was beating up on the other guy, causing trouble."

"Well, you're mistaken. He was only defending himself."

"We don't allow anyone with weapons in here," the guard with the toupee said tightly.

Berryman shook his head. "The kid had a knife," he said evenly. "I saw it."

There was a prolonged silence, during which the guards looked back and forth between one another. It was the lumpy-nosed man who finally spoke.

"All right, Berryman, you've given us the information and set us straight. Now you and the others can go back to bed."

"I believe I'll wait for my friend here."

"It's all right, Dave," Bone said quietly. "Thank you. I'm leaving now."

Berryman frowned. "Leaving? It's the middle of the night."

"I think I've worn out my welcome. But I want to leave; it's time. You go back to bed—and thank you again."

Berryman remained where he was. "Maybe I'll go with you," he said quietly.

"No, Dave. We're traveling in different directions, to different places."

The boyish-faced man stared at Bone for some time, sadness moving in his expressive brown eyes, then slowly nodded his head. "Yeah, you're right. Thank *you*, Bone."

"For what?"

"For showing me how it's done. A lot of us who end up in places like this think we've lost everything, but we really haven't. *You've* lost a hell of a lot more than any of us have, but you still have the pride, guts and dignity to keep going after what you want. You reminded me of—and taught me—a few things. People listen to you."

"And to you," Bone said softly as the other man waved to him, then turned and walked from the room.

"I hope you realize how easy you're getting off, pal," the

146

lumpy-nosed guard said as he closed the door after Dave Berryman. "We could give you a summons for fighting like that."

"Yeah, I noticed the kind of summons you were about to give me," Bone replied evenly. "I'd like to go now."

"You can go; but you're not leaving on your own, like your bum friend who just walked out of here. We're throwing you out for being disorderly. We're blackballing you from this shelter, and we'll make sure the word gets around that you're a troublemaker. If you're a reporter like some people say you are, now you've got nothing to report that we can't deny. If you're just what you say you are, then I sure as hell hope you enjoy living like an animal on the streets, because you've had your last bed and meal in a city shelter. You're history to us, pal."

"I understand."

"You got any accusations to make, let's hear 'em now."

"I have no accusations."

"Good. Then get the hell out of here. We don't want to see your ugly face in here again; if you try to come in, we'll just boot you out again."

"You have some things that belong to me. The package I was given with underwear and—"

"Forget it. Troublemakers like you aren't entitled to gifts from the city."

"My bone."

"Your *what*?"

Bone pointed to the right of the guard with the chapped lips, to his gray metal basket with his name tag on it. "There's a bone in there that belongs to me. It's a personal belonging, and I'd like it back."

"Why the fuck don't you split while you're ahead of the game, pal?" the guard with the toupee and dandruff growled as he stepped forward threateningly.

"The bone is mine. Give it to me."

"Jesus Christ," the thin guard said to no one in particular. "There was something in the papers the other day . . . Jesus H. Christ."

The lumpy-nosed guard unlocked Bone's basket, removed the femur and hefted it with both hands. "What the hell's the matter with you?" he said to the thin guard, who was gaping at Bone. When there was no response but a nervous shake of the head, the lumpy-nosed guard came back across the room and handed the femur to Bone. "Here's your fucking weird personal belonging, pal. Now get the hell out. We don't want you here."

Bone took the femur, noting how familiar it felt in his—the stranger's—grasp. He went to the door and opened it, then turned back to find the three guards huddled together, with the thin guard urgently whispering to his companions. When the man realized Bone was standing in the doorway watching them, he suddenly stopped speaking. The eyes of all three guards now reflected curiosity—and fear.

"What the fuck are you staring at, crazy man?" the lumpy-nosed guard said in a low voice. "We told you to leave."

"Who's Lobo?" Bone asked in an even tone.

"We don't know anybody named Lobo!" the guard with the toupee snapped.

"Please," Bone said quietly. "I don't intend to cause any trouble; I won't be back, and I don't intend to say anything to anybody about what's happened here. But I do need to find this Lobo. It's very important to me."

The lumpy-nosed guard laughed tightly, without humor. "You better hope Lobo doesn't find you, you fucking lunatic. He'll cut *your* head off for you, and that's for sure."

"Please," Bone sighed. "Can you tell me where to find him? Or can you at least tell me what he looks like?"

The guard with the chapped lips strode quickly to a telephone mounted on the wall, snatched up the receiver. "Split, you!" he shouted at Bone. "If you're not out of here in the next five seconds, I'm calling the cops and telling them their crazy headhunter is here causing trouble!"

There was nothing here of value to the stranger, Bone thought. At least, nothing that he could discover. Nothing at all. He walked out of the room, leaving the door open behind him. He turned left, walked down a short flight of stone steps, past the metal detectors and across the vestibule, then out the narrow entranceway into the New York City night. He didn't look back.

(iii)

Bone stood very still at the corner of Third Street and the Bowery, probing the stranger's mind as dawn broke; the sun was rising behind him, just over his left shoulder. The stranger was used to being up at dawn, Bone thought, and he experienced the rising sun as a deep emotion. And it was more than just a natural, daily event; dawn was something which provided the stranger with a good deal of information.

But what information?

Direction: north, south, east, west.

At night, Bone thought, the stranger could get this information from the stars.

He looked up. The glow from the rising sun was already washing the sky with light, but Bone doubted that here, in this city, there would be many nights when he could see the stars in any case. Then why, he wondered, should the stranger feel this sense of *importance* attached to the sun and stars? How had he used the information? It was doubtful that he would have needed it in the city, and it would not have been available to him underground.

He waited patiently for more than a half hour, eyes half closed, waiting for something more to come to him. It didn't. It was time to move on, he thought, time to find a place to . . . camp.

Camp. In the stranger's mind, he thought, there was an emotional valence to that word.

Bone looked to his left, to the southwest. According to his maps, that route would lead to the southern tip of the island of Manhattan, and there was no indication that the stranger had been sighted there. He turned right on the Bowery and headed uptown, instinctively drawn toward a single, tall building that shot up into the sky, higher than the buildings surrounding it, a soaring rectangle of steel, stone and glass that seemed to exude an almost mystical aura for him, drawing him to it.

He had no sense that the stranger had ever been in the tall building, and yet the way it stood apart from the other buildings reminded him of . . . something; it was important to the stranger. Height, depths; sun and star light, utter darkness. Seeming contradictions.

He kept walking, noting that the Bowery was slowly angling to the west. He continued northwest, angling from street to avenue, before coming to what a sign identified as Park Avenue South, stopped and looked all around him. The thoroughfare was different from the Bowery, he thought—and markedly so.

149

In this city, it seemed that walking only a few blocks could mean an abrupt change in the appearance and atmosphere of one's surroundings; there were neighborhoods within neighborhoods, parallel worlds with virtually nothing in common except for the fact that even on this elegant avenue there were ragged people sitting on the sidewalks or sleeping in doorways. Park Avenue was much cleaner than the Bowery, the shops larger and less flashy, much less cluttered. The lanes were divided by park-like malls with shrubs, trees and flowers which also, he noted, had a strong emotional valence for the stranger.

But the thing that most impressed him was the buildings lining both sides of the street as far as he could see, buildings so high that he had to crane his neck in order to look up at those closest to him, buildings that formed a canyon of stone, glass and steel.

Suddenly he experienced a strong sense of familiarity, immediately followed by an equally strong sense of alienation. The canyon of buildings, he thought, made him feel at home—and yet far from home; he belonged here, and he did not; the stone canyon was home to him, and totally alien.

It made no sense at all, he thought, suddenly frustrated and disgusted by the fact that his random thoughts and feelings remained maddeningly ephemeral and would not coalesce into anything he could call a *memory*.

Once again he wondered if he was insane.

He continued walking up Park Avenue, slowly, trying to push away the anxiety the seeming contradictions in his sensations and feelings caused him, trying to relax and yet still struggling to capture the essence of the strong emotions the stranger was experiencing in this man-made canyon.

In the distance, another huge building loomed in the very center of the landscape, seemingly blocking the way. High atop it, in large blue letters, were written the words *Pan Am;* the words meant nothing to him, yet once again the sight of a tall building standing out from the others exerted a powerful emotional pull on him.

Suddenly, without knowing why, he abruptly stopped walking and looked down at his gnarled hands. Had he broken his hands in a building? For almost a full minute he stood, alternately glancing up at the building in his path, then down

150

at his hands with their twisted bones and scar tissue nails. But nothing came to him, and he resumed walking.

He had assumed Park Avenue would end at the building with the blue letters on it, but what he found when he reached that point was a smaller—but equally impressive—building of grayish-brown stone, with intricately carved stone balustrades and columns forming its facade; it was quite unlike any of the buildings around it. He stood for a few minutes on the sidewalk, staring at the building with the words *Grand Central Terminal* carved into the stone above the entrance. This building, he found, also reminded him of something, but it was a different feeling from the sensations evoked by the other buildings—the same, yet different, as this building was different from the others.

Contradictions.

He felt no desire or urge in the stranger to enter the stone building up ahead, but he did feel the need to go on to the place where he would make camp. Park Avenue here diverged in two directions; one part of the road appeared to circle Grand Central Terminal, while the other angled down into darkness.

Underground.

This is where the stranger wanted to go, Bone thought, and he started walking down into the underpass. There was no sidewalk, but only a narrow concrete ledge on the right to walk on. The volume of traffic on the street was increasing, and as he descended down into the roadway he had to press closely against the stone wall on his right in order to avoid being brushed by the cars that swept past.

Suddenly, with no warning, he experienced a strong sensation of belonging—and yet *not* belonging—in this man-made cave, pressed against a stone wall. Suddenly he felt dizzy, and he almost fell off the stone ledge onto the roadway and into the flow of traffic. Carbon monoxide and burning oil fumes assaulted his senses, burning his nostrils, clogging his lungs and making his eyes water, nauseating him. He had made a mistake in coming this way, he thought. It was all wrong.

Peel off!

And yet he felt *natural* here, pressed against the wall with his gnarled fingers digging at the smooth stone, the flesh tingling on his back, his buttocks and the backs of his knees as he balanced on his toes.

He could die here!

Suddenly his fear, confusion and nausea combined into an explosive mixture that flashed into panic. He had to get out of the cave.

He stumbled off the ledge into the path of an oncoming car, and barely managed to leap back again and press himself flat against the stone as the car, horn blaring, sped past him, brushing his shirt. More horns blared. Sickened by the fumes and gasping for breath, he crab-walked as fast as he could along the stone ledge, occasionally stepping down into the roadbed as he lost his balance, hopping and staggering along as fast as he could as more cars sped past, their bright lights creating a surreal, nightmare glow throughout the underpass. The noise from the blaring horns was deafening, and served to fuel his panic. Finally, when there was a small break in the traffic pattern, he simply jumped down into the roadbed and sprinted, arms pumping and heartbeat racing, toward the sunlight a hundred yards away. In the opposite lane, onrushing cars in the narrow tunnel seemed about to hit him, and Bone was dimly aware of drivers staring out their windows at him in shocked amazement. Behind him, brakes squealed, and he was conscious of a car almost directly upon him. A horn sounded, seemingly right behind his head; the shrill, abusive blare echoed off the stone walls, pounding at him. He could do nothing but keep sprinting. The light was closer now, closer . . .

And then he was out of the tunnel.

He collapsed against the side of a building, crumpled to the sidewalk and lay there, gasping for breath in the smog-filled air with his eyes tightly closed. He fought to control the panic he had felt in the underpass, and gradually came to sense that the terrible fear had come not so much from being in the darkness of the underpass as from the impossibly contradictory sensations and emotions he had experienced there; even though the roadbed had been only inches below the narrow ledge he had tried to walk on, he had somehow felt that as he clung to the stone wall he was also hanging over an abyss . . .

Light and darkness, high and low, at home and alienated . . .

When he opened his eyes, he found that he was being stared at by curious onlookers on their way to work in the city

152

morning; people carrying briefcases, in suits and ties or dresses and heels, stared at him as they walked by—but all gave him a wide berth, sometimes glancing back over their shoulders before hurrying on. Nobody stopped to ask if he needed help.

Embarrassed, Bone struggled to his feet. He picked up the femur, walked quickly around the corner and stopped there, leaning against a second building with his forehead against the cool brick until he was breathing normally and once again felt in control of himself. Suddenly he felt terribly alone—and lonely. He wanted desperately to have a sanctuary where he could rest, hear the voice and perhaps feel the touch of someone who was neither hostile nor suspicious.

He desperately wanted to talk to, see, Anne. His most vivid memory now was of the brief moment in the park when her breasts had pressed against his arm, when she had unhesitatingly placed herself in a position of potential peril in order to defend a stranger who might be a killer. At this moment, in the wake of the panic attack in the underpass, he would have given almost anything to feel her breasts brush against him once again. Perhaps he would—should—even give up his quest. Ali Hakim had given him the construct and suggested the psychological tools he might use in the search for his identity, but at this moment he was no longer certain he wanted to know. In that direction, perhaps, lay madness.

He would need change. He started toward the entrance to Grand Central Terminal—then slowed, finally stopped and once again leaned against the side of a building.

He—not the stranger, but he—was a fool, Bone thought. And a coward. He had been ready to give up his search so quickly, and in the midst of an emotional storm which could very well provide vital clues to his identity. And if the stranger had been mad, there was no guarantee that he was not still so.

He had no right to involve the woman further; also, even if he did have the right, it wouldn't be a good idea. He was obviously very vulnerable to the feelings she had aroused in him, but those feelings were part of *this* life—not the one he had lived on the streets, or the life even more deeply buried in the past. His feelings for the woman could be a severe hindrance in his search for the stranger's feelings in the past. Until he had the answers he was searching for, he could belong to no one, and no one could belong to him.

Finally, he had already, in a way, betrayed the stranger by panicking and bolting when he had experienced precisely those kinds of strong emotional surges Ali Hakim had told him to look for. To search for, in a moment of weakness, solace—a woman—who might further weaken his resolve and confuse his memories would be another kind of betrayal, and he would not do it. He continued walking up Park Avenue, deeper into the forest of soaring buildings.

Further uptown he used a portion of his emergency funds to buy two changes of underwear, jeans and another shirt. In addition, thinking he felt a vague urging in the stranger, he purchased other items: cans of food, Sterno, two large boxes of wooden matches, soap, a comb.

Closer to his destination, his arms filled with packages, he passed an army and navy store, abruptly stopped and stared in the window at a display of hunting knives. And he felt the strongest urge yet in the stranger.

The stranger wanted a hunting knife, Bone thought—and immediately felt a surge of fear. For what reason could the stranger want a knife? To cut what? He could not think of any good reason why a man should want, or need, a hunting knife in New York City, except for self-defense—and he already knew that the stranger had effectively used the femur for that. Increasingly uneasy with the urge, he turned away from the window and started walking quickly away. He crossed an intersection and was halfway up the next block when he halted, then stepped back into a doorway to get out of the way of the increasingly heavy flow of pedestrian traffic. It took him only a few moments to make his decision.

He walked back to the army and navy store and used twenty-five dollars out of his diminishing emergency funds to purchase a large hunting knife that his instincts told him was good, made of quality materials. He also bought a sharpening stone and a small can of fine machine oil with which to hone the knife, for the vague urgings of the stranger told him that a fine knife should be kept sharp at all times.

The idea of possessing such a weapon still frightened Bone, and he suspected that he could be put in jail if the police found him with it. Still, there was no doubt in his mind that the stranger had wanted the knife, and Bone was, if not content, at least willing to risk waiting to see what its purpose would be.

He was the stranger's only ally, his only defender besides Anne, whom he could not afford to contact, and he had to trust the man.

He had already betrayed the stranger once, and he would not do it again.

CHAPTER NINE

The night before, while he slept, somebody had stolen his three-wheeled shopping cart, after—inexplicably—removing two garbage bags filled with his belongings and dropping them on the filthy marble floor of the waiting room in Grand Central Terminal. He had been almost overwhelmed with relief to find that he still had his possessions, and had decided to leave Grand Central; the next time he fell asleep on the hard wooden benches at the rear of the waiting room, he might not be so lucky.

Besides, it was time to return to God and the intergalactic television station, anyway; the people on all the other planets who watched him speak with God probably wondered what had happened to him.

Gasping for breath as he dragged his two bulging garbage bags behind him on the sidewalk, Michael Goodman finally made it to the Chrysler Building, which he knew was actually God with His brightly lighted, multi-faceted spire of a head that was also a television antenna broadcasting his image, thoughts and words to the other beings of the galaxy. It was because of God that he knew that on other planets the streets and sidewalks were made of soft material, and there were beds in all the doorways of the buildings, toilets on every corner, and nobody who lived on the streets was ever cold or hungry. There was no need for the terrible shelters, where other men had hurt, raped and robbed him. Michael was fifty-eight years old, and he wished he lived on one of those other worlds. Sometimes, he wished he were dead, and he often wondered if committing suicide would enable him to get to another world.

He did not hear the voices yet, but that was not unusual, for he was not yet safe deep inside the great domed arch of the entranceway. Once there, he would take his blanket and small pillow out of one of the bags, curl up with his bags on either side of him and then listen to the voices and talk back to them until dawn, when sometimes he would fall asleep and dream sweet dreams of his childhood until a policeman shook or prodded him awake and forced him to move on. But where would he go the next day? Not back to Grand Central, where his things might be stolen. He decided he would not worry about it until morning, when he was shaken awake.

Almost totally exhausted, but now within yards of his goal, Michael slumped down on the sidewalk of Forty-third Street and leaned back against the building, panting for breath. It was past midnight, and not many people were on the streets on the East Side. But there were some. A well-dressed couple walked past, stopping when the woman tugged at the man's sleeve. The man turned around, walked back and stopped in front of Michael. He withdrew a wad of bills from his pocket, thumbed through them until he found a single; he dropped the bill in front of Michael, then walked quickly away. Michael picked up the bill off the sidewalk, stuffed it into the pocket of one of the three shirts he wore.

He was hungry. The dollar would buy him a doughnut, but he was too tired to walk any distance to find a store that was open. He would have to sleep with his hunger, he thought, and maybe in the morning he would have the energy to walk the few blocks to the headquarters of Project Helping Hand, where Anne or Barry or one of the other workers would give him something to eat. Maybe they would help him find another shopping cart, which was even more important to him. First, he would have to listen to their lectures and pleas for him to go to a shelter, and he might even have to take a card and promise to go before they would help him. But he would not go to a shelter; he feared the shelters more than anything else. He did not want to be raped again.

He was so very tired, Michael thought. But he had to get to God and hear the comforting voices before he could sleep. Feeling as if he were moving under tons of water at the bottom of an ocean, he slowly struggled to his feet. He breathed deeply a few times, reached down and grabbed the necks of the garbage bags, had to use all of his strength to tug them along the sidewalk; but finally he was into the almost total darkness under the Chrysler Building's entranceway arch.

He immediately began to hear the soft, soothing voices on the intergalactic television station.

"Get the hell out of here, motherfucker! You smell like a goddamn sewer! Get the fuck out! Go find someplace else to crash!"

It was not a voice from another world, Michael thought; this voice had drowned out all the other voices, frightening them away. He tugged at his bags, trying to move off to the opposite corner. Suddenly a foot landed on his thigh, and a fist hit him hard between the shoulder blades, narrowly missing the base of his skull. His head jerked back painfully.

"Shit, man, you *stink*!" another voice said. "Get *out* of here! *Jesus!*"

"But I can't," Michael murmured. "I'm so—"

He was kicked again. And then there was a chorus of voices, all belonging to men like himself from this wretched world.

"Take your stink out of here!"

"Get away from me, you stinking motherfucker!"

"Get the fuck out of here before I cut your balls off!"

The doorway under the arch was crowded with other homeless men, and Michael felt despair when he realized this meant he would not hear the voice of God or kind people on other worlds this night. With tears of exhaustion and sadness streaming down his cheeks, Michael once more gripped the necks of the garbage bags and hauled them back out onto the sidewalk.

He was so tired, so hungry . . .

There was a half-filled wire trash basket halfway up the block, near Park Avenue. Michael leaned over it, reached down and began poking around in the debris, pushing papers around and wriggling his fingers until he felt something soft and sticky. He grabbed this scrap of paper and brought it to his mouth, licking it; it tasted sweet, of apples and crumbs—the

158

remains of a slice of pie, which only served to whet his appetite and make him even more hungry. Now he reached down into the basket with both hands, and again touched paper with something on it that felt like food. He pulled out the paper, eagerly put it to his mouth. He smelled what the substance was a second too late, after he had already put his tongue and lips to it. He gasped and spat, hurling the paper covered with dog excrement away from him as he desperately wiped at his mouth with his sleeve. The horrible taste would not go away. He slumped down on the sidewalk, over his garbage bags, bowed his head and began to sob uncontrollably.

He couldn't help it if he smelled like the dogshit he'd just eaten, he thought as he continued to sob. Twice he had allowed people at the shelters to strip him and put him under a shower. The first time he had been scalded, and the second time the water had been so cold that he had come down sick soon afterward. He feared the shelters, and would not go to them again. He couldn't help it if his fingers didn't always work right and he couldn't drop his pants before he urinated or defecated. Sometimes he defecated without even being aware of it. Also, in the winter the urine and feces that collected in his pants and ran down his legs was so deliciously warm that he welcomed it. And after a while he could no longer smell himself.

A sound caused him to look up—and he cried out in terror.

They were back—the young ones with the gray jackets and black boots. The last time they had caught him alone, he had been on his way to a soup kitchen; but he had left his belongings and his shopping cart behind, in a safe hiding place, and his smell had caused them to leave him alone. Now they would take everything he owned.

Without a word, two of the four Wolves stepped forward, reached down and grabbed his two full garbage bags. Michael lunged for the bags, but it was too late; his fingers grabbed nothing but air, and then a fist shot out and struck him on the side of the head. Pain shot through his skull, flashed down into his jaw and neck, and he fell over on his side.

"Oh, God," he moaned, "please don't make me take your thing in my mouth again. Please don't stick it in me."

"Shut up," one of the youths, a white, said as he reached down and began to undo the buttons of Michael's heavy outer shirt. A moment later the youth gagged, quickly stepped back.

"Man, if any of you guys want to search him, be my guest. Not me. This guy stinks of shit; even his breath stinks of shit."

"Fuck it," a black Wolf said. "Let's just take the bags and get out of here."

"That fucking Lobo is crazy," another Wolf said. "Can you imagine him wanting *this* guy to give him a blow job? How could he stand the smell?"

"Lobo will stick his prick into anything that moves," the white wolf said. "You know that. He *is* fucking crazy, and he's always got a hard-on. I once watched him fuck a Big Mac; he said he wanted to see what it felt like. And he likes to fuck old ladies."

"Please," Michael whispered, crawling across the sidewalk toward the booted feet of the youths. "Please give me back my things. That's all I have in the world. Please don't take them. Please, please . . ."

A black-booted foot was placed on his shoulder, and he was shoved face-down on the sidewalk. Through the tears that filled his eyes, Michael watched helplessly, one trembling arm held out in useless supplication, as the gray-jacketed youths hurried to the end of the block, turned the corner and disappeared from sight.

Numb with grief and a paralyzing sense of loss, Michael crawled back to the trash basket, leaned his head against it. Then he closed his eyes and began to sob again. Everything he had in the world was gone: his two blankets and pillow, his extra coat, the three books he couldn't read but which had given him a sense of belonging to a world where people did sit and read things, his collection of TV antennae which he liked to lay out on summer days and watch gleam in the sunlight, his collection of smooth pebbles, the brush with its yellowed mother-of-pearl handle which, for some reason, he thought had once belonged to his mother.

All gone.

Now he would have to go to a shelter like the one where the youth with the chalky skin had raped him, Michael thought. He would be forced to stand under water that was always too hot or too cold. They would jeer and laugh and curse at him, and they would make him throw away these familiar clothes which he had—

Suddenly there was a loud *whoop-whoop* which sounded as if it was just behind his right ear. Michael started, opened his

160

eyes and turned his head to find a police car standing at the
curb beside him. Michael knew that if the police picked him
up, he would be taken to a shelter—after being washed off at
the nearest fire hydrant, where the water would be freezing. It
had happened before. He was not ready to go to a shelter yet;
he still had too much fear. And he did not want to feel the touch
of the icy water.

He struggled to his feet. He wiped away his tears with the
back of his hand, then staggered up the block and went around
the corner at the first side street. He sighed with relief when he
heard the police car pull away.

Once more lost in his grief, Michael began to wander aim-
lessly down the street, looking for a place—any place—where
he could lie down and sleep.

"Michael?"

Michael shook his head and kept walking. His mind was
playing tricks on him, he thought. He never heard the voices
when he was away from God.

"Michael, why don't you stop and listen to me?"

Michael stopped, slowly turned and looked around him,
trying to determine where the voice was coming from. It
seemed to be coming from a distance, which meant that it
could be somebody from another world . . . but this voice
sounded oddly familiar.

"Where are you?!" he shouted.

There was no reply. A lone pedestrian, a middle-aged man
shivering inside a light topcoat, came around the corner,
glanced nervously at Michael, then hurriedly crossed the street
and walked on.

And then the voice came again.

"There's no need to shout, Michael. I can hear you, as you
hear me. I'm across the street. Come over and talk to me. I saw
the Wolfpack take all your things. I know how you're feeling.
You need me now."

Once again, Michael had the odd sensation that he knew this
person who was speaking to him. Although the voice carried
clearly across the street, it seemed strangely muffled; still, it
was a voice Michael associated with help, with caring.

He waited for two cars to go by, then crossed to the other side
of the street.

"Here, Michael; to your right. Come over here."

Michael walked in the direction of the voice, which he could now tell was coming from a wide, deep doorway cloaked in night-shadow. He went into the doorway, abruptly stopped when a figure draped all in shining orange stepped forward. Michael tried to look into the features of the shining figure, but could not see the face behind the flap of material which was pulled up around the neck. Michael decided that, after all, it had to be a being from another world, in some kind of uniform.

"Hello, Michael," the being said gently.

It was not a being from another world at all, Michael thought as he finally placed the voice. He smiled. "It's you. I haven't seen you in a long time. I thought you'd gone away."

"No. I've just been busy elsewhere. I haven't had a chance to visit you."

"I didn't know you were one of them."

"One of whom, Michael?"

"I always thought you were part of this world, but now that I see your clothes, I know that you're not. You're from another world, aren't you?"

There was a prolonged silence, then: "You believe there are better worlds than this one, don't you, Michael? We've often talked about it."

"Yes," Michael replied in a hollow voice. "I hate this world."

"I know you do, Michael. There's just no way to properly care for you here; you can't help yourself, and you won't let others help you. You suffer terribly, but there's no way to ease your suffering."

"I'm afraid," Michael whispered.

"Of me?"

"No. I'm afraid of the shelters."

"Would you like me to send you to a better world?"

Once more, tears flooded Michael's eyes; but this time they were tears of joy. "Oh, yes," he sobbed. "I've waited so long. Can you do that?"

The shiny orange figure stepped back into the darkness. "Come back here with me, Michael. This is the doorway to a better world."

CHAPTER TEN

(i)

Beyond the Turtle Pond, Belvedere Castle rose into a cloudless sky painted orange by the rising sun, a fairy-tale structure of stone courtyards and balustrades that was a dwarf cousin to the towering skyscrapers ringing Central Park. Stripped to the waist, Bone crouched in the dawn shadows and peered about him; this section of the park appeared to be empty. He walked to the edge of the pond, pushed the brackish surface water away with his hands, then scooped up handfuls of water and splashed it over his face and under his armpits. It was enough; he had already bathed, during the night, in the small lake he had found further to the north. Next, he filled one of the two canteens he carried with water which he would use for shaving; the second canteen had already been filled with fresh, clean water from a drinking fountain he had found near his campsite. This done, he headed back to his camp in a wooded section which a map posted outside the park had told him was called The Ramble.

He had less than ten dollars left of the money Anne had given him, Bone thought as he headed back up the park, but he was not concerned. The money had been well spent purchasing goods or equipment which he felt the stranger wanted or needed, and he felt good, certain that he was slowly but surely settling ever deeper into the stranger's mind, doing the things that the stranger would do, behaving as he would behave.

For food, he had discovered a soup kitchen nearby where he could get both lunch and supper—but he had found that he did not require much food. Also, to his astonishment and delight, he had discovered that the stranger could recognize edible and nourishing berries, fruits and roots among the flora growing in the park. With food available and facilities to clean his clothes and body, he had all he needed. He was free. He found he was reasonably content, satisfied—and, most important, optimistic that he would eventually succeed in his search for his identity.

Back at his camp beneath a footbridge in a heavily wooded section of The Ramble, Bone shaved himself with an old but sturdy straight razor he had bought, along with a leather strop, in a pawn shop. The stranger liked these simple but most useful implements, he thought; there was an elegance to the razor's simplicity, utility and durability. The stranger liked to be out-of-doors, but he also liked to be clean and well groomed even when he was alone; it was, Bone had found, very good for his morale.

His shaving done, Bone dressed in the worn shirt he had originally been given, then took the metal cup filled with hot tea brewed from herbs he had found in the park off the small stove he had constructed with scraps of metal and the can of Sterno. He squatted on his haunches, sipped at the tea, shuddered with pleasure.

It was a Sunday morning, and from the position of the sun he estimated that he had better than two hours before he was scheduled to be at Ali Hakim's office on Lexington Avenue. And so he relaxed, continuing to sip at his tea while he thought about what he had—and hadn't—learned in the five days that had passed since he had walked out of the Men's Shelter down on the Bowery.

The footbridge was in a relatively secluded area, and even now in early May the mornings and evenings were chilly enough to keep pedestrian traffic in The Ramble to a minimum, but Bone, in order to guarantee the security and privacy of his retreat, had taken the further step of using his large knife to cut brush along a nearby stream bed, then weave the brush into a series of mats which not only protected the site from view but provided a windscreen. With the small but effectively smokeless fire he built from hardwood each night, he slept very comfortably. Now, he thought as he followed the progress of two early-rising bird-watchers coming over a small rock outcropping to the east, he could see, but not be seen.

The stranger had excellent outdoors skills and craft, Bone thought. And he had not learned these things in any city.

On the other hand, there was the continuing and powerful sense of familiarity he experienced whenever he gazed at the towering walls of the soaring buildings that were everywhere in Manhattan. Once again it occurred to him that he belonged here; but he did not. He was obviously an outdoorsman, but he applied his skills in a forest of steel and concrete.

Where had he come from? What had happened to him?

The stranger's affinity for the outdoors, his survival skills and meticulous hygiene, simply did not correlate with the panic attack he had experienced in the underpass near Grand Central Terminal—nor with his dreams of graves, bones, death and a gleaming, orange-crimson figure. The affinities, the things he had learned about the stranger's habits, did not correlate with the way he had *felt* when he had been pressed against the stone wall in the underpass; before the panic had swept away his reason, he had been aware of a keen sense of balance while stepping along the narrow ledge; he had pressed against stone walls before.

What had happened to his hands?

And there was a dark side to the initial delight he had experienced as he'd discovered the stranger's abilities. Following increasingly strong urges, the stranger's instincts, he had almost effortlessly found a suitable place to set up a campsite, and he had hidden it well. He certainly knew how to build a secure stash.

Perry Lightning had told him he had such a cache, and now Bone knew it must be true. Somewhere in the city, there could be another hiding place like this one, a place where the stranger, if he was the serial killer, had hid his weapon, and perhaps even his grisly trophies.

But it was not yet proven that the stranger was a killer; nothing even remotely resembling a memory of killing anyone had occurred to Bone, and until it did he was determined to keep on trusting the stranger.

When he had walked out of the Men's Shelter, he had not

known precisely where he had wanted to go, but had ended in Central Park. It was just as well. It was in this park that this new life had begun, and thus it was here—or close to here— where the keys to the two previous lives might lie. From the shelter he had gone directly to the Sheep Meadow, to the spot where he had been squatting when Anne, Barry Prindle and Ali Hakim had come to him. He had stood there for almost two hours, slowly turning to look in all directions, thinking, trying to find something that looked familiar, some hint of memory to tell him where he had come from, or where he should look next.

There had been nothing.

After hiding his packages, he had spent the better part of the day wandering through the park, searching for some sight, sound, smell or other sensation that seemed familiar.

There had been nothing.

But he had immediately recognized what would be a safe, secure campsite at this site beneath the footbridge in The Ramble. He had retrieved his packages and brought them here, then spent the remaining hours before nightfall cutting brush and taking steps to protect the site from the eyes of others.

He had been up at dawn the next morning—and had found himself very hungry. He had bathed and shaved himself, then—using the maps Anne had given him—he had walked out of the park, emerging on the East Side at the Eighty-fifth Street exit, just above the Metropolitan Museum of Art. He had walked to Ali Hakim's office on Lexington, just to see how long it would take him, but had not gone in or left word that he had been there. In Bone's mind, the neuropsychiatrist had already given him all the ideas and psychological tools he needed to carry on his search, and he did not feel there was a great deal else to discuss with the man until he was further along in his quest. He had also walked further downtown, to the storefront offices of Project Helping Hand—but, again, had not gone in. He had merely wanted to see the place where the woman who so occupied his thoughts worked. There had been three blue vans parked along the curb, each with a smiling, yellow "happy face" painted on its side. Bone had stood across the street, in the shadow of a doorway, for twenty minutes; then he had quickly walked away in disgust when he realized that he was wasting precious time simply because he was hoping to catch a glimpse of Anne Winchell. He had not, he had thought, the time—or emotion—to waste thinking about a woman.

The places on the maps where Anne had noted that he'd been seen on at least one occasion had indicated to him that the stranger had wandered over a large territory. Consequently, he had decided to break down each day to correspond to a grid on the map, then systematically search along every street in that grid, walking and looking, talking to other homeless people he might meet. All five days had been spent searching the Upper East Side.

And he had found other soup kitchens along the way; each time he had eaten at one, often drawing curious stares from both hosts and clients, he had sought to pay for his meals by working for one or two hours in the kitchen, serving others.

At one of the soup kitchens he visited, a woman volunteer reported that she had seen him eat there once during the past year. He had not spoken; carrying his bone, he had simply lined up with others for his food, eaten, then walked away. He had been alone. The woman did not know where he had stayed at night, where he came from or what he did during the day. Occasionally, Bone's questions were met by questions. Bone had been vague in his answers, and had moved on. Nothing the woman had told him had been of any use. Bone had concluded that he had indeed walked the streets of the Upper East Side, but not often.

During these five days, responding to the urging of the stranger, he had made additional purchases, and he kept these items at his campsite. His stash.

And as he had systematically searched the Upper East Side, he had systematically looked for a job. He had anticipated being able to find work, but obtaining a job proved to be a far more difficult task than he had imagined without means of identification or a Social Security card. When giving a false name hadn't worked, because of suspicions raised by the fact that he had no papers, he had tried telling the truth about his loss of memory. But this had only served to arouse more suspicion—and, sometimes, fear and open hostility.

After three days, he had stopped asking shopkeepers for a job. The clothes he had, he knew, would last him a few months. He could walk wherever it was he wanted to go, and, if he needed money, he could always collect discarded soda cans and turn them in to stores. He could always go to the soup kitchens for food, but he was not totally dependent on them, for he had learned other strategies: he knew which supermarkets threw out near-fresh produce at the end of the day, and he had observed that many schoolchildren were in the habit of throwing their bag lunches into the nearest trash basket upon arriving at school in the morning.

He had shelter and clothing, and knew how to obtain food; Bone had decided that he could afford to spend all his time searching for the stranger's identity.

As he had walked the streets, he had studied the faces of teenagers, searching for the youth in the gray jacket who had tried to kill him at the Men's Shelter. *Lobo*, the youth had said; Lobo wanted him dead. Either Lobo or the youth who had come after him with a knife would have valuable information about the stranger, Bone thought, and might even be able to tell him who he was.

But he had not lost sight of the fact that Lobo and the youth with the knife, and perhaps others, wanted to kill him; consequently, Bone always wore dark glasses and a floppy, oversize hat—items he had picked up at a Salvation Army center. However, he had not seen the youth, and Bone suspected that he confined his activities to lower Manhattan. Still, he had kept looking.

Now Bone finished his tea, once again glanced up at the morning sun. He judged that he still had at least an hour before he was due at Ali Hakim's office, and he decided that he would use the time to walk the perimeter of one of the grids he had drawn in that area around Lexington and Sixty-fourth Street— new territory for him; the grid he had arbitrarily drawn was bounded by Fifth and Third avenues to the west and east, Fifty-fourth to Forty-second streets to the north and south.

He washed his metal cup in the narrow stream that flowed beneath the footbridge. Then he carefully wrapped everything in a sturdy plastic garbage bag, which he placed in a hole he had dug with his knife. He covered the hole with a mat of brush, peered through his brush screen to make sure nobody was about to observe him, then climbed up out of the ravine. Then he started walking south, toward the exit at that end of the park.

(ii)

Later, he would take a bus to visit his sister across the river, in Rockland County, where he would stay for a week. But for now

Zulu was at his usual post in front of St. Thomas Church, preparing his mind, meditating, searching for the stories he would tell the crowds he expected to see on the streets this morning of what promised to be a fine, sunny Sunday.

The church service inside St. Thomas would be over in a few minutes, and then the worshippers would stream out and join the other people strolling up and down Fifth Avenue. Not a few would stop to listen to him.

His stories on this day, he thought, would be devoted to the pleasures of spring and summer in New York City—concerts and Shakespeare and opera in Central Park, strolling along the boardwalk at the South Street Seaport, warmth, street festivals, a time when even the homeless could be relatively comfortable. His stories this day would be about happiness and satisfaction; cruelty and misery in the city were things he could talk about any day, and usually did.

Suddenly, the seven-foot street performer had the distinct sensation that he was being watched. Unwilling to come out of his trance just as a new story was forming, he tried to ignore the sensation, which was growing increasingly stronger. After all, he thought, he was being watched all the time; a seven-foot-tall black man dressed in flowing ceremonial robes and carrying a seven-foot staff made for a rather imposing sight, even in New York City. Indeed, he depended on his presence to initially gather audiences which he would then captivate with the sound of his voice and the content of his stories. So it was only normal that people should be staring at him, and he hoped they could continue to stare until he was ready to rap his staff on the sidewalk and begin . . .

But this was somehow different; some*one* was staring at him, a single pair of eyes, from a distance . . .

And then the story that had been forming in his mind was lost in confusion and distraction.

Still without moving his body, Zulu slowly let his eyes come back into focus. Already, a crowd—including many "regulars" who knew that his Sunday morning stories were often his best—was gathering around him, staring up at him with anticipation.

But these were not the eyes he had felt.

Without moving his head, Zulu looked to his left and his right. As expected, people crossing the street, moving up and down the block from both directions, usually fixed their gaze on him while they were still a distance away.

But these were not the eyes he had felt.

Then Zulu looked across the street, and was mildly startled to see a slender but solidly built man about six feet tall standing at the very edge of the sidewalk, staring intently at him. A moving wall of pedestrians flowed behind the man, often jostling him, but the man remained still, staring . . .

These were the eyes.

The man wore dark glasses and a floppy-brimmed hat that was probably one or two sizes too large for him and which covered his forehead, making it impossible to make out his features. Zulu did not immediately recognize the man, and yet he had the strong feeling that there was something definitely familiar . . .

And then the man, still keeping his gaze locked with Zulu's, slowly took his hands out of his pockets and folded them across his chest—and in that moment Zulu saw the twisted, gnarled fingers.

It was the bone-man.

Zulu frowned. He had not seen the bone-man in more than two weeks, and then it had only been a fleeting glimpse of the bone-man's bewildered face looking out the window of one of the blue vans operated by Project Helping Hand. After that had come the newspaper stories, with the police claiming that they had captured the killer responsible for beheading homeless men and women—a murderer who carried a human bone. Zulu had had his doubts, but had assumed that the police had strong evidence against the strange man. He had also assumed that the bone-man was locked away in jail, or in a mental hospital. Obviously, Zulu thought, he had been wrong; the police had been wrong. The clothes of this man staring at him were decidedly unfamiliar, and his long hair had been cut, or was folded up under his hat—but the man standing on the edge of the sidewalk across the street was definitely the bone-man. Nobody else had hands like that.

Zulu could not understand why the bone-man did not come across the street. The bone-man had spent many hours sitting on the steps of St. Thomas, in all kinds of weather, listening to his stories. The bone-man had never spoken, but Zulu had always had the sense that the bone-man was listening intently, absorbing everything. And, of course, considering the other

170

way in which their lives had intersected, Zulu found it decidedly odd that the bone-man did not seem to even want to
acknowledge his existence, much less come over to sit and
listen again. More strange behavior from a very strange man
who was unbelievably lucky just to be alive.

Unless something else had happened that he didn't know
about, Zulu thought. Unless something else had changed in the
bone-man, and the bone-man might once again need his help.

Zulu was about to raise his staff in greeting, to beckon the
bone-man across the street, when the figure in the dark glasses
and floppy hat abruptly turned and said something to a man
who had stopped at the intersection to wait for the light to
change. The man glanced at his watch, said something to the
bone-man, who then quickly turned away from the curb and
walked away.

Zulu, thoroughly puzzled, gazed after the bone-man until he
disappeared in the crowd. Something had, indeed, changed in
the bone-man, Zulu thought; for one thing, he now spoke. But
Zulu could make no sense of the bone-man's new pattern of
behavior, and he found that it troubled him. Suddenly, Zulu
felt concerned and anxious, for reasons that he did not fully
understand.

There would be no more stories today, Zulu thought, for the
story that now held the most interest for him was unresolved,
with large sections unknown to him. He would go to his sister's
home early. Offering a smile and half nod as a kind of apology
to the expectant crowd gathered around him, Zulu picked up
his empty wooden bowl and quickly walked away.

(iii)

"Just before I came here, I saw something that gave me a
strong impression that I'd been there before; and one of the
maps Anne gave me confirmed that I had been spotted there—a
number of times. It was a church on Fifth Avenue, at the corner
of Fifty-third Street. I was walking down Fifth, I looked across
the street . . . and I just felt this strong sense of association.
There was a man standing in front of the church—a very tall
black man wearing brightly colored robes and holding a long
pole, or staff. A lot of people were gathered around, staring at
him, but he just stood there, without moving. When he looked

at me, I had a very strong feeling that I'd met the man before, that I knew him."

Ali Hakim looked up from the yellow legal pad on which he had been making notes. Warm sunlight streamed in through a large window directly behind his desk, filling the spacious chrome, glass and oak-lined office with a golden glow. The slight Pakistani psychiatrist with the lilting voice was dressed in jeans and sneakers, with a brown corduroy jacket worn over a maroon polo shirt. As usual, his features were impassive, his large, black eyes revealing nothing.

"Did you speak to this man?"

Bone shook his head. "I was going to; but I'd committed to coming here to see you. I didn't want to break my word, and I didn't want to be late. I'll go back there after I finish here."

"Oh? How do you know he'll be there?"

"I think he spends a lot of time there; I spotted him there before, from the window of the van when Barry, Anne and you were taking me to Bellevue."

Ali made a note. "Obviously, you like to be punctual for appointments. And you have a sense of honor; it's important to you that you keep your word."

"It seems so. I hadn't thought about it that way; I just experienced it."

Ali made a very slight clucking sound with his tongue. "Then you are not concentrating hard enough; experience things, yes, but then ponder the experience. These are the kinds of things you must attend to. Little things. I believe it's more likely that an accumulation of little impressions and reactions will help you, rather than any sudden, dramatic breakthrough. When you fail to observe, or dismiss, such important character traits as punctuality and honor, I suggest that you are off the track. The big 'event' you are waiting for may never happen. Stop waiting for a mountain to appear to you; you must build it yourself."

"I understand."

Ali put down his pen, then folded his hands and rested them on top of his thick glass desktop, which was bare except for the yellow pad on which he had been writing. "The black man in the robes calls himself Zulu," the psychiatrist said easily. "And you're right; he will most likely be there, at least during the day, if and when you wish to speak with him. Of course, I can't guarantee that he'll wish to speak with you; if he doesn't, you'll be met with nothing but silence. Zulu is a most interesting fellow."

"Homeless?"

"He's classified as such by the city agencies that try to keep track of such things, but he really doesn't fit into any neat category. You'll find a small percentage of otherwise rational people living on the streets who are there precisely because they want to be, people who have made a conscious, balanced decision to live outside the parameters of what we call civilized society, and who are reasonably—sometimes extremely—self-sufficient. Zulu is such a person. You, albeit under radically different circumstances, were another. Zulu was approached a few times by Project Helping Hand personnel, and he was highly offended. He's what you might call a street performer, and he's been virtually a landmark on that corner for the past five or six years."

"What does he do?"

"He tells stories about the city. But 'tells' isn't quite the word. He *performs* them, almost like an opera singer. He's really quite good. I've stopped to listen on occasion, and have always been very impressed. Judging from the amounts of money I've seen in his bowl, I'd say that he does quite well at his chosen profession."

Bone frowned, remembering the black man and the strange sense of familiarity—almost kinship—he had felt. Now he was sorry he had not taken the time to cross the street and try to talk to the man. But, as Ali Hakim had pointed out, the stranger was both honorable and punctual. And he had said that he would be here.

"Where does this Zulu live?"

Ali shrugged his frail shoulders. "Perhaps in a split-level in Queens. I don't know, and I doubt that any city worker knows—just as we don't know his real name. The two of you seem to have—or had—those things in common. However, if I were to take a guess, I would say that the man's background includes some classical acting training; his voice and mannerisms are those of a well-trained performer."

Bone said nothing. Now he wanted to get out of the psychiatrist's office as quickly as possible so that he could go back to the church on Fifth Avenue and talk to the robed black man.

"I'm very happy to see you, Bone," Ali continued after a pause.

173

"You sound as if you weren't sure I'd show up."

"The abruptness and manner in which you disappeared from the shelter took us all a bit by surprise. Then, when you didn't get in touch . . ." The psychiatrist finished the sentence with a shrug. "We've all been very concerned about you."

"I wasn't aware that I had to check in with anyone," Bone said evenly.

"You don't. But may I ask why you left the shelter?"

Bone matter-of-factly related the events that had occurred during his first night at the Men's Shelter. Ali listened with growing concern on his face.

"You must be very careful," Ali said when Bone had finished. "The gray-jacketed boy you mentioned is a member of a particularly vicious youth gang which calls itself the Wolfpack. Their leader is a psychotic young man who calls himself Lobo, but whose real name is Rafael Billingsley. Lobo might be described as the ultimate neo-conservative, or Social Darwinist; I'm told he actually views himself as a reformer culling out the weak from the herd, as it were. He's spent most of his life bouncing in and out of foster homes and mental institutions. The Wolfpack has made a specialty of preying on the homeless, and each member must be considered very dangerous. There are a lot of them out there. You must be especially careful to avoid Lobo; he's apparently made a blood oath to kill you, and he won't be thinking about much else until he does."

"Lobo knows something about the stranger— me. It seems I had a serious run-in with him while I was living on the streets."

Ali shook his head. "Pursue your other means of investigation. I repeat: the Wolfpack is extremely dangerous. They usually pick only on those who can't fight back, and who won't report the attacks to the police. But if this Lobo has a personal grudge against you, every member of the Wolfpack will be on the lookout for you. And Lobo will kill you; make no mistake about that. He's a very disturbed young man who never should have been set free in the first place."

"I'll be careful."

The psychiatrist again shook his head, sighed. "You say you've been living in Central Park for the past week, under a bridge?"

Bone nodded.

"*Why*, Bone?"

174

"I've been following my instincts. It's what you told me to do."

"Yes," Ali replied evenly. "That's true."

Now Bone related the incident that had occurred in the underpass near Grand Central Terminal—his panic, his initial sense of balance and its loss, his instinct to try to dig his fingers into the smooth stone. Ali listened intently, occasionally making notes and nodding, but did not interrupt.

When Bone had finished, Ali leaned back in his leather swivel chair and studied him, his features impassive but his large eyes displaying heightened curiosity. It occurred to Bone that there was something on the other man's mind, something the psychiatrist was holding back. He considered asking Ali if that was true, decided not to. If Ali Hakim was hiding something from him, Bone thought, it would not be revealed to him until he had at least discovered its bare outlines for himself; it was how the other man worked.

"How is Anne?"

"Anne is fine."

"Barry?"

"Also fine, as far as I know. They're not working together any longer, and Barry has been assigned to another project working in the Bronx. I don't see him anymore."

"Please tell Anne I said hello— and Barry, if you do see him."

"Why don't you tell Anne yourself? I know that she'd like to hear from you; she's been very worried. Also, by this time your emergency grant should have been approved; she may have some money for you. However, I guess you know that you'll have to have some permanent address before you can get further financial aid. Perhaps it's time for you to check into a residence. Anne can help you with that, too—as you know."

"I'll give it some thought. Thank you, Doctor."

"You're afraid, aren't you?" Ali said softly.

"Of a residence?"

"Of Anne."

Bone said nothing. After a few moments, Ali opened a drawer, took out a set of cards and what appeared to be two or three questionnaires.

"I'd like to run some tests on you, Bone—Rorschach blots and two personality profiles. It will take about two hours."

"If you think it will help, sure," Bone replied, hoping his disappointment did not show on his face or in his voice.

"Frankly, Bone, it will probably help me more in my research protocol than it will in your search. You seem to be doing just fine on your own. However, the personality profiles may give us some indication of preferences and aversions you're not aware of."

"Will it wait, Doctor? I'm kind of anxious to get back to the church and try to talk to this man you call Zulu."

Ali again leaned back in his chair, crossed his legs. "Of course it will wait," he said, his tone flat.

"But you don't think it should."

"You will find Zulu at St. Thomas Church later in the day—or any day. But, if you'll take these tests now, I may have any information they can give me for you next week when you come in. The tests might be useful, or they might not—but you will lose that week if you don't take them now. This is the only time I have available to administer them."

"All right," Bone said. "Let's do it, Doctor."

"Are you aware that there was another killing two nights ago?" Ali asked in a casual tone as he began laying the questionnaires out on the desk in front of him.

Suddenly Bone felt stunned and short of breath, as if someone had punched him in the stomach—and the easy manner in which the psychiatrist had asked the question only added to the impact. He wondered why the other man hadn't raised the issue as soon as he'd come in, then realized that throughout what had seemed to him an almost casual conversation the psychiatrist had been studying him, gauging his words, demeanor and reactions. Bone felt a surge of resentment and anger, and he remained silent as the other man continued to rearrange the papers on the desk.

Finally Ali looked up, raised his eyebrows slightly. "You weren't aware of it, were you?"

"No," Bone replied curtly.

"Yes. I can see that."

"Was it a . . . decapitation?"

"Yes. It was in all the newspapers, on radio and television."

"I haven't been reading the newspapers, listening to the radio or watching television, Dr. Hakim. All the time I've been sitting here and talking, you knew there'd been a killing and you didn't tell me; you've been sitting there watching me and wondering if you were talking to a murderer."

"Isn't that what we've both been wondering since we met, Bone?" Ali asked in a mild tone.

"I did *not* know about this, Doctor."

"I believe you." The psychiatrist hesitated for a few moments, then began to replace the packet of cards and questionnaires in his desk drawer. "On second thought, I believe we will leave these until next week."

"You're playing games with me, Doctor," Bone said in a low, tense voice, "and I don't like it."

"I'm not playing games with you, Bone," Ali replied with uncharacteristic forcefulness as he leaned forward, resting his forearms on his desk. "Now that the subject of the killing has been brought up, you're upset—and that could effect the outcome of the tests. Frankly, I wasn't sure until I said it if I wanted to mention the killing before I gave you the tests. However, as I watched you, it become apparent that, at least from the time you walked into the office, you were not aware that there had been another decapitation murder two nights ago. Waiting a week to take the tests will do no harm; as I said, you seem to be doing quite well on your own. Simply continue what you have been doing. However, I do strongly suggest that you let HRA put you in a permanent residence; it will make things easier for you. But that's up to you."

"Lieutenant Lightning must be looking for me."

"I would assume so, but I don't really know; he hasn't contacted me."

"Is that it for today?"

"Unless there's something else you wish to talk about, yes."

"What if I tell you I want to take those tests now?"

"That is not your province. I don't know what they may reveal about you, but the result would almost certainly be skewed if you took them now."

Still feeling a strong residue of resentment, Bone rose and walked stiffly to the door leading to the small outer office. He opened the door, then turned back to the psychiatrist, who remained sitting behind his desk, legs once again crossed, watching him.

"Why don't you tell me what else is on your mind, Doctor?"

"What's on *your* mind, Bone?"

"You were very careful to say that I didn't seem aware of the murder when I *walked into your office.* The implication is that

I may have committed that murder, but simply don't remember it."

"I was simply stating a fact, Bone. I meant to imply nothing."

"Is it possible that I killed somebody two nights ago, chopped off the head, then went to sleep, woke up and don't *remember* it?"

Ali took some time to reply, as if he were giving very careful thought to his words. "Let me put it to you this way, Bone," he said at last. "As bizarre as they may be, there are far more documented cases of people with multiple-personality disorders than there are of people—one person, you—suffering global anterograde and retrograde amnesia and still being able to function perfectly normal in the present. You're a case unto yourself."

"Then it is possible?"

"I would say most definitely so."

Bone took a deep breath, slowly exhaled. Initially, mixed with resentment toward the psychiatrist for withholding the information, there had been elation at the fact that, considering his new state of awareness, he had proof that the stranger was not the serial killer. Now his old anxieties about the stranger had returned, and were multiplied. "What should I do, Doctor?" he asked quietly.

"You are a free man, Bone. I have no answer for you. I can only address you—or this personality you display to me—to help you search for your answers, your memory. Even if you were to enter a residence, where your movements would presumably be monitored, that would not guarantee anything. If you do have at least one other discrete personality, and that personality is a killer, it's obvious that that personality is very crafty, and cautious. If that personality is a killer, he hides his deeds very carefully—not only from witnesses and the police, but from you; from this personality. It seems to me that there is nothing for you to do but continue doing what you have been doing."

"What you're saying is that if I . . . if the stranger is a killer, then it's up to me to unmask and catch him."

"Yes, Bone. That is what I'm saying."

Bone turned and walked out of the office, closing the door quietly behind him.

(iv)

Bette Greer Simpson sighed with contentment, weariness and relief as, after days of walking, she finally arrived home. She pulled the garbage bag containing her few belongings—including a towel, an extra set of underwear and a heavy sweater, all things she had stolen from the sanitarium—under the bench in the middle of the traffic island at the intersection of Broadway and Eighty-second Street, then sat down on the hard and worn, comfortably familiar wood.

Traffic was heavy today, and cars sped by on Broadway, on either side of her home. Then the light changed, and people began crossing, walking through her home on their way to the other side of the street. Tomorrow, Bette thought, she would confront these trespassers as she had in the past, warn them not to walk through her home. But for now she was simply too tired to get up and yell at them—and she was just happy to be back here on her traffic island, the only place in the world where she felt safe.

Once, in a time long ago that now seemed to stretch back through the years, she had felt safe in her apartment. If she turned around, Bette knew that she could look directly at the building where she had once lived, could see the windows of the small but comfortable apartment on the fifth floor which once had been hers, before her landlord had put all her belongings out on the street and placed a padlock on her door.

But looking at the building where she had once had an apartment always made Bette very sad, so she never did; she always sat on her bench in the middle of the traffic island with her back to the building. Somebody else lived in her apartment now. But at least, she thought, she had found another home, here on this bench across the street from her apartment building; she remained in the neighborhood where she had grown up and with which she was familiar; she remained close to the neighbors and shopkeepers who knew her, and who occasionally gave her food and even blankets when it became very cold. And she was usually able to keep people off her island; even though she was old, very old, she had found that people grew afraid of her when she started screaming at them, and then they were content to stay in the street as they crossed it, staying out of her home. This bench on this traffic island was the only home that remained to her, and she would defend it.

They might take her away, Bette thought, because she was too weak to fight back when the men pinned her arms to her sides and carried her away. They might put her in places where she did not feel safe, but she somehow always managed to find her way back to her home. Nobody seemed to be able to understand why she kept slipping away from places where she was given food, a bed to sleep in and medical care; they did not seem to be able to understand that this traffic island, this bench, was her *home*. She preferred to be here, even if life sometimes became difficult.

"Oh, *Bette*!" a woman's voice called from behind her. "I don't believe this! Are you *back* again?!"

Bette was happy to hear the voice; it belonged to a friend, somebody who truly cared about her. But she did not turn, for then she would have had to look at her former apartment building.

Anne walked around to the other side of the bench, squatted down in front of the old woman and took both her hands. In Anne's bright hazel eyes was a mixture of affection, frustration and pity. She brushed a strand of gray-streaked brown hair away from her eyes, shook her head and sighed.

"Aren't you going to talk to me, Bette?"

"Nothing to talk about today," Bette replied, her voice characteristically shrill, her words clipped. "Like some food, if you got it."

Anne nodded, patted Bette Greer Simpson's hands, then walked back around the bench to the blue van parked at the curb with its motor running. She took a sandwich and a carton of orange juice from Hector Gozando, the young, bespectacled, fresh-faced Hispanic who was her new partner, then returned to the old woman, gave her the food.

"Where's the heavy guy who's always with you?" Bette asked in a sullen tone as she greedily bit into the sandwich, then took a sip of juice.

Anne again squatted in front of the woman, rested one hand lightly on Bette's knee, which trembled with palsy. "Barry? He's working up in the Bronx. I have a new partner now, a very nice young man named Hector. I'm not going to introduce him to you right now, because I know you don't like strangers—and,

180

frankly, I'm afraid you'll scare him. But you'll like him a lot when you get to know him."

"Don't like nobody."

"Oh, come on, Bette. You like me. And I know how much you liked Barry; if you didn't you wouldn't have asked after him."

"Don't like nobody."

"Bette," Anne said with a deep sigh as she gently pressed the woman's trembling knee, "what on earth are you doing here? Somebody at the nursing home was supposed to bring you in to the hospital for a checkup last night. I went to the hospital to say hello, but you weren't there."

"Got away."

"You left?"

"Got away."

"Obviously. But *why*, Bette? You have no idea how long it took for Barry and me to find that nursing home for you, and how much trouble we had getting them to agree to take you for what the city could afford to pay. We thought that home was perfect for you—nice people, trees, even a lake for you to look at and walk around."

"Didn't like it. Wanted to come home. Want to stay here, and want you to leave me alone."

Anne bowed her head, took a deep breath, then looked up again into the old woman's face. "Bette, you *can't* stay here. In January you lost two toes and three fingers to frostbite. You could have died of gangrene, and you're lucky you didn't lose your left hand and your right foot; the doctors worked very hard to save them."

"This is my home. I want to stay here."

"If you'll come along in the van right now with Hector and me, maybe we can just take you back to that nursing home and all will be forgiven. Whoever was supposed to bring you to the hospital and keep an eye on you may have lost his job because you walked away."

"Wanted to come home."

"You know what's going to happen if you don't come with us. Dr. Hakim is going to come and talk to you— "

"I'll kick him and spit at him, just like I did the last time."

"—and then you're going to be taken someplace anyway, whether you like it or not. And the next place might not be anywhere near as pleasant as the nursing home you just left."

"Don't like Dr. Hakim. He makes me leave my home."

"It's because he cares about you, Bette. We all care about you." Anne paused, again took the woman's frail hands with their missing fingers in hers. "We just don't want you to suffer. But you have to cooperate with us. If you keep sneaking back here every time you get a chance, one day something may happen to you that we can't prevent. You could even be killed."

"Leave me alone!" Bette shouted, snatching her hands away from Anne's and cringing on the bench. "Get out of my home!"

Anne, recognizing the warning signals and not wanting to goad the old woman into a screaming frenzy, straightened up and took a step backward. "I'm going now, Bette. It's all right. Calm down. Maybe I'll stop by later to see how you're feeling. Okay?"

"Go away! Get out of my home!"

Anne walked around the bench, to the van, then turned back. "Bette?" she said softly, tentatively. "I don't want to upset you any more, but I would like to ask you one question. Have you seen the man who sometimes used to sit here with you and keep you calm when there were a lot of people on the streets? We called him Bone. I know you liked Bone, or you wouldn't have let him sit with you in your home."

"Don't like anyone!"

"But have you seen him?"

"Just got here, stupid woman! Go away!"

Then Bette Greer Simpson struggled to her feet, turned toward Anne and began to spit. She continued to scream and spit until the social worker climbed back into the van, and the van pulled away and disappeared into traffic.

Bette collapsed back onto the bench, exhausted. All she wanted was to be left alone, she thought. She couldn't understand why people couldn't just let her be, and why they couldn't learn to stay out of her home.

Walking all night, combined with her sudden outburst, had drained all of Bette Greer Simpson's energy; she slumped over on the bench, promptly fell asleep. She remained semiconscious, drifting in and out of deep sleep, all day long, and into the night. She was aware of many people tramping over her traffic island, but she just didn't have the energy to get up and chase them away.

And she dreamed. She dreamed of what it had been like as a little child growing up in this neighborhood, and she dreamed of how beautiful she had been as she grew into womanhood;

and then all the dreams and all the years jumbled together as she got old and sick and she couldn't pay her rent any longer and her landlord had thrown her out into the street.

Bette Greer Simpson dreamed of how her father had once picked her up in his strong arms—as he was doing now in this dream that wasn't a dream. The sudden lifting of her body caused her to open her eyes, and she saw that her cheek was nestled against someone's bright orange skin which felt rubbery against her own flesh. This was a strange dream, she thought, but she did not want to wake up; this bright orange, rubbery figure was not her father, but the strength and gentleness of the arms carrying her reminded her of him. It was a pleasant sensation, and she did not want it to end. She drifted back into deep sleep, and never felt the touch of the razor that sliced through her neck.

(v)

The black man Ali Hakim had called Zulu had not been on the sidewalk in front of St. Thomas Church when Bone had gone back after his meeting with the psychiatrist. He had not been there the next day, or the day after that.

Now Bone sat in a carrel in the main reading room of the New York Public Library on Forty-second Street poring over the various volumes on archaeology and anthropology he had, with the help of an attractive, stern but patient, young librarian, ordered up from the institution's vast subterranean stacks. He knew what he was looking for, but was not certain where to look—or even if the information he sought had been recorded.

For a year, he had walked around with a fossilized bone that was centuries old. According to Lieutenant Perry Lightning the bone was that of an American Indian, and Bone assumed it must have come from some ancient burial site, someplace underground. If he could find a recorded site somewhere near any of the areas Anne had marked on the maps, he felt he might have a better idea of precisely where to continue his search for the stranger's identity.

He gave up after three hours; there was considerable information on Indian burial sites, but they were all a considerable distance away from any of the places where the stranger had been sighted.

Next he turned to texts on what lay beneath New York City—and was amazed to find that there was, in effect, what amounted to another vast city in the darkness under the sidewalks.

Public and private utilities had provided underground facilities in New York City since the 1700s. There were literally hundreds of miles of subway tunnels, water, steam and sewer mains—some so large that two trucks could easily drive through them side by side. In the city's history there had been three separate water systems, each with its own system of drains. There were ancient aqueducts underground near the Wall Street area, where the first settlers had established themselves; there were wells, high- and low-pressure mains—some going as deep as two hundred and eighty feet below the surface, through solid rock and vast underground bogs of quicksand. There were eighty thousand miles of electric, telephone and traffic cables, gas mains, rapid-transit structures, police and fire alarm systems. Shallow excavation techniques had been used to construct some systems, deep bore tunneling for others. Beneath Grand Central Terminal, near where he had experienced his panic attack, there were seven levels, each radiating snaking railroad tunnels. Beneath the Hudson River were the Lincoln and Holland tunnels, linking New York City and New Jersey. And beneath Penn Station there were more levels, more tunnels.

He could have been in any of these places, Bone thought—or none of them. Indeed, perhaps he had simply picked the bone out of some trash can, for no logical reason whatsoever. This was, after all, New York, and he was rapidly learning that New York was a huge, bizarre city where virtually anything could happen. He was convinced now that he wouldn't find the answers he sought in books; he must continue to search the city, try to experience it the way the stranger had.

The Empire Subway Company was mentioned frequently in regard to the work they did in exploring and mapping the underground systems for the utility and construction companies. Bone made a note to himself to speak to Barry Prindle, whom Bone remembered had once worked for this company, and then he returned the books and walked out of the great stone building into the warm New York evening. He turned left, then headed down Sixth Avenue; he would go to the church across from Penn Station, where there was a soup kitchen.

Suddenly he found that he was lonely, and he picked up his pace, as if by doing so he could somehow outdistance the chasms of emotion and need that kept yawning open unexpectedly in his heart.

(vi)

Harry Boniface sat, his head lolling back and forth, in a drunken stupor at the curb on the Bowery, just above Fourth Street. He wanted to cry—and finally did; tears rolled down his cheeks, and sobs racked his body. The bottle which he had counted on to last him through the night had just tipped over and was lost somewhere in the darkness of the gutter at his feet, its precious contents spilling out into the street. He knew that without the bottle he would realize before too much longer that he hadn't eaten, and he would begin suffering hunger pangs; without the bottle he would be cold, but he had nothing else to give him warmth. There was no way they were going to allow him into the Men's Shelter, for he was drunk; he had known that when he'd started drinking early in the morning, but he hadn't cared; he'd had money, a pocketful of quarters given to him by motorists who, trapped at the red light on the corner, had tipped him for wiping—or for not wiping—their windows with the filthy rag he carried in his pocket for that purpose. He couldn't drink and expect to get into the Men's Shelter at night, but he preferred to drink. He always preferred to drink, preferred drinking to anything. He had long ago ceased to care about anything but the need to come up with money for his next bottle.

Finally Harry allowed himself to fall down off the curb, and he began crawling on his hands and knees along the gutter, searching in the trash and dirt there for the familiar feel of the bottle—and he found it at last. Still on his knees, he clutched the bottle with trembling hands and lifted it to his mouth. There was still some of the raw, cheap liquor left in the bottle, and he swallowed it thirstily. Then it was gone, and he threw the bottle away from him into the street; there was the sound of shattering, then glass shards skittering along the concrete. Harry struggled to his feet, lurched back up on the sidewalk and staggered to the south, often pausing to peer into the darkened storefronts he passed along the way; with luck, he thought, he just might find somebody who'd passed out and left a bottle nearby.

He went into the next block, stumbled into a darkened storefront—and suddenly found himself clutched by strong arms. Startled, he cried out in fear and tried to pull away, but the arms and hands held him firmly. Maybe he was hallucinating, he thought with hope born of panic and desperation; the skin that touched his didn't feel like skin at all. Whatever held him was not human.

"It's all right, Harry," a low voice said. "I've got you. You won't fall. You're safe with me."

Harry blinked, searching in his liquor-soaked mind for the memory of where he had heard that voice before. A car passed, and in the brief flash of headlights Harry saw that he was being held by a figure dressed all in shiny orange, with the same material that he had thought was skin coming up around the figure's neck and partially obscuring his face. One hand left Harry's arm, went up and pulled down the collar. Immediately, Harry recognized the face.

"Hi," Harry said, smiling self-consciously.

"You're drunk, Harry. Have you eaten anything today? I know they won't let you into the shelter."

Harry shook his head. "Maybe if you'll just lend me a couple of bucks, I'll go get myself something to eat. Now that I think of it, I am kind of hungry."

"Harry," the deep, gentle voice said with a note of resignation, "if I give you money, you'll just use it to buy more liquor. Isn't that true?"

Harry started to sway, but both of the other man's hands were once again on his shoulders, and they held him firm. The man's features were blurred, but came back into focus when Harry blinked. "How come you're dressed like that?" he said. "It ain't raining."

"You'd use the money I gave you to drink, wouldn't you, Harry?"

"Aw, come on. You've helped me out before. All I'm asking you for is a couple of bucks. I'll pay you back. I promise."

"Harry. Poor Harry. What more can people do for you? You've been given food and shelter, picked up off the street again and again and taken to the hospital where they've had to

186

pick the fleas off you. Twice you've contracted tuberculosis, and been sent away to be cured. You've been put into rehabilitation and Alcoholics Anonymous. Nothing works. Every time, the moment you get out you make a beeline for the nearest liquor store. If you won't make even the slightest effort to help yourself, how can anyone else hope to help you?"

"Tomorrow I'm going to start pulling myself together. You'll see."

"Don't you suffer? You've got scars from rat bites on you, Harry. Don't you have even a shred of dignity left?"

"I need a drink. Can you help me out?" He waited, but there was no response from the man in shiny orange. Then Harry felt anger surge within him. "Fuck you," he continued. "I don't need to hear any sermons from you about dignity. I used to be an engineer. In Cleveland. I made more money than you'll ever see. I was somebody. I had a wife, a new home and three good kids. But I liked to drink, and so I lost it all. You want me to tell you something, pal? I don't give a shit about what I lost, and I don't give a shit about clinics. I *still* like to drink, and that's *all* the fuck I like to do. So don't preach to me, pal. If you want to give me a couple of bucks so I can get a bottle, fine. If you don't, that's fine too."

Harry tried to pull away, but the rubber-gloved hands held him firm.

"Goddamn you, let me go!"

"I've decided to help you, Harry," the soft voice said with an air of resignation.

"Good," Harry replied.

But only one hand came away from his shoulders, and he never even had time to cry out as the razor came out of the darkness and bit deeply into his flesh, sinew, cartilage, arteries and veins. Three more quick slashes, expertly delivered, severed the remaining muscles and the spinal cord, and Harry Boniface's lifeless head toppled off the gushing stump of his neck and fell to the sidewalk.

CHAPTER ELEVEN

(i)

Police Detective Lieutenant Perry Lightning glanced up from the papers on his desk, raised his eyebrows slightly when he saw the two men standing just inside the doorway to his small office in the midtown precinct station house. "Well, well, well," he said quietly to the man on the left, a uniformed policeman. "You finally found him."

The uniformed policeman shook his head. "He found us. He came up to me in Times Square and asked if I'd bring him to you."

"I saw the newspaper headlines this morning," Bone said evenly to the impeccably dressed, powerfully built black man with the shaved head and milky left eye. "I figured you might want to talk to me."

"You figured right!" Perry Lightning snapped. He stared hard at Bone for a few moments, then nodded to the uniformed policeman, who turned and walked from the office, closing the door behind him. "We've been looking for you, Bone," Lightning continued in a low voice.

"You couldn't have been looking very hard."

"Where have you been?"

"On the streets, doing what I told you I was going to do. I've been trying to regain my memory."

"And have you regained your memory?"

"No—not from before the time I woke up in the park."

"We've had three more homeless people killed and beheaded in the ten days since you walked out of the Men's Shelter—two loonies and one hopeless drunk. The heads are missing, Bone. You know anything about that?"

"No. I told you I read about it in the newspapers—at least the last two. Dr. Hakim told me about the twenty-ninth victim. Like I said, I knew you'd want to talk to me."

"Why didn't you come to me after Hakim talked to you?"

"I probably should have. I knew you'd think it was me."

"The beheading killings stopped when we had you locked away, Bone. And they started again after you were released and dropped out of sight; three murders in a little more than a week. How do you explain that?"

"I can't."

"Then why are you here?"

"I told you."

"Why are you cutting out the genitals? That's a new trick."

The words struck at Bone with the force of a physical blow delivered by a fist of ice, chilling him. He felt paralyzed, transfixed by the other man's steady, accusing stare. Finally, he managed to shake his head. "I . . . didn't know that. It wasn't in the papers."

Perry Lightning sat silently for almost a full minute, staring at Bone, then nodded to a straight-backed wooden chair against the wall to the left of his desk. Bone hesitated, then sat down in the chair.

"Bone," the detective said evenly, "I'm thinking now what I thought at the beginning: you're lying. You want us to stop you—or you're playing games with us, to show your superiority. Serial killers love to do that."

"If I was playing games, why would I be so stupid as to kill three people right after I left the shelter?"

"Because you think you can get away with anything."

"I came in voluntarily. I think you're the one who's playing games; when you don't have an explanation that you believe in, you cook one up."

"Why did you sneak away from the shelter?"

"I didn't 'sneak away.' I just left—or I was thrown out. It depends on how you look at it, and who's doing the telling."

"Why?"

Bone told the detective about what had happened at the shelter, of the bribe-taking guards and the member of the Wolfpack who had tried to kill him. Lightning listened intently, his good eye gleaming with a kind of black light. When Bone had finished, he nodded his head slightly.

"So, since you left the shelter you've been walking the streets and sleeping at night in Central Park?"

"That's right."

"Why sleep in Central Park?"

"Why not? I had no place else to go."

"Where in Central Park?"

"Under a bridge, in a section they call The Ramble. I'll be happy to take you there."

Lightning studied him, made a dismissive gesture with his left hand. "If that's where you kept the heads and the murder weapon, you wouldn't very well take me there, would you?"

"I didn't kill those people, Lieutenant," Bone said with more assurance than he actually felt. His conversation with Ali Hakim still haunted him; but he had no choice but to continue to trust the stranger and defend him until he was proven wrong. And locked away.

"Anybody been sleeping under that bridge with you?"

"No."

"Anybody with you on the streets?"

"No."

"Then you don't have any witnesses to back up your story about where you've been and what you've been doing?"

"No."

"Then this conversation looks like a waste of time for both of us, doesn't it?" Lightning said, a hard edge to his voice. "If you've really got nothing to say to me, why come in?"

"Because I knew you'd want to question me. You've asked me a few questions, but mostly what you've done is accuse me."

"What good are more questions when you can't even prove where you've been and what you've been doing for the past ten days?"

"I had another reason for wanting to come and talk to you, Lieutenant."

"What's that?"

"I'd like you to help me find a kid by the name of Rafael Billingsley. They call him Lobo."

Perry Lightning's eyelids narrowed. "What do you know about Lobo?"

"He's the leader of a youth gang which calls itself the Wolfpack. The kid who came after me in the shelter was a member."

"You told me about that; you still haven't told me how you know so much about Billingsley and his Wolfpack."

"Dr. Hakim told me. Will you help me find Lobo? Will you bring him in so that I can talk to him?"

Perry Lightning folded his hands behind his head, leaned back in his chair and stared at the ceiling. "Lobo's as hard to find as you are, Bone," he said tersely. "And as tough to prove anything against."

"But will you help me look for him? Lobo could have a lot of answers we both want."

Lightning lowered his gaze, leaned forward and picked up a pencil, which he began to roll back and forth between the fingers of his right hand. "You're trying to manipulate me," he said softly.

"What?"

Suddenly the detective's eyes glinted with anger, and he snapped the pencil in two. "The killings started at the same time you surfaced in New York, pal. They stopped when we had you locked up, and they started again when you got out."

"I know that," Bone said in a flat voice.

"And now you've got the balls to ask me to cooperate with *you* and go chasing after Lobo just so you can talk to him. I think you're trying to make a fool out of me."

"No, Lieutenant."

"If you were me, what would you think?"

"I'd think that my prime suspect should at least get some points for coming in voluntarily to talk about it. And I'd think that it couldn't hurt to pick up this Lobo and see what he might have to say about my prime suspect; Lobo might even give you a clue as to where to look for evidence. If I were you, I'd pick him up—for my own reasons, not the suspect's."

"I fully intend to do that, Bone. But it *still* occurs to me that my prime suspect may be trying to make fools out of the police;

I told you that's partly how serial killers get their jollies—until they get caught. We'll get you eventually."

"If I were you," Bone said quietly, "I think I'd also not want to make a fool out of myself; that can be worse than having somebody else make a fool out of you."

Perry Lightning flushed. "Get out of here. Stop wasting my time."

"I'd like to say something else, Lieutenant. I had one more reason for coming in."

"Bullshit."

"Will you listen?"

"If it's fast."

"Suppose I'm telling the truth, Lieutenant?"

"That's it, pal. Now you just—"

"I grant you that it's a very large and damning coincidence that these beheading murders began with my appearance in New York, and have continued since I've been free," Bone said quickly. "So, even if I'm *not* the killer, the murders could have something to *do* with me."

Lightning, who had started to rise to his feet, slowly sank back down in his chair. "A most interesting thought on your part," he said in a low voice still heavily laced with suspicion. "Go on."

"One of two things is true," Bone said, suddenly feeling slightly light-headed and short of breath, for the first time voicing the idea that had begun to grow in his mind shortly after his last conversation with Ali Hakim. "Either I'm the killer—knowingly or unknowingly—or I'm not. Grant me again, as you once did, that I'm telling the truth when I say that I can't *remember* killing anyone, and I'll grant you the possibility, as I always have, that it's possible, considering my head injury and history of bizarre behavior, that I could still be murdering those people and not even be aware of it; Dr. Hakim and I have considered that possibility from the beginning."

"It's more than a possibility, Bone," the detective said wearily. "You're the killer. The timing of the killings is just too much of a coincidence."

"But that's what I'm trying to get at. What if I'm not the killer, and the timing of the killings is *not* a coincidence?"

Perry Lightning slowly blinked. "What?"

"The killings began around the time I showed up in New

192

York, walking the streets and carrying a human femur; they stopped when I was hospitalized, and there have been three in the ten days since I left the shelter."

"You sound like your own prosecutor," Lightning said in a flat voice.

"I'm only stating the obvious—what's known, and what makes you absolutely convinced that I'm the killer, consciously or unconsciously. I'm saying that it's possible for the killings somehow to be linked to me, even if I'm not the killer—which I don't believe I am."

"How?"

"I don't know, Lieutenant," Bone said, feeling the frustration grow in him. "Maybe it's something connected to the year I spent on the streets; maybe there's a connection to my past— where I was or what I was doing in the years before I ended up on the streets. It's just a thought that occurred to me; even if I'm not the killer, I could somehow be the key to the killings."

Lightning ran the palm of his right hand back over his shaved head. "That's crazy, Bone."

"I didn't kill those people, Lieutenant. Even if I had some other personality that took over at night, it still means I'd be wandering around at all hours covered from head to toe with blood. So then I'd have to tidy myself up and hide everything in order to keep the truth from *this* personality. At the very least I'd be damn *tired* when I woke up in the morning—and I'm not. I slept well last night, and I sleep well most nights."

"In Central Park, under a bridge?"

"Yes."

"Eating garbage?"

"Everything that's thrown away isn't garbage, Lieutenant."

"If you'd stayed at the shelter, or checked into some residence like those HRA people wanted you to, we'd all have a hell of a lot clearer picture of what you've been doing—day and night."

"I've never been in a shelter before, Lieutenant; I'm sure of that. If I'm ever going to regain my memory, I have to live and keep doing things in the context of how I was living and what I was doing during that lost year. That's the only way I have of finding out who and what I was before."

"What if you never regain your memory?"

"Will you pick up Lobo and arrange a meeting between the two of us?"

"I'll give it some thought. But I'll tell you right now that Lobo won't tell you anything—especially after we pick him up. And if he and his buddies are after you, you're in trouble."

"You won't do it?"

"I said I'd give it some thought. Why won't you let the HRA people help you? Maybe you just have to start all over building a new life. Why don't you give *that* some thought?"

"Am I free to go?"

Lieutenant Perry Lightning nodded curtly, and Bone rose and walked from the office.

(ii)

"Bone!"

It was a voice Bone hadn't been sure he would ever hear again. He looked up from the map he'd been studying, turned toward the street as Anne, her face flushed, stepped out of one of the blue Project Helping Hand vans, then slammed the door shut behind her. Her hazel eyes flashed with anger as she stepped up on the curb, strode quickly up to him and stopped, her hands on her hips.

He had not fully realized how very badly he missed this strong yet vulnerable woman until now, with her standing before him, obviously angry, and just as obviously deeply hurt.

"Hello, Anne," he said quietly, feeling very vulnerable himself, foolish and slightly ashamed.

"You've got a hell of a lot of nerve!" Anne snapped, her voice even huskier than usual. "You walk out of the Men's Shelter in the middle of the goddamn night without telling a soul, you walk around for better than a week, and it's the *police* you go to see! You go to see Ali, but you don't even bother calling me to say you're all right! Do you have any idea how many hours I've spent driving around looking for you?"

"I'm sorry," Bone said in the same soft voice. "I just wasn't sure—"

"Oh, you're *sorry*. Well, I'm really glad you're *sorry*. I suppose I should be grateful for that." She sighed deeply, let her hands drop to her sides. The anger had drained out of her face and voice, leaving only a residue of pain. "Christ, do I sound like a bitch," she continued in a voice so low Bone could hardly hear her. "Worse, I sound like Barry. I had no right to talk to you like

194

that; I'm not your mother. I just thought maybe . . . I gave you my card, Bone."

"I still have it."

"Why . . . ?" Anne's upper lip with its pronounced cleft had begun to tremble slightly. She bit it, tossed her hair back, then stood up very straight, spoke in an even tone. "Why couldn't you at least have called to let me know you were all right? Didn't you think I'd be worried?"

"Yes. I was afraid."

Anne frowned slightly, cocked her head to one side. "Afraid of what?"

"Of you, Anne. I feel too much for you, and I don't know what to do with that feeling; not only does it distract me, but until I find out more about just *who* it is that's feeling these things, I'm not sure I have the right . . . " He let his voice trail off, looked away and shrugged. Suddenly he had a lump in his throat, and he swallowed hard. "It wasn't that I didn't want to call you, Anne; I didn't call because I felt I wanted to too much. It was thoughtless of me, and I apologize."

He waited, but there was no reply. When he looked back at Anne, he was startled to find her grinning, her hazel eyes very bright.

"All *right*!" Anne said, and thumped him playfully on the chest with both her fists. "Now we're getting somewhere!"

Bone smiled back. "Uh . . . did I manage to say the right thing?"

"You said the perfect thing; your head may be all screwed up, but your tongue works just fine. How about lunch? I'll spring for hot dogs."

Without waiting for a reply, Anne walked back to the van and spoke to the young man behind the wheel. The man nodded, and then drove away. Anne took Bone's hand, led him across Broadway to the corner where a Sabrett vendor was selling hot dogs from his cart."

"I haven't forgotten the money I owe you," Bone said.

"It never occurred to me that you had. How do you like your hot dogs?"

"With everything."

Anne bought two hot dogs for Bone, one for herself and two Cokes. Then they walked back to the traffic island in the center of Times Square, where people were lining up at the TKTS booth waiting for theater tickets for the evening's perfor-mances. They sat down on a bench, started eating.

"This is pretty rich fare for me," Bone said, picking a strand of sauerkraut off his lower lip. "I was just getting ready to head for a soup kitchen."

"Jesus Christ," Anne said around a mouthful of hot dog. She swallowed, took a sip of her Coke. "You are stubborn."

"There's another reason I didn't call you," Bone said seri-ously. "It's still not proven that I'm not the serial killer. Until I find out the truth about myself, I don't feel I have the right to . . . involve myself too much with other people."

"Bullshit," Anne said easily. "You're no killer. Even that police lieutenant doesn't believe it."

"You're wrong about that, Anne; he believes it."

Anne shrugged. "He touched base with me a few times after you walked out of the shelter; he wanted to know if I'd heard from you. I know he likes and respects you—and that bothers him. Hell, it's hard not to like and respect you." She paused, looked at him and grinned once again. "I know all about that."

"Even if I'm not the killer, Anne, the murders could somehow have something to do with me; they occur when I'm on the streets."

Anne's grin faded, and she shook her head slightly. "Strange; I'd never thought about it in that way. I just didn't believe you were the killer. But *how* could they be connected to you?"

"I don't know. If—when—I get my memory back, maybe I'll have the answer."

They finished their hot dogs and soda. Bone took their papers to a trash can, then came back to the bench and again sat down beside Anne.

"That wasn't Barry driving the van," Bone continued care-fully. "Is Barry sick?"

"No. He's working with another unit up in the Bronx. That's my new partner—a very nice young man by the name of Hector. I should have introduced you, but I had other things on my mind." She paused, then reached out and gripped Bone's hand. "I didn't know how much yelling and screaming I was going to have to do before you realized that all the very nice chemistry going on between us is a very rare and very wonder-ful thing—especially in this city. Bone, I'm just too old, and I've experienced and seen too much misery, to be coy. I like you enormously. In fact, I'm probably in love with you—and that's that. When you live as close to death and suffering as I—as we—do every day, it tends to make you want to cut out all the bullshit in personal relationships."

Bone looked into the woman's hazel eyes, smiled. "You're very direct."

"Yep. Bother you?"

"No. You've known all along how I felt, haven't you?"

"Yes. And I was pretty sure I understood your reasons for not contacting me. But I was still pissed."

Bone squeezed Anne's hand. "Thank you."

"Thank *you*."

Bone lowered his gaze. "The fact that you're not working with Barry any longer has something to do with me, doesn't it?"

"Not really. Considering the circumstances, it was probably inevitable that Barry and I wouldn't be able to work together much longer. Barry has a wonderful heart when it comes to humanity as a whole, but he doesn't know much about women; I don't think he's had much experience with them. Maybe it was all the years he spent preparing for the priesthood. Anyway, he seems perfectly content now with his new assignment. We talk on the telephone, and he sounds just fine. Actually, I think he's kind of secretly relieved to be away from me."

"Next time you talk to him, tell him I said hello."

"I will. Now I think it's time you told me what you've been up to." She paused, frowned slightly. "Are you making any progress?"

Bone shrugged. "Some. I think."

"You're remembering?"

"I'm feeling things."

"Why did you walk out of the shelter in the middle of the night?"

"Actually, I didn't exactly walk out; I was thrown out. But I was ready to leave anyway. The city has some very nasty and corrupt people working in its shelters. I—" He stopped speaking when Anne put her hand over his mouth.

"It's going to take you some time to tell me about it," Anne said quietly, "and I want to hear everything. But not here."

"Where?"

In response, Anne rose from the bench, stepped to the curb and raised her hand to signal for a taxi.

(iii)

The moment they reached Anne's apartment they flowed over and into each other's body, like two streams drawn together by the gravity of passion to form a surging river of longing and need. They stripped off their clothes and left them in piles on the floor, clung to each other, lips, tongues and hands already exploring the flesh of the other as they fell onto the bed, kissing, stroking, exploring. When Anne finally rolled over on her back, spread her legs and drew back her knees and guided him into her warm, passion-slick center, Bone felt he must come immediately. But he did not. He did not want to ejaculate—not yet; not for a long time. Not only did he want to totally satisfy Anne, but he enjoyed teetering on the cliff edge of passion, and wanted this exquisitely painful feeling of explosive fullness just before orgasm to last indefinitely. He found he could control this tide in him by stopping movement just before the beginning of an ejaculation spasm and pressing down on Anne's body, holding her buttocks to prevent her from moving.

"Come, come, come," Anne murmured in a kind of incantatory chant. "I want to feel it."

Then, very slowly, he would begin to move again, once more riding the wave of his passion just below its foaming crest. With Anne's slender yet strong legs wrapped around his waist and with his member deep inside her, he would press forward and knead her soft breasts, cup them as he licked and kissed her firm nipples with their large, dark brown aureolas. Then he would kiss her lips, probe her eager, open mouth with his tongue as Anne fought back against his weight, matching his passion with her own, writhing under him, thrusting up her hips to meet his.

He rose higher on the wave, closer to the crest . . .

"I want you to come now," Anne gasped, locking her knees against his ribs, reaching around and under him to cup his testicles with her left hand. "I know you're holding back. I started coming in the taxi on the way over here, so you don't have to worry about me. Come in me, Bone. Then we can start all over again."

And finally he did, bursting with an orgasm that made his

198

whole body shudder, carrying out of his body with his semen his tension, loneliness, fear, so much weight . . . During the course of this new life it was the first time he had been free of tension, loneliness and anxiety, the first time he had felt happy, and for a moment he thought he would begin to cry. Instead he collapsed into Anne's arms, reveling in the sensation of Anne's vaginal lips spasmodically contracting around his penis, the warm slick of juices from both their bodies on his thighs and belly.

After a few minutes he sighed deeply, rolled off. Then he wrapped his arms around Anne's sweat-smooth body, buried his face in her thick brown hair, rested his lips against the musky-smelling flesh of her neck.

"My *God*," Anne gasped, letting her right hand fall with a hard slap across his firm buttocks. "I think it's absolutely safe to say that you've done this kind of thing before, and your stranger does it exceptionally well. You're *incredible*."

"Yeah," Bone murmured, his lips trembling against Anne's neck, hot tears welling from his eyes to mix with her sweat.

"Bone," Anne said softly, "you're crying."

"Yeah. It seems so, doesn't it?"

Anne gently but firmly turned his head so that she could see into his face. Tears continued to well in Bone's deep blue eyes; they rolled down his cheeks, dripped off his chin. Through the mist of his tears, Bone gazed back at her.

"Are you all right, Bone?"

"Oh, yeah," he said, stroking the back of Anne's hand as she gently wiped at his tears. "I don't know why I'm crying, Anne. I just feel . . . very full; so full that it pushes out tears."

"Your stranger was very lonely," Anne whispered as she kissed both his cheeks. "He had to be. Your stranger is an incredibly strong man."

Bone kissed Anne's cheeks, her lips, her hands, then held her close to him. "I knew I was lonely," he whispered in her ear. "I guess I just didn't realize how lonely. Thank you for filling me up, for giving me you."

"Everybody needs somebody, Bone. And you . . . I can't understand where you found the strength to hold yourself together as long as you did."

"Yeah," Bone said, and laughed. "We can both see how strong I am right now; I'm crying like a baby."

"I'm not sure the rest of us can even begin to guess at the

terror you must have felt when you woke up in that field, in the rain and mud, and didn't know the first thing about who you were, where you came from or what you'd been doing. Then you were accused of being a killer, and locked away. You've been living on the streets, sleeping only God knows where and eating only God knows what. I know something of what you've seen and experienced, Bone. Is it any wonder that you might just feel a little needy?"

"I can't afford to be weak, Anne. Not now. If I am, I could end up just another one of those broken people out on the streets."

"I don't believe you could ever end up just a broken person on the streets."

"That's what I was."

"No." Anne paused, gently stroked his cheek, then continued in a voice just above a whisper: "Do you believe I've weakened you, Bone?"

He rolled over to face her. His eyes were dry now, his voice firm. "No. You'd made me feel stronger. I told you; you've filled me."

"Good," Anne said, and smiled. "And now that we've taken care of the most important business, at least for the time being, you can tell me what you've been up to."

He did, beginning from the time he had left the van to enter the Men's Shelter, his odyssey to Central Park, his still-fruitless search for his identity and the two men who might provide information that could help him find it—Zulu and Lobo.

Through it all, Anne had listened in silence, but with a growing sense of both wonder and unease. Now she leaned her head on Bone's chest, stroked his heavily muscled thighs.

"I don't know what could have happened to Zulu," she said, and shook her head slightly. "He's at St. Thomas nearly every day, rain or shine—at least in the morning. I hope he's not sick. As far as Lobo is concerned, you have to stay away from him. He'll kill you."

"He probably thinks he has good reason; it seems I put his eye out. But I still have to find him."

"You need a safe place to stay, and a base of operations. You'll stay here, with me."

Bone laughed. "Barry was right; you spend too much time on me. You're going to get yourself fired."

Anne didn't smile. "I spent a year on you, Bone-man. I got you back, and I find that I like you very, very much. Living in this city teaches you that you really have no time to play around; life goes by too fast, and it can end in the blink of an eye. I want you staying with me because I enjoy having you around—but also because I'm not about to let you get yourself killed before we find out who you really are. Do you need money?"

"I need a job."

"I'll work on that. Will you accept my offer to put you up?"

"No," Bone replied evenly. He bent over to kiss Anne, but she pulled away.

"Why not?"

"Because it might be dangerous for you."

"Lobo isn't going to find out that you're here, and he wouldn't come around here even if he did. He's a street punk. And I'm a big girl who doesn't really care what people think or say."

"It isn't Lobo I'm worried about."

"Then who, or what?"

Bone did not reply.

"You?" Anne continued. "I thought we were both agreed that you're not the killer."

"Dr. Hakim says it's possible that I have a multiple personality, maybe as a result of my head injury; it's possible that there are times when I become someone else without being aware of it."

"Ali *believes* that?"

"He says it's possible. That's enough. Until I can find all the answers I need, I have to stay alone."

Anne's response was to grasp both his hands. She gently kneaded the backs and palms, then the crooked, gnarled fingers. "You still have no memory of what you did to your hands?"

"I have no real memory of anything—only impressions, sensations."

"But nothing about your hands?"

"No. Maybe I was a manual laborer or machinist and had an accident."

"You didn't get these hands by doing manual labor; an accident, maybe."

"Why not manual labor?"

"You've got small scars all over your body. I'm no expert, but some of them look older than others."

Bone's only response was a shrug; he had found that it was useless to try to force memories. He would need to recapture the experience before he could recapture the memory, somehow relive pieces of his past before he would remember it.

"You are going to stay with me, of course," Anne continued.

Bone raised his eyebrows slightly. "I thought we'd been over that."

"No; you just thought we had. I know this dreadful and magnificent city as well as anybody—and a hell of a lot better than most. I have a relationship with Zulu—not a good one, but at least he knows and trusts me. He might not even talk to you; with Zulu, you never know. I know you're not a killer, and *you* know you're not a killer. There's just no reason for you to eat in soup kitchens and sleep in Central Park anymore; you've *had* that experience, and there's nothing more to be gained from doing those things. Hey, Bone, I like you a lot, but I'm not asking you to marry me. We'll work *together*, when I'm off duty, on helping you to get your memory back. I'll help you find a job. Then, when you do get your memory back, you can do what you want. I'm doing what *I* want. I say you're going to accept my offer because you're no fool. It's time to take the pressure off yourself, and I say you'll make more progress now if you have a safe, warm and dry base of operations to work out of. I'll bet Ali would agree with me. He's your shrink; check with him to see what he thinks."

She had already weakened him, Bone thought. She had filled him up, brought him in from the cold—and now he didn't want to go back. At least not all the time. Anne was right about the experience; he had found that the stranger was comfortable and could take care of himself out-of-doors. But the stranger had not lived in Central Park; he was sure of that now too.

"All right," he said at last. "Thank you, Anne."

"You're welcome, you silly man. Don't you know how much pleasure this gives me? Now I don't have to be constantly distracted wondering if you're all right."

"I do need a job so I can pay you back, and so I can pay my way." He did not add that he was becoming increasingly discouraged at the slowness of his progress, the realization that it might indeed be a very long time before he recovered his memory. And he might not recover it at all.

"I'll see what's around when I go in to work tomorrow. I have good contacts."

"I have to get my stuff," Bone said, starting to rise from the bed. "It's the femur I really need; I still believe that's the key to what happened to me."

Ann reached out, gently but firmly pulled him back onto the bed. "That'll wait; after all, it's not going to walk away by itself, and you said your camp is well hidden. Later, we'll both get dressed and go get it. In the meantime, I'm using up half a vacation day, so I think there's something else we should take care of first."

"What's that?"

"This," Anne said, and reached between his thighs. Then she bent forward.

(iv)

With Anne beside him, Bone stood at the side of the stream, beneath the bridge, and stared at the area that had been his campsite. The brush mats he had so carefully woven had been torn away from the depression in the ground where he had slept, and the garbage bag containing his belongings was gone.

"Oh, Bone," Anne said softly, "I'm sorry."

Bone said nothing. He was filled with a very strong sense of foreboding that was completely out of proportion to the value of the things he had lost. Only the femur meant anything to him, and that value lay in the fact that it was the only physical link he had to the year he had spent on the streets. But its loss was not what made him uneasy.

"Did anyone else know you were here?" Anne continued.

"No."

"Then who . . . ?"

"Maybe the lieutenant is playing games with me," Bone said, not really believing it. "I told him the general location where I'd been sleeping, and he didn't seem particularly interested. Maybe he changed his mind."

"If he wanted to examine your belongings, wouldn't he have come here with you?"

"I believe so."

"Then it must have been someone else, just somebody who was passing by and saw you come down here under the bridge. The person waited until you left, then came down and found your belongings." Anne paused, looked into his worried face, tugged at his sleeve. "Come on, Bone. The clothes and other things can easily be replaced, and you can pay me back from the job I'm going to find for you. It's not important. From what you tell me, even the femur wasn't helping you all that much."

"No, it wasn't," Bone replied distantly as he took Anne's hand and climbed back up the bank. His sense of foreboding was growing even stronger.

CHAPTER TWELVE

(i)

Dr. Ali Hakim, absorbed in the task of laying out and organizing the battery of psychological tests he planned to administer to Bone that morning, started and looked up when he heard the door to his empty outer office open and close. He glanced at his watch; it was nine-forty, twenty minutes before Bone was scheduled to arrive, and he knew Bone to be punctual. Ali could not imagine who else would be coming to his office on a Sunday morning.

The mystery was solved a few moments later when the door to his inner office opened and Barry Prindle, carrying a large blue nylon duffel bag, stepped through. Ali, who had not seen the other man in weeks, was shocked by the social worker's appearance, and he could see that Barry was deeply troubled. The burly young man appeared to have lost a considerable amount of weight, and the tendons in his neck stood out like wire cables. His face, normally full and ruddy, was now gaunt, and his bright green eyes seemed oddly blank. Barry, walking stiffly, came across the office and stopped in front of the desk, dropping the duffel bag to the floor, out of Ali's sight.

"Good morning, Dr. Hakim," Barry said in a hollow voice.

"Good morning, Barry," Ali replied, frowning slightly. "How can I help you?"

"I need to talk to you."

"How did you know I'd be here this morning?"

"Anne told me. We talk on the phone a lot, and she told me you meet with Bone at ten o'clock on Sunday mornings."

"She shouldn't have told you that, Barry," Ali said quietly in his lilting voice. "It was not her place. Who I meet with, and when, is confidential. You, of all people, should be able to appreciate that."

"I don't think you should be angry with her, Doctor. She was just trying to be friendly to me. Since I was one of the people who picked Bone up, I think she just wanted to keep me up to date on what was happening with him. Is he making progress?"

Ali said nothing, but he continued to study the face of the other man. He did not like what he saw.

"Did you know that Anne has taken that man in to live with her?" Barry said in the same hollow voice as he sat stiffly in a leather-padded chair, pulled it up close to the desk.

"I wasn't aware of that," Ali replied carefully, resisting the impulse to push back in his own chair. "And I'm not sure it's anyone's business. Do you think so?"

"Yesterday, she found him a job. He'll be working in the stockroom of Bloomingdale's. They drive around a lot, looking at places where he's been. And then they go home and fuck all night. I wonder how that feels." Barry blinked slowly, shuddered slightly, and then his green eyes came into clear focus on Ali, who clearly saw the madness there. Barry laughed softly, continued: "It sure as hell beats sleeping under a bridge in Central Park, doesn't it?"

Ali raised his eyebrows slightly. "How do you know where Bone has been sleeping?"

"I knew he was walking around midtown, trying to find someplace he could remember. I took a couple of days off, walked around until I spotted him, then followed him. I made sure he didn't see me."

"Why did you do that, Barry?" Ali asked softly.

"I'm sick and tired of having things taken away from me, Doctor. God's not playing fair with me, so I don't see why I have to play fair any longer."

"Barry, has Dr. Potter prescribed medication for you, as I did?"

"I don't take it. If God played fair with me, I wouldn't need medication."

Ali smiled easily as he slowly reached out for the telephone at the edge of his glass-topped desk. "Barry," he said evenly, "I'm going to call Dr. Potter right now. I know she'll want to talk to you, and I think you'll feel a lot better after you talk to her. You look very tired and stressed. I wouldn't be surprised if she recommended that you take some time off and go into a hospital."

Almost casually, Barry reached out and snatched away the telephone, ripping the cord from its base, then tossed the phone across the office. The muscles in his jaw and neck writhed, but his voice was soft. "If I wanted to talk to Dr. Potter, I'd have gone to see her, Dr. Hakim, not you. You were the one who was supposed to take care of me in the first place."

Ali, his heart beating rapidly, forced himself to slowly lean back in his chair, casually cross his legs and fold his hands in his lap. He knew it was important that he appear relaxed, but in fact he was afraid. Very afraid. He did not dare to glance at his watch, but he estimated that he had perhaps fifteen minutes before Bone arrived.

He had to keep the other man talking.

"It's true, as you know, that I sometimes see troubled city workers on a volunteer basis, Barry," Ali said quietly, still smiling. "That's how you first came to me last year. But after our second session together, I recognized that you were going to need far more extensive treatment than I was in a position to provide. Dr. Potter is a fine psychiatrist, and I knew that she could do far more for you than I ever could. My turning you over to Dr. Potter was not a rejection, Barry, but an attempt to get you the best treatment. Your unresolved homosexuality is a most difficult condition to—"

"Don't say that!" Barry shouted, his face turning scarlet as he abruptly leaned forward in his chair. "I'm not a homosexual! I want *Anne*! If Bone hadn't taken her away from me, you'd know I wasn't a homosexual!"

"Perhaps a poor choice of words on my part, Barry," Ali said softly. "But it was your unresolved desires, and the commission of at least one homosexual act, that got you thrown out of the seminary, wasn't it? Sooner or later, you're going to have to deal with that fact, and resolve the conflict in your own mind. I'm sure Dr. Potter has suggested the same thing."

Barry Prindle's response was to bend down toward the floor,

and Ali heard the nylon duffel bag being unzipped. The gaunt, wild-eyed social worker drew out a gold-ornamented, purple priest's chasuble. He took off his light outer jacket, donned the chasuble. Next came a heavy gold cross on a chain. Barry kissed the cross, then draped it around his neck.

"Jesus was a homosexual," Barry said with a kind of a sigh as he leaned forward on the heavy glass top of the desk. "Did you know that, Dr. Hakim?"

A few more minutes, Ali thought. Perhaps Bone might be early. "I'm familiar with that speculation, Barry. Is that something you'd like to talk—?"

"But I'm not!" Barry snapped. "God told me to do those things precisely because He wanted me to be cast out of the regular channels to the priesthood! He planted those yearnings in my heart so that I would understand what it meant to feel compassion for *all*, men and women equally, as Jesus did. I didn't understand that at the time. I was devastated that I would want to make love to a man. Then, a year ago, I came to understand how God had been using me for His own purpose; He had another mission for me, and it was for this mission that He ordained me personally. I was to be His instrument here in this wretched city, and I was to minister solely to the most wretched of His children."

Ali took a deep breath, trying to relax and project a semblance of calm. "And you've done just a marvelous job, Barry," he said, smiling broadly. "In my opinion, you're as fine a social worker as this city has. You've shown endless patience with the homeless, which is a most difficult group to work with. I wish I had your patience. Perhaps you have so much compassion because you've suffered so much yourself. It's something you might want to discuss with Dr. Potter. Are you sure you don't want me to call her? I have another phone in the outer office."

Ten more minutes. Maybe five. A distraction might at least allow him to get out from behind the desk and run from the room. He had come face-to-face with Bone's nightmares.

Next, Barry withdrew from the duffel bag a large rain hat with a floppy brim, ear flaps and chin strap. He put on the hat, drew it down tightly over his forehead. "You don't understand, Dr. Hakim," he said in a low voice. "You never did."

"I don't understand why you killed all those people, Barry. Would you like to tell me?"

Barry took out a large, lined raincoat made of the same bright orange oilcloth as the hat, put that on over his purple priest's vestments, began to button it up. "I've been sending those people home to God," he said in the same low voice. "They were of no use to either God or themselves here on earth. They had lost the capacity to care for themselves, and they refused to let others help them. It was time for them to die and go on to their reward. They were suffering, and God wished for me to demonstrate to them His infinite compassion. He told me to send the most wretched on to Him. I have been performing acts of great mercy."

"What does Bone have to do with all of this, Barry?"

"Nothing," the other man replied curtly as he pulled up the collar of his raincoat. "I am God's messenger, not Bone."

"But—"

"Bone knows. Or he did know."

Ali swallowed hard; his mouth tasted of copper. "Bone knows what? Does he know that you're the one who's been killing those people?"

Barry Prindle slowly nodded. "He'll know—if he gets his memory back. But that won't happen until God wills it."

"How does Bone know that you're . . . that you've been committing these acts of mercy, Barry? What happened to Bone?"

"It's not important."

Ali shook his head slightly. Somewhat to his astonishment, he discovered that his fascination with the other man's murderous pathology was slowly overtaking, outweighing, his fear. "But you were around him for weeks. Obviously, he poses a threat to you. Why haven't you killed him?"

"He's never posed a threat to me. God took away his memory precisely so he wouldn't be a threat to me, the same as He spared Bone's life because Bone was not mine to send home to Him. That was fair, and I understood what God was doing. Now I don't. That's why I'm not playing fair. That's why I'm killing Bone now."

"Barry, you have to make it clearer for me if you want me to understand."

"It's not necessary that you understand, Doctor—but I will try to make it clearer. Bone should have died a year ago, when we first met. But he didn't. Believe me when I say that it is a miracle that he's alive. When I first saw him on the streets, I understood that he was alive because God had not meant for me to kill him. And when I realized that he had lost his memory and was mute, I understood that God had forgiven me for what I'd tried to do to Bone, and that He wished for me to continue my ministry. That day in the park, when Bone awakened, I thought it meant that God wanted my ministry to end. I was ready to accept that. If Bone had recognized me and remembered, I was ready to find a way to kill myself and go on to my own reward. But Bone didn't recognize me, and he didn't remember. The message was clear to me—at least, I thought it was. But then I quickly learned that God was using Bone to torment and humiliate me. Or so it seemed. I couldn't understand why God would play tricks on me—unless He expects me to fight for what is mine, and unless He doesn't expect me to play fair any longer. That's what I now believe."

"Anne," Ali said in a voice just above a whisper.

Barry nodded. "I've been in love with Anne from the first time I met her. To love a *woman* had been the most joyous, wonderful feeling I'd ever had in my life. I've never been in love before, you know."

"I know, Barry."

"Up to that point, all of my sexual attractions had been for men."

"I know that too."

"But that wasn't right; I knew that. Homosexuality is a mortal sin. But when Anne came into my life, I saw that she was going to make everything all right for me. Anne was going to be my reward for faithful service; I'd been forgiven for what I did to Bone, and was to continue my mission. For the first time in my life, *my* suffering was going to be alleviated; God had sent me a woman to love, and to be loved by. And Anne did love me—before."

Ali watched in horrified fascination as the other man withdrew a pair of orange rubber gloves, slipped them on. "Life doesn't work that way, Barry," he said in a voice that cracked. "Because you love somebody doesn't mean that she has to love you. You just have to keep searching for somebody who can love you in return."

Barry shook his head angrily. "Anne is right for me. But God is testing me! He's challenging me by holding out the promise of a reward, then seeming to punish me for the accident with Bone by having Bone take my reward from me. It's like the testing of Job! The difference is that I'm to fight back in order to prove I'm manly enough for Anne!"

"But why kill me, Barry?" Ali said softly, slowly raising his

210

hands with the palms upward. "Or isn't that what you plan to do? Are you waiting for Bone to arrive so that you can kill him?"

"I'm sorry, Doctor," Barry said curtly as he pulled back a sleeve of his oilcloth raincoat to glance at his watch, then once more reached down into his bag. "I'm afraid there's no more time to talk."

(ii)

At three minutes past ten Bone entered Ali Hakim's outer office, knocked on the closed door of the inner office. He waited, knocked again, then opened the door and stepped in. Instantly he was assailed by the hideous sight of carnage, the fetid odor of death. He gagged and was almost sick. He swallowed bile, forced himself to look even as his mind raced and he tried desperately to absorb and somehow go beyond the horror, to think.

Ali Hakim's decapitated body was slumped over his desk, and blood, pooling and pebbling on the glass surface, still oozed from a stump that was a horrid pallet of severed flesh, dangling ivory-colored pieces of tendon, the cable-like end of the vertebrae. Directly overhead, blood dripped from the ceiling where it had spurted; blood, as if shot from a spray can, was splattered over the wall to Bone's left, and over the windows directly behind the desk, as well as over a half-open door a few feet to the right of the desk.

Suddenly Bone became very conscious of the fact that he was standing just inside the entrance, and that the killer could be inches away from him, on the other side of the half-open door. Another shudder passed through him, and then he suddenly threw his weight against the door, slamming it back against the wall. There was nobody there.

Still feeling stunned and short of breath, Bone slowly walked into the office, approached the desk. On the glass surface, next to the bloody torso of the dead neuropsychiatrist, were a bloody pair of rubber gloves and blood-spattered rain gear, hat and coat, all of brilliant orange oilcloth.

The orange and crimson of his dreams.

On the floor in front of the desk was a large blue nylon duffel bag stained dark with blood. Using the toe of his shoe, Bone

211

spread open the unzipped top; inside were Ali Hakim's head, along with Bone's hunting knife, his razor and the ossified human femur.

Bone walked quickly to the door to the right of the desk and peered through the crack between the door and the jamb; the doorway led out into a small vestibule with a private elevator and emergency fire stairs. There was nobody there. He turned back to again survey the carnage inside the office, trying to marshal his cascading thoughts, slow down his racing heartbeat and decide what to do.

The stranger was definitely not the killer, Bone thought. That was now certain, and this, at least, offered him a sense of relief which was as profound as it was short-lived.

He knew now that he had been right when he'd speculated that the killings and the killer were somehow connected to him; the orange-and-red-clad demon-figure that had chased him through his flickering, candlelit nightmares was the murderer. He had met him—somehow, somewhere.

Perhaps underground.

But why was Ali Hakim dead? he wondered. The psychiatrist was certainly not homeless, and this made him radically different from the other victims of the serial killer, an anomaly in death. One of the doctor's patients? Bone considered the idea, then rejected it. The psychiatrist had made it clear to him that he preferred research to people, and had no real private practice. Yet the presence of his personal items in the bag made it clear to Bone that the killer had been following him, had stolen the items from his campsite in the park and had left them here in an attempt to frame him. But it made no sense to him for the murderer to kill Dr. Ali Hakim. If the man was his enemy, if he feared discovery, then why hadn't *he* been the victim?

But he was to be the victim, Bone thought when he suddenly heard the sound of police sirens approaching from at least three different directions. The ultimate victim. Ali Hakim, it seemed, was to be the last person beheaded, and he was set up now to take the blame for all the murders. There wasn't even time to call the police, for the killer had already done that for him. He was to be caught inside the building, or trying to somehow hide the damning evidence inside the duffel bag, or trying to run away.

Now Lieutenant Lightning would have the "proof" for which

he had been so diligently searching. Nobody could now possibly believe that he was innocent—not even Anne. He would be executed, or locked away for many years—perhaps for the rest of his life. And he would never find out who he really was. He had to run.

And then Bone had a thought which made him nauseated and light-headed and caused his heart to hammer even faster. If he managed to escape, Ali Hakim might not be the last victim; if he was free, the murderer would be able to continue slaughtering helpless people, secure in the knowledge that Bone would be blamed. If he ran, he might be condemning an unknown number of innocent people to death.

But if he did not run, Bone thought, the innocent stranger would never be free again; he would remain locked away in two prisons, one of concrete and steel and the other of his mind, until he died. The stranger did not deserve that—and the only way to clear the stranger was to find the killer himself; he had to run, return to the streets.

Besides, he thought, just because the killer apparently intended to stop after framing him for the murders did not mean that the killer might not start killing again at some time— perhaps years—in the future; if he did *not* run, it could mean the future murders of innocent people. He had to find the killer, and he could not do that behind bars; imprisoned, he was certain he would never recover his memory.

He would not even try to hide the duffel bag, Bone thought. There was no time. Trying to do so would only slow him down, and to be caught with it in his possession would only be more damning—if that were possible. Also, he realized that it was improbable that he could leave the building undetected, since by the time he got to the ground level the police would have all the exits covered.

So he would have to leave from another building. Even the precious femur, the only solid link to his past, would have to be left behind.

Halfway up the emergency stairs he climbed through a window onto a fire escape. He quickly climbed to the top of the building, sprinted across the roof, gathering speed and timing his approach, and then without hesitation leaped up on the brick cornice at the edge and hurled himself off into space twenty stories above the ground. He caught the parapet of the adjoining building with his hands, absorbed the shock of

213

hitting against the stone surface with his left hip and thigh, noted with satisfaction that his gnarled fingers held their grip firmly. Exhilarated, feeling adrenaline surge through him, he flexed the muscles in his arms, back and shoulders and easily pulled himself up over the parapet and onto the tar-papered roof.

The stranger's skills, courage and strength thrilled him and filled him with pride—but this was only a fleeting thought, one which made him feel even stronger and more confident but not something he could afford to dwell on at the moment.

There was no time now for thinking about anything but the need to get far away.

He continued on his journey across the roofs of the other buildings in the block, often making leaps of twenty feet or more. When he reached the building at the end of the block, he crouched behind a parapet, then raised himself slightly and looked down.

There was a subway entrance halfway up the block, and no policeman in sight.

He found a door on the roof, went through it and found himself on stairs. He descended, came out in an alley. He went out to the sidewalk, turned and hurried toward the subway entrance. He knew where he had to go.

(iii)

Anne, feeling very cold, small and foolish, sat on the floor in a corner of her bedroom with her arms wrapped around herself, shuddering as she stared in horror at the unmade bed where she and a man who cut off the heads of people had made love and slept together.

So it had been Bone all along, she thought as a new shudder moved in a wave through her body, and she hugged herself even tighter. He was the killer, as everyone—including Bone— had suspected might be the case. Everyone except her. Finally he had been betrayed by the "stranger" he had fought so hard and bravely to clear.

She wondered what it was Ali had said, or what they had discovered together, that had finally caused the killing person in Bone to emerge. For that matter, she wondered what it was that Bone had used to sever the psychiatrist's head; whatever the weapon, he had obviously been carrying it on his person, for they had risen late, and she had driven him directly to Ali's office.

Perhaps, she thought, there had never been a "stranger" inside Bone at all. If he had been carrying such a deadly murder weapon with him all along, it had to mean that he had always known exactly who he was, what he had done—and what he was prepared to do. His "awakening" and pretending not to remember anything had all been a game.

He could have killed her at any time.

Anne wondered how she could have loved such a man. Perhaps she still loved him; she was not sure exactly how she felt at the moment, and was not sure she wanted to know. Perhaps, she thought, it would be a good idea to see an analyst herself. She had been so *certain* that Bone was innocent . . .

A cold-blooded killer who had probably been laughing at her all along . . .

Suddenly the phone rang, startling her. She let it ring— seven, eight times. Finally one of the homicide detectives who had been searching her apartment answered it. He listened for a few moments, then covered the mouthpiece and looked at Anne.

"It's somebody named Barry Prindle, ma'am," the detective said gruffly. "He says he works with you. You want to talk to him?"

Anne thought about it, finally nodded. She rose, walked across the room and took the receiver from the detective's hand. "Hello, Barry," she said in a soft, slightly quavering voice.

"Anne!" Barry Prindle's voice was strained, breathless. "Thank *God* you're all right! I was on my way home from playing tennis when I heard the news on the car radio. God, I was just about to hang up and come over . . . I was so afraid that . . . I'd heard that you'd taken him in to live with you. *Are* you all right?!"

"Yes, Barry, I'm all right," she said with a small sigh. She felt foolish, embarrassed.

"But what if he comes back?"

"There are police detectives here now, Barry; I called them right after I heard. I think they plan to keep the apartment building under surveillance. In any case, there's good security here, and there's a doorman. But I don't think he'll try to come back. If he'd wanted to kill me, he could have done it anytime during the . . . he could have done it easily enough. I think he's gone for good now—until the police catch him."

"Anne, the man is insane. You can never be certain what a madman is going to do."

Anne swallowed hard. "Barry?"

"What is it, Anne?"

"Barry, I just want to apologize to you for . . . acting the way I did. You were right all the time; all the time, you were just trying to protect me, and I said—and did—some things I shouldn't have."

"Forget it, Anne. I'm the one who should apologize; I acted like a bonehead—if you'll pardon the expression. Now I realize just how immaturely I behaved. I was just—well, I was just worried about you." He paused, laughed nervously. "Also, if I may say so, I've never felt the way I feel about you, so I didn't know how to handle it."

Anne gnawed at her lower lip. There was something in the back of her mind that was bothering her, and she knew what it was: guilt. She felt as if she were now somehow betraying Bone, and she felt anger at herself for being so stupid. "I don't understand how I could have been so wrong about him," she said distantly, almost to herself.

"He had a lot of people fooled, Anne."

She laughed bitterly. "Not like he fooled me, Barry." She paused as tears welled in her eyes, rolled down her cheeks. Suddenly, she was no longer sure of anything. "Or maybe he really wasn't fooling anyone; maybe he was telling the truth when he claimed not to remember. Something must have happened during his session with Ali. Ali must have said something that set Bone off, something that released that other, terrible personality in him." She paused again, shuddered. "He was always referring to himself as 'the stranger.' I guess he must have finally met that stranger."

"I guess he must have."

"Barry," Anne said, and sighed again. "I could use some friendly company real bad right now. Would you like to come over and have some coffee with me?"

"I'd like that very much. I'll see you in a few minutes."

CHAPTER THIRTEEN

(i)

In order to remain free long enough to prove the stranger's innocence, Bone knew that first he had to disappear. He had seen enough, learned enough, to believe that he knew how to do that.

He had headed for the Bowery.

Finding different clothes had certainly not been a problem. Within twenty minutes of his arrival in the lower section of Manhattan he had found a drunk about his size, bleary-eyed and searching through trash cans for cans to redeem, who had been more than happy to exchange his clothes for Bone's. The man's clothes—torn shirt, outer jacket, baggy trousers and plastic shoes—were filthy, and reeked; but Bone had known that was precisely what was needed, and so he had overcome his revulsion and donned the fetid rags. He'd known that now he had to be truly homeless, drifting deep in the bowels of the city, if he was to escape detection. In order to protect the stranger, he had to ignore the stranger's uncanny survival skills, as well as his love for cleanliness, for as long as it took to find—to remember—the real killer. Until his quest was finished, he would now have to lead the life of the most wretched of the homeless.

For three days he remained on the streets, his features still hidden behind dark glasses and under a floppy-brimmed hat, clustered with groups of men, some of whom occasionally wandered in and out of the Men's Shelter. At night he slept huddled in doorways, arms wrapped around himself for warmth.

And he thought of Anne.

He knew she would, of course, have to assume that he was guilty; after all, he had been the one to repeatedly point out to her the possibility Ali Hakim had raised that his was a multiple personality, his mind host to a savage killer. He missed Anne terribly, but knew that to contact her would not only place her in jeopardy, but would also confront her with a terrible dilemma. If he contacted her, no matter what she believed, she would have to report that contact to the police, or risk charges of abetting a fugitive. Really, he had nothing to say to her—but the time he had spent with her, sharing her bed with its clean sheets, the softness and musky smell of her body, her passion, only made his present misery more acute.

His one solace, the thought he clung to during his stench-filled days and cold nights, was the certainty that the stranger was innocent.

What he had sensed before instinctively was now confirmed: cleanliness was an all-important factor in maintaining the stranger's morale. Clothed in filthy rags, he was a constant affront to his own senses and sensibilities. Nor was he able to eat properly; he could not risk going to any of the soup kitchens for fear of being recognized. Like the other homeless, sick men down on the Bowery, he ate from garbage bins and trash baskets.

And he learned what it felt like to be invisible; as he had hoped, few people gave him a second glance, and those who did usually walked quickly away.

But he was making no progress. Clearly, the stranger had never been in a situation like the one he was in now, and, aside from escaping detection, there seemed to be no value in the situation, no reference points to aid him in his search for his memory. He had to expand his range, move about the city.

But he wondered how long he could continue to live this way before he became ill—perhaps seriously so.

The impulse to move on from the Bowery came on the morning of the fourth day, when one of the city's blue vans pulled up to the curb next to him. Bone quickly ducked down an alleyway, then watched from the shadows as two Project Helping Hand people got out and began to talk to three drunken men sitting on the sidewalk in front of a storefront. When the van left, Bone walked out of the alley, pulled his hat down low over his forehead and began walking uptown; he would go to another place he had heard of, where he would be invisible.

(ii)

Bone stood across the street from the Forty-second Street entrance to Grand Central Terminal and shuddered slightly. It was in the underpass near here where he had suffered his panic attack on the morning after leaving the Men's Shelter, Bone thought. Now he knew that the terminal itself was a gathering ground, like the Bowery, for the most wretched and helpless of the city's homeless men and women. At the time it had happened, and since then, Bone had attributed his panic to the close proximity of speeding cars, suffocating fumes, darkness, and perhaps the fact that he was underground. Now he wasn't so certain it had been those things which had triggered the attack; now he wondered if it was the building itself and its hidden memories. Looking at the facade of the massive stone structure he felt no sense of familiarity, no indication that it meant anything to the stranger.

But it might be different for him inside.

Bone sucked in a deep breath, then, in the shuffling gait which he had adopted for walking on the streets during the day, he hobbled across the street and went through the vaulted entrance. He found himself in what appeared to be a waiting room, old, with a musty but unmistakable atmosphere of grandeur. It was close to four in the afternoon, and he found himself going against the flow of heavy pedestrian traffic: well-dressed men and women carrying portfolios or briefcases who hurried on past him with their gazes fixed straight ahead, their faces tense, not looking at each other and not looking at him, yet parting smoothly as they walked past him like rushing water around a stone, giving him a wide berth. A few made visible gestures of distaste; one woman turned her head away and held her nose.

He stank, Bone thought. And he felt deeply ashamed.

And he was exhausted. He could not last much longer living like this, he thought; he felt feverish, weak, profoundly depressed. He was losing his soul down the holes he was seeking to hide in. He was swimming in the sea of the wretched, but he was losing it; now he was *becoming* wretched, and he was drowning.

His initial reaction as the stream of well-dressed commuters swirled past him was fear of exposure, fear that somebody would look more closely and recognize him as the man whose drawn likeness was on the front pages of all the newspapers. But nobody gave him a second glance—and soon he was standing alone, but still feeling conspicuous dressed in his rags. He looked around him, saw rows of benches like church pews on both sides of the waiting room.

In front of him, at the opposite end of a short but wide connecting corridor, he could see part of what appeared to be a very large, brightly lit room where a large, ornate clock was suspended over an information booth. But Bone did not want to go there with his filthiness and his shame and his wretchedness; it was too open. For now, all he wanted to do was sleep.

He thought: he was escaping, all right—disappearing right down the drain into himself. Now, for the first time since he had awakened, he actually felt like one of the homeless, the dispossessed. It was horrible.

He shuffled to his left, past the first three rows of benches where well-dressed men and women sat reading newspapers or idly staring off into space, waiting for their trains. It was when he reached the rear pews, those close to the entrance to the men's toilet, that he saw what, where, his quarters would be for the night, and he felt a renewed sense of despair. It was the same here as on the Bowery, he thought, except here everyone was jammed together, and there was no place to walk to. At least a dozen homeless, ragged men and women were huddled on the worn wooden benches at the rear of the waiting room. Despite the fact that it was a relatively warm afternoon, all of the people appeared to be dressed in multiple layers of clothing, shirts and jackets buttoned or zipped up to the neck, scarves wrapped tightly around their necks, dirty woolen caps pulled down low over ears and foreheads. Two men and four women had shopping carts pulled up beside them, the baskets overflowing with clothing and flotsam from the street. Everyone seemed to be either sleeping or in a stupor.

Stupor, Bone thought. That was where he was headed—to a kind of death in life where, like these people on the back benches near the toilet, all he could hope for in each day was simply to survive it.

He had no energy left; all he wanted to do was rest.

He found a narrow space between two men, sank down on the bench, leaned back and pulled the floppy brim of his hat down over his eyes. Almost immediately he fell into a troubled sleep of exhaustion and despair sharply punctuated by fever dreams of darkness, flickering lights, bones and a crimson-streaked orange figure stalking him.

(iii)

Grand Central Terminal was closed from one-thirty to five-thirty in the morning; at around one-fifteen, members of the terminal's Metro North Commuter Railroad Police came to prod and shake Bone, and the other sleeping men and women sharing the rear benches with him. The manner of the police was firm, but not rough; the eyes of the police, when Bone looked into them, were oddly glassy, as though the men were not really seeing what they were looking at.

He had expected to be hustled out onto the streets; instead, he and the others were herded down the wide corridor opposite the entrance and into the vast rotunda, now only dimly lit, that Bone had glimpsed earlier. They were herded across the rotunda and under an arch at the far end into another large area, with marble tunnels branching off in various directions. Here, more homeless men and women were rousted from their cold marble beds and forced to join the main group. They were herded down a tunnel to their left, down onto a wide platform sealed off at one end by a high, wide gate. The police left, and a few minutes later Bone heard another gate slam shut somewhere back in the area they had come through. They were sealed off, Bone thought, and immediately he began to experience a feeling of claustrophobia. He knew that the guards had meant to be kind in affording them this place to sleep while the terminal was closed, but Bone wished he had left the building when he'd had the chance.

Bone stopped in the center of the platform, which was really a gently sloping ramp, and looked around. Bone estimated that there were perhaps a hundred and fifty people in the area, shuffling about, searching for a place to lay down their few belongings and their bodies so that they could return to their stupor-sleep. Bone walked down the ramp, sat down on the stone with his back resting against the gate.

But he did not sleep.

Grand Central Terminal was like an open psychiatric ward, he thought as he watched a half-naked man with scabs covering his body dig into his nose with a dirt-encrusted finger and pull out a large, slimy mucous clot. When the man had cleared one nostril, he started on the other, wiping his fingers on his filthy, torn trouser legs. A young, wild-eyed man with greasy black hair that hung to his waist was furiously masturbating as he rocked back and forth, singing to himself. Gradually, since it was even stronger than his own smell, Bone became aware of the cloying stench of unwashed bodies, urine, vomit, feces.

The four hours Bone waited through the night for the terminal and the gate at the opposite end of the ramp to open seemed an eternity, and during that eternity he kept going over and over in his mind the events that had happened, searching for some clue—any clue—to the stranger's identity. It was, he decided at last, hopeless. He had made a mistake in trying to lose himself in this sea of the most wretched of the homeless. The stranger, he well knew, was meticulously clean, and only a few days of being dressed in filthy clothes, eating rotting food and not washing himself had drained him of his will. He now knew that there was no way the role he was playing could help him find the stranger's identity. Instead, he was in real danger of losing the only identity he really had, this identity of the ghost-eyes inside the stranger; as he slipped further and further away from the stranger's habits, he was losing himself.

By the time he heard the gate at the opposite end of the ramp open, he had decided what he had to do. In fact, he had made the decision two hours before, and had spent the remaining time quieting himself, searching for his center. He had removed his floppy hat and dark glasses.

He could not—would not—continue to live this way; he was going to turn himself in to the police and tell his story. Of course, Perry Lightning would not believe him, and he would almost certainly be locked away. But he had decided that a state prison, or a mental hospital, was infinitely preferable to this prison, this out-of-control mental ward, he was now in. He simply had to be clean in order to have peace of mind to think clearly.

If nothing else, Bone thought as he walked with the others up the ramp toward the network of tunnels leading to the concourse and the adjoining waiting room, he had at last convinced himself of the futility of searching for the stranger's memories, traces of his lives before and after the injury that had certainly precipitated the amnesia, on the streets of New York. He had certainly given it his best shot, and all he had really managed to discover were places where the stranger did *not* belong. And, despite the ambivalence he had experienced while gazing down the great stone canyons of the streets, he was now convinced that the stranger did not even belong *in* the city. He had come from somewhere else.

But, wherever he had come from, there was obviously no one there who missed him; the stranger had been alone even before the injury to his head. He had been all over Manhattan, had revisited the places where he had been seen, and had experienced only negative impressions. Of the two men who might be able to help him, Zulu and Lobo, one had disappeared, and the other desperately wanted to kill him. And so he would go to prison, or a mental hospital. Eventually, perhaps, he would be put to death. But until that time, it now seemed clear to him that he had no choice but to give himself up to the police and hope that one day his memory might return of its own accord. There would be other psychiatrists, other forms of treatment. All his hopes had not died with Ali Hakim, and the neuropsychiatrist had hinted at the existence of certain drugs that might . . .

Suddenly Bone stopped and turned to his left as a huge display along the east wall flickered, then lit up. He stared at the display, abruptly felt light-headed and short of breath. But his reaction was not caused by fear this time, he thought; it was something about the display.

Taking short, shallow breaths and with his heart beating wildly in his chest, Bone ran across the remaining distance of the concourse and bounded up a short flight of marble steps to a balcony on the west side. Then he spun around to once again look at the huge display that looked to be almost half the size of a football field, and was situated beneath a soaring bank of windows.

The display consisted of what appeared to be a single, huge, photographic transparency, with a sign below it that read *America's Parks*. The photo itself, now brightly lit in the gray dawn light, showed a young man, obviously a hiker or climber, standing on a high ledge, shielding his eyes against the rising sun as he gazed out over a vista of purple-hued, craggy mountain peaks. Nearby, an eagle soared.

Bone found that his mouth was suddenly dry, and he licked his lips. Almost unconsciously, he found himself reaching behind his back for something that wasn't there, something he felt should be hanging from his belt . . .

He looked down at the marble railing of the balcony, ran his hands back and forth over the smooth, hard, cold surface. Then he crouched down and ran his hands through a small pile of debris at his feet, rubbing the dirt over his gnarled fingers.

Not dirt, he thought; it wasn't dirt he was looking for; dirt wasn't what he carried.

Chalk!

Why chalk? he wondered as he straightened up and resumed staring at the gargantuan photo transparency.

Mountains. A youth on a ledge; an endless ocean of sky; a soaring eagle.

Chalk up!

Peel off!

5.5.

All traces of weakness, fear and exhaustion had vanished. He felt exhilarated—but also frustrated. He was, he thought, so very, very close . . .

It was there, he thought, right on the tip of his mind, and it was what was causing the tears to well in his eyes and roll down his cheeks.

He brushed away his tears, bowed his head and closed his eyes, trying to rein in the excitement and anxiety which seemed to be blocking the final leap in his mind.

Leap.

Mountains. What did mountains have to do with this city?

He opened his eyes, once again gazed at the transparency and the bank of windows above it. The concourse was filling now with the light of dawn, with rays of sunlight streaking through the dozens of dirty windowpanes above the transparency. His gaze went up further—and he let out a little gasp. High above him, very faint, there were markings on the vaulted, green ceiling. The constellations, he thought. But there was something wrong with the paintings; they were not as they should be.

It was the winter Zodiac, but it showed a left-handed Orion, which was wrong, and Pegasus was charging from the west instead of the east, which was wrong. It was the winter Zodiac in reverse.

But how did he *know* it was wrong? Bone thought as he swallowed hard, trying to work up some moisture in his mouth. Because he had obviously spent a great deal of time out-of-doors, looking up at the winter Zodiac. He knew the stars, the constellations . . .

He slowly lowered his gaze, once again fixed his stare on the photograph of the youth on the mountain ledge.

Why did the picture move him so much? Bone thought. Why did it seem so familiar? Because . . . because . . . it was home.

The voice that came from behind him was low, but taut with excitement. And hatred. "Is that you, Bone-man?"

Bone slowly turned around, started slightly when he found himself facing an albino youth who could have been white, Hispanic or black. A black patch covered his right eye, but his pink left eye glinted with light like some strange jewel of evil. He wore a gray leather jacket, jeans, black boots. Behind the one-eyed albino were two other youths, dressed identically, and they now moved in opposite directions to flank Bone.

"Christ, Johnny was right," the albino youth said, his voice betraying a slight lisp. "He said he saw you come in here the other day; he said you were dressed funny, but he was sure it was you. We wanted to get here early so we could check out everybody coming in over the concourse. We come in the door, and look what we find right off the bat."

"You're Lobo," Bone said quietly.

The youth raised his eyebrows slightly. "So you talk now. Found your tongue, huh?" He paused, sniffed, wrinkled his nose. "But you smell like a fucking sewer, just like all the other worthless, lazy bastards on the street who're fucking up this country, giving the Russians something to laugh at. Hey, are you really the guy who's been cutting off the heads of all those people?"

Bone swallowed. The other two gang members were very close to him now as they leaned on the railing, almost brushing his sleeves. "I lost my memory," he said evenly, staring into the pink eye in front of him and seeing nothing but cruelty and madness. "I don't remember anything that happened to me, or what I did, during my time on the streets. And I don't remember who I am, or where I came from. I believe you can help me remember—if you will. I've heard that I . . . hurt you. I'm sorry. I don't remember what happened."

Lobo's thin lips curled back in a sneer, although the light in his pale eye remained cold, implacable. "You're sorry?" he lisped. "That's nice, you parasite; that's really nice. There I was in the alley about to get me a good little blow job from that toothless old broad when you pop up out of nowhere and bang me in the eye with that fucking bone you used to carry. You busted another guy's jaw, and knocked four teeth out of another guy's mouth. But it was my eye you burst. The doctors had to scoop it right out of my head. Now, what do you think I ought to scoop out of you, Bone-man?"

Bone remained silent. There was nothing further to say, he thought. Three more gray-jacketed youths had come in the swinging doors behind Lobo and were fanning out, forming a tight phalanx around him, screening him from view.

Lobo took something out of the pocket of his leather jacket, flicked his wrist. There was a sharp click as a six-inch steel blade snapped from the thick bone handle of the knife.

"You want to talk, we'll talk, Bone-man," the albino said in a voice that was just above a whisper. "But we won't do it here. You're going to come with us nice and quiet, and then we can talk all you want to—when you're not screaming. I have business to take care of with you."

Bone threw back his arms, smashing the knobby knuckles of his gnarled hands into the faces of the two gang members flanking him at the marble railing. At the same time he kicked Lobo in the groin—but not before the albino had thrust at him with the knife. The blade slashed through his shirt. He felt a brief, stinging sensation in his stomach, then numbness as blood began to flow, warm against his belly.

But Lobo was doubled over, both hands clutched to his groin, and the youths flanking him had been stunned—but the other three were now lunging for him. Bone wheeled around, planted both his hands on the stone balustrade and jumped up.

226

Peel off!

He leaped out into space, over the stairway, and landed on his feet on the marble floor, instinctively collapsing and rolling to absorb the shock of the landing. Instantly he was up on his feet and racing across the concourse as early-morning commuters scattered to get out of his way.

Two leather-jacketed youths were closing in on him from his right. Bone, holding his right hand against the wound in his belly, cut to his left and bounded up an escalator, dodging around startled commuters. Hearing running footsteps close behind him, he pushed through a set of swinging doors and ran out of the building. With the cursing youths racing at his heels, he glanced down at the blood staining the front of his shirt. He knew that the knife had not punctured the stomach wall, but it had given him a good slice, and he was losing blood rapidly; he couldn't go much further, and if the youths caught up with him he suspected he would be immediately and unceremoniously butchered.

He dashed across the street, looking around in vain for a police car or a patrolman on foot. He reached the sidewalk, ran left, then darted right into a passageway over which was a sign that read *Helmsley Walk*. Still holding his hand tightly over his bleeding flesh wound, he sprinted to the end of the covered walk, came out on Park Avenue.

The members of the Wolfpack were so close now that he could hear the heavy, rasping breathing of two of them, one just off his right shoulder and the other off his left. A hand grabbed at his sleeve, missed.

In another second or two, he thought, he was going to die.

Directly to his right was a wall of glass panels enclosing the Chemical Bank Building's four-story-high terrarium—a bright, airy rectangle of sculpted space fronting on Park Avenue and encasing a charming mini-jungle of trees, ferns and plants in striking counterpoint to the shrubbery malls which bisected the elegant thoroughfare. As the hands on the left reached for him and a knife blade sliced through his coat, Bone instinctively leaped up on the side of the building. His toes found the narrow ledge at the base of the panels; his fingertips found a groove in the lead strip between the panels above his head, and they held their grip. But he knew he was not high enough to escape a knife thrust to his legs, and he did not have the strength or leverage to pull himself higher. Looking down, he saw the stunned expressions on the faces of Lobo and the other five members of the Wolfpack as they stared up at him.

"What are you?" the startled Lobo said, shaking his head slightly. "A fucking human fly?"

Bone looked back the way he had come, then up the long, canyon-like street. Park Avenue at dawn was virtually deserted, and there was no sign of the police.

Lobo recovered from his shock, then slashed at Bone's calves with his knife. Bone, his fingertips digging into the lead strip above him, leaped over the arcing blade, then nimbly danced down the length of the concrete ledge and around the corner of the building, looking and feeling above him for a grip, a route up the side of the glass wall, that would enable him to escape the slashing knives below him.

A few yards down the length of glass panels was the adjacent building on Forty-eighth Street, a brick structure. Between the panels and the adjacent brick wall was a narrow fissure perhaps three or four inches wide. As Lobo and the other five youths below him slashed at his legs, Bone unhesitatingly jammed his gnarled left hand into the fissure, then clenched it into a fist; muscles and tendons expanded like a wedge, forming a tight lock in the fissure. He leaped up, jammed the fingers of his right hand into the fissure and clenched his fist, pulled himself up as he relaxed his left hand. And he kept going. In less than five seconds, using only his hands as wedges and the tremendous strength in his arms, Bone had hauled himself ten feet up the narrow space between the buildings.

But he could go no further. The front of him was covered with blood; the wound in his stomach burned, and his legs felt as if they were filled with sand. Gasping for breath, he tried to yell for help, but could not summon the strength.

"I'm going to kill you, you fucking freak!" Lobo shouted, and flung his knife at Bone.

With both his fists now wedged into the fissure to support his weight, Bone could only duck his head and hunch his shoulders; the knife bounced off the brick a few inches from his left ear. He looked down, watched as one of the gang members hurried to the corner to act as a lookout. Forty-eighth Street was empty.

A car came around the corner, slowed as the driver cast a puzzled glance up at Bone, then sped away when two of the gang members stepped toward him threateningly.

Lobo motioned to one of the other gang members, who quickly handed over a straight-edged razor to the albino Wolfpack leader. A second Wolf stepped forward and leaned against the building, his hands flanking the fissure, his legs outstretched, his back arched slightly. Lobo backed up a few paces, then ran forward, leaped up on the other youth's back and planted his feet on the youth's shoulders. Now he was only a few feet below Bone, within striking distance of Bone's legs. Lobo glanced at the Wolf on the corner, who gave a thumbs-up sign to signal that he saw no one. Then Lobo reached up, slowly ran the gleaming blade of the razor along the sole of Bone's shoe.

"Now I'm going to open up the arteries in your legs and let some more blood out, you fucker," the albino said softly as he raised the razor.

"Hey, Lobo!" the Wolf at the corner shouted, tensing and reaching into his pocket. *"Watch out! Here comes—!"*

At that moment the huge black man Bone recognized as Zulu came sprinting around the corner, his multi-colored robe billowing behind him. Without slowing, he raised his great staff and brought it crashing against the side of the lookout's head. The gray-jacketed youth flew off his feet, landed sprawled and splay-limbed in the street.

Both Lobo and the youth supporting him cried out in surprise and alarm, and then the two-man tower began to quaver and crumble; its collapse was helped along by Zulu, who in three great bounds was down the sidewalk, his staff swinging sideways and forming a blurred arc in the air. The Wolf on the bottom ducked out of the way, and the thick staff caught Lobo's ankles. There was a sharp crack, then Lobo screamed as he flipped in the air and landed on his back on the sidewalk.

Bone's vision blurred, came back into focus, then blurred again. He screwed his eyes shut, shook his head slightly, opened his eyes. Below him on the sidewalk, three gang members had drawn their knives and were cautiously circling Zulu. The giant black man, his staff now held in both his hands, was slowly turning, occasionally jabbing or sweeping the air with the weapon, keeping the youths at bay.

"All of you charge him at once!" the crippled Lobo screamed from where he lay on the sidewalk, clutching his shattered left

229

ankle. "Rush him! One of you has to get to him! Stick the bastard!"

The three other gang members looked at one another—but they continued only to circle. Lobo picked up the razor that had fallen beside him on the sidewalk, then began to crawl the short distance separating him from Zulu, whose back was to Lobo, and whose attention was focused on the other three youths in front of him. Lobo continued to crawl forward, reaching with the razor beneath Zulu's flowing robe, searching for the legs . . .

Peel off!

Bone relaxed the tension in his fists, and as his hands slipped out of the narrow fissure he pushed against the glass and brick on either side of him, launching himself through the air. He fell, landed with both his feet on the back of Lobo's neck. There were two sharp, almost simultaneous, cracking sounds—one as the albino's neck broke, and the other as his face smashed into the sidewalk. Bone fell sideways, crumpling to the sidewalk as the staff whirled through the air over his head and smashed into one of the circling Wolf's ribs, crushing his rib cage. Virtually in the same series of movements, Zulu brought the staff up over his head and prepared to attack again.

But the two Wolfpack members who were still on their feet were already running away down Forty-eighth Street.

Two cars had stopped across the street, and a small knot of early-morning pedestrians crowded together on the opposite sidewalk, staring in astonishment. Bone, his vision blurring once again, struggled to get to his feet. A huge hand reached down and grabbed the back of his jacket, then lifted him to his feet as though he were no more than a child.

"Can you walk, Bone-man?" Zulu asked in his deep, rumbling voice. When Bone nodded, he continued, "Then let's start walking."

With a sweep of one huge arm, Zulu cloaked Bone with his robe. Holding his staff in his right hand and supporting Bone with his left, he began walking back toward Park Avenue.

Moving his legs as best he could, leaning against Zulu for support, Bone was half led, half carried to the corner, where Zulu turned left and headed back in the direction of Grand Central Terminal. Bone felt like he was floating, and he tried even harder to move his legs, which had gone numb. His vision cleared just as Zulu turned left into a doorway a half block from the entrance to Grand Central.

"You're lucky I was just leaving from home for the office, Bone-man," Zulu mumbled as he moved with Bone down a sloping concrete ramp.

People coming up out of the terminal quickly moved aside, some staring open-mouthed at the sight of the giant Zulu with his staff in one hand and his closely held companion wrapped in the folds of his robe. At the bottom of the ramp Zulu turned right, and now Bone could see that the ramp they had come down was one of dozens connected to the labyrinth of tunnels that radiated from the concourse at Grand Central. They passed a newspaper kiosk, already doing a brisk business with early-morning commuters, a coffee shop, a sign that read *Oyster Bar*. Then they went down another sloping ramp that led to gated entranceways with numbers above them. Bone glanced through one of the doorways, saw people, tracks, trains.

Zulu guided Bone to the left, down a wide corridor. They turned a corner, into another corridor which seemed to Bone to lead nowhere, and which was empty of commuters. Then Zulu stopped in front of the wide, closed doors of a freight elevator.

"This is risky business at this time of the morning," Zulu continued in his deep, rumbling voice as he produced a ring of keys from somewhere beneath his robe. He glanced around to make sure they were unobserved, then inserted one of the keys into the lock of the freight elevator, turned it. The door opened. Zulu raised the wooden gate, helped Bone into the huge box, then quickly lowered the gate and pressed the Basement 3 button on a panel to his right. The door swung shut, and the elevator began to descend.

"Where are we going?" Bone murmured as he leaned heavily against the side of the box. He felt very faint, dizzy.

"My home, six stories down," the black man replied in a voice that to Bone seemed almost like the low rumble of trains that reverberated in the walls around them. "I've got quite a spread here, don't you think? Forty acres in all, seven levels. Of course, I have to share it with a few million people who traipse in and out all year long, but they don't bother me, and the rent is just right."

The freight elevator bumped to a stop, and the door opened.

231

Zulu lifted the gate, poked his head out into the dimly lit corridor, looked back and forth.

"We're in luck, Bone-man," Zulu continued quietly as he reached back, took a firm grip on Bone's elbow and gently pulled him forward. "Come on; we don't have far to go now."

They went left, down a short wide corridor that led to a large storage area, then through an opening which led onto tracks now shrouded in darkness. Bone watched Zulu reach down for something on the ground, close to the concrete wall. There was a soft click, and suddenly the beam of a powerful flashlight cut through the darkness. Zulu led Bone down the tracks for fifty yards, then up a short flight of metal stairs which ended on a catwalk stretching away into the distance beyond the beam of light. They moved on down the catwalk, often, to Bone's horror, having to step over or around piles of newspapers or rags which turned out to be covering people who stared up at him with vacant eyes.

Finally Zulu stopped in front of a large iron door. Zulu again produced his key ring, inserted one of the keys into the lock in the iron door, turned the key and pushed on the door, which swung open easily and silently on its well-oiled hinges. Bone, whose vision was completely blurred now, staggered, felt Zulu's strong hands holding him up, guiding him into the darkness beyond the iron door. Then he was eased down onto a soft surface that seemed to swallow up his body. Bone tried to speak, but could not. He closed his eyes and let himself disappear into the darkness.

CHAPTER FOURTEEN

(i)

There were the usual nightmares of darkness and flickering torches or candles, bones, an orange-clad figure stalking him; but Bone slept, and finally in his dreams there was pain that brought him back to semiconsciousness. Then the pain eased and he drifted off into deep sleep, dreamless, restful, healing. It was the smell of food that finally caused him to wake.

He opened his eyes, found himself lying on an air-inflated mattress in one corner of a spacious, concrete area that had no windows but was filled with the low hum of what Bone assumed were large ventilation fans. It was quite warm in the room, but two large fans at opposite corners whirred quietly, producing a pleasant breeze. Behind him, off to his left, there was an opening in the concrete wall, but it was dark beyond. There was a wardrobe made of heavy cardboard off to one side, and bookcases constructed of wooden packing crates piled on top of one another. Books, magazines and newspapers were everywhere, overflowing from the bookcases, stacked in neat piles around the room. Against one wall was a pile of cartons containing canned food. There was a rocking chair, another air mattress and pillows, sheets, blankets. Light was provided by two bare bulbs screwed into fixtures in the high ceiling; wires and electrical cables of varying thickness snaked along one wall and through the opening in the wall into the darkness. Paintings of sea- and landscapes hung from nails driven into the concrete walls. Everything was very clean—which only made Bone more conscious of his own stench.

Against the far wall next to the cartons of canned food were two hot plates, as well as a small stove beneath which two Sterno heaters burned; the delicious aromas that had awakened him had come from two pots that were simmering on the stove. A card table had been set up, complete with tablecloth and two place settings. There was only one chair at the table, but an overturned milk crate had been placed in front of the second setting. Bone sucked in a deep breath, savoring the smell of the cooking food. He could not remember ever being so hungry.

He pulled back the single cotton sheet that covered him, found that he was naked. His clothes were nowhere to be seen. The wound in his belly had been attended to, seemingly by an expert. The cut was perhaps six inches long, just above his naval, and the area all around it had been swabbed with what looked to be either iodine or Merthiolate. It was held closed with six small shiny butterfly clamps.

Suddenly there was the sound of metal clicking against metal, and the door noiselessly swung open. Zulu stepped in, closing the door behind him. He was carrying his staff in one hand, and an armful of packages. He looked at Bone, smiled thinly.

"Bone-man," Zulu said evenly. "I didn't think I'd find you awake yet."

Bone started to sit up, then grimaced and clutched at his belly as fiery pain stabbed through his stomach. Then the pain subsided. He exhaled slowly, leaned back against the wall.

"You'd best take it easy, Bone-man," Zulu continued as he came across the room and placed the packages next to Bone's air mattress. "That's only a flesh wound you've got there, and you're damned lucky the knife didn't pierce the stomach wall. But those things bleed like crazy; if you move too suddenly and pop those clamps open, I'm going to have a lot of cleaning up to do all over again."

"You're Zulu, aren't you?"

The huge black grunted, raised his eyebrows slightly.

"You've gotten to be a regular chatterbox, Bone-man. This is the first time I've ever heard you talk."

"But you do know me?"

"Know you?" Zulu laughed—a deep, booming sound that echoed in the concrete chamber. "Picking you up off the sidewalk and bringing you home with me is getting to be a habit."

Bone felt his heart begin to pound, and he swallowed hard, took a deep breath. "When did you pick me up before?"

"You don't remember, do you?" Zulu said, studying Bone's face.

Bone shook his head. "No. I . . . God, Zulu, I don't know where to start. I've been looking for you for almost a week, from the time when I learned that you might know something about me."

"I've been on vacation," Zulu replied evenly. "It was you staring at me from across the street the other day, wasn't it?"

Bone nodded. "I should have come over to you then, Zulu. I can't remember anything that happened to me over the course of a year. A few weeks ago I woke up, as I describe it, in Central Park. It was like I was born at that moment. I didn't—and don't—remember anything that happened to me during a year I lived on the streets, and I don't remember who I am, or where I came from, or what I did. I've been searching for my identity ever since. Somebody told me your name, and when I saw you that day I had a strong feeling that I should know you—or had met you before."

"Mmm. You've changed, Bone-man, and that's for sure. You look different, because you got your hair cut. You haven't got that blank look in your eyes, you speak—and, frankly, you smell like a goddamn goat. Before, you were always clean."

The words cut to Bone's heart, and he lowered his head. "I know. I'm sorry. There was a reason—or I thought there was. Is there someplace down here where I can wash?"

"Did you cut the heads off all those people, Bone-man?" Zulu asked in an even tone.

Bone's head snapped up. "No," he replied flatly.

"I thought you just said you couldn't remember anything you did for a year."

"And I still don't. For a time I was afraid I had committed those murders, and even after I 'woke up' I was afraid I might have another, hidden, personality and was still killing people.

235

But the last killing—Dr. Ali Hakim—I know I didn't do. That murder was committed to frame me. Dr. Hakim was treating me. I was on my way to see him, and he was dead and mutilated when I got there. It was then that I knew I hadn't killed anyone—but I would never be believed. The reason I'm so filthy is because . . . I just haven't been able to take care of myself the way I should."

Zulu was silent for some time, staring into Bone's eyes. "Okay," he said at last.

"Okay?"

"I believe you, Bone-man. I always thought you were a decent man. I never believed you were killing those people like the first news reports said, but that last killing seemed to nail you good. Now you've explained it to me."

"I have an awful lot of questions to ask you, Zulu."

"They'll wait. You must be very hungry. I've got some food for you over here."

Bone nodded, gestured around the chamber. "Where are we?"

Zulu smiled thinly, pointed to the ceiling. "Beneath the metropolis of New York City—specifically, beneath Grand Central Terminal. Incidentally, I'm sorry it's so hot in here. There are steam pipes beneath the floor, and they make things quite cozy in the winter. But it's uncomfortable when the weather changes. In another week or so I'll be moving to my summer quarters—two blocks west of here, in another room like this that's right next to some air-conditioning ducts."

"But this room . . . ?"

"It's what's called a junction terminal room. Abandoned. All the switching equipment that was here has been moved out. You ready for some food? I'll bring it over to you."

Bone shook his head, then struggled to his feet. "I'm not a dirty person, Zulu. I want to wash first."

"Sit down, Bone-man, before you open up that wound. I'll bring water for you to wash with later. There are clothes in those packages. I'll help you get cleaned up, and then we'll get you dressed. But first you eat. I don't want you opening that cut—which, if I do say so myself, I think I did a pretty good job on. I don't want you messing it up. I've got first-aid supplies down here, and you learn how to take care of yourself. It costs you a fortune to go to a hospital, and they ask you a lot of questions that are none of their damn business."

Bone again shook his head. "I'll be careful, Zulu. Please; this is important to me. Is there someplace down here where I can wash?"

Zulu sighed, opened a trunk that was set between two bookcases and took out a huge bath towel, a bar of soap, a razor and a small mirror. He put the articles into a plastic bag, draped the towel over his arm, nodded toward the door. "Come; I'll take you."

"I'll take myself, Zulu. Tell me where I can go to wash."

Zulu studied Bone for a few moments, then slowly nodded. "Don't you get that wound wet."

"I won't."

Zulu handed Bone the towel, which Bone wrapped around his middle, wincing slightly when the rough material touched his cut. Then Zulu handed him the toilet articles and a large flashlight.

"When you go out of here, turn left. Go up on the catwalk, and stay on it. About a hundred yards down you'll find a tap. You can wash up there." Zulu paused, held up a huge hand as Bone walked past him toward the door. "Be careful, Bone-man," he continued. "You won't find any alligators in these tunnels, but there are mutant cats, and rats the size of dogs. But it's the humans you have to watch out for."

"God, I remember seeing people on the way here. I don't understand how anyone could live down here."

"Why? I live here, don't I?"

"Yes, but—"

"Most of the men who find their way down here are quite mad, Bone-man, and they can be dangerous. Avoid them."

Holding the plastic bag in one hand and the flashlight in the other, Bone walked out of the junction terminal room, then up a narrow flight of stairs to a catwalk beneath three massive pipes. He had gone perhaps twenty yards when he suddenly stopped and sucked in a deep breath.

Ahead of him, just barely visible at the end of the beam of light, a half-naked man sat in a pool of urine, idly rocking back and forth as he stared off into the darkness. He did not turn toward the light as Bone approached, then, with his back to the metal railing, edged past. The man gave no indication that he even saw Bone.

He passed three more men on his way—all of them simply sitting or lying down in the darkness. Bone saw no food or water near the men, and he wondered how they survived, how they managed to come and go, in this eternal night far below the city streets.

He found the tap, braced the flashlight against the railing and quickly washed himself. He found he was already feeling stronger, more confident. He shaved, washed his hair, then vigorously toweled himself off, being careful to avoid the wound on his stomach.

When he returned to the concrete chamber that was Zulu's "winter home," he found the black man dressed in flannel shorts, thongs and a T-shirt. The clothes Zulu had bought for him were laid out on his air mattress.

"Thank you," Bone said simply.

Zulu nodded, then pointed to the clothes. "Get dressed."

"I have a thousand questions to ask you, Zulu."

"First we'll eat, then we'll talk."

(ii)

"When I first found you, it was at about the same time of morning as when I found you today. You were lying on the sidewalk with your face in a mud puddle next to a construction site at Thirty-third Street and Ninth Avenue. You were absolutely covered with mud, which first made me think that you'd injured yourself down there in the foundation pit that had been dug, and had somehow managed to crawl out. But you weren't dressed in construction worker's clothing; you had on leather shorts, a T-shirt and hiking boots with heavy woolen socks. You had no identification on you, and the side of your head was bashed in.

"I don't usually go that way; normally, I walk from here directly to St. Thomas Church, where I work the corner. But that day they were having a convention of booksellers at the Jacob Javits Convention Center, and there were some displays I wanted to check out. I don't know if anybody else had seen you and walked on by, but there wasn't anybody attending to you when I found you. You were semiconscious, and when I touched your shoulder you moaned and tried to get up. I helped you to your feet, and then I tried to take that bone away from you. No way. You'd kept a tight grip on that thing even while you'd been unconscious, and there was no way you were going to let go of it.

"I had a decision to make. I hailed a taxi, figuring to check you into a hospital. When we got to the nearest one, there were problems—just like I knew there were going to be—in the emergency room; they didn't want to accept you because you had no identification, and obviously had no money to pay. They said I should take you someplace else, to a clinic that I'm familiar with; but I knew you were going to be hassled there too. By this time you were conscious most of the time, but couldn't talk. Well, some of the charity hospitals in this city can be dangerous places even for people who *can* talk. I figured you had a pretty good concussion, but that if you were conscious and walking around the most dangerous time had passed, and that you'd be all right as long as you got a lot of rest. So what I did was bring you down here, clean you up and otherwise take care of you. As long as you didn't slip into a coma or develop a very high fever, I figured the care I could give you was as good—or better—than you'd get on some of the charity or welfare wards around here.

"Eventually you did get stronger, and you stopped sleeping so much. You'd been eating okay when you were awake, so I figured you were healing. I got you some clothes, a razor and some other stuff, and you started taking care of yourself. You ate the food I cooked for you, slept and spent a lot of time just watching me, but you didn't talk. Well, I do talk—a lot; you listened, and for some reason I thought you understood what I was saying, but you didn't respond.

"Then one day I came back down here after work and you were gone—along with one of my flashlights. It scared the shit out of me. I didn't know where you could have gone, and I was afraid you wouldn't be able to find your way back here; I was afraid you'd get yourself lost down here in these tunnels, which is damn well easy to do. So I took another flashlight and some extra batteries and went looking for you in the tunnels. The first thing I saw, about twenty yards from here, was a big black X someone had marked on a wall with a piece of charred wood. I'd never seen that X before, so I figured you'd put it there. I kept walking in that direction, found another X. I finally found you about three quarters of a mile from here, at the junction of a maze of tunnels that are part of the third water system they're building. There you were, big as life, holding the flashlight in one hand and your bone in the other, just looking around. Hell, you weren't lost; you were exploring. You seemed happy enough to see me, but not exactly relieved. *I* was the one who was relieved, not only because you weren't lost, but because what you were doing seemed to indicate that you weren't retarded as a result of your injury—just mute. Hell, you led me back here; you knew exactly where you were.

"After that, on some days you'd come out with me to St. Thomas. Sometimes you'd be content to just sit on the steps with the others and listen, and other times you'd go wandering off—I don't know where you went to, because you never spoke; at least not to me. The first few times you wandered off, I was a little worried—but I always found you here waiting for me when I got back; you'd found your own way of getting down to this level without using the freight elevator, and I was leaving the door unlocked. Other days you'd stay here, and when I got back I knew you'd been exploring the tunnels again. But you always managed to find your way back to this transformer room at night. Quite frankly, I'd really gotten used to having you around. I knew that you had more than your share of wits about you, and that you could take care of yourself. As you can tell, I'm a pretty solitary fellow. But I did like having you around—even if it did mean a big raise in the budget for flashlight batteries.

"Then one evening you didn't come back. Even though I'd learned that you were well able to take care of yourself, I've got to admit that I was still upset. I stayed up most of the night waiting for you, but you didn't show up. The next day I started searching through the tunnels—every place I knew you'd been—looking for you. I followed the marks you'd already made, and I looked for new ones; I couldn't find any, and you weren't in any of the tunnels."

"Blaze marks," Bone said distantly. "They're called blaze marks."

"Aha," Zulu said, sitting up straighter. "You remember something?"

It was some time before Bone spoke. "Go ahead with your story, Zulu," he said at last. "Please."

Zulu grunted, then rose from the table. He placed the pots and dishes in a plastic bag, which he set down by the door—to be taken later to the tap to be washed. He produced a pipe from a foot locker, filled it with tobacco, lit it and puffed thoughtfully for a few moments as he studied Bone. The other man seemed lost, he thought . . . struggling so hard to remember.

"I didn't see you for a week, Bone-man," Zulu said softly, waving smoke away from his face with his hand, opening the iron door to let the smoke be wafted away into the darkness of the train and subway tunnels. "I have to tell you, I was very upset. I figured you'd suffered a relapse, and were lying sick or dead in the darkness. I figured you'd been run over by a train, beaten up, or whatever. I spent almost that entire week looking for you. But there was no trace of the bone-man. So there was nothing for me to do but go back to work. I was on my corner one Sunday morning, almost exactly a week later; I'd just finished a story. I looked around, and—son-of-a-bitch—there you were. It was as if nothing at all had happened. You were sitting on the third step, and you were wearing different clothes—Salvation Army, from the look of them. And you still had your bone with you. You'd been listening to me. When I looked over at you, you smiled and raised your bone to me.

"You sat there on the church steps all day listening to me, Bone-man, and in the evening you came back here with me. I made us something to eat, and then we talked—or I talked—for hours. It was just so damn good to see that you were all right. Then, after a while, you got up, came over and hugged me. And then you left. That was when I knew for certain that you had your own place somewhere.

"I saw you quite a few times after that; after all, even though you never talked, I knew we were friends. You'd stop by the church just about every day to listen to me and exchange a nod or a wave. Then you'd be off about your business—whatever that was." Zulu paused, smiled broadly. "It's good to see you, my friend. I'm sorry about your troubles."

"I owe you my life," Bone said quietly. "Twice."

The huge black man merely shrugged. "Is there anything in what I said that makes things come back to you, Bone-man?"

Bone closed his eyes, absorbing the warmth of his surroundings and his closeness to Zulu. "For a time earlier, this morning just before Lobo and his friends showed up, I felt I was very close to it; to remembering who I was, and where I'd come from." He paused, opened his eyes and quickly looked away as they misted with tears. He felt filled with emotion. Zulu had told him a story of the stranger; now he knew much more

241

about the man, and it was like meeting an old friend. And he knew now exactly what he had to do.

"Are you all right, Bone-man? You look kind of funny."

"I'm all right, Zulu."

"Did any of what I told you make sense?"

"Some. But I still don't remember anything. I've learned that I have to experience things, Zulu; that's what makes the circuits close. When I saw you from across the street, you looked *familiar*, but that's all. But when I was in the terminal, looking at that picture . . ."

"The Kodak exhibit?"

"Yeah. There was just this tremendously strong sense of identification with those mountains and the boy on the ledge. It felt like home."

"Those mountains are a long way from New York City, Bone-man."

"Yes. But I felt as if I'd been there, as if I belonged. Then, when you told me I'd been exploring the tunnels under here, I remembered what blaze marks were. So the mountains felt like home—but I also seemed to be at home here, underground. I seem to know how to get around. The Zodiac painted on the ceiling in Grand Central: I recognized it, and I knew it was wrong."

Zulu grunted. "Not many people know that. I know it, because I've read about it; but you recognized it."

"I'm at home out-of-doors, Zulu. It has to be. I can handle myself on mountains, and maybe in caves."

Zulu nodded, then tapped the ashes from his pipe into an aluminum saucer. "It sounds to me like you're getting warm. But it doesn't begin to explain why you were in New York City, or what you were doing at that construction site." He paused, looked up, added quietly, "And it doesn't explain why you stay."

"I stay because I have no place else to go. I know the place where you found me; that area is marked on a map a social worker gave me. The building is completed now, and there's nothing about it that feels familiar. Maybe I came up from somewhere under the ground. The problem is that wherever I may have been down there is now part of the foundation of the building. There may be no access."

"The Penn Central tunnels run down there, Bone-man, as well as the Hudson tubes. Man, you've got a real spiderweb of

242

tunnels in that area. We can check it out, if you want, but there's a lot of territory to cover."

Bone nodded curtly. "And there's no guarantee that's where I found the bone I carried, and that bone may be the key to open a lot of locks. I'll look—"

"*We'll* look, Bone-man. You're my friend. I want to help you."

"Thank you, Zulu. We'll look. But I have a strong suspicion that I have to *do* something in order for my memory to come back." He paused, looked down at his hands, remembered how the twisted fingers had held their grip on the side of the Chemical Bank Building—and how his instincts had led him to leap up there to escape the Wolfpack. He remembered how deeply the picture in Grand Central's concourse had stirred his emotions, and he now felt certain he knew how his hands had become gnarled. "Zulu, I need to climb," he continued quietly.

"Climb?"

"Yes," he said, remembering something Ali Hakim had said. *Stop waiting for a mountain to appear to you; you must build it yourself.* But not build it, he thought. He had to climb it. "I need . . . a mountain."

"There aren't too many of those in New York City," Zulu replied drily.

"Then a cliff; something high, and sheer."

Zulu pointed to Bone's stomach. "You aren't going to be climbing anything for a while, Bone-man; not with that slice in you. You do, it'll pop and you'll be squirting blood again."

"Then I'll do it when the wound heals. Can you find me something to climb, Zulu?"

The black street poet nodded. "I'll give it some thought—as long as you promise not to do anything too soon that could pop that wound open."

"I promise," Bone said, and smiled.

"It goes without saying that you'll be staying with me for a time, Bone-man."

"This could eventually get you into a lot of trouble with the police."

Now it was Zulu's turn to smile. "Don't you worry about it."

"What about those gang members? I killed Lobo."

"Lobo needed killing. I'll be the one all the witnesses will remember, not you. If the police want to ask me any questions, they know where to find me. I'll tell them I came across Lobo and his scumbag friends molesting some homeless people, and the gang members attacked me. The cops know there was bad blood between Lobo and me, and my guess is that they won't make too much of a hassle about what happened. In the meantime, let's you and me try to noodle out what we can do to help you jog your memory."

Bone leaned back in his chair, half closed his eyes. "There are two key areas, Zulu, like geographical bookends. There's the neighborhood around Penn Station and the post office where you found me on the sidewalk with my head bashed in, and there's Central Park, where I came out of whatever kind of trance I was in. There's quite a distance between those two places."

"For sure."

"My waking up seems to have had something to do with the killing of the old woman whose name was Mary Kellogg." Bone paused. He had almost forgotten the locket around his neck. Now he touched it, brought it out from under his shirt. "I had her blood and the old man's who died with her on my sleeves and the cuffs of my pants, Zulu. And I was wearing this locket around my neck; it belonged to Mary Kellogg. For the longest time, even though the police finally released me, I wasn't sure myself that I hadn't killed her, and the others. And then I walked into Ali Hakim's office and found his corpse, and I knew I hadn't killed him. But the incident that cleared me in my own mind is the one killing that absolutely convicts me in the minds of the public and the police."

And, surely, in Anne's mind.

Zulu shrugged his massive shoulders, made a deprecating gesture with his hands. "You kill Mary? I could have told you you didn't do that. The two of you were friends."

"Friends?"

"That's what I just said. She *gave* you that locket."

"How do you know?"

"She told me—the same as she told me how you rescued her from Lobo and a few other gang members. It seems you beat the shit out of them with that bone of yours."

"Lobo said something in Grand Central . . ."

"That's right. Shit; I keep forgetting that you don't remember any of that."

Suddenly Bone tasted blood, and he realized that he had bitten his lip. "Tell me about the woman, Zulu."

"Mary was what I call a 'waster.' Gone. Human Resources

people kept picking her up, getting court orders and putting her away in nursing homes. She kept walking away and coming back to St. Thomas Church. She slept there, at the top of the steps. She was probably schizophrenic. She told me she heard voices, and that the only place she felt safe was up there under a statue of Jesus. That's what she told me, and I imagine it's what she told you."

"I don't remember," Bone said tightly.

"Hell, she was a real chatterbox with you—and it made no difference to her at all that you never did anything but sit there and listen. There were two people Mary really liked— you and me. She liked a couple of the social workers well enough, but she said that you and I helped her clear her mind. She spent her nights up there under the statue, covered with newspapers or whatever she could find; I used to buy her sleeping bags, but she kept losing them or having them stolen, and finally she just said she didn't want to be bothered. During the day she'd usually wander around the city, doing whatever she did. But if it was a nice day, she liked to sit on the steps and listen to me. When you stopped around, which was pretty often, she liked to sit with you. You'd sit there with your arm around her, and she'd lean her head on your shoulder and talk to you about all her troubles. Then she told me what had happened with Lobo. That crazy fucker and his gang had roughed her up a little, and for some reason Lobo took it into his head that he wanted her to give him a blow job. Lobo was just getting ready to shove his pecker in her mouth when you showed up. You must have been one righteous act to see. You had the advantage of surprise, and you just banged away at them with your bone. Later, there were rumors—which turned out to be true—that you'd knocked out Lobo's eye. It was right after you'd saved her from Lobo that she gave you the locket. You also helped her in other ways, taking her with you to soup kitchens, and just generally trying to watch out for her welfare. That's what she told me, Bone-man. So you didn't kill that poor old lady. Incidentally, I'm pretty sure she isn't the only one that you helped. There are a lot of wasters out there, you know—people who are totally out of it, but who, for one reason or another, won't accept help. But I think you helped them in little ways, however you could. That was another reason why I liked you so much, and why I never believed what they were saying about you in the newspapers."

Bone reached up and wiped tears from his eyes. Zulu's words had touched him deeply; like Zulu, he found that he too now liked the stranger very much. "I know I didn't kill those people, Zulu, but I have a strong feeling that all the beheading murders are somehow connected to me—to my life."

Zulu frowned slightly. "Why do you say that?"

Bone told him, drawing connections between the killings and his time on the streets, how the killings had stopped when he had been locked up, and how they had started again when he had been released. Finally he again told of finding Ali Hakim's body—with the head in the bag, along with his razor and his bone.

Zulu nodded thoughtfully. "Maybe you're right. But this Dr. Hakim definitely didn't fit into the pattern of the other killings."

"No; obviously, he wasn't homeless."

"And he wasn't a waster."

Bone glanced up sharply. "What do you mean?"

"What I said. Just the fact that Hakim wasn't homeless isn't the only thing that made him markedly different from the other victims—at least judging from what I read in the newspapers about the other killings. This is a very, very tough society we live in, Bone-man—in case you hadn't noticed. But not everybody who lives on the streets is a waster. Even those who refuse help sometimes make out all right—people like you, for example. You and I can take care of ourselves. But wasters can't take care of themselves. Awake and asleep, they're covered with their own filth. They get frostbite and gangrene in the winter, and they have to have limbs amputated. They eat out of garbage cans. When they do get rounded up, they take off at the first opportunity from whatever treatment facility they've been placed in. Mary Kellogg was a waster, and she probably survived in large part for as long as she did because of you and me. Now, these beheading murders sold a lot of newspapers for a year. Every victim I read about, with the single exception of Ali Hakim, was not only homeless, but appeared to be a waster."

"I hadn't realized that," Bone said distantly, knitting his brows in concentration. It was another thread, a connection—but he did not know where it led, what was connected to what.

"How could you?"

"I have to find the killer in order to clear myself, Zulu. But there's an even more important reason why I have to find him."

Zulu said softly, "Because if you don't, more people are going to die."

"Yes. I believe so. As long as I'm free, he has me to take the blame for the killings. I have to get my memory back quickly, Zulu. I have to climb."

"Not yet; you'll kill yourself. I told you I'd give it some thought. In the meantime, there are other things that we can do."

"Like what?"

Zulu shrugged. "We can go over and check out whatever's underground at the corner of Thirty-third and Ninth Avenue."

"The police are looking for me, Zulu. I can't walk on the streets."

"Who said anything about walking on the streets?"

(iii)

"This is the IRT we're walking now," Zulu said as, powerful flashlight in hand, he led Bone through the subway tunnel. "This will intersect with the Penn Central and Conrail tracks; when we reach them, we'll walk west. Anything look or feel familiar?"

"Yes," Bone replied simply. "I've been in places like this."

From the time they had left the junction terminal room that was Zulu's home and begun their bizarre journey in the perpetual darkness beneath New York City's streets, Bone had felt a familiarity with the underground world. The stranger had indeed explored these tunnels, just as Zulu had said, and so it was not surprising to Bone that these surroundings should be familiar. Also, although he could not remember, it would not surprise him to learn that the stranger, like Zulu, had lived somewhere in these tunnels, perhaps in a room similar to the one where Zulu lived.

But that did not address the question of why he had been underground in the first place, as he strongly felt he had, before his injury. There was still no clue to who the stranger really was.

There was always ample warning when a train was coming, and when they heard the approaching roar of sound they ducked into recesses in the walls and covered their ears as the trains rushed past. Occasionally, huge Norway rats as big as puppies scurried away from the beam of light. Bone and Zulu walked to the right, away from the electrified third rail and the safety trip switches that jutted out every quarter mile or so.

"Cats," Zulu said as three white-furred creatures flashed through the cone of light. "They're mutants. Around the turn of the century, when they were building these lines, the workers brought down cats in an attempt to get rid of the rats. Obviously, the rats survived—and now there are thousands of these mutant cats down here. They live all their lives in the darkness. Every once in a while a humane society will send members down and trap a few to adopt out, but the few they catch don't begin to make a dent in the cat population."

"You seem to know a lot about what goes on down here, Zulu."

"I used to be what's called a 'track walker' for the MTA. In the fifteen years I spent with them, I must have walked a couple of thousand miles down here. It was my job to walk the tracks looking for gas, water or sewage leaks, and pick up trash. Also, the friction between the wheels and the rails creates a kind of dust that sticks to the steel, and that has to be constantly scraped away; if it isn't, you get track fires and short circuits. Would you believe that track walkers collect up to fifteen hundred fifty-pound bags of trash every twenty-four hours?"

"How did you end up on the streets, Zulu?"

Zulu's response was a laugh that Bone thought contained more than a trace of bitterness. "You think of me as one of the homeless, don't you, Bone-man?"

"I'm sorry, Zulu. It was a very personal question, and it's none of my business. Actually, I meant the question as a compliment. You seem to be a man of many talents who certainly doesn't need to be living under Grand Central Terminal."

They walked in silence for some time, until they finally came to the junction of the Penn Central and Conrail tracks, which ran east and west. Bone, who was certain he had offended the man who had twice saved his life, did not speak for fear of making matters worse.

Finally, Zulu said: "Bone-man, how many people do you know who can make a living doing exactly what they want to

248

do—doing what they'd do anyway, for nothing, if they couldn't get paid for it?" If Zulu had been offended, there was no trace of it in his voice now.

Now it was Bone's turn to laugh. "Zulu, you're talking to a man who doesn't know *who* he knows."

"Right."

"But I suspect that I don't know many."

"Right again, Bone-man," Zulu said, and grunted with satisfaction. "Well, you're talking to one of those few. I always wanted to be a writer. Do you know how many writers there are in this country—published authors—who can make a living at it? Damn few. Anyway, there I was with a job I hated and a dream of being a writer. I'd been writing ever since I was a kid, and I kept writing through the years—early mornings and evenings, before and after work. I'd walk these tracks, and the ideas would just keep tumbling over and over in my head. But I couldn't make them come out right on paper. I never got a single thing that I wrote published. Then I realized that I was a different kind of writer—I write things in my head, on the spot, and that's how I publish them; I publish my stories in sound, just as they come to me, on the spot. And I found I was damn good at it. One day I just decided that that was what I damn well wanted to do, *all* I wanted to do, and I've been doing it ever since. I've been supporting myself with my writing for better than seven years now. I guess some people would call me a performance artist. As you saw, I kept my keys from the time I worked for the subway. In the beginning, after I started writing full-time, I just kind of hung out down here when things were tough. Then things got better, I started to get regulars coming to hear me and I started to make money. But I'd gotten used to living down here. It's a place to sleep, I have everything I need and, like I said earlier, the rent is exactly right. I'm doing exactly what I want to do, and I'm satisfied with my work and life. I tell stories on the street because I want to, and I live under Grand Central because that's where I want to live."

"It's called success," Bone said, and then abruptly stopped walking.

Zulu stopped, turned and put a hand gently on Bone's shoulder. "What's the matter, Bone-man? You look funny. You all right?"

"Success is making a living doing what you want to do," Bone said distantly.

"Yeah," Zulu replied, and frowned. "So what?"

Bone lifted his left hand into the beam of light, studied the scar tissue and calluses there, the bent fingers. "I think I am—or was—successful in the same sense, Zulu."

"You remember something, Bone-man?"

Bone shook his head. "It's just a feeling I got when you were talking about doing what you do, and living where you live, by choice. Suddenly I got the feeling . . . that I'd been like that. I think that's how I made a living—doing what I wanted to do."

"Mountain climbing?"

Bone brought his other hand up into the light, turned it over, slowly nodded.

"Then what are we doing down here, Bone-man? A tunnel is not a mountain."

Bone thought—about his dreams, the panic attack in the underpass, his sense of familiarity with the darkness. "In a certain sense, it is," he said at last. "From the way you describe it to me, all of this intricate network of tunnels, on many levels, is like a huge, inverted mountain beneath the city."

Zulu shrugged. "I never thought of it that way. I guess you're right."

"I feel I have to climb to help myself remember; climbing may be the key to memory. But I also feel that whatever happened to cause me to lose my memory, and that the connection between me and the killings and the murderer . . . it happened to me here, underground. You found me after I'd somehow managed to come up to the surface."

"I hear you, Bone-man," Zulu said with quiet intensity.

Bone thought about it some more, then realized that he was pressing too hard. He let it go, turned and looked up into the chiseled features of the other man. "Are you African, Zulu?"

Zulu laughed. "Harlem—East Hundred and Sixteenth Street. My *nom de plume* is part of the performance. My real name is Horace Thorogood—and I'd just as soon you kept that to yourself."

"It's forgotten, Zulu."

They walked for another five minutes, and then Zulu reached out and gripped Bone's shoulder, at the same time sweeping the area with the flashlight. "As close as I can figure it,

Bone-man, I'd say we're just about under the area where I found you on the sidewalk."

Bone took a few steps forward, then stopped and looked all around him—but there was nothing to see but the tracks and walls of the subway tunnel stretching back and forth into the darkness beyond the beam of light. It looked no different from any of the other tunnels, and he felt no particular sense of familiarity. He could not understand what he would have been doing here—or how he could have climbed through solid rock to the surface.

"I think we wasted our time," Bone said with a sigh.

"There sure doesn't seem to be much here—and it looks about the same for a half mile or so in either direction. I know."

"There's no access route to the surface?"

"Not in this area."

"What's between us and the surface?"

"It's hard to tell," Zulu replied, pursing his lips. "Probably phone lines and power cables packed together tight as cooked spaghetti."

"What about below?"

"God and maybe a couple of dead engineers only know, Bone-man. I just know the subway system. But there are probably sewer and water mains, all sorts of things. Some of those pipes are big enough to drive a truck through. Even if you were in one of those, what would you have been doing there? And how could you have gotten out?"

Bone shook his head. He felt he was slowly finding pieces to the puzzle, and yet the identity of the stranger remained as elusive as ever. "You're sure we're under the spot where you found me."

"In the general area, yes. You were on the sidewalk, next to a construction project."

"The femur is another key," Bone said almost to himself.

"You sure as hell weren't about to let go of that thing."

"I had to hold on to it because it was important; it provided the answer to the question of where I had been, and what had happened to me."

"Maybe the construction people accidentally uncovered some old graveyard when they were digging down for the foundation."

"What was on that site before they put up the new building?"

"A parking lot— and before that, a grocery store."

Bone again shook his head. "I didn't find the femur at the construction site; I'm sure of it."

"How can you be so sure of that?"

"I've been having recurring dreams, Zulu. There's darkness, torchlight—and the bones are jutting right out of the floor, walls and ceiling of what seems to be a cave; it's definitely not a subway tunnel. Then there's a figure dressed all in orange . . . and streaked with blood."

"Maybe it's something you ate, Bone-man."

Bone smiled thinly. "I need to find a way to get further down."

"There may not be anything below us but dirt and granite, Bone-man—and even if there is something else down there, I sure as hell don't know how you're going to get to it. There are probably access routes to the sewage and water mains, but I don't know anything about them. If I *did*, I wouldn't want to go down there. I don't know anybody who knows a lot about everything that's under Manhattan."

But he knew somebody who did, Bone thought as he turned with Zulu and started to walk back the way they had come. But he didn't know how to contact Barry Prindle—and probably couldn't get the man's cooperation if he could contact him. There seemed nothing else to do but wait for the wound in his stomach to heal. If he could not go down below the ground any further, then his only hope was to go up, toward the sky, and hope that he would finally meet and know the stranger there. And hope that searching for the answer wouldn't cost him his life.

CHAPTER FIFTEEN

(i)

Softly humming a hymn to himself, Barry Prindle—wearing a new black oilcloth raincoat with matching hat—turned left off Broadway, onto Fifty-seventh Street. Walking quickly, keeping to the shadows cast by the building, he went halfway down the block, then turned into a narrow alleyway. Three quarters of the way down the alley he set down the plastic garbage bag he was carrying, reached down and into a niche in the brick wall of the building on his right, came out with a crowbar. Then he got down on his knees and brushed away the dirt and refuse concealing an ancient manhole cover, chipped and rusted around the edges. Just barely visible in the worn metal was the date, 1917. Prindle slipped the end of the crowbar into the notch in the cover, pried up the heavy steel and slid it to one side. He paused to wipe sweat away from beneath his pronounced widow's peak, then clambered into the hole, pausing on the third bent, iron rung to reach back and haul the cover back over his head. Then he climbed the long distance to the bottom and stepped into a spacious concrete chamber which housed the old, broken valve system for a part of the Croton water system—New York City's first successful attempt to tap bountiful upstate waters to sate the thirst of its population and flush its wastes. He drew a flashlight out of a pocket of his raincoat, turned it on.

The joints on one of the steel panels covering one wall of the room were rusted away. Prindle pushed his shoulder against one side of the panel, and it gave way. He stepped through the narrow opening into the interior of a dry water pipe more than seven feet in diameter. He moved to his left, walked a hundred yards to where sections of the pipe had separated to allow dirt to trickle in over the years, finally piling up to the height of a man's waist. Prindle tossed his garbage bag through the space between the pipes, then climbed up the dirt pile and squeezed through the opening, sliding down the sheer rock wall on the other side onto the smooth, cold stone of an ancient underground riverbed. He propped the flashlight on a rock, aiming it toward the ceiling so that the light would reflect off the limestone roof of the cavern, which was perhaps eight feet high. He flicked flakes of dried blood off his black slicker, then opened the garbage bag to once again examine the three heads inside.

They were the heads of two old women and a young man: Trixie Fein, Elma Dockowicz and Richard Green—two schizophrenics and a homeless teenager whose brain had been irreparably damaged by PCP. Time after time, Prindle thought, he and Anne had tried to help these people. With Ali Hakim's help, they had put these people away into safe places; but they had not stayed there, as they should have. These three people had returned to the streets to suffer needlessly. But now he had taken care of their problem, sent them on to the same God who had played such nasty tricks on him. He was still God's messenger, the arbiter of who had suffered enough and deserved to be relieved of further misery.

The thought gave him an erection. He'd always had erections, some of them painful, after executions; but he had always ignored them as best he could, realizing that the sexual excitement was a burden he had to bear. He'd been taught that it was forbidden to relieve himself, and he'd had to remain pure for Anne. But now things had changed; God had shown him that he didn't have to play fair. Now nothing was forbidden, at least not to him. Anne would still be his, one way or another.

He unzipped his pants, took out his stiff penis and began to furiously masturbate as he gazed down at the three severed heads. Within moments he ejaculated. Trembling with pleasure, Prindle zipped his pants back up, picked up the plastic bag and headed down the dry riverbed toward his cathedral.

He certainly felt very strange, Prindle thought as he moved along the water-scoured stone. He had believed that Ali Hakim would be his last gift to God; Bone would be caught and sentenced for the killings, and he would at last be free of his terrible burden of responsibility—and consequently free of his terrors. Without the burden of Bone, he would be free to pursue and marry Anne. He was certain it would have worked if Bone had been caught. Even with Bone free, he'd been certain that Anne's attitude toward him would change. Yet, when he had asked her to have dinner with him that evening, she had once again refused. Worse, he had detected something in her voice that had enraged him. She was, Anne had told him, feeling regret that she had been so quick to condemn Bone; she'd shared with him Bone's conviction that the killings were somehow connected to him, and Anne had gone on to ask if he, Barry, didn't think it possible that the real killer had murdered Ali in an attempt to frame Bone. The more she thought about it, Anne had said, the more she could not understand how, or why, Bone would have killed Ali. She'd said that she desperately wanted to talk to Bone.

Talk to Bone indeed, Prindle thought. He had never imagined it possible that Bone would manage to escape from the office building, and he could not understand why the police had not found him yet. He had never imagined that Anne would ever again consider the possibility that Bone could still be innocent. It made no sense.

Things were all falling apart for him once again, Prindle thought. His response had been to go out and search for more of the city's wretched to send on to God; after all, as long as Bone was free the police would assume that it was Bone doing the executions. He recalled the surge of excitement he had experienced when he had realized that Bone's release meant that he was free to continue with his mission. He enjoyed his work. He enjoyed the power. His work was not better than sex; it had become the same as sex. And it was not as if he were doing something wrong; he was carrying out God's mission. Except for the time when Mary Kellogg had come upon him right after he had sent one of her fellow wretches on to God, he had never before killed more than one person in a night. Now he wondered why he had been so reticent; there were certainly enough wretched people in the city who deserved to be put out of their misery, and he knew exactly who they were, and he usually knew where to find them. He had been wrong to limit himself. He decided that he would kill a minimum of four the next night. The number meant nothing as long as he did what God required, which was to give them—or at least their heads—a decent burial, and he had always done this.

Suddenly the riverbed widened, and the ceiling of the ancient subterranean waterway became higher. Prindle came to the first of the Coleman lamps he had hung on nails driven into cracks in the rock walls. He checked the level of kerosene in the lamp, then lit it with a match. The lamp flared, and he adjusted the flame to its highest level. He walked around the perimeter of the circular, domed stone chamber, taking care to avoid the quicksand pit in the center, and lit three other Coleman lamps, one at each point of the compass. Then he squatted down in front of the flat stone that was his altar and looked out over his cathedral with its two crypts—one very old, and one he had begun and consecrated. A year ago.

Here, in the great chamber deep below Manhattan's West Side, the bedrock granite had given way to more porous limestone, as well as veins and pockets of soil. To his right, ancient, ossified bones from some aboriginal graveyard jutted at odd angles out of a large lode of moist earth that had, over the centuries, sunk down to this level; bones lay scattered on the rock floor, occasionally having been shaken free from the soil by subterranean tremors. Light from the Coleman lamps flickered eerily, reflecting off the tangle of bones and the slick, dark surface of the large quicksand pit in the center of the chamber. The pit was his burial ground, Prindle thought; this was where he buried the heads of all his victims.

It was at the opposite end of his cathedral, at the narrow mouth of one of three smaller channels, that the man known only as Bone had suddenly, inexplicably, appeared out of nowhere.

Prindle still remembered the thrill he had experienced when, while doing some mapping of the Croton water system for one of Empire Subway's clients, he had discovered this uncharted, serpentine river channel and the great crypt-cathedral that was its heart. He had instantly recognized it for what it was—a gift from God, a sign, the church of his own that had previously been denied him. He'd been certain that God had guided him to this, his own, cathedral for a purpose—and he had soon discovered that purpose, which was when he had left Empire Subway and gone to work for the city's Human Resources Administration.

He recalled how his mission, God's purpose, had almost been thwarted near the beginning. He had chosen his second gift to send on to God, and had brought the head back here for proper burial. He had unbuttoned his raincoat, but had not removed his hat. Eager to get on with the service, his penis painfully erect and throbbing, he had removed the old man's head from the plastic bag with trembling hands, placed the still-dripping object on the smooth, stone altar. Startled by a sound, he had looked up to find a tall, lean and muscular man, dressed in leather shorts, a T-shirt and heavy hiking boots, standing in the mouth of the middle channel, staring. The man had a knapsack draped over his left shoulder, wore a miner's lamp strapped to his forehead and carried a large, powerful flashlight; both the miner's lamp and the flashlight had been turned off. He had not heard the man approach, and Prindle had assumed that the man had seen, then cautiously approached, the glow from his own Coleman lamps.

"What the hell?!" the man had shouted, his features twisted with shock and horror.

And then he had panicked. He'd had no permission to execute anyone who was not in need of God's final solace, but this sudden and totally unexpected appearance of a stranger out of nowhere had made him fear for the loss of his cathedral and the termination of his mission; once again he would be thwarted in his desire to serve God, just as he had been at the seminary. He could not let everything be taken from him once again. He had reached into the plastic bag and grabbed the straight razor he had sanctified and used for the executions, then raced around the quicksand pit toward the other man. The man, still numb with shock, had simply stared at him for a few seconds, then, at the last moment, had snatched one of the bones protruding from the earthen wall to his left and used it to defend himself.

Prindle had lunged at the man, slashing at his body with the razor. Displaying great speed and agility, the man had jumped back, at the same time striking him a glancing blow on the left shoulder. Then the man had swung at his head, narrowly missing, brushing the rim of his rain hat and causing him to stumble and slip on the loose bones, which had clattered away into the darkness.

Prindle recalled how the man had kept coming at him, swinging the rock-hard bone. He had ducked and scrambled to his feet, slashing at the man's midsection, at the same time trying to shield his eyes from the beam of the powerful flashlight which the man had turned on and was using to blind him. In frustration he had picked up one of the heavy bones and hurled it at the man; there had been a solid thud of bone against flesh, and the flashlight had fallen from the man's hand to shatter on the rock floor. Then he had attacked again with his razor, forcing the man, now obviously dazed and disoriented, to stagger back into the narrow confines of the third channel on the man's left.

Unwilling to follow the man into the darkness, he had hesitated at the entrance to the channel. Suddenly he had heard a shout of dismay—a sound which abruptly became muffled and distant, as if the man were falling. There was a sound of a body hitting against rock, and then a faint splash. Then there was nothing but silence and the sound of his own heavy breathing.

He'd gotten down on his hands and knees and crawled slowly into the third channel, which he had never explored. Ten feet in he reached out with his hand and touched nothing but air; he was at the edge of a chasm of uncertain width and depth. The man had fallen into an underground stream, and he'd been certain that the man would soon be dead—if not from drowning or being buried alive, then from the injuries he had sustained in the fight and during his fall.

He'd taken what he'd presumed to be the stranger's death as a good omen; it had been God Himself who had taken the man's life in order to keep him from interfering with the mission.

He'd been thoroughly astounded when, weeks later while riding in the van with Anne, he had seen the man, still clutching the bone he had wielded, on the streets. He'd had no idea how the man had survived, but he obviously had—and Anne had insisted that they stop and investigate this "newcomer." In that moment he had envisioned all his plans—God's plans—coming to naught. But the man had turned out to be mute. Prindle recalled how readily the man had accepted the sandwich, apple and carton of juice Anne had offered, but would not speak. Nor had his glacial blue eyes betrayed any sign of recognition when they had passed over his own face. It was then that he'd realized that the man with the bone was obviously brain-damaged as a result of his fall.

God's will, he had thought.

Or perhaps the man was God's messenger; the stranger had appeared out of the darkness, in a place he had assumed no one else even knew about, much less could find a way into. Also, the man's life had been spared in some unfathomable way, perhaps by a miracle of divine intervention; and now the man had shown up on the streets and was living in a way that, because of Anne's strong interest and determination, caused them to frequently be in close contact. Prindle recalled how puzzling it had all been to him, and still was. If the man with the bone was a messenger from God, what was the message?

He'd fallen in love with Anne soon after he'd met her, but had not known how to proceed. Up to that time, his sexual desires had always been directed toward other men; he'd loathed the desires, and himself. With Anne, finally, he had come to desire a woman. He'd been sure Anne would be able to help him change his life, and he'd been convinced that she was God's gift to him. She was there for him, and so he'd decided that he did not have to be in any hurry to draw her to him. God would make everything turn out all right.

But the continued presence of the homeless man with the bone, the man who had come upon him in his stone cathedral, had continued to disturb him, even as he continued to ponder the question of what message God was sending him.

What had become unmistakably clear was that Anne, from the first time they confronted him, was strongly attracted to the man with the bone. Frequently, Anne had asked him to drive out of their way so that they could go past St. Thomas Church, where the man could often be found listening to the madman Zulu as he sat with other homeless people and pedestrians who had paused to rest. Anne was always giving the man sandwiches. When the man was not sitting on the steps, Anne would ask Zulu about him—but Zulu had never had much to say to her. When they drove around the city, Anne had always been turning in her seat, her gaze restlessly wandering over the crowds on the sidewalks, and he'd known that she was searching for the man with the bone.

Helplessly and with growing resentment, he had watched as Anne's obsession toward the man with the bone had increased. When she had known where he was, Anne had often spent her lunch hours with him, talking, trying in vain to get some response from a man who would listen with apparent attention and even interest, but who would never reply. Still, he had been certain that the obsession would pass, God's will would be done and Anne would be his. And in the weeks, months, the seasons that passed, he had found fulfillment in his role as God's bringer of lasting peace to those who, it could be said, were of no further use to themselves or anyone else on earth.

But then he had suddenly been faced with a new crisis and dilemma, Prindle thought: the morning after he had committed his first double execution, the man with the bone had suddenly and mysteriously appeared in Central Park.

It had been nine in the morning when a call had come into the Project Helping Hand office from a patrolman who was concerned about an apparently homeless man, motionless and mute, who was squatting in the mud in the Sheep Meadow, grasping a bone. Anne and he had gone there, and he had immediately seen that something had happened to, or changed in, the man with the bone. His blue eyes seemed haunted, out of focus, and he would not look at Anne when she spoke, or even give any indication that he heard her voice. At one moment his features were twisted in anguish, but then his expression would change to one of fierce concentration—as if he were trying to remember something. Anne had stayed with him for almost two hours that first morning, talking constantly, pleading, but getting no response, and had finally left behind three sandwiches for him. Anne had been constantly distracted all through the day, and when she insisted that they go back in late afternoon, the man with the bone was where they had left him, in the same position, the sandwiches in front of him shredded by birds and squirrels, or by the huge Norway rats which migrated each spring from the tunnels beneath the city to Central Park.

Anne had been beside herself, and had again begun talking to the man, begging, cajoling, even tugging at his coat sleeve. The man had remained mute and immobile, the changing expressions on his face the only indication of the tempest that was going on inside his mind.

He had not known what it meant, Prindle thought, and he remembered his increasing uneasiness.

As night fell and the man had still not moved, Anne had begun calling various city agencies, asking for help—but, despite the incessant rain, the temperature had been relatively mild, and Anne had been told there was nothing that could legally be done; if a man wanted to squat in Central Park, and refuse to talk, eat or drink, that was his business.

They had returned early the next morning—to find the man with the bone exactly where they had left him. Again Anne had pleaded with the man, and again there had been no response. It had taken most of that day to enlist Ali Hakim's assistance, and then Ali had said that they should wait until the next morning in order to make a better case for forced removal to a city agency.

And it was on the morning of the third day that the man with the bone, to everyone's astonishment, had spoken.

Prindle recalled how, in those first moments, he was certain that the man would recognize him, and that his mission would be ended. But it had not happened; the man with the bone not only failed to recognize him, but did not remember the incident in the cathedral. The man with the bone did not remember anything.

He had not understood it then, Prindle thought, and he still did not understand it. God seemed to be playing with him.

Then had come the days, stretching into weeks, of anxiously waiting to see if the man would regain his memory and condemn him; finally there had been the torment of Anne's rejection, and then making the terrible hurt even worse by sending him away and taking Bone in to live with her. To make love to her . . .

A man could only take so much, Prindle thought. *That* much God had certainly taught him. He'd had to do what he did to Ali Hakim, for Ali too had rejected him. God had given him a mission to end the suffering of the wretched, but God obviously expected him to take care of himself.

Prindle sighed, then shook his head violently, as if to banish all the memories of Anne, Bone and his own seemingly endless torment. Then, without even going through the customary ritual, he removed the three heads from the bag and tossed them out into the middle of the quicksand pit, where they landed with a soft *splush-splush-splush*, floated for a few seconds, then slowly sank beneath the dark surface.

The message, Prindle thought as he stared at the flickering lights reflected in the dead eyes of the sinking heads, was that God enjoyed playing tricks on him.

Now it was his turn.

(ii)

Each day on her way to work Anne had to pass the building where Ali Hakim had worked. In the ten days that had passed since the neuropsychiatrist had been murdered, Anne had avoided looking at the building, since it stirred so many nightmarish thoughts, memories and fears. Now, according to the news bulletin she had heard on the radio, the horror had started again. There had been three homeless people decapitated during the night. The killer was following the same pattern of cutting off the heads, and sometimes the genitals, but he was obviously picking up the pace.

But was Bone really the killer?

On this morning Anne stopped on the sidewalk, deliberately looked up at the floor where Ali had had his offices, and she frowned.

The serial killer was back to killing the homeless, but he had broken that pattern once, with Ali. Why?

"The killings have something to do with me."

For the first few days, while the shock of Ali's death was still fresh and numbing, she had believed that Bone was indeed the killer; the evidence had seemed incontrovertible.

Then why was there still this gnawing uncertainty? she wondered.

Why did she still love him?

She remembered the year she had spent trying to make contact with him, trying to get him to respond to her; she remembered how, from the first time she had gone up to him, she had sensed such a feeling of *decency* in him.

But there could have been another, murderous, personality in him. Ali had said so; Bone had said so.

With Ali's severed head, Bone's femur and razor found in the same bag, how could she still believe he might be innocent?

Precisely because, she thought, the evidence seemed almost *too* incontrovertible, and precisely because Ali's murder did not fit into the pattern. Bone was certainly not stupid—and, if there was a killer inside him, the killer would not be stupid either. Killing Ali, and then allowing himself to be trapped, would be very stupid. And she had been with Bone when they had gone back to his campsite in the park and found his belongings missing. Had that just been a show put on for her benefit? Had the killer in Bone, the secret self in his "stranger," taken those belongings to another place?

Possible—but she didn't believe it, not now. She hadn't really believed it even in the first days of her initial shock.

"The killings have something to do with me."

Someone had framed Bone, and Anne felt ashamed of herself for reacting the way she had, for not thinking clearly after Ali had been murdered. Now Bone was staying away to protect her, she thought; but if he had contacted her in the first few days, she would not have been available to him. She would have been terrified of him.

But not now, she thought as she turned away from the building and hurried on down the sidewalk. Now she must once again begin searching for him, for he certainly needed her help.

Ten minutes after she sat down at her desk to clean up some paperwork before going out in the van, the phone on her desk rang.

"Project Helping Hand," Anne said as she picked up the receiver and cradled it between her neck and shoulder.

"Anne," the voice on the other end of the line said softly.

"Bone!"

"Shhh!"

Anne wrapped her fingers tightly around the receiver, breathed a deep sigh. "It's all right, Bone. There's nobody else in the office right now. Are you all right?"

"I didn't kill Ali, Anne. He was dead when I walked into his office; his head, my razor and the bone were in a bag by the desk. It was a setup. And I didn't kill the three people who died last night, either. But the latest killings meant that I had to call you."

"Bone . . . why didn't you call me at home?"

"I thought your phone might be tapped. Also, I thought it might be less . . . frightening . . . if I called you here."

"I'm not frightened of you, Bone."

There was a long pause on the other end, then: "You wouldn't be human if you weren't frightened of me after what happened to Dr. Hakim. *I* was frightened of me *before* I walked into that office, because it wasn't until that moment that I was absolutely certain I wasn't the killer. But then, of course, I knew that everyone else would be convinced beyond a doubt that I *was* the killer."

"Bone, where are you? I'll come to you."

"No."

"Trust me, Bone. Let me help you."

"I do trust you, Anne, but that's not the point. If I tell you where I am, and you don't inform the police, then you'll be aiding a fugitive. But you can help me; I need you to help me."

"Just tell me how."

"Anne, listen to me; I wouldn't be calling you unless I had to. I didn't want you involved in any way, because I sense there's great danger here. Whoever killed Dr. Hakim knew that I was going to see him Sunday mornings. If he knew about Dr. Hakim, then he probably knows about you. You must be very careful, Anne."

"I'll be careful, Bone," Anne said evenly. "Just tell me what you want me to do."

"I had to leave Dr. Hakim's office, because I didn't have any choice. Since then, I've made some progress."

"Bone—!"

"Just listen. I can't give you details, because I want you to immediately report this conversation to Lieutenant Lightning after we finish talking, and I don't want you in a position of having to lie. There's something I must do, but there are certain reasons why I can't do it yet. But I knew, after I was told of the latest killings, that I had to act; that's the reason for this call. I'm convinced that the killer knows me, or is connected to me in some way, and I'm also convinced that the killings would have stopped if I'd been caught. That was the point of killing Dr. Hakim; the killer wanted to retire, and he wanted to make sure I'd take full blame for everything he'd done. That means that every moment I'm free, more homeless people are in danger of being murdered. I believe the killings will stop if I turn myself in, but then I'll never be able to clear myself, and I'll never be free again."

"Oh, Bone," Anne breathed, "how you must be suffering."

"I have to catch the killer myself, Anne—or at least be able to prove who it is. I have a witness who'll testify that I couldn't have committed the murders last night, but if I turn myself in the police will still want to charge me with all the other killings."

"Bone, who's the witness?" She paused, listening to the silence on the other end of the line, then added: "You're right; I don't want to know."

"All of the murder victims that I know of seem to have been—with the single exception of Ali Hakim—the most helpless of the homeless, people who have fallen right off the ladder; they were absolutely wretched people who couldn't help themselves, and who refused help. Am I right?"

"I hadn't thought about it," Anne said after a pause. "Now that I do, I think you may be right. Really, I'm not sure."

"I'd like you to try to check it out for me—every victim. What I think you'll find is that every single victim, except Ali Hakim, was hopelessly mentally ill or alcoholic, and had consistently refused to accept any kind of help. Find out how many had walked away from mental institutions, or drug treatment facilities; see if you can get agency and hospital records on them, if there are any. And see if they might have anything else in common. I'm not sure what it would mean if I am right, or if the information will do me any good, but it's a start. Can you do that for me?"

"I'll do the best I can, Bone. I'm not even certain all of the victims have been positively identified, and the records on the rest are likely to be pretty scanty."

"Call Lieutenant Lightning. Tell him I've been in touch with you, and report exactly what we've discussed. That will protect you. He won't believe I'm not the killer, but he just may help you get the information I want."

"I think I'll ask him for the information first."

"Handle it the way you feel best, but remember that Lightning is no fool. He'll want to know why you want the information, and he'll probably suspect right off that you've been in touch with me. I'd tell him up front."

"Okay."

"How are you getting on with Barry?"

"Fine," Anne replied after a slight pause, somewhat surprised by the question.

"I need other information which he may be able to supply. I

recall him saying that he used to work for a firm that does underground surveys for the utilities and other companies that want to dig into the ground."

"That's right; Empire Subway Limited."

"Barry has always thought I was the killer, so I'm not sure how you should approach him on this. If you tell him it's for me, he may not help you."

"What do you need, Bone?"

"All the information I can get about structures—natural as well as man-made—in a broad area underground, with an epicenter under the building at the corner of Thirty-third Street and Ninth Avenue. That's where I was found, unconscious, on the sidewalk next to a construction site a little more than a year ago."

"Bone! Who found you?!"

"There's no time now, Anne, and I can't give you information that I don't want Lightning to have. But I need to know what's under that area. I thought Barry might know, and he might even be able to steer you to some maps of the general area, say nineteen or twenty square blocks. I know there are subway tunnels that run under there, but I'm looking for something else."

"Do you think you were hurt somewhere down there?"

"I'm almost certain of it."

"Can you tell me how you found out?"

"Not now. I got lucky. Do you have any idea how long it will take you to start getting the information?"

"I'll start right now, and we'll see how much I can find out by, say, five o'clock. How will I get in touch with you?"

There was a prolonged silence at the other end. Finally, Bone said: "Lightning will probably have this phone tapped right after you talk to him—if he doesn't already. I guess it doesn't make any difference. He'll ask you to cooperate with him, and that's what you'll be doing. I'll call you at this number at five."

"Bone, let me come to you."

"No."

"If Barry can get me maps, I'll have to hand them over to you anyway."

"First see if you can get the maps. I don't want you to lose your job, and I certainly don't want the police to charge you with aiding and abetting a fugitive. I think you should be in the clear as long as you keep Lightning informed of what you're doing, and why."

"Considering the fact that we're talking about saving lives, I find I really can't get too excited about what the police may do to me."

"I can."

"Do you really think this phone could be tapped?"

"Probably not now—but it will be. I may have to call you a few times, from different phones, and only speak for short intervals."

"That sounds very clever," Anne said, and smiled thinly. "You go ahead and call here at five. If I'm not around, it probably means that I've gone for a walk—and that walk should take me somewhere around the boathouse in Central Park at about six o'clock."

"Anne—!"

"You can withhold information and refuse to meet in order to protect me, but you can't tell me I can't be at the boathouse at six o'clock if I want to. I'm just telling you that. But call here first to see what I may have for you. Oh, incidentally, I've decided that I'm in love with you."

There was a long, deep, clearly audible sigh on the other end of the line. "Anne, thank you. There are so many things I'd like to say to you, but I can't. Not now; not yet. I know the stranger will love you."

"Well, thank you for saying that. There's no stranger, Bone. There's just an honest, decent, courageous man who's been hurt and lost his memory. We're going to find the real killer and prove you innocent. Now, let me get going and see what I can dig up for you."

"Anne?"

"Yes, stranger that I love?"

"There's one other thing I'd like you to think about."

"You name it, I'll think about it."

"I need a place somewhere close by where I can climb."

"Climb?"

"A very high, sheer surface; a cliff."

(iii)

"Homicide. Lieutenant Lightning speaking."

"This is Bone, Lieutenant."

There was a sound like a sharp intake of breath, but Bone could not be sure; there was a great deal of background noise on the street just behind the bank of pay phones from which he was calling. When Perry Lightning did speak, his tone was even. "It's good to hear from you, Bone. I thought I might."

"Why do you say that?" Bone asked tightly.

"Because, as I've told you, I've always believed that you were basically a decent man with a big problem. Somehow, I think those three people you offed last night might have been just a little too much for you. You're ready to give up and come in, and I salute you for that; that's the truth. Tell me where you are, and I'll come and pick you up."

Bone clenched his jaws in frustration, then glanced at Zulu, who was shielding him from the gaze of passersby at the same time as he acted as a lookout and timekeeper. The huge black man held up two fingers.

"Lieutenant, since I don't care to have you trace this call, I don't have a lot of time to talk; I don't want to use my time trying to convince you that I'm not the killer."

"Let me bring you in, Bone. Give yourself—"

"Did Anne Winchell, the social worker with HRA, call you today?"

There was a short pause, surprise in the police lieutenant's tone when he answered. "No. Why?"

"Are you sure? Maybe she called when you were out."

"Every call is logged, and I check in every hour or so. Anne Winchell's call would have been forwarded to me; she's high on my list of priorities, since she's a link to you. She didn't call me. Now, you tell me why she would have wanted to call me."

Bone again glanced at Zulu, who held up one finger.

"I was in touch with her this morning— which, incidentally, she was going to report to you. Besides you, I asked her to get in touch with Barry Prindle, her ex-partner, to try to get some information that I need."

"What information?"

Zulu put a hand on Bone's shoulder, used his other hand to make a slashing motion across his throat.

"That's not important now. What's important is that I was supposed to be in touch with her at five—and, if not five, then six."

"It's past eleven, Bone."

"I know that. She wasn't at either place where I was supposed to be in touch with her, and she's not home."

Zulu's fingers began to press more tightly into Bone's shoulder.

"I haven't heard from her, Bone," Lightning said, his tone suddenly very hard. "I'm thinking this may be another little game of yours, pal. If you're really worried about the woman, you'll let me come and get—"

Bone angrily slammed down the receiver, then turned around and followed Zulu—dressed less flamboyantly than usual, in jeans and a sweatshirt—through the crowds of people in Times Square. They turned right on Forty-second Street, and Zulu stepped in front of him just as a police cruiser sped up the block, lights flashing, and screeched to a halt in front of the pay phone where Bone and Zulu had been only moments before.

"You like to cut things pretty close, Bone-man," Zulu said under his breath as they reached Sixth Avenue, waited for a light and then walked on toward Grand Central Terminal.

"He's got her," Bone said, his heart racing and his breath rasping in his lungs for reasons that had nothing to do with their fast pace.

Zulu stopped, put a hand on Bone's shoulder and drew him into the shadows of a storefront. "Take it easy, Bone-man; just take it easy. You look like you're about to have a heart attack. We're safe now. Tell me what the good lieutenant said."

Bone took a series of deep breaths, then reached up and wiped a sheen of sweat off his forehead. "He says Anne never called him."

"Maybe he's lying."

"Why should he lie?"

"Because he's trying to lay a trap for you; he wants you under a lot of pressure."

Bone shook his head. "She was supposed to be at the boathouse at six, and she wasn't there. Also, she never called Prindle. You heard my conversation with him, when I was finally able to get a number where I could reach him." He paused, took another series of deep breaths in order to fight the sense of panic that threatened to engulf him. "She may have spoken to someone else first, Zulu. The killer."

"Before she called Prindle or Lightning? Come on, Bone-man."

"It has to be. She wasn't able to reach Prindle, and the thought of talking to Lightning made her uneasy. So she tried to get the information for me some other way. She had to have called somebody else: the killer. Their conversation tipped him off that I might be close to finding out—or remembering—who he is, so he panicked and took Anne." He paused, then forced himself to say the words that were in his mind, haunting him. "Maybe she's already dead."

Zulu squeezed both of Bone's arms. "Easy, Bone-man," he said in his deep, resonating voice. "You're not going to help her by getting all hyper."

"If she's dead, Zulu, I killed her: my call to her, the things I asked her to do. I killed her."

"No, Bone-man. I hear your grief talking, and that's just a waste of time. If you're right about the killer having her, and I think you are, then one of two things is true: she's either dead or alive. If she's dead, there's nothing you can do about it; if she's alive and being held somewhere, then it seems to me that the best thing for you to do is keep working to get your memory back. What about calling this Prindle guy back and asking him yourself for information about what may be under that West Side section of the city?"

Bone thought about it, shook his head. "Prindle never much cared for me in the first place, and he's been convinced all along that I'm the killer. I'm sure he must have reported our last conversation to the police. The first thing he'll do if I talk to him again is call Lightning back and report on what I said; there'd be cops all over the place around there, and I don't need that."

"Then we'll go back to that section again tomorrow, and we'll keep walking through the subway tunnels until we find something that looks familiar to you. Maybe we can find a way to get down to another level—if there is another level."

Bone again shook his head. "Too time-consuming, and we might never find what I'm looking for." He paused, looked up into Zulu's face. "Tomorrow I climb. Have you got a place for me?"

Zulu clucked his tongue, pointed to Bone's stomach. "If you try to do any serious climbing, you're going to rip yourself right open."

"You know I have to do it, Zulu. Have you got a place?"

Zulu sighed, slowly nodded. "I've got a place. It's in Nyack, across the river in Rockland County where my sister lives. It's about an hour away. We'll get you disguised again and take a bus there in the morning. It's a state park, but it's early in the season, and it's a weekday, so we should have the place pretty much to ourselves."

"The climb—is it steep enough?"

Zulu raised his eyebrows slightly, smiled thinly. "You'll tell me. It's called Hook Mountain."

CHAPTER SIXTEEN

(i)

"That high and steep enough for you, Bone-man?"

Bone stood in the small meadow, gazing up at the sheer escarpment before him, feeling his heart hammer with excitement.

They had gone to the Port Authority early, boarded a bus to Nyack. They had gotten off in the center of the small waterfront town, walked the two miles to where North Broadway ended at Nyack Beach State Park. While still a mile away, the mountain had suddenly come into view as they'd rounded a bend in the road. From the time when he had first glimpsed the escarpment soaring up into the sky, time had begun to collapse in on Bone, and he had kept his gaze firmly fixed on the mountain as they had approached. Now he stood in the clearing at its base, staring up, taking deep breaths, trying to empty his mind of everything but the challenge which faced him. The stranger had stood in places like this before, he thought—not at Hook Mountain in Nyack, but before other cliff faces that were even higher and more sheer.

He felt at home.

This was a "new" mountain, Bone thought, one that had

thrust up out of the earth in fairly recent geologic time. There was this plateau on which they stood, and behind him the mountain dropped off at a steep but easily climbable angle to the Hudson River; the cliff face before him was almost perpendicular, perhaps seven hundred feet high.

It was exactly what he had wanted.

"I figured you could get your exercise clambering up and down that stuff at the base," Zulu said, pointing to the hundred feet or so of jagged rockfall at the foot of the escarpment. "Just take it easy, Bone-man. I've got you taped up pretty good, but you could still split open that wound if you put too much stress on the stomach muscles. Do about ten minutes on that loose stuff and see how you feel. Okay? Just watch out you don't break an ankle."

Bone did not reply. He was deep within himself now, his eyes scanning the face of the escarpment as he planned his ascent. He removed his floppy hat, dark glasses, slacks and coat, leaving himself dressed only in leather shorts and a T-shirt. The wind blowing up the Hudson River swept over his body, chilling him, but at the same time filling him with exhilaration. He would not be cold for long, he thought as he opened the canvas bag at his feet, took out smooth-soled black sneakers which were among the items they had purchased before leaving New York, put them on over his two pairs of heavy socks. Next he took out a muslin bag of powdered chalk which he positioned against his spine on the belt he had looped around his waist.

He was aware of Zulu speaking to him—but now all of his concentration was focused on the cliff face as he searched for the best angles, finger- and toeholds.

Once he started up, he thought, there would be no way back. Somehow he knew that a cardinal rule of what he was about to attempt was to keep moving at a steady, fluid pace, in an almost continuous flow of motion where his body would become as one with the stone and flow upward, defying gravity, to the top. If he found the right angles, took the proper route. To stop for too long, to make one wrong decision, was to die as muscles cramped and fingers lost their grip.

All of this he knew.

His mind now cleared of everything but the terrible knowledge he possessed of free climbing, Bone abruptly started walking away at a rapid pace, angling off to his right toward the base of the route he had chosen.

"Hey, Bone-man, where the hell are you going?!"

Bone reached the base of the sloping rockfall, stepped up on a rock wedged between two huge boulders and began picking his way through the loose, jagged rocks, remembering as he climbed to breathe deeply, flex his knees slightly and push with his legs in order to conserve energy.

This was, he thought, about a 5.1 climb—very difficult, for top experts only. But he was a top expert, and he had executed climbs of 5.5 difficulty, which would have been considered impossible only a decade earlier.

He effortlessly climbed to the top of the loose rockfall, reaching the base of the escarpment itself where he unhesitatingly reached up with both hands and gripped a tiny, narrow ledge jutting out from the rock face.

"Bone-man, what the hell do you think you're doing?! You're going to fucking kill yourself! Get back down here! Nobody can climb that!"

Zulu's shouting voice was close, Bone thought, right beneath him, at the base of the rockfall; but this was the last time he actually heard Zulu, for now he was totally immersed in the challenge posed by his free climb. There could be no hesitations, no pauses to rest except for those which were planned, when he reached places where he could hang by his legs. He could not climb too fast, for that would deplete his energy too quickly— but he could not climb too slowly, for this too would exhaust him before he had reached the top. Pace and rhythm were everything. He had no rope, no equipment whatsoever to help him in his climb; there was only his body and his mind to pit against the sheer rock face, and to make a misjudgment with either his mind or body was to die.

The momentum of his initial swing took him out over the rock face, and at the apogee of his swing he released his right hand, reached up and gripped another minuscule outcropping of rock. A split second later he released his left hand, and as he swung again like a human pendulum he flexed his knees, brought his legs up slightly and pressed the toes of his left foot into a small niche. With this leverage he pushed himself up to his next handhold and immediately moved to his right. Then he repeated the same series of motions, this time moving to his left, driving with his legs, pulling, following cracks in the rock, flowing up the bottom third of the escarpment in nonstop motion.

He knew that now he could no longer peel off, no longer voluntarily release his grip and fall back to the ground to search for another, safer route; he was far too high for that, and if he dropped now, his body would be broken on the jagged rockfall below.

He reached a relatively wide, deep ledge. Here he swung his legs up and over the outcropping, then released his grip and lay back in space, letting his arms hang loose in order to rest them, regain strength and circulation. It was a planned rest stop, one he had spotted from the ground as he had planned his route. If his eyesight and planning had been good, he thought, he would come to two more such rest stops on his way to the top.

Hanging upside down, his arms dangling, he looked up at the azure sky, then arched his back slightly and looked below him—at Zulu, who was very still, his head back and an absolutely disbelieving look on his features as he stared up at him.

But it was not Zulu's voice he heard in his mind.

"You should go to New York, boy. You like to roam around caves? Well, you should see some of the interesting shit that's under that city. I know; I've been down there."

Caves? Climbing. Climbing up, and climbing down. He did both, Bone thought. It was what he did for a living.

No, more than that. Climbing, exploring: these things were his life.

His arms felt better, stronger. He reached behind him, took some chalk dust out of the cloth bag hanging from his belt, wiped it over his hands to dry the moisture there and thus provide him with a better grip. Then he took a series of deep breaths, abruptly reached up and gripped the rim of the ledge with his right hand, kicked his legs off the ledge. He used the momentum of his swinging legs to carry him to his right, swung back again and then in a single motion grabbed the ledge with his left hand, pulled himself up and onto the outcropping. He felt something rip in his belly, a sharp stab of pain. He looked down, saw that the front of his T-shirt was stained with blood.

There was nothing to be done about that now, Bone thought. Indeed, he could not even afford to think about his wound and the bleeding, for then he would risk losing his concentration, risk falling from the escarpment and dying. This was the beauty of free climbing, the essence of what had always attracted him to the sport. It was pure, with no room for error. Grace was rewarded, while clumsiness or loss of concentration was punished by death. More than once he had been told he was crazy by people who did not understand. All rock climbers were crazy, he had been told.

Sure, he thought as he smiled grimly. Rock climbers were crazy. But in what other sport could one find such purity?

On the next leg of this route there was nothing but a narrow cleft running perhaps twenty feet straight up, ending at another narrow ledge. Bone jammed his left hand into the cleft, clenched his hand into a fist. With only this clenched fist serving as a piton, anchoring him to the face of the cliff, he swung out and up, reached over his head and jammed his right hand into the crevice, clenched it into a fist. Then he planted both feet against the smooth rock on either side of the crevice, pushed with his toes as he pulled. Little by little, foot by precious foot, he "punched" his way up the face of the cliff.

By the time he reached the second ledge the flesh on the backs of both hands was raw and bleeding, and the muscles in his arms and shoulders burned with uric acid buildup from fatigue. He hooked his legs below the knees over the rim of the ledge, released his grip and once again allowed the upper two thirds of his body to dangle loosely in space.

Zulu now appeared as little more than a black dot on the grassy plateau below. Zulu still remained motionless in the same spot, as if he were a great black tree which had taken root, a silent witness.

"You're a good man, Granger; a little weird, maybe, but I respect what you do, and you're certainly a free spirit. Since you explore caves as well as you climb cliffs, check out the New York City underground. I work for a company there called Empire Subway Limited; we find and map out what's down there for the utilities, subways and construction companies."

He had started free climbing when he was a freshman at the University of Colorado. There had been a club at the university, and the instructor had started him off climbing huge boulders, using no equipment and carrying nothing but a bag of chalk powder to keep his hands dry and his grip firm.

He had soon discovered that he had a natural talent for free climbing, possessing not only tremendous upper body strength

276

and agility, but grace in his movements and an almost uncanny instinct for finding the "right" route to take him to the top of unforgiving barriers of stone. He had "graduated" from boulders to the buildings on campus, and from these sheer but predictable columns of brick and window ledges to the sheer and unpredictable faces of rock cliffs. Each weekend all during the school year he had driven, often with other enthusiasts, to various cliffs in the region. It soon became apparent to all that he was the best—better than the other hobbyists, better than any of the instructors. Fourteen months after his first tentative crawl up the face of a boulder, he'd been executing 5.0 climbs—climbs which were then considered at the very edge of the possible, the ultimate in difficulty.

"You're a hell of a guide and teacher, Granger, and you've shown me one hell of a lot down there in the places you've taken me. Now I'd like to show you a good time. I'll send you some maps from the company. You walk around under New York and you'll see more than a bit of history; in lower Manhattan you can see wooden waterworks designed and built by Aaron Burr. Check it out. If you do decide to come, give me a call when you get there. I know how to show you a good time above ground, too. If you've never been to New York, it's an experience you'll never forget."

Indeed, Bone thought—and once again smiled grimly.

He had dropped out of college at the beginning of his junior year, for he had already discovered what it was he wanted to do with his life. He'd worked at some odd jobs to earn money, and when he had saved enough he would quit and travel, searching for new cliffs and mountains against which to pit his skills, living in rooming houses and YMCAs, wherever he could find a bed.

His fame had spread, and soon he had found himself much in demand as an instructor of free-climbing techniques at various mountaineering schools, in Europe as well as in the United States. The pay from these free-lance assignments was very good, and he had used the time the money had bought him to pioneer new techniques and to free-climb rock faces previously scaled only by climbers with traditional mountain-climbing equipment. It was because of him that the rating scale of difficulty had to be expanded beyond the 5.0 range, to 5.5. He was constantly on the move, traveling around the world to teach and to climb. He had become friends with people around the world, and had become increasingly more famous among rock and mountain climbers. But his friends had long grown used to not seeing or hearing from him for long periods of time, for he might be camped in desolate mountain ranges anywhere from Colorado to the Himalayas; his friends had learned to expect him when he appeared, and they would never question an extended leave of absence; they would assume he was climbing somewhere in the world.

"Come to New York, Granger. Check out what's under the streets there. If you find anything down there we don't already know about, the company will lay some money on you."

Caving—spelunking—had somehow seemed a natural extension of his talents; instead of climbing up, he would climb down. He liked to explore and climb, regardless of the direction in which he was moving. Indeed, he had soon learned of famous cave systems, such as Fantastic Pit at Ellison's Cave in Georgia, which could be reached only by someone using mountaineering techniques. He had astounded the world of climbing by free climbing down four hundred and fifty feet into the Valhalla Pit, in Alabama.

Once introduced to this underground world, he'd discovered that he enjoyed exploring there almost as much as he enjoyed climbing sheer cliff faces toward the sky. Caving had its own unique challenges and fascinations, and before long he had become a top expert in underground explorations. He was an important contributing member of the Cave Research Foundation, and was on the Cave Rescue Commission—ready to fly on short notice to any site in the world to assist in the rescue of lost or stranded spelunkers. He had discovered dozens of new cave systems, helped map hundreds of miles of caverns in Carlsbad, Mammoth Caves, Shenandoah and Curry Caverns, as well as other, lesser, cave systems.

Now he could feel the warmth of his own blood spreading across his stomach; the front of his T-shirt was stained a dark crimson and was sticking to his flesh. As he hung in space, blood was flowing down his arms, dripping off his fingertips. Strength and feeling had returned to his arms—but he knew that it was much diminished. He was in great danger, Bone knew, and if he did not pick up his pace he would never make it to the top; the value of the flood of images that was now engulfing his mind would be lost. Finally, he had found the stranger—but the stranger was going to die if he did not get moving.

And if he died, Anne would die. If she was not dead already.

He flexed the muscles in his legs slightly, pulling himself up far enough so that he could see the next ledge and rest stop; it was perhaps seventy-five yards above him. From that stop it appeared to be a fairly easy climb the rest of the way to the top—but those seventy-five yards were extremely difficult; in his present, very weakened, condition, they could prove to be deadly. He would need all of his remaining strength, will and—most of all—concentration. If he was going to make it, he had to flow . . .

He wiped blood away from his eyes, then arched and grabbed hold of the edge of a narrow crevice off to his right. Then he released his legs and once more swung out into space. He searched with his feet for a toehold, found one, lost it. Then his grip on the crevice began to loosen.

It looked like he might not make it, Bone thought dreamily as he swung back and forth, his fingers slipping. One mistake usually meant death. He had not climbed for more than a year, and he was growing very weak from loss of blood.

He reached up and out with his left hand, jammed it into a crevice; that served to stop his side-to-side motion, and he braced himself with his feet against the rock. He released his right hand, reached back into his chalk bag. He chalked his right hand, then his left. He had to increase his pace, Bone thought. But he mustn't struggle against the rock, only flow faster over it . . .

Now!

He reached up with his right hand and found a grip. He surged up, found another grip, scrambled with his feet, pushing, pulling up again. *Flow;* pull, push, swing, grab hold, *flow* . . .

Blood, warm and sticky, was running down his legs now. Still he kept going, his ears ringing with distant, dissonant music. One slip . . . don't think about it. Keep moving! Flow!

And then he reached the next rest stop. Panting with exhaustion, he hooked his legs over the ledge, lay back and struggled to breathe. His arms and fingers felt as if they were on fire, but he knew that he could not afford to rest for long; not with his blood draining out of him at an ever-increasing rate.

Then one day the maps had arrived, sent by the New Yorker whose party of amateur cavers Bone had guided through a little-known section of Carlsbad Caverns, forwarded to him at the Utah mountaineering school where he had been teaching. He had studied the maps, and had indeed been intrigued by the strange world, part natural and part man-made, beneath the streets of New York City—especially the borough of Manhattan. He had never been to New York; indeed, he generally avoided big cities altogether, preferring the mountains and open country of the West. Almost as a whim, he had decided to visit New York City, perhaps to do some exploring of its subterranean world on his own. He had told no one where he was going, and had not contacted the man who had sent him the maps, for he was not certain how long he would stay.

In New York he had checked into a YMCA, paid a couple of days in advance, and then proceeded to go out on his own to walk the streets and see the sights. He'd been impressed by the incredible energy of the city, regretted that he had not come before.

And he had begun to use the maps to explore underground.

He had started in the Wall Street area, where there were underground structures dating back to the times of the earliest Dutch settlers who had colonized the tip of the island of Manhattan.

He had been fascinated by what he found, and he had decided to branch out, to try to go beyond the routes indicated on the maps. Eventually, by repeatedly daring to crawl into very narrow, natural fissures in the limestone and granite, he had discovered an ancient, natural cistern into which wells had been drilled hundreds of years before. There were natural tunnels radiating out from the cistern, and he had explored them—eventually finding the unmapped, dry bed of a river that had carved its way through the bedrock of Manhattan in prehistoric times. Excited by his discovery, he had spent day after day exploring the riverbed and its narrow tributaries, traveling south to north, heading further and further up this dark artery beneath the island.

Almost a week after he had begun, when he estimated that he had worked and mapped his way almost halfway up the island, he had been thoroughly startled to hear what sounded like muted chanting. Someone was in the darkness ahead of him— and with his own lights off, he could now detect a faint glow from that direction. Using the glow as a beacon, he had cautiously gone forward, feeling his way in the darkness. He had groped through a narrow channel, then suddenly found himself standing at the entrance to a vast, stone rotunda that the swirling water of the vanished river had carved from the surrounding soft, almost pure, limestone. Coleman lamps anchored in the walls at the four points of the compass cast an eerie, flickering glow throughout the chamber, and he had suddenly realized that he was standing in the center of a field of bleached bones that were not only beneath his feet, but jutting from the walls and ceiling of what appeared to be a geological anomaly—a small core, or pocket, of earth veining the stone; an ancient burial ground that had steadily sunk over the ages.

From this surrounding thicket of bones he had found himself staring out over a horrifying tableau. In the center of the chamber was the dark, shimmering surface of what Bone thought was almost certainly a quicksand pit, another oozing anomaly which would be deadly for the casual and unsuspecting explorer, probably fed and lubricated by fresh springs even further beneath the ground. On the opposite side of the pit a man knelt; the man was dressed all in blood-streaked, orange rain gear, open at the front to reveal what appeared to be a brocaded purple priest's chasuble. Bone had watched in horror as the man had reached into a black plastic garbage bag and drawn out the severed head of an old woman whose long, white hair was matted with blood.

"What the hell?!"

The man in blood-streaked orange had looked up and seen him, then once again reached into the plastic bag and drawn out an object which had glittered in the flickering light cast by the Coleman lamps; the man was already halfway around the quicksand pit, running toward him, before Bone had realized that the object the man held was a straight-edged razor. He had snatched one of the bones from the earth wall to his right, hefted it; the femur he had drawn from the earth had felt as heavy and hard as stone.

The man had slashed at him with his razor, and he had jumped back, away from the deadly steel. Then he had leaped forward and swung at the man's head, missed, but hit the man's arm. At the same time he had used his other hand to turn on the flashlight and shine the beam straight into the man's face; he had seen, beneath the floppy brim of the rain hat and above the upturned collar, a pair of bright green eyes which had glittered with madness, panic and rage. The man had slipped and gone down, but had immediately picked up a bone and flung it at him. The stone-hard bone had hit him over the left temple, stunning him. He had dropped the flashlight, heard it smash on the stone floor. His vision blurred, hands to his head, he had known only that the man with the razor would be coming at him again, and he had staggered backward to his left, into the mouth of a narrow channel which was not the one he had come through. He'd continued to back up, left foot, right foot—and then he had stepped into nothing. Suddenly he had been falling away into darkness, colliding with stone walls on his way down, banging his head again, listening to what sounded like the roar and whistle of a freight train rushing through his skull, threatening to crush him. Pain had exploded somewhere behind his eyes in a blinding white flash that had abruptly blinked out, leaving him suspended in a void of nothing and nowhere.

He did not know how long he had been unconscious, but he realized that it couldn't have been more than a few seconds, or he would have drowned. As in a dream that he'd known was not a dream, he had found himself immersed in icy water that chilled him to the bone and was moving very swiftly. He'd desperately wanted to close his eyes, to somehow shut off the pain in his head and the cold in his body; the dissonant music in his mind seemed to be playing in counterpoint to the boiling hiss of the water that roiled all around him, sucking him along. But he knew that if he closed his eyes to darkness in darkness, if he allowed himself to give in to it, to sleep, to pass out, he would surely die. Then the will to live surged through him, and he struggled to turn over on his back, coughing, spitting water, arching his back, kicking slightly, treading water with his hands, fighting to stay afloat in the foam of the hissing water. Just as he had done countless times when dangling by his fingertips from some tiny ledge hundreds of feet in the air, he struggled to concentrate on just one thing—what he had to do to stay alive. Keep his head above water, and not worry about where this gelid underground journey would end.

He'd lost track of time and space, had no longer even known who he was, where or what he was; all that was left in the pain and the wet and the darkness was a terrible will to live, to conquer this new peril. For what had seemed an eternity he had ridden the surging water on his back and fought against the blackness threatening to engulf his mind.

And then, finally, it gradually came to him that he was no longer moving; he was in mud, and he was sinking. He'd twisted and floundered, struggling to keep his head above the clinging ooze, and had caught a glimpse of a sliver of light above him and to his right. Blue sky. And then he'd realized that he was still clutching the femur. He'd used the bone to dig into and pull himself through the mud, slowly inching forward, up an incline that was part muddy earth, part stone. He'd come to the narrow opening, used the femur to dig at and widen it even as the narrow tunnel through which he had crawled had begun to melt and collapse around his body, threatening to bury him alive . . .

And then he had surged forward, toward the sky, out of the ephemeral tunnel that had opened and closed so quickly. He had crawled through more muck until he had come to a concrete wall, then a wooden ramp that led up and out of the pit. He'd continued to crawl, pulling with the bone, scratching with his fingertips, pushing with the bone, up the rough wood . . .

It was the last he remembered.

But it was enough, Bone thought as he wiped more blood from his eyes, again reached to the bag dangling from his belt for a handful of chalk dust. Then he swung up, grabbed the rim of the ledge, swung free and started up the last leg of the journey to the top of the escarpment and his identity.

The sky seemed inexplicably to be growing dimmer, he thought, and wondered why. He wondered why the terrible ache in his arms and shoulders and the pain in his belly had vanished; he wondered why he could barely feel anything at all . . .

(ii)

Zulu's first reaction upon seeing Bone unhesitatingly grab hold of a narrow ledge at the top of the rockfall and swing up onto the face of the escarpment had been to attempt to scramble up the loose rock in order to grab Bone, whom Zulu was certain had become demented and wished to die.

Zulu had dashed forward, then stopped at the base of the rockfall. It was too late to try to stop the other man; even if he could climb up through the loose rock without slipping—a feat which Zulu considered doubtful—there would be nothing to grab for but rock and air. In the space of only a few seconds, Bone had somehow managed to climb out of reach up a rock face that to Zulu seemed almost absolutely sheer, except for a few cracks and slight protuberances.

Zulu had never seen anything like it—or initially thought he hadn't, until he considered the leap Bone must have made to the side of the Chemical Bank Building in order to escape Lobo and his Wolfpack—and now Bone had not only managed to cling to that smooth surface, but even moved along it.

He'd shouted repeatedly, but the man steadily ascending the rock face gave no indication that he heard. Finally Zulu lapsed into stunned silence, watching what was happening before him with amazement and disbelief.

Zulu tried to think of something comparable to what he saw, but could not; he could not see what it was that Bone was clinging to, and yet the man kept moving up the face of the escarpment with virtually nonstop, fluid motion that exuded enormous self-confidence. Indeed, it was this fluidity of motion as much as the feat itself that filled Zulu with awe. To him, Bone seemed to be defying gravity as he unhurriedly, almost effortlessly, ascended the cliff face like some graceful white ape, his hair waving like a flag in the breeze off the Hudson.

Zulu, mesmerized, continued to stand and stare until Bone reached his first rest stop; it was when Bone hooked his legs over the ledge and hung back in space that Zulu saw the blood staining the front of the other man's T-shirt.

The bone-man was going to die this day, Zulu thought, suddenly numb with foreboding. The bone-man had been lucky to get as far as he had, but he was less than a third of the way up. Despite what he had seen, Zulu still considered it impossible for any man *without* a gash in his belly to climb all the way to the top of the escarpment, and he could not see how Bone could climb back down before he became weakened from loss of blood and tumbled off the cliff face to be mangled on the rocks below.

And there was absolutely nothing he could do to prevent it, Zulu thought, stunned and chilled by this feeling of helplessness. It was useless to even shout; all that was left to him was to stand here in silent witness to an incredible feat of courage and uncanny skill that could only end in death.

Zulu was still staring up, his mouth hanging open, when

Bone reached his second rest stop, once again locked his legs over a ledge and hung back in space. The other man was now so far up the rock face that Zulu could barely make out his features; but Zulu could see the crimson stain that was his T-shirt, making Bone appear like a blotch of white and red smeared on the brown stone.

When Bone, after what seemed to Zulu a very long time, finally left this perch and once again resumed his climb, it occurred to Zulu for the first time that the man actually might make it to the top.

Then, with perhaps no more than twenty yards left to go, Bone slipped. His feet shot out from under him, his right hand lost its grip—and yet the fingers of his left hand remained locked over the rim of a small ledge. His breathing rapid and shallow, his heart hammering, Zulu watched as Bone's right hand slowly came up, found a grip; his legs moved as he searched for a toehold—and found it. And then Bone once again began to climb. But the fluid motion was gone. The arm and leg movements had become laborious, and Zulu knew he was watching a man who could pass out at any moment from pain, loss of blood and exhaustion.

For the last ten yards of Bone's journey Zulu was shouting incoherently, jumping up and down, urging the other man on, and when Bone finally clambered over the upper rim of the escarpment and rolled away out of sight, Zulu began to sob with joy.

He abruptly stopped celebrating when it occurred to him that *he* did not know how to get to the top.

"Shit!" Zulu shouted as he spun around and sprinted back across the grassy plateau toward the access road leading down to North Broadway, and to Nyack Beach below. He continued to curse to himself, at himself, as he raced down the road. He had been so convinced that Bone could not reach the top of the escarpment that he had given no thought to what he would do if Bone *did* reach the top. And now his friend was in imminent danger of bleeding to death. He had to get the bone-man to Nyack Hospital, Zulu thought, but the hospital was more than two miles away—and he did not even know how to get up to the bone-man. He needed help, and quickly.

Zulu reached the entrance to North Broadway, kept going past the empty guard's kiosk, down the access road toward the beach. A hundred and fifty yards down he came to the small brick structure that was the information building; he cursed again when he saw that the receiver on the pay phone outside the building had been torn loose from the housing.

He turned back just in time to see a patrol car of the Nyack Police Department brake to a stop in front of the steel barrier across the road. The officer, a young man with a thin moustache and a wary demeanor, got out of the patrol car and stood behind the open door, his hand near the gun on his hip, obviously not knowing quite what to make of the fact that there was a seven-foot black man with a fierce expression on his face, panting with exhaustion, sprinting up the steep hill right at him.

"My name's Horace Thorogood," Zulu gasped as he reached the top of the hill and sagged on the metal barrier across from the police officer. "A friend of mine is bleeding to death up on top of the mountain. We've got to get up there."

The young officer backed up a step, swallowed hard, squinted, "You on drugs, man?"

"There's no time to talk about it, sir," Zulu said as he ducked under the barrier, opened the car door on the passenger's side and slid onto the seat. "I told you there's a man bleeding to death up there. Let's you and I go get him."

The officer stared uncertainly at the gasping, black giant who was occupying the front seat of his patrol car, then made his decision. He jumped behind the wheel, put the car in reverse and gunned the motor. The car screamed backward. The officer braked, shifted gears, and the car raced forward onto North Broadway. He turned right at the first street, put the accelerator to the floor.

The patrol car, tires screeching, sped to the top of the steep hill, where the officer made another sharp, hard turn onto an access road. He straightened the car out, then picked up his radio handset and called for an ambulance.

"Over there!" Zulu shouted, pointing ahead and to his right, toward a copse of fir trees. "Stop up there! He should be in there someplace! I saw trees from the bottom of the cliff!"

The policeman braked the patrol car to a skidding, shuddering halt by the side of the road. Instantly, Zulu was out of the car and running toward the trees, then through them, hoping against hope that he was not too late. He suddenly found himself past the trees, standing at the brink of the cliff.

Bone was nowhere in sight.

"Where's this friend of yours?!" the policeman snapped as he came up beside Zulu. "Man, if you're trying to jerk—"

Zulu turned and began running to his left, along the rim of the escarpment—until he saw blood stains on the stone and adjacent grass. He darted into the trees, stopped and groaned aloud when he saw Bone on the ground, leaning against the trunk of a tree, doubled over and pressing the blood-stained folds of his T-shirt into the open gash on his belly.

"Bone-man!" Zulu cried, dropping to his knees beside the other man. "Can you hear me?!" When Bone nodded slightly, Zulu bowed his head, closed his eyes and took a deep breath in an effort to control his trembling. He could hear an ambulance siren in the distance, approaching fast. "Help's on the way," he continued in a low but steady voice. "Just hang in there."

Bone's head came up, and he whispered hoarsely, "My name's John Granger, Zulu. You have to call Anne . . . warn her. Also call Lightning and tell him where I am . . . have to see him. Barry Prindle's the killer."

CHAPTER SEVENTEEN

(i)

Lieutenant Perry Lightning, his mouth set in a grim line, stepped out of the elevator on the second floor of the hospital. Accompanied by a Nyack policeman, he strode quickly and stiffly to his left, to the room at the end of the corridor. He was surprised to see Bone—looking extremely pale, with dark rings around his blue eyes—sitting up in bed, his back braced by two pillows. Beside the bed was a rack holding a bottle of plasma which was draining through an intravenous tube and needle in Bone's left arm. The huge black man Lightning knew as Zulu was sitting in a chair near the foot of the bed, looking at once both concerned and just slightly bemused.

"Before you ask me anything, Lieutenant," Bone said in a soft but firm voice as Perry Lightning entered the room, "tell me if you've been able to locate Anne Winchell."

Lightning glanced at Zulu, who stared back at him impassively. Then he turned and whispered something to the uniformed policeman. The policeman stepped out of the room, but remained standing near the open door.

"No," Perry Lightning announced evenly as he turned back toward the other two men. "Barry Prindle's missing too."

"Oh, Jesus, Lieutenant," Bone whispered, closing his eyes and breathing a deep sigh. "Then I was right; Prindle has her—or she's dead."

The police detective pulled another chair over by the bed, sat down, leaned back and crossed his legs. His face and his one good eye revealed nothing. "So you say," he said in the same even tone. "Your buddy Zulu here is pretty persuasive, Bone—which is why you've got me here in person. But the story he told me over the phone sounded pretty incredible; I'm not sure I believe it."

"You're a real piece of work, Lieutenant," Zulu said drily. "If you don't believe it, go get yourself some heavy mountain-climbing equipment—or a derrick. We can drive up the road to Hook Mountain and you can climb that cliff following the bone-man's blood stains right to the top. What do you say?"

Lightning's gaze flicked over Zulu's face, came back to Bone. "Like I said, your friend is pretty persuasive. I've got a citywide APB out on both the Winchell woman and Prindle. We're talking lots of manpower and man-hours."

Bone shook his head, clenched and unclenched his fists. "You won't find them. If Prindle hasn't killed her, he's got her somewhere underground; he's as at home down there as he is up on the streets." He paused, swallowed hard, looked away. "And Anne has a phobia concerning darkness."

"You listen to me, Bone," Perry Lightning said with quiet intensity. "I told you we've got a lot of men looking for those two, so don't you worry about it; you've got more than a few problems of your own to attend to. You're a fugitive from justice, and a story from a friend about you climbing some cliff without any equipment doesn't prove—or change—anything."

"There was a bit more to my story than that, Lieutenant," Zulu said. "I told you he was with me during the night those last three people were killed. I'm his witness."

"All that means is that you've aided and abetted a fugitive; it doesn't mean he didn't kill the other people."

"I didn't kill anybody," Bone said impatiently. "Would I have asked Zulu to call you if I had?"

"I'm not sure what you'd do. I've never accused you of not being clever."

"If you think he's just clever," Zulu said with the faintest trace of amusement, "you should see him climb cliffs."

Lightning continued to study Bone. "You sound pretty convinced when you say you didn't kill any of those people; that hasn't always been the case. Do you remember now?"

"I do," Bone replied evenly.

"So, let's hear it," the lieutenant said, raising his eyebrows slightly.

"My name's John Granger, Lieutenant, and I happen to be an internationally known free climber."

"What's a free climber?"

"I climb cliffs, mountains—whatever—without benefit of equipment."

"Bullshit."

"Whooee," Zulu said, his tone flat. "I hope you didn't swallow any stupid pills before you came across the river, Lieutenant."

"Watch your mouth, Zulu."

"I'm also a pretty good spelunker—cave explorer," Bone said impatiently, distracted by thoughts of Anne. "You can check that out by calling the National Cave Rescue Commission. Ask them to describe John Granger, ask them what he does and then ask when was the last time anybody saw him. When you get finished with that call, I'll give you the names of a few dozen mountaineering schools and organizations around the world. You check out John Granger, and then tell me that what I've told you is bullshit."

Perry Lightning stared hard at Bone for a few moments, then abruptly rose, walked to the door and spoke in low tones to the policeman standing outside the room. The man nodded, then walked away. Lightning returned to stand at the foot of the bed. He passed a hand over his shaved head, absently rubbed his milky left eye. "Considering the fact that you've supposedly got a stab wound in your gut, and you supposedly pumped blood all over the face of some cliff, you don't look in such bad shape to me."

"It's not a stab wound, it's a gash. Zulu patched me up. It's not that deep, but it's true that I bled a lot. I'm told that I lost a little more than three pints during the climb. The doctors have already put two back in, and they're working on the third. If you don't believe Zulu, ask the cop and ambulance attendants what they saw when they picked me up."

"The bone-man's tough, Lieutenant," Zulu said quietly. "In fact, he's just about the toughest man you're ever likely to meet. Give him a break."

Lightning grunted. "Who cut you, Bone? Lobo?"

Uncertain of what to say, Bone looked away.

Lightning continued, "I don't suppose the cut on your belly has anything to do with the three dead Wolfpack members we found cluttering the street a few days ago, would it? Lobo's neck was broken, and the other two had their skulls bashed in. How about you, Zulu? You know anything about that?"

"As a matter of fact, I do, Lieutenant," Zulu replied, his tone flat, his manner casual. "I killed two of them, and the bone-man killed Lobo by accident. It was self-defense. First they were trying to kill Bone-man, and then they came after me. Bone-man saved my life when he jumped on Lobo."

"And Zulu saved my life, Lieutenant," Bone said.

"I don't suppose it occurred to you to report it," Lightning said drily as he inclined his head in Zulu's direction.

The street poet shrugged his massive shoulders. "It slipped my mind; I'm reporting it now. If it hadn't slipped my mind, we wouldn't be sitting here now, would we? And the bone-man wouldn't have found your killer. If you're going to charge me with anything, it should be for littering."

"We'll talk about it later," Lightning said quietly, after a long pause, and almost smiled. "If it doesn't slip my mind."

"Whatever you say, Lieutenant."

"What else do you remember, Granger?" the policeman asked, turning back to Bone.

"I've been free climbing for almost fifteen years, exploring cave systems for ten. I'm a professional. I climb, around the world, for my own pleasure, and I get paid for teaching at various mountaineering and caving schools in this country and others. How long I teach depends on how much money I need to get to the next mountain I want to climb or cave system I want to explore. I move around a lot. I have a post office box in Denver, but it doesn't get used a lot. My friends are used to having me drop out of sight for long periods of time, which is why I was never reported missing.

"Occasionally, if I'm offered enough money, I also guide parties with members who have advanced climbing or caving technique and want to see some unusual cave systems. Two years ago I guided a party of New Yorkers. We spent a week exploring parts of Mammoth Caverns, in Kentucky, that few people have ever seen. One of the men and I hit it off pretty well. He works for a company called Empire Subway Limited. Have you heard of it?"

"I've heard of it," Lightning replied.

"Barry Prindle used to work for them, before he went to work for the city; it's how he gained his knowledge of what's under New York's streets. Anyway, this man in the party I was guiding said I should come to New York and check out the underground; later, he sent me some maps."

"What's this man's name?"

"Matthew Tolovich, and I'm sure he still works for Empire Subway. If he doesn't, they'll know how to reach him. He'll verify what I'm telling you."

"You didn't tell him you were coming?"

"No, and I didn't contact him when I got here. I'm not very social, and I wasn't sure how long I wanted to stay. I was mainly interested in seeing some of the aqueducts the Dutch settlers built in the seventeenth century—they're under the Wall Street area."

"Where did you stay?"

"I rented a room in the YMCA down there."

"Why didn't they report you missing when you didn't show up to claim your stuff?"

"You'll have to ask them."

"All right; go ahead."

"While I was poking around down there I worked my way into a very large and complex natural tunnel system which wasn't indicated on any of the maps Tolovich had given me. From all indications, it was virgin territory.

"I took my time, charting the system as I worked my way northward. About a week after I started I was startled to hear what sounded like someone singing somewhere ahead of me. And there was a faint glow. I turned off my own lights, headed toward the glow. What I found was a huge chamber, a dome-like structure, that the river had carved there out of the softer limestone. There were also bones from some prehistoric grave-yard. Prindle was there."

"You saw his face?"

"No. He was wearing orange rain gear, including a hat with a floppy brim. He'd unbuttoned the coat, but left his hat on."

"If you didn't see his face, how can you be so certain that the man you saw down there was Barry Prindle?"

"I saw his eyes; not many men have eyes as green as

Prindle's. Also, he was wearing a priest's vestment under his raincoat; Prindle once studied for the priesthood. Finally, there was his body build. The man I saw down there was Barry Prindle."

Perry Lightning thoughtfully stared off into space for a few moments, then nodded. "Go ahead."

"I saw him take a severed head out of a plastic garbage bag. He put the head down on a ledge beside the quicksand pit in the center of the chamber."

"How could you see all this?"

"There were kerosene lamps anchored to the walls around the chamber. What with the singing and the purple priest's vestment, I think he was performing some kind of ritual with the head—a burial service. That's why the heads have never been found; they're in the quicksand pit."

"Interesting speculation," Lightning said in a flat voice. "Our killer considers himself a priest, and he wants to ensure that his victims have a proper burial. He can't drag a whole body down there, so he just takes the head."

"I called out. He grabbed a razor out of his bag and came after me. I grabbed the only thing close at hand to try to defend myself—one of the bones that was sticking out of an earth wall beside me. We fought, and Prindle threw a bone at me and hit me in the head. I ended up backing down a narrow channel, and I fell down into a chasm. I fell a long way, and I think I banged my head at least one more time against a rock wall on my way down. From there it gets pretty foggy, but I must have fallen into a fast-moving underground stream—the same one that percolates up through the rock and earth to form the quicksand pit. I managed to stay afloat as the stream carried me along, and the next thing I remember is finding myself on a rock ledge, at the base of a narrow tunnel that led up to the surface; I could see daylight. I don't clearly remember just how I managed to crawl up, but I did. Zulu found me on the sidewalk next to a construction site. This is only speculation, but the underground stream must have connected with other streams that ran under the construction site. The digging above must have just clipped off the top of a natural fissure in the earth below. That was what I must have crawled up. I hadn't been carrying any kind of identification with me, and I'd lost all my equipment during the fight and the fall—but I'd managed to hold on to the bone. Afterward, even with my memory gone, I instinctively kept the bone because, even if it was unconsciously, I knew that it was a link to what had happened to me. That's just a guess; I don't know why else I would have hung on to it and carried it with me everywhere."

"You're saying you still don't remember what you did for a year while you were living on the streets?"

"That isn't what I said. I said I can't remember exactly why I kept the bone and carried it with me. I can only guess—and I think it's a good guess—that I instinctively, unconsciously, held on to it because of where I'd found it, because it was a key to my identity. As a matter of fact, I do remember that year—but it's like a dream. Or somebody else's dream. But I remember enough to know that I didn't kill anyone. I lived in a tunnel under Penn Station; I'll take you there when I get out of here. You'll find the few clothes and other possessions I had; but you won't find anything with blood on it, and you certainly won't find any severed heads."

The Nyack policeman reappeared in the doorway, softly cleared his throat. Lightning went to him, had another whispered conference, then returned to Bone's bedside.

"All right," the detective lieutenant said softly. "You check out, Granger."

"I didn't kill anyone, Lieutenant."

"I believe you."

Zulu, his lips drawn back in a thin smile, slowly, deliberately, clapped his hands three times.

Lightning clasped his hands behind his back, nodded slightly. "Granger, can you take me to this underground chamber?"

"Yes." Bone paused, smiled thinly. "Just be sure that you wear your old clothes."

"You say you're certain the killer—the man you saw underground—is Barry Prindle."

"Yes."

"What's his motivation?"

"I haven't got the slightest notion of what's going on inside Prindle's mind, Lieutenant. How would I?"

"You may not have seen the killer's face clearly, but he certainly saw yours. If it's Prindle— "

"There's no *if*, Lieutenant. Prindle's the killer—and he's got Anne."

"If it's Prindle, why didn't he kill you sometime during the year you lived on the streets?"

"I don't know," Bone replied softly, averting his gaze.

"It must have come as quite a shock to him to see you alive."

"I'm sure. But I'd lost my memory; I wasn't a threat to him. And I wasn't the . . . kind of victim he was looking for."

"You were homeless."

"But not helpless. Except for Ali Hakim, who was killed in an attempt to frame me, I think Prindle limited himself to murdering only the most wretched. That was something I wanted to ask you—or have Anne ask you."

"All right, but what about after you came around in the Sheep Meadow? You certainly posed a threat to him then."

Bone thought about it, remembering Barry Prindle's tension—a tension he had attributed at the time to the man's obvious concern for Anne. Now he realized that the social worker's reaction could be interpreted two ways. "I just don't know for sure, Lieutenant," he said at last. "Obviously, he couldn't have killed me right then, in broad daylight—and not unless he was also ready to kill Anne and Hakim at the same time. He wouldn't kill Anne, because he loved her. Then, of course, after a short time he realized that I *still* wasn't a threat to him; I was alert, and I spoke, but I still couldn't remember anything."

"But you were working on it."

"So why didn't he kill me later? Maybe because he wasn't certain he could. If I'm right about the pattern of his killings, none of his victims were even remotely able to defend themselves—except for Ali Hakim, who may have been taken by surprise."

Lightning grunted, and when he spoke there was a new note of respect in his voice. "I think you are right about the pattern, Granger. But why did you start to come around a year later? Do you remember?"

"I think it . . . was because of Mary Kellogg. I think I . . . remember stumbling across her body, and that of the old man. I recognized her clothing. It was a tremendous emotional shock to me, and I think that must have triggered despair at first; I think I wanted to die. Then, after Anne reached through to me, that same emotional shock triggered my will to live, which was the start of my recovery."

"Bone-man and Mary Kellogg were very close, Lieutenant,"

Zulu said. "It was Bone-man who saved her from being raped by Lobo, and out of gratitude she gave Bone-man that necklace you found him wearing. The woman told me."

"Another reason he didn't try to kill me," Bone said, "was because I was the prime suspect for all the other killings; when I was set free, he knew I'd be blamed for any future killings. As long as I had no memory of what had happened, I was no threat to him; and as long as I was free, I was a convenient scapegoat."

"All right, Granger," Perry Lightning said with quiet intensity. "I think I'll buy it."

"Bone-man," Zulu said, his deep baritone rising slightly in alarm as he watched Bone grimace in pain, sit up and try to swing his legs over the side of the bed, "just what the hell do you think you're doing?"

"I have to get out of here, Zulu."

"No, man. You heard what the doctors said when they were pumping blood back into you; you have to stay here for a while. You need lots of rest."

"If he hasn't killed Anne, Zulu, he's got her with him in the underground chamber—or someplace else underground. I'm sure of it."

"Why, Granger?" Lightning asked. "How can you be so sure? He went underground to play priest and bury the heads of his victims. Why would he take a live hostage down there? He'd be trapping himself."

Bone thought about it, found the answer. "He's at home down there," he said at last. "Remember that he's a madman, anyway, and after Anne called him—which I'm sure she did, because I asked her to—he knew that I was getting close to remembering. He panicked, grabbed Anne and ran. But where was he going to run to? He feels safe down there. He worked for Empire Subway, which is how he found that cavern system in the first place, and he's done his own exploring. He feels powerful there. Maybe most important, he'll feel that he has complete control of *Anne* down there. Even if she wasn't phobic about the dark, she still couldn't hope to find her way out of there without him. That's what I think he would want most: complete control over Anne. He's down there with Anne, Lieutenant—in what he considers his world. I've got to go get her."

"I'm just a poor street performer, Lieutenant," Zulu said in a flat voice, "but what the bone-man says seems to make sense. Except, that is, for the part about him going down there."

Perry Lightning glanced at Zulu and nodded, then looked back at Bone, who was sitting on the edge of the bed, doubled over with pain. "Tell me how to get to this chamber."

Bone shook his head. "I can't tell you; it's too complicated. I can't even draw you a map—at least not one that would guarantee that you and your men might not get lost and killed."

"Don't patronize me, Granger," Lightning said tersely. "You think you can handle this better than the NYPD?"

"I'm not questioning your abilities, Lieutenant, or those of your men," Bone replied through clenched teeth. "But I doubt that you have too many men on the force who are trained in caving techniques—and if you do, you'll find out they're hobbyists. I think Prindle may have found a way to get into the cave system from somewhere in midtown; I don't know that route. The only route I know starts down around the Battery. It took me two weeks to work my way to where I found that chamber, and—"

"Jesus Christ, Granger. Are you saying it will take us two weeks to get there?"

"No; I was taking my time, and I was mapping. My point is that it's a very complex system, with a lot of offshoots and dead ends that an inexperienced caver could easily get lost in. If you get lost down there, you'll die. I left blaze marks along the direct route, but—"

"Then we'll follow your marks."

Bone again shook his head. "It's not that simple. Even if you could follow my blaze marks, there are some very difficult passages to get through; they're dangerous, and you need very good technique. Miss one blaze mark, make one wrong turn, and you're dead. I would have to guide you—and even then, there's no guarantee that you could follow."

"Well, we're just going to have to take a chance that we can follow your blaze marks, Granger, because you're not going anywhere for a while. You can't take a chance on opening that wound in your belly again; it's not going to do anyone any good for you to climb around down there and suddenly start gushing blood all over the place."

"You let me and the doctors worry about me, Lieutenant. I think you're missing my point. There's no way for you or your men to find that chamber without me to guide you; that's definite. But it would be too difficult and time-consuming for me to take a whole party of novices through there. Alone, I can make it from the Battery to the chamber in under twelve hours. I don't know how long it might take with novices; they're clumsy. Also, sound carries a long way through rock; novices make a lot of noise underground. We can't afford to give Prindle any indication that someone is coming after him. Our only hope is that Prindle has kept Anne alive because he wants to spend some time with her, and maybe even win her over. But he has nothing left to lose by killing her; one flick of that razor he carries, and she's dead. So the problem is not only one of getting there, but of getting there making as little noise as possible."

Lightning bowed his head and studied the floor for some time. "You can't even stand up," he said at last. "You're just going to have to do your best to draw a map, and we'll call in some other caving expert to guide us."

"No. I should have a good part of my strength back in a day or two. The doctors can put another set of stitches into me, and then wrap my middle with pressure bandages. That should hold me together for at least twelve hours, and that's all I need."

"Jesus, Bone-man," Zulu said softly. "What about the pain?"

"My problem; I'll handle it, Zulu. I'll go in alone—with a rifle equipped with a sniper scope and, if the Lieutenant can get me a pair, a set of those infrared goggles the Army uses for night fighting. No lights. If I can manage to sneak up on him, I should have him."

Lightning said, "You'd have to shoot him, you know. He'd give you no choice."

"All right, then I'll shoot him."

"Have you ever shot a man, Granger?"

"Don't worry, Lieutenant; I won't freeze. I'll shoot him, if I have to."

Perry Lightning thought about it, pursed his lips and shook his head. "The City of New York can't allow a civilian to substitute for its police department in entering a dangerous situation, much less allow a civilian to perform duty as a sniper. It can't be done."

"Lieutenant—"

"One man, Granger. Could you still make it to the chamber

in under twelve hours if you had to take along just one other man?"

"If that man was in good physical condition, had a lot of guts, wasn't claustrophobic or afraid of the dark— and if that man would do exactly as I say—yes. It might take an extra hour or so, but that wouldn't be a problem; finding the right man is the problem."

"Me, Granger," Perry Lightning said evenly. "I'll go with you. You make a list of the equipment we'll need, and I'll get it for us. I'll also do any shooting that needs to be done. That's what I get paid for."

"Have you ever done any caving at all, Lieutenant?"

"No—and I can't say that I much care for the idea of climbing around in the dark for twelve hours or more, either. But it has to be my responsibility. As far as guts are concerned, let's just say that I'll use you as my role model, Granger. I'm your man."

"Okay," Bone replied simply. "I like your choice, Lieutenant."

"And me," Zulu said.

Both Bone and Perry Lightning glanced sharply at Zulu, who was now sitting back in his chair at the foot of the bed, his legs crossed.

"The bone-man here is hurting," Zulu continued, looking at Lightning. "He's going to have all he can do to keep going without busting his belly open; he can't carry anything. Lieutenant, you'll be carting around a rifle with a bulky scope; I say that's all you'll be able to safely handle. You'll need supplies— water, medical equipment, maybe even a litter that can be tightly folded. You don't know what kind of shape the woman's going to be in when you find her, and if you take Prindle alive you're going to have to restrain him while you take the two of them out. You need at least one more pair of hands." He paused, sighed, raised his eyebrows slightly. "I'll be your bearer on this expedition. That would amuse me."

"You're too big to go down there, Zulu."

"You're not so teeny yourself, Lieutenant, and I bend very nicely. I notice you don't question my reasoning."

Lightning looked at Bone inquiringly, and Bone nodded slightly.

"The bone-man says okay, Lieutenant," Zulu continued.

"Thanks for the offer, Zulu," Lightning said after a pause.

"But I'll take one of my own men to carry the supplies. This is a police matter. I need Granger, but not you. There's no reason for you to risk your life."

Zulu straightened up in his chair, leaned his elbows on the railing at the foot of the bed. "Bone-man? You're the white hunter in charge of this expedition. I'm telling you I want to go. I'm the right man. You know I can handle myself underground. As far as being sneaky is concerned, I've been living under Grand Central for seven years, and nobody's caught me down there yet. What do you say?"

Lightning looked at Bone, smiled thinly. "What's the word, B'wana?"

"All right," Bone said, nodding to Zulu. "It will be the three of us down there—and I may be able to make things easier for us. Lieutenant, I need you to talk to the doctors; explain why I need a second, very tight, stitching job. I'll make a list of equipment we'll need, and you might also see if you can find me a Niele-MacLain map; the city's environmental department may have one."

"What the hell's a Niele-MacLain map?"

"You'll see. If we're lucky, it's something that could make things a lot easier for us."

(ii)

Anne sat on the hard, cold stone, staring blankly at the fire that blazed on the slightly elevated rock shelf in front of her. Beyond the shelf, firelight reflected off the dull, khaki-colored surface of what seemed to be a large pool of mud. She had thrown a stone into the mud, watched it sink from sight; she wondered how deep the pool was.

She had considered killing herself, exploring the depth of the mud pool by throwing herself into it, but had not found the courage. As terrified as she was, she was not yet prepared to take her own life. In the beginning, the terror of Barry Prindle and the world of night he had taken her into had been so great that she'd thought her heart would burst, stop. Now she merely felt . . . numb. And cold. But she suspected that the cold was more in her mind than her body.

It seemed, she thought, that there were limits even to terror.

And now it was time to give some thought to the question of survival.

She allowed herself a grim, wry smile as she reflected on the thought that any future choices she made had better be an improvement on the one she had made in deciding to call Barry Prindle before Perry Lightning. She had caught Barry in his office just as he was about to leave to cruise in the van. Now she realized that he had made the connection, guessed that Bone had been in touch with her, as soon as she'd made her request for information—but his reaction had fooled her completely. He had sounded excited and enthusiastic—and had assured her that he now believed Bone was innocent. When he had suggested that she not tell the police until after he had met with her to show her the maps she had asked for, she had readily agreed. He had assured her that Bone and she now had an ally, and that it might be better for the three of them to proceed alone without notifying the police, who would only complicate matters further.

Right.

She remembered wondering how he had gotten permission to leave his assigned duties, for he had been at her office within thirty-five minutes. She had gotten into his van, started to turn toward him when a soft rag with a strong medicinal smell had been clamped over her nose and mouth. She had struggled briefly, but that was the last thing she remembered before waking up—here. The bruises on her body suggested to Anne that it had not been easy for Barry to carry her to wherever this place was; she had been bumped and scraped along the way a good many times.

She wondered where Prindle was, remembered the suffocating panic she had experienced upon awakening to find herself alone and surrounded by darkness. Her first thought had been that she had been left alone to die, but then she had seen that there were ample supplies of food and water in the great stone chamber.

Anne looked around her, shuddered once again as she saw the tangled bones protruding from the ceiling and walls of the cavern on the opposite side of the mud pool, to her right. Bone had been here, she thought; it was where he had obtained his femur. She understood now that the man she loved had stumbled across Barry Prindle doing—something.

But what, she wondered, had *Bone* been doing down here?

Her gaze fell to the blood-stained rock shelf before her, and she trembled. She heard a sound off to her left, started, then scrambled across the rock to her right, braced against a wall beneath a flickering Coleman lamp as Prindle approached her.

"Don't come near me, Barry," she whispered hoarsely. "Please don't come near me."

Prindle stopped a few feet away. He shut off the miner's lamp he wore strapped to his forehead, then squatted down, forearms resting on his knees, and stared at her. Reflected light from the Coleman lamps danced in his bright green eyes.

"I wouldn't hurt you, Anne," the man said quietly. "I love you."

Anne swallowed hard, trying to work up moisture in her mouth. "If you love me, why did you bring me down here? I'm terrified of the dark and closed-in places. You know that."

"I had no choice, Anne. It was clear to me that Bone was close to remembering."

"He came across you down here, didn't he? You were carrying a severed head."

"Yes," Prindle replied in the same quiet tone.

"What was *he* doing here?"

"I don't know."

"What happened to him, Barry?"

"I don't know; I mean, I don't know how he survived. We fought. He backed off into that narrow tunnel across the way, and he fell down into some sort of hole. I thought he was dead." He paused, then murmured, "Nothing is ever as simple as it seems."

"What?"

"Nothing. It's not important."

"Barry, why did you kill all those people? I would never have thought of you as being someone who would hurt anybody."

"I never hurt them, Anne; I was putting them out of their misery. I sent them home to God." Prindle removed the miner's lamp and sat it down next to him, then passed a hand back over his widow's peak and sighed deeply. "I was certain you'd understand."

Anne again swallowed hard, her mind racing as she wondered how one went about trying to reason with, or outwit, a madman. "I guess maybe I do," she said at last. "All of the people you killed were . . . like that?"

"Except for Ali, yes."

"How could you have killed Ali, Barry?"

"He betrayed me once. I was angry."

"Ali betrayed you? How?"

"Never mind. I don't want to talk about that. It's not important."

"But what about all the others? Were you angry at them?"

"Oh, no, Anne. My heart was filled with pity for them."

"Then *why*?"

"I'm a priest, Anne, and I have a special commission from God Almighty. That's why I sent all those poor, helpless people home to God; because that was my job. As far as Bone and Ali are concerned . . . I was confused for a while, Anne. I thought God was trying to trick me by sending Bone to take you away from me."

"I was never yours to be taken from, Barry. Can't you understand that?"

Prindle shook his head. "You're wrong. The fact that you're with me now proves that you're wrong. God was testing me, using Bone. I failed once—but now He's given me another chance. You called me first, remember? It was meant for me to bring you down here with me, to my church."

Anne looked around her, suppressed a sigh. When she spoke, her voice was firm. "Barry, you say you love me. Okay. I accept that, and I thank you. Now I'm telling you that I don't *want* to be in this place. If you love me, you'll take me out of here right now. I'll stick with you; I promise you that. But we have to go to the police and tell them what you've done. You need help, Barry. You'll get it, if you take me out of here. That would make me happy."

Prindle slowly shook his head. "Please don't talk to me like I'm a fool, Anne."

"Barry, I promise that I'll stand by you and do everything in my power to see that you get the help you need."

"At the least, I'd be put in a mental hospital because people wouldn't understand. How could we be together then?"

"I didn't say we'd be together, Barry," Anne said softly. "I said I'd stand by you."

"But you don't love me?"

"You asked me not to talk to you like you were a fool. Would you believe me if I told you I loved you?"

303

"No. That's why we have to live here for a while."

"*Live* here?"

"Yes," Prindle replied matter-of-factly. "This is my church, given to me by God. I promise that you'll be comfortable. I'll take care of you. You don't have to be afraid."

"Barry," Anne said, licking her lips, struggling to remain calm, "what if something happened to you? I don't know how to get back. I'd die down here."

"Nothing's going to happen to me, Anne," Prindle said, smiling boyishly. "You can see all the food and water we have. There's good ventilation, plenty of kerosene for the lamps, and I bring down wood for fires. Also, there are plenty of blankets to keep you warm. I've saved several thousand dollars, so I have money to buy anything we need. When we do need things, I'll just go up to the surface and get them."

"Oh, God. Barry. How long will we have to stay here?"

Prindle slowly straightened up, and his smile vanished. He stepped forward, reached out and tentatively touched Anne's shoulder.

"You're trembling."

"Yes, Barry, I'm goddamn trembling. What the hell do you expect? I'm afraid."

"Of me?"

"Of you; of *this*."

"We'll stay here until you're no longer afraid—and until you learn to love me, Anne. I'll know when that time comes, so it won't make any difference what you say. I'll know in my heart when you truly love me." He paused, then hesitantly reached down and rubbed the back of his hand against Anne's left breast. "We'll be happy together, Anne. You'll see. When I know that you love me and won't try to run away when I take you back up to the surface, then I'll take you out of here. By then, the police will have stopped searching for us; they'll think we're both dead. We'll travel to another part of the country to live. We'll be married, and we'll have lots of children. It's God's plan."

"Barry," Anne said in a voice just above a whisper, "you're forgetting about Bone. His memory is returning; he'll find his way back here."

Prindle shrugged, then turned to look behind him at the narrow tunnel he had just emerged from. "I think that's unlikely, my love. But even if, in the unlikely event, he does remember how to get back here, he'll find a few nasty surprises waiting for him. He won't survive all of them."

"Barry, what have you done?"

"A man has a right to defend his home," Prindle said, turning back to Anne.

"Traps," Anne said in a small voice.

The big man reached down with both hands, stroked Anne's shoulders. "I've wanted you for such a long time," he said hoarsely. "You're the answer to so many of my problems."

Anne shuddered at Prindle's touch, but she began to unbutton her blouse with trembling fingers. "I'm not the answer to any of your problems, Barry. But if you intend to rape me, there's nothing I can do about it; we might as well get it over with."

"Please don't do that," Prindle said tersely, wrapping his fingers around Anne's wrist and pulling her hand away from her blouse. "Not yet. I don't want to take you like that."

Anne watched anxiously as the man turned and stepped back toward the rock shelf, where he had placed a black plastic garbage bag. He reached into the bag, drew out an embroidered, purple priest's chasuble, which he slipped over his head.

"Barry, what are you doing?"

"I'm a priest, Anne. I'm going to marry us before we make love."

"And if you marry us, then it won't be rape?"

"That's right; a man can't rape his own wife."

Despite her lingering terror, Anne suddenly found herself wanting to laugh. "Barry, unless there have been changes in the church that I haven't heard of, I don't think priests are supposed to marry."

"I have special permission. God wants us to marry."

(iii)

Bone, the gash in his belly secured with a second set of stitches, clamps and a pressure bandage, sat at the small table that had been brought into his hospital room. Zulu and Perry Lightning looked over his shoulder as he pored over the detailed drawings he had laid out over the surface of the table and the surrounding floor.

"So that's a Niele-MacLain map?" Zulu said in his low, rumbling voice. "It looks to me like a whole lot of maps."

Bone grunted as he drew his index finger along a line on one of the maps. "You're right. Niele-MacLain is constantly being updated. These are maps of all the underground streams, lakes and what-have-you that are *known* to exist under Manhattan. The maps also indicate man-made structures that were built in the last century and might have been forgotten. Matthew Tolovich sent me maps like this. I just wanted to check to make certain that that cavern system I found isn't listed. Unfortunately, it isn't."

He shifted in his chair, grimaced against the pain in his abdomen, then took a felt-tipped pen from his shirt pocket. He searched around on the floor until he found the sheet that he wanted, put it on the table and drew a small circle over the center of Broad Street. "This is where I first went in," he continued. "An aqueduct built by Aaron Burr's water company is down there, and I wanted to see it. Then I branched out. I happened to find a very narrow cave high up on one of the walls of the main tunnel; it wasn't the kind of opening many people—especially those working for a salary–would care to go into, for fear of becoming stuck. I gave it a try, and I found the dry river channel."

"Which isn't on the map," Lightning said. "Shit."

Bone searched among the sheets until he found one indicating a small area under Manhattan's West Side. He drew a large circle in the center of the map. "My best guess is that the chamber where I ran into Prindle is somewhere down here."

Lightning said, "We found Prindle's HRA van collecting tickets at the corner of Ninth and Forty-eighth."

Bone nodded. "Obviously, Prindle found his own way into the system, and for some reason never reported it to Empire Subway."

"I'll have some of my men start searching underground there."

"Don't bother, Lieutenant. All they'll find are the subway tunnels, water and gas mains that are indicated here. They could look for months and never find the route he uses to get into that system; he may even have it disguised now."

Lightning sighed heavily. "Then we have to go the long, hard way."

"Yes," Bone replied evenly. "We go the long, hard way."

(iv)

Naked, Anne lay in a pool of flickering firelight staring up at the pitted stone of the domed ceiling high above her. In her was a mixture of fear and pity.

She had known that it would be useless to resist Barry Prindle's advances; also, she suspected that he could shift emotional gears at any time. Her life depended not only on the man not killing her, but on his eventually being persuaded to take her out of this massive stone coffin. She was, she thought, totally dependent on him. She did not know if Bone would ever remember how to return to this place, and did not know if Bone and the police would even realize that she was being held prisoner. Indeed, now that she knew that Prindle had set traps, she was not even sure that she wanted Bone to try to rescue her.

Realizing that her most realistic chance for survival lay in somehow persuading the serial killer, her former partner, to lead her out, she had done her best to respond to him sexually after their "marriage."

Their attempted coupling had been a disaster, and it had not taken her long to realize that Prindle was impotent. No matter what she had done to him, or allowed him to do to her, he had been unable to get an erection. Exhausted, he had finally stopped trying. He had not dressed. Now he squatted in silence, unmoving, a few feet away, facing the opposite wall. He had been that way for almost an hour. Once or twice she thought she had heard him sob, but she could not be certain.

What she was certain of, without knowing exactly why, was that she was in considerably more danger now than she had been before the man had "married" them and tried unsuccessfully to make love to her.

CHAPTER EIGHTEEN

(i)

There obviously hadn't been too many seven-foot underground workers in the eighteenth and nineteenth centuries, Zulu thought with a wry smile as, bending low, he followed Perry Lightning and Bone through a wooden aqueduct that had been constructed before the Civil War.

It had been three days since Bone's ascent of Hook Mountain. The doctors had wanted him to wait at least a week before attempting this journey through the cavern system beneath Manhattan, but Bone had insisted that he was ready. Zulu knew that his friend was in pain, although Bone's face and manner gave no indication of it.

Zulu had felt his heart begin to pound from the moment they had entered the very old Croton water system, and then proceeded into and through even older structures. Zulu carried two backpacks, one across each shoulder, filled with medical supplies, food, water, a collapsible litter and various pieces of equipment Bone had asked for. Perry Lightning carried a rifle with a sniper scope, while Bone, in the lead, carried a large coil of strong but lightweight nylon rope slung around his shoulders. At Bone's direction, they each wore heavy canvas pants

BONE

and shirts, and sneakers. Each man wore a miner's lamp strapped to his forehead, and carried a powerful flashlight. In Zulu's backpacks were extra batteries, and infrared night-vision goggles for later use.

There were rats in the tunnels—lots of them. Huge Norway rats skittered over the wood, rock and earth as the beams of light passed over them. Bone appeared to pay no attention to the animals, while Lightning was constantly starting and cursing under his breath. Zulu found that he was getting used to the rats—but he had tucked the cuffs of his pants into the tops of his sneakers.

Suddenly Bone stopped walking and pointed the beam of his flashlight high on the earthen wall to their left. "There," he said curtly.

Zulu and Lightning looked up to where remnants of wood piling and siding had rotted away to reveal what appeared to be the mouth of a small tunnel.

"That goes about twenty yards," Bone continued, "and it connects with the riverbed. Zulu, you'll go first. Take out some of that olive oil and smear it over your shoulders."

"Why does he go first?" Lightning asked.

"Because of his size," Bone replied, turning to Zulu. "If you get stuck, it will be a lot easier to pull you out from here than it would be to push you from the other side. It'll be a tight squeeze all the way, but if you use the technique I talked about, pushing with your heels and the palms of your hands, you should be able to make it through. Your shoulders may tend to swell. Just remember to stay calm, breathe regularly with your mouth to the side, and don't force it."

"What if I can't make it through, Bone-man?"

"Then you miss the trip."

Zulu removed the miner's lamp from his head, set down the backpacks, opened one and took out a bottle of olive oil. "I'll make it," he said quietly.

Zulu smeared oil over his shoulders and chest, turned to allow Bone and Lightning to smear his back. Next, Bone knelt on the floor and tied one end of the rope loosely around Zulu's ankles.

"Whatever happens in there," Bone said, straightening up, "don't panic. If you get stuck, we'll get you out; count on it. But you mustn't try to force your way through. If you think you're in trouble, you probably are. If things get too tight, don't push;

309

you'll just wedge yourself in deeper. Just stop, give us a call, and we'll get you back. If you do make it through, you'll pull through the equipment, and we'll follow. Still want to do this, Zulu?"

"Yeah. Uh, what are the chances that I'll meet up with rats in there?"

"The chances are good," Bone replied evenly, "but it's best not to even think about them."

"Oh," Zulu said, and smiled wanly. "Then I won't think about them."

"You'll go head first, arms to your sides, shoulders as sloped as you can make them. No sudden movements with your head. It's all wrist, ankle and heel action; everything will start to ache like hell after a short distance, but just keep pushing away. Again: don't try to force anything."

"Jesus, Bone-man. You went in there like that *alone*?"

Bone shrugged. "Sometimes you have to risk going into small places so you can find the big places beyond. Ready?"

"Ready," Zulu said, and stepped close to the wall. With a boost from Perry Lightning, he pulled himself up to the mouth of the tunnel, twisted around, put his arms to his sides and began to squirm backward into the tunnel.

As Bone had predicted, he suddenly found his heart beating very fast, his mind filled with fear of being buried alive. He turned his head to the side and concentrated on breathing regularly and deeply in an effort to calm himself.

Don't panic, Zulu kept reminding himself as he kept flexing his ankles, digging in with his heels and pushing. The passageway seemed to be getting even tighter. Or perhaps, he thought, it was only his imagination.

Don't panic; panic would make him swell.

If you think you're stuck, you probably are.

Zulu stopped when he realized that he was gasping for breath.

Take it easy!

He had once read somewhere that a man's shoulders could almost always go through a space big enough to admit his head; he'd read it, but he'd never believed it.

If you get stuck, don't try to force it. You'll only wedge yourself in.

Well, Zulu thought as he resumed digging in and pushing with his hands and heels, he wasn't stuck yet. And his fear must certainly be insignificant compared to the woman's. He had to make it to the river channel; he was needed.

Suddenly Zulu felt something soft and fine brush across the top of his head. At first he thought it was a spider's web, but then it moved. A rat was sniffing at his scalp, Zulu thought, and he screamed.

"Zulu?!" Bone's voice sounded oddly distant to Zulu, muffled as it was by his own body filling the passageway. *"Zulu, are you all right?! What's the matter?!"*

The matter, Zulu thought, was that he was chickenshit. Indeed, the rat had probably been more frightened of him than he had been of it, for the whiskers were gone.

"I'm all right!" he shouted, his voice echoing in the stone and earth tube that reminded him very much—too much—of a coffin.

"Do you want us to pull you out?!"

"No!" Zulu shouted, and resumed digging and pushing with his heels.

He wondered how far he had gone, wondered how long he had been in this tunnel, sandwiched in earth. Then, suddenly, he felt rock press against both shoulders.

If you think you're stuck, you probably are. Don't try to force it.

Then this was it, Zulu thought. He was finished. He had crawled all this way for nothing. He would have to be pulled back out, and he suspected that could take an hour or longer. He was needed, but he would have to stay behind.

He should try to wriggle further ahead.

But if he *really* got stuck . . .

If he really got stuck, Zulu thought, he would die. And his corpse would block the passageway.

But he was needed.

He slowly exhaled, then stretched his arms down along the sides of his body, sloping his shoulders until pain shot up into the muscles of his back and neck.

Then he flexed his ankles, dug his heels into the earth and shoved with all his strength.

He felt the stone pinch his arms even more, and for one terrifying moment he was certain he had made a foolish, deadly mistake that was now going to cost him his life. Then he realized that his head was free of the tunnel; he was able to move his head around, and there was a faint, dry aroma that was startlingly different from the rich, damp odor of the tunnel. He—or his head, at least—had reached the underground river channel.

Now he had to get the rest of himself there.

Adrenaline surged through him, momentarily dulling the fierce pain in his shoulders, wrists, ankles and heels. He wriggled furiously, at the same time digging in and pushing with his heels. In a few moments he had worked his way back far enough so that his arms were free. He planted his hands against the smooth stone of the river channel, on either side of the tunnel from which his body protruded, and pushed with all his might. Finally his hips slipped free. He did a half twist, rolled over on his left shoulder and tumbled down a concave incline, finally coming to rest in a heap on a hard, pebble-strewn surface. Howling with triumph and joy, he leaped to his feet in the darkness, removed the rope from around his ankles and followed its length until he felt the edges of the mouth of the tunnel he had emerged from.

"I made it!" he shouted into the opening, amazed at how his voice boomed and echoed in the cavern. "Tie up the equipment, and I'll pull it through! And don't worry about a thing, Lieutenant! It's a piece of cake!"

(ii)

She was cold—colder than she could ever remember being in her life. Wrapped in blankets, she was huddled beside a fire a few feet from the edge of the quicksand pit, her arms wrapped around herself. She should eat, she thought, but she was not hungry, and she was not sure she could keep food down. She wondered if she was sick.

She was almost certain now that she was going to die, for something had died in Barry Prindle. Hope. He had tried two more times to have intercourse with her, but each time his penis had remained limp. From the few things he had muttered during his feverish attempts to become hard, she gathered that he had counted on her to make him what he considered to be a whole man. But she had failed, Anne thought, and now he avoided her, sitting by himself in the cold and dim light on the opposite side of the quicksand bog, brooding.

His impotence could kill her, Anne thought. If she was to remain alive, her only chance was to somehow find a way to

please the man sexually, convince him that she was still his
best hope for a normal life.

"Barry," she called out softly in what she hoped was a
seductive voice. "Come over here. I'm cold, and I want you next
to me. Let's try it again."

She waited for some response, but there was none. She
opened her mouth to call again, but stopped when she suddenly heard Prindle begin to breathe heavily. The rasping
breathing grew even heavier, and when she heard the sound of
flesh slapping against flesh it dawned on Anne that the man
was masturbating. She wondered what it was he was fantasizing in order to arouse himself, then decided that she didn't
really want to know. Suddenly she felt even colder.

(iii)

Much to his chagrin, Lieutenant Perry Lightning was discovering that he was physically odd man out in this rescue and
hunting party. He was very tired, although he did his best not
to show it.

In the first hour or two after his terrifying transit through the
narrow cave into the river channel, he had been awestruck that
he was only the third man—or fourth, if Prindle had been
here—ever to see the underground labyrinth of stone; even
with his companions, he felt isolated and lonely. Above him, he
knew, was a city filled with millions of people; indeed, at this
hour of the day the streets and sidewalks would be crowded
with people hurrying on their way, drivers cursing and honk-
ing their horns in anger at the traffic congestion. But down
here in this underground world there was nothing but awe-
some silence broken only by their heavy breathing and their
rubber-soled footfalls on the stone.

But now he was no longer awestruck, only exhausted.

John Granger had been right, he thought. Without him
acting as guide, nobody else would have found this way;
indeed, he would not even have been able to work up the nerve
to crawl through the tomb-like access tunnel. He was still
amazed that Zulu had made it.

But Lightning was glad that Zulu had come, for the man was
more than carrying his own weight. The seven-foot giant was
showing himself to be not only strong, but surprisingly lithe

313

and agile. Indeed, although he was sweating profusely, it seemed to Lightning that the street poet was enjoying the physical challenge of tiptoeing along ledges, climbing up and down, listening intently to John Granger's precise instructions on how to walk, climb and squeeze through narrow openings.

Mountain climbing and cave exploring, Lightning thought with a wry smile as he hefted his cotton-padded rifle into a more comfortable position, were not for sissies.

Granger, he thought, was absolutely remarkable in terms of the strength and stamina packed into his wiry body. Lightning knew that the man had to be in considerable pain, and yet he gave no indication of it as he stoically, steadily, led them through the maze of caverns. Lightning frequently glanced at the front of their guide's shirt, but there were no signs of bleeding; not yet. Only the pallor of Bone's face and the tightness of the muscles in his neck and jaws indicated his exhaustion and pain.

He was in the company of two of the most remarkable men he had ever known, Perry Lightning thought—and he would never have known it except for the bizarre chain of circumstances that had led to John Granger's recovering his consciousness in his precinct. He was proud to be with these men, ashamed of what he considered his own weakness at having all he could do to carry himself and the rifle. But he knew that his time would come, and that he had to pace himself, save his resources. Finally, in the end, he would require the nerve and strength to aim, and then to shoot straight.

"Rest break," Bone said curtly as he paused, sat down wearily on a boulder in the middle of the riverbed, which was quite wide at this point.

"It's about time," Zulu said wryly.

"Drink some water and eat some food, gentlemen. And we'll wait until you both feel well rested. The next leg is going to take about two hours, and you're not going to be able to eat or drink anything; if you have to piss, it's going to be down your leg."

Lightning, sprawled out on the stone, aimed his flashlight around, frowned slightly. "What's the problem, Granger? You could drive a train through here."

"But it's a dead end." He paused, aimed his flashlight against the opposite wall where there was a narrow crevice Lightning hadn't even seen. "That's where we have to go—straight down, on the rope. It's about seventy feet, and you'll be scraping rock against belly and ass all the way down."

"Shit," Perry Lightning mumbled, and reached for his canteen.

(iv)

Once again they lay together, sweating and exhausted after Prindle's failed attempt at lovemaking, in the flickering light from the Coleman lamp above their heads.

"Barry, you shouldn't try so hard," Anne breathed against the wet flesh of the man's chest. "Maybe if you hadn't tried so hard right after masturbating—"

"I wasn't masturbating!" Prindle snapped, and abruptly rose to his feet.

"You don't have to be ashamed of it, Barry. You need sexual release, just like everyone else. Maybe . . . you should let me do it to you."

"*Don't* say that! Don't talk like that, Anne! I wasn't masturbating!"

"All right, you weren't masturbating," Anne said with a sigh as she sat up.

Prindle picked up his clothes and stalked away, returning to the shadows on the opposite side of the quicksand pool. Anne dressed slowly, found that she was both hungry and thirsty. Earlier, Prindle had gone to the surface to replenish their supply of drinking water, and Anne had estimated that it had taken him less than an hour. It meant, she thought, that the route to the surface was relatively close by; but then, it might as well be a million miles away, for she knew she could never find it without Prindle's help. And there was nowhere to run, except to her death in a darkness which was even more fearful than the nightmares that had terrified her all her life.

She opened a can of tuna fish, ate that and drank some water. She would have liked a cup of tea, but she could not get up the energy to light the camp stove.

She lay back on the blanket, stared up at the ceiling, then let her gaze wander around the chamber, across the pool of quicksand to the mouths of the three smaller caves and the tangle of bones protruding from the walls and ceiling of the cave to her right. That was where Bone must have entered, she thought. Would he come again? Had he finally regained his memory? If so, would he realize that Barry Prindle had brought her here? What could he do against Barry's razor?

What could *she* do against Barry's razor?

What kinds of traps had Barry set?

She heard a sound somewhere off to her left, close by, and it startled her. She glanced around, and was surprised to find Barry there, dressed in his priest's vestments. She had not heard him approach.

"Barry, what is it? What are you doing?"

"It doesn't work, Anne," Prindle said in a strained, hollow voice. "It won't work. I'm closing the church. I have to put . . . everything . . . into my past. And you will, at last, please me."

He brought his right hand out from behind his back, and the razor he was holding glinted in the flickering light.

Now Anne knew what Prindle fantasized about when he masturbated—and she also knew that she had run out of time. If she was to live, she had to act; she had to run. But where? Prindle would simply chase her down.

Unless he, too, had to move in total darkness. To risk her own death in terrifying darkness, she thought, was her only chance to live.

Having made her decision, she moved with deliberateness and speed. She darted off to her right, to where all the supplies were stacked, and began throwing them out into the quicksand; flashlights and batteries, and all of the canteens—except for the one she had slipped by its strap around her neck—were thrown into the mire, and immediately began to sink. Then she grabbed the Coleman lamp closest to her, threw that out into the center of the deadly pool of mud.

"What are you doing?!" Prindle shouted. "Stop!"

Prindle's shock, and his shouting, gave Anne the time she needed to throw in the last of the flashlights and batteries. Then she moved around the narrow perimeter of the quicksand pool toward the second lamp.

"You'll kill us both!"

"You're going to kill me anyway!"

Then Prindle recovered from his shock and came running after her—only to stumble when he came to the section of the ancient graveyard, then slip and sprawl in the tangle of bones.

316

Anne reached the second lamp, threw that into the quick-sand pool.

"Don't be a fool!"

Anne threw in the third lamp, and came to the fourth and last a split second before Prindle reached her. She ducked away as he slashed at her face, then shoved the flaming end of the lamp into his face. Prindle screamed with pain and stumbled backward as Anne threw the lamp out into the quicksand.

Suddenly she found herself shrouded in a darkness more absolute than any she could have thought existed.

And there was complete silence. Prindle, she knew, could be no more than a few feet away, and yet she heard no sounds of breathing or movement. Moving very slowly, holding her breath, she crouched slightly and backed away toward the network of tunnels behind her.

She had gone perhaps ten yards when she heard Prindle's voice, barely a whisper, in the darkness.

"Now we're both dead, Anne. You've killed us both."

Anne took a series of measured, deep breaths, squatted down and felt the ground beneath her feet; it was still smooth stone. Knowing that she had to get as far away from Prindle as possible, she continued to move backward.

"Anne? Where are you? We're both dead anyway, so at least let's die together. Even I can't get back without light. I guess I don't know any more than you do about what it's like to die of thirst, but it can't be very pleasant. Anne, where are you? Please talk to me. I don't want to die alone; not like this. I'm . . . afraid. Please be with me. I know how afraid of the dark you are, and I can make things easier for you. I'm not going to die of thirst, so I'm going to kill myself. I'll kill you so that you won't suffer. It won't hurt, I promise you. Please don't leave me alone like this, Anne."

Prindle was still talking when Anne, who had continued to move backward, reached back and touched the craggy edge of one of the smaller, tributary caves behind her.

"Anne? Are you there?"

Anne almost cried out. She had not heard the man move, but Prindle's voice was suddenly much closer to her. She turned, ducked and moved into the smaller cave.

CHAPTER NINETEEN

(i)

Bone held up his hand, indicating that Zulu and Perry Lightning should stop and remain silent. Then he squatted and stared intently at the rock formation just ahead of him in the narrow passageway. The configuration of rock was not as he remembered it.

Something was wrong.

Bone closed his eyes and took deep breaths, trying to restore strength to his burning limbs and banish the searing pain from his stomach wound. He glanced down, saw that the front of his heavy canvas shirt was stained with blood. However, the doctors had done a good job; as far as he could tell, the majority of the stitches still held, and the wound had not torn open completely. He only needed to hold himself together a short time longer—and hope against hope that he would find Anne in the great stone chamber, and that she would be alive. He opened his eyes, again studied the stone formation in their path—and then he knew what it was.

He turned to look at the two men behind him, and was shocked by what he saw; both Zulu and Perry Lightning seemed to be on the verge of collapse. Both were bleeding from multiple cuts, bruised on their hands and faces, obviously near exhaustion.

"He's done something to the rocks up ahead," Bone said, surprised at the rawness of his voice. He had not spoken for hours.

"What?" Lightning asked.

"Take some water; both of you."

Zulu said, "There's not much left, Bone-man."

"Drink some anyway," Bone said in a low voice. "And eat some of the jerky. Keep your voices down. The chamber is about seventy yards ahead, but it's a tough seventy yards. You rest. I have to find out what Prindle's done here— it's either a warning system or some kind of death trap."

The men opened their canteens and drank, and Zulu produced some foil-wrapped packets of food from the packs. Bone took a swallow of water, then crawled forward. He was certain he remembered a crevasse in the center of this passageway, and to get past it one had to balance on one's toes and inch along a narrow ledge while bracing one's hands on the opposite wall. Now the crevasse was covered with a slab of stone that was in turn covered with pebbles. But the pebbles were not the same color as the surrounding rock; they had been placed there, like the slab over the crevasse. Anyone stepping on the delicately balanced slab would plummet to his death, or at the least send the rocks crashing into the abyss as a warning of his presence.

Zulu's deep, hoarse voice was suddenly close by his right ear. "What's the matter, Bone-man?"

Bone held his flash steady on the rock in front of them. "If I'm right, that slab is balanced on the lip of a crevasse; it will tip if anyone steps on it. Or if any of those pebbles fall, Prindle will hear it and know we're here. Can you brace the edges of it?"

Zulu grunted, then got down on his stomach, extended his arms and gripped the edges of the slab.

"Got it," Zulu said quietly. "You were right; it wouldn't take much to tip this thing."

"Hold it steady," Bone said, then knelt down and painstakingly began to pick the small pebbles off the slab's surface. When he had finished, he touched Zulu's shoulders, felt the bunched muscles. "Can you pull it back—easy—just far enough so that it won't tip if we step on it?"

In response, Zulu sucked in a deep breath, hunched his shoulders and began to pull on the slab. There was a slight grating sound, and he stopped. The slab had been moved almost two inches.

"Bone-man? I don't want to make too much noise."

"That may be enough. Very carefully, slowly, release the pressure and see what happens."

Zulu slowly began to release his grip—and the slab began to tilt. He grunted softly, pulled the rock back another inch, again relaxed his grip. The slab began to tilt, then held.

"Okay, Bone-man," Zulu said with a deep sigh. "I think she'll stay there as long as we don't do too much tap dancing on it."

Bone motioned for Lightning to come closer, then addressed the two men, turning away slightly so that they could not see the blood on the front of his shirt. "Are you two okay?" When Zulu and Lightning nodded, Bone continued, "If you watch what I do and move exactly as I do, neither of you should have trouble getting past this section. Then we put on the night-vision goggles. Stay close behind me, step where I step and try not to make a sound. When we reach the other side of this little hole in the ground, we'll be very close."

(ii)

Bone, wearing his infrared goggles, sat in the darkness, his back braced against cold stone, trying to slow the beating of his heart and fight against the feeling of despair that threatened to overwhelm him. Throughout their long journey, which had now stretched to almost fifteen hours, his energy reserve had been fueled principally by hope. Now that hope was almost gone. He was at the top of an incline, fifteen yards from the edge of the ancient, sunken graveyard and one of the entrances to the vast stone chamber. If there was anyone in the chamber, flickering light should clearly be visible from this vantage point. But there was only darkness. It seemed he had risked all their lives on a journey that had led to nothing but more empty darkness.

He took a deep breath, signaled for Zulu and Lightning to follow, then started down the incline, taking care to avoid stepping on the ossified bones underfoot. He came to the entrance to the chamber, pressed back against the wall, peered around the edge of the mouth of the tunnel—and almost cried out.

Barry Prindle, wearing his purple priest's chasuble, was lying prostrate, sprawled in front of his stone altar.

But there was no sign of Anne.

At Bone's signal, Lightning—who had removed the cotton padding from his rifle and fitted the scope—came forward, followed by Zulu. Lightning nodded to Bone and Zulu; all three men stripped off their goggles. Bone and Zulu turned on their powerful flashlights while the police lieutenant raised the rifle to his shoulder and sighted on the still figure on the far side of the quicksand pit.

"All right, you son-of-a-bitch!" Lightning snapped in a voice that was clear and powerful despite his obvious exhaustion. "You move a muscle, and you get a rifle slug right between the shoulder blades."

"Don't kill him!" Bone said in an urgent whisper.

Lightning shook his head, whispered, "I won't; I just want him to think I will." He paused, then barked: "All right, Prindle, sit up slowly!"

The draped, still figure of Barry Prindle did not move, and Bone could not tell if the man was breathing. He played his flashlight around the great chamber, still saw no sign of Anne.

"You two wait here," Perry Lightning continued curtly. "Now it's my show."

Lightning, his rifle held at the ready, went into the chamber, circled the pool of quicksand, cautiously approached Prindle and poked him in the ribs with the toe of his shoe. When there was still no response, the detective knelt down beside the figure and reached for Prindle's right wrist to feel for a pulse.

Bone felt a prickly sensation at the back of his neck. "Be careful, Lieutenant!" he called out. "There's something—!"

Suddenly there was a blur of motion. Prindle spun around, and the razor in the hand Lightning had been reaching for glinted in the beams of the flashlights. Lightning leaped backward, raising his arm to protect his throat, and the blade slashed across his wrist and forearm. Blood spurted. Lightning cried out and fell backward, the rifle dropping from his hand and skittering off into the darkness. Prindle was instantly on his feet. He grabbed Lightning's flashlight, played it across the stone behind him until he saw the rifle and headed for it.

Both Bone and Zulu, at Prindle's first movement, had started running forward. Zulu slipped and fell in the field of bones but Bone kept running, sprinting on the narrow ledge around the quicksand, past the bleeding, dazed Perry Lightning, toward the robed figure who was stooping down to pick up the rifle. Suddenly Prindle spun around, and Bone ducked as the razor slashed through the air over his head. He dove for Prindle's legs, missed. But he had his hands on the rifle—for a moment. Prindle kicked it away. Bone scrambled to his feet, crouched and slowly backed away as Prindle, his bright green eyes gleaming with madness in the light reflected from the walls, came at him, slashing with the razor. Bone sidestepped the first attack, but then, his strength almost completely gone, his legs buckled under him and he crumpled to the stone. A moment later Prindle was bending over him, raising the razor to slash at his face and throat.

The fingers of a huge hand wrapped themselves around the wrist of the hand holding the razor, twisted and pulled. There was a cracking sound that echoed throughout the chamber, and the razor fell to the stone. Prindle screamed in agony and rage; he continued to scream as Zulu effortlessly lifted him off his feet, marched him to the edge of the quicksand pit and threw him out into the air. Prindle's body described an arc; he landed splay-limbed, on his back, in the center of the pool of quicksand, and immediately began to sink. His screams became even more high-pitched.

"I'm all right!" Bone shouted as Zulu started back toward him. "See to the Lieutenant!"

Zulu nodded and went to Perry Lightning who, although his eyes were glassy with shock, had had the presence of mind to wrap his fingers tightly around his forearm, just above the gash; the spurting from the severed artery had stopped. Zulu quickly stripped off his belt, wrapped it around Lightning's arm to form a tourniquet, tied it off.

"You're going to be all right, Lieutenant," Zulu said quietly. "I've got my own medical kit in one of the packs, and the bone-man will tell you I'm real good with cuts."

"Thanks, Zulu," Lightning said, sitting up and grasping the end of the belt. "Go see if Granger's all right."

Bone, one hand over his bleeding stomach, walked to the edge of the quicksand pit, looked out at Prindle, now almost three-quarters submerged. Prindle had stopped screaming, and was beginning to whimper like a child. His eyes were wide with terror.

"Don't struggle," Bone said calmly as he played the beam of his flashlight over the other man's head. "If you don't struggle, you won't sink so fast. Actually, I've been told that a man can swim in quicksand, if he knows how to do it. I've never done it, so I'm afraid I can't be of much help to you. Also, it looks to me like you may have sunk in a bit too deep to do any swimming."

Prindle began to scream again.

"Jesus Christ," Zulu said, shaking his head. "How long is it going to take him to go under?"

"I don't want to die!" Prindle shrieked.

"Neither did any of the people you killed," Bone said in the same soft tone.

"I did it for them!"

"What about Ali Hakim?"

"Please . . . I don't want to die like this! This is where I buried all the heads! They're down there, waiting for me! I can feel their teeth in me!"

Bone swallowed, found that his mouth was very dry. "What happened to Anne?"

"She's dead! Please don't let me die like this! Don't let me be buried alive in a graveyard!"

"Did you kill her, Barry?"

"No! She threw all the lamps and supplies in here, then ran off into the tunnels behind you! She killed herself!"

Bone felt his heart beat faster, and he suppressed a grin. A smart woman, he thought. And a very brave one.

"Bone!" Prindle screamed as the quicksand rose to his chin, and he had to arch his head back to breathe. "I'm sinking! Help me!"

"How's the Lieutenant, Zulu?" Bone called back over his shoulder.

"I'm all right, Granger," Perry Lightning said.

"Did you hear this man's confession?"

"I wouldn't have come down here with you, Granger, if I hadn't thought I'd been wrong about you. You know that."

"Just checking," Bone said as Prindle's head finally sank beneath the surface of the quicksand pool.

Bone walked quickly back to where he had dropped his coil

of rope, then returned to the spot where he had been standing, looped one end of the rope around his chest. "Give me a hand here, Zulu, will you? Take the other end of the rope."

"Bone-man, what the hell do you think you're doing? You can't save Prindle. He's gone."

But Bone was already leaping through the air. He landed in the center of the pit, almost directly over the spot where Barry Prindle's head had disappeared from sight. He kicked with his legs as he hit the surface, slapped at the surface with his hands to keep from sinking too deeply. Then he groped beneath the surface until he felt the top of Prindle's head, grabbed a handful of hair.

"Okay, Zulu, pull; low angle, steady pressure, easy does it."

Zulu crouched and braced his legs, then began pulling on the rope. Slowly, Bone began to move, pulling Barry Prindle up after him; after a few seconds Prindle's head broke the surface. His face was a deep crimson, and his eyes bulged from the effort of holding his breath. The pent-up breath came out of him with a loud, whooping sound—and then he began to scream once again, mindlessly, and wouldn't stop.

It would probably have been more merciful to let the man die, Bone thought as he reached the rock ledge at the edge of the pit, dragged Prindle up and out of the quicksand. Prindle had indeed felt the sharp teeth of his many victims, and was now hopelessly mad, beyond the reach of any other human being.

Zulu silenced Prindle with a left hook to the point of the chin. Then the street poet wiped the mud from Bone's face and body.

"Jesus, Bone-man," Zulu said, shaking his head. "I don't know why you did that. You should have let the fucker die. The lieutenant's in a state of shock. He'll keep his arm as long as I keep tending to his tourniquet, but I don't know how we're going to manage to get everybody back the way we came."

"Don't worry," Bone said wearily, bracing himself with his feet slightly apart so that he wouldn't sway. He'd felt stitches tear loose as he'd dragged Barry Prindle to the surface of the quicksand pit, and he wondered how much longer he had before he lost consciousness. If only Anne had somehow kept her wits about her as she'd run away in the darkness, there was still hope.

"Don't *worry*?"

324

"We're not going back the way we came. There's an easier way."

Zulu thought about it, said: "The way Prindle came in?"

"Right."

Zulu nodded toward the unconscious man in the priest's chasuble. "He's a space cadet now, Bone-man; he's gone. I don't think he'll be telling us anything."

"He won't have to. The way will be marked."

"Huh?"

"Handcuff Prindle, Zulu, and take care of the lieutenant. I'll be back in a little while."

"Bone-man—?!"

"Keep the faith, Zulu. I'll be back. If for any reason I'm not, search the mouths of the caves at this end. You should find some kind of marks. Follow them."

He found Prindle's blaze marks almost immediately—large, thick Xs drawn in red oil crayon on both sides of the cave on his far right. Ten minutes later he found what he had not dared to hope would be there.

In the middle feeder cave, beginning almost at the mouth, there was a piece of a woman's silk handkerchief anchored beneath a small stone. Ten yards further there was another piece.

He found Anne fifteen minutes later, perhaps an eighth of a mile down the length of the tunnel. She was sitting on the floor of a small chamber, knees drawn up to her chest, sipping from a canteen of water. As he came around a bend and shone his light on her, she smiled wryly and gave a weak salute.

"Boy, am I glad to see you," she said as Bone knelt down beside her and wrapped her in his arms. "I heard a lot of fussing back there a while ago, and then I heard you coming down the tunnel."

"Why didn't you call out?" Bone asked in a rasping voice.

"I . . . I was afraid it was a dream, Bone. If it was, I didn't want to wake up. Barry . . . ?"

"He's not ever going to hurt anybody again."

"Lord, are you a mess," Anne said, pulling away slightly and looking over Bone's body. Then she saw the fresh blood marbling the drying mud and she uttered a sharp cry. "Bone, you're bleeding!"

Bone wearily rose to his feet, put both hands over the wound in his stomach. "I'm all right—or I will be. I don't think we're that far from the surface. Come on."

Anne got to her feet, managed to get her shoulder under Bone's right arm as he staggered and sagged. "It's my turn to do a little rescuing," she said as they made their way back toward the stone cathedral, and the way out.

Bone, Anne, Perry Lightning and Zulu—resplendent in his flowing, multi-colored robes, holding his staff—stood just outside the security checkpoint at the boarding gates leading to the American Airlines terminal at John F. Kennedy Airport.

"Oh, John," Anne said, wrapping her arms around Bone and holding him tight, "how I'll miss you."

"And I you," Bone replied softly, gently stroking her hair. "But it's time for me to go back to where I belong—at least for a while."

"You belong anywhere, John; you can survive anywhere."

"I belong where I feel at home, Anne."

"Yes, I know," Anne said, and sighed. "I shouldn't be greedy. This has been a wonderful month we've spent together."

"And, thanks to the three of you, I've certainly seen plenty of New York City—the right way. You have vacation time next month, Anne. Then you'll come to visit me, in my world."

Anne stepped back, shuddered slightly. "But *no* poking around in caves, my love."

"I promise; no caves. Just some hiking on gentle slopes. I

have a chalet up in the mountains." He paused, winked at Anne. "We'll have a good time."

"*I'm* the one who's going to do some caving," Zulu announced proudly. "I think I showed some talent down there. Right, Bone-man?"

Bone grinned at his traveling companion. "Without doubt."

"I'm going to miss you, too," Anne said, squeezing Zulu's hand. "I'm going to think about you every time I drive past St. Thomas Church. Who can ever take your place?"

Zulu bent over and kissed Anne on the cheek. "It's time for me to move on, Anne. The bone-man says that I'll make out like a bandit in Denver with what he calls 'my act.' I want to try it out, as a change of pace. Hey, if I get tired of all that scenery, I can always come back and live under Grand Central."

"You see *me* before you ever go underground again, Zulu," Perry Lightning said. "If you come back to New York, you'll always have a place to stay with me—for as long as you want. Got it?"

"Thanks, Lieutenant."

"That goes for you too, Granger."

Bone nodded. "When are you coming out to visit me, Lieutenant?"

Perry Lightning smiled thinly. "We'll see. I'm afraid all that fresh air might make me sick. Good luck to both of you."

Lightning shook hands with Bone and Zulu, and Bone kissed Anne. Then the two men picked up their bags and started down the ramp. They stopped at the bottom to turn and wave, and then they turned a corner and were gone. Anne and Perry Lightning, arms linked, walked from the terminal.